"Sheriff?" Erin called. "I need to talk to you."

Nothing.

She glanced around. The light came from deeper in the house, sputtering as if from a candle or lantern, maybe a fireplace. There was no furniture, no curtains, no heat. No sign of life save for the flicker of light and the open door.

"Sheriff?" Her voice echoed and she realized the floors had been stripped. She followed the light through an archway down a wide hall, the scent of burning firewood touching her nostrils and luring her deeper into the house. "Sheriff?"

She rounded a corner and nearly jumped from her skin. A man sat in the center of an empty room—a large, black silhouette sprawled on a wooden chair, the fire glowing behind him. The shape of a giant pistol in hand.

"Rumor has it you almost got shot once tonight," he said. "You looking to try again?"

ACCLAIM FOR KATE BRADY'S NOVELS

LAST TO DIE

"A winning combination of complex characters and an intricately woven plot."
— ***Publishers Weekly***

"The author seems to have an innate talent for creating gripping suspense with witty and determined characters. *Last to Die* is a roller-coaster ride, full of ups and downs, twists and turns. Hold on tight!"
— ***RT Book Reviews***

"A dark, twisted suspense story...starts off at full speed and doesn't let up until the very end...Full of sexual tension, devious villains, and a thrilling plot that will have [readers] up all night, flying through the pages."
— **FallenAngelReviews.com**

"Kate Brady has created another thriller that features heart-pounding action with just the right amount of sizzling romance."
— **BookIdeas.com**

ONE SCREAM AWAY

"Brady weaves a tight and gripping mystery...[with] an emotionally satisfying conclusion...endearing and intense."
— ***RT Book Reviews***

"A wonderful debut author...gripping romantic suspense...I read all night with my heart in my throat...fast-paced and scary."

—DearAuthor.com

"A nail-biting story...a powerful novel full of terrifying details and chilling revelations...edge-of-your-seat intensity."

—CoffeeTimeRomance.com

"*One Scream Away* has it all: rich, multilayered characterization; a harrowing, serpentine plot; and a diabolical and cunning villain...the sexual tension absolutely smolders...Kate Brady brings a fresh and incredibly skilled voice to the romantic suspense genre and is on the fast track to the top."

—BookLoons.com

"A suspenseful romantic thriller. It also reads like a good police procedural...The suspense is chilling, with page-turning action. The dialogue is snappy, with just enough romance."

—MyShelf.com

Also by Kate Brady

One Scream Away
Last to Die

WHERE ANGELS REST

KATE BRADY

FOREVER

NEW YORK   BOSTON

Forever
Hachette Book Group
237 Park Avenue
New York, NY 10017
www.HachetteBookGroup.com

Printed in the United States of America

First edition: November 2012
10 9 8 7 6 5 4 3 2 1
OPM

Forever is an imprint of Grand Central Publishing.
The Forever name and logo are trademarks of Hachette Book Group, Inc.

The Hachette Speakers Bureau provides a wide range of authors for speaking events. To find out more, go to www.hachettespeakersbureau.com or call (866) 376-6591.

The publisher is not responsible for websites (or their content) that are not owned by the publisher.

This one's for Alta. She and the angels know why.

ACKNOWLEDGMENTS

Many thanks to my wonderful editors—both of them. To Celia Johnson, thanks for the start, and may your new path be filled with joy. To Selina McLemore, thanks for being there in the middle of the stream, and may our new path together be filled with success. No good things happen to writers without great editors, and I am twice-blessed.

My deepest gratitude to my agent, Jenny Bent, who makes me the envy of writers everywhere I go. How did I get so lucky?

To Carol Whitescarver, whose devotion to the process of writing and commitment to our friendship and salad bars made these characters possible. Her patience is unmatched.

To Elaine Sims, who forged the path before me and taught by example.

To Joyce Lamb, who hangs out with me even though more famous, interesting, and exciting people are always knocking at her door. Her support, her experience, and her sense of humor are godsends.

And of course, to my children and husband, whose love and devotion keep me going. It's pretty amazing that they are proud of such a twisted mind, but I'll take it.

WHERE
ANGELS
REST

PROLOGUE

A LONELY ROOM, naked wires clawing from the outlets and a heap of cold ash huddled in the fireplace. The ceiling joists crisscrossed in a matrix ten feet up, the floors and walls stripped to bare concrete and plaster, making the tiniest sound ricochet in the rafters. Even the faint moans of a woman nearly dead echoed like whispers in a cathedral.

The Angelmaker studied the woman, faceup on a wooden table with duct tape binding her wrists and ankles. Her eyes stared at nothing in the rafters.

What do you see now, bitch?

Nothing, of course; she was almost finished. It rankled, actually. She should have held up better.

But it was too late to worry about that now. The clock was ticking, lives counted in minutes. A week ago, who'd have thought the grand finale would come so soon, or be so exhilarating? And yet, here she lay, ready for her transformation.

The Angelmaker pried a hunk of cold earth from a pile, kneaded it like artist's clay, then smeared it onto her jaw. Got another handful and pushed it over the edge of the first, thumbing it smooth with practiced strokes—not too thick and not too thin. Over the slender nose, over the high cheekbone, over the seam of ugly stitches at her temple. The Angelmaker smiled at that. On the inside of this mask would be something special: the imprint of stitches and the swell of a nasty welt on the side of her face. When the authorities found this mask, there would be no doubt whose face had provided the mold.

The mighty Erin Sims. Her death would come just in time to join her brother in hell. A twofer.

That thought brought a snicker and the Angelmaker worked faster. *Tick-tock,* Dr. Sims.

Time's up.

CHAPTER
1

Seven days earlier . . .
Thursday, November 8
Outside the Florida State Prison, Starke, Florida
11:42 p.m.

L ET ME *GO*."
Erin Sims jerked against handcuffs, the metal rings
biting into her wrists. Tears rose to her throat but she held
them back: Time was almost up. What was it, twenty 'til
twelve? Quarter 'til? She couldn't see her watch but it was
late. God, she had to stop them before midnight.

She took a step and a guard snagged her arm. "No,"
he said. He was a burly black man with tattoos vining his
neck and an earring winking in the darkness. His tag read
Collier but people called him Collie. Erin had been coming here long enough to remember when his son made the
varsity football team and his wife beat breast cancer. Now
he and another guard stood on either side of her, each with
a hand on her elbows. Just in case she decided to throw
herself at one of the demonstrators or incite a riot.

"Stay back here," he said. "You're already hurt."

She followed his glance to her legs, where her jeans were torn and the skin of both knees ripped open. Sheriff's deputies had dragged her from the prison entrance. "I won't do anything this time," she said. "Just let me go back to the front. I need to see." *I need to be close to him.*

"There's nothing more you can do," the second guard said.

The words brushed a chill over Erin's skin. There had to be something more. Eleven years of fighting couldn't end with—

"Kill him!"

The chant started up again, cycling through thirty friends and relatives of Lauren McAllister, all gathered to witness justice, cheering and crying and waving handwritten signs: *Death to Justin Sims, An Eye for An Eye, We Love You, Lauren.* Nine reporters, the most permitted at an execution by law, wove among the demonstrators with their photographers trailing behind like cyclopes. On Erin's side of the drive, three people—strangers—carried worn signs reading *Stop the Death Penalty* and *Two Wrongs Don't Make a Right.* Otherwise, Justin had no supporters. He was the murderer of a senator's daughter.

Erin drew a shuddering breath. "What time is it?"

"Quarter 'til," Collie said. "Fifteen more minutes."

Illogically, as if to confirm the time, Erin glanced to the sky. It was a night made for tragedy: black clouds grumbling with thunder, security lights casting the air in thin shades of gray. A slivered moon had slunk out of sight, as if cowering from the travesty about to happen.

"They can't do this," Erin said, her voice coming out on a thread. "Victor Santos is still with the Attorney General. He's presenting new evidence."

Collie shook his head. "That might not matt—"

"It has to matter." She rounded on him. "Damn it, I found John Huggins. After all these years, I know where he is and gave them more evidence. *He* murdered Lauren McAllister, not Justin. How can the Attorney General ignore that? He has to listen."

Her own words stopped her. *You have to listen, Mommy. Please. He scares me.* She'd learned long ago that people don't listen to things they don't want to hear.

A finger of panic touched her heart. Even if Justin's attorney had gotten a last-minute audience with the Attorney General and convinced him there was enough evidence to warrant investigating John Huggins again, even if just now they were waking up a judge and working through paper or chewing through levels of bureaucracy, what if it was too late? Where was Justin? Strapped to a gurney already, an IV dripping into his arm, awaiting the toxins that would end his life?

The unspeakable passed her lips. "What if it's not enough? What if—"

She couldn't finish. She had to save Justin. People didn't see him the way she did; no one else would keep up the fight. He needed her.

No, he didn't. And he didn't want her, either.

Erin cursed. Damn it, she was a shrink, an advocate. She'd made her career unearthing the emotions of people who were victims, and serving as their voice when they couldn't do it themselves. She ought to understand why Justin had pushed her away.

But she didn't.

"I should be in there," she said, tears stinging the backs of her eyes. "He could have had three people in there with him. Why didn't he let me—?"

A siren cut her off. She whirled and the crowd turned en masse to see a deputy's car swing in, the wail of the siren lopping off with a *whoomp*. A guard stepped out, talked to the driver in the strobe of blue and red lights, then waved the car through and picked up his radio. From a nearby tower a voice roared through a bullhorn, commanding people to clear the way and make a path.

Erin held her breath. Three men spilled from the car. Deputies who had been stationed outside the prison to aid security guards swooped in to provide escort, and the group rushed through the gates. Erin rose on tiptoe trying to see. She caught Victor Santos's eye a second before he was swallowed into the maximum security prison.

A wave of hope washed over her. "Oh, God," she whispered. Collie and the guard behind her stood like pillars. A pall of silence lowered on the larger crowd—the McAllister camp—like a damp wool blanket on fiery coals.

Please. *Please*, Erin prayed. *Let me have done enough.*

Moments passed, the crowd holding its collective breath; then the front doors opened. Erin's throat tightened into a knot. From the black maw of the entrance, a handful of people plodded outside with their heads down. The sobs of a woman scraped the air.

"It's the senator," Collie said, and Erin could hardly believe it. She noticed hands at her back, and heard the cuffs jangle as the second guard said in her ear, "That means they didn't do it. They stopped it."

Erin stared, her hands coming free. What? It was over?

Like a giant beast that had been thrashing just seconds before, the crowd gaped at their fallen warriors emerging from the prison. Senator and Mrs. McAllister made their way through the inner and outer gates, and as realization crept through the bystanders, the great beast collapsed into groans and sobs and curses. Erin stood rigid, afraid to move. Beside her, the three anti–death penalty activists issued kudos, but their triumph was bathed in macabre tones, like a dream that wasn't yet real. Lauren McAllister's father, supporting his wife with an arm, glared at Erin as they drew near, a security guard handing them off to a local police escort. McAllister stopped in front of her.

"You," he said, his voice like chipped ice. "You did this."

She nearly wilted with relief. Dear God, Justin was alive.

"Yes," she managed, and couldn't suppress the joy that bubbled into her voice. It was over. At least for now. "Justin didn't kill your daughter, Senator. I've found the man who did."

McAllister's head moved back and forth, the hot emotion Erin had seen in the early years now gone cold. He'd heard it all before. Never listened.

His wife stepped forward. "May you rot in hell," she said to Erin, her voice trembling with emotion. "My angel is dead. He should have paid. *Someone* has to pay—"

A cop nudged her and piloted the couple past. Mrs. McAllister walked as if a steel rod held her, her skirt tangling below her knees as she twisted to keep her eyes glued to Erin. News cameras flashed, catching it all.

Erin steeled her spine. She ought to be used to it; she and the McAllisters had faced off more than once over the years, sometimes in public and other times in private. But this time, Erin realized, they'd believed Justin would finally be put to death.

Dear God. This time, so had she.

The crowd fragmented, clusters of mourners following the McAllisters, others trailing to the parking lot with defeat dragging their steps. Erin pushed through a handful of lingering reporters and saw Victor. He paused outside the prison gates to give a statement to the press, then said "no more" with his hands and walked over to Erin.

Collie gave her a nod and both guards stepped away. She could hardly speak.

"Thank you, Victor," she began, but he held up a hand.

"Seven days."

She blinked. "What?"

"The judge stayed the execution for a week."

"No." The momentary high of knowing Justin had escaped death gave way to a surge of alarm. "That's not enough time."

"It's more than I thought you'd get. Even if you're right and this man you found on the Internet in Ohio really *is* John Huggins, it doesn't mean he's the man who shot Lauren McAllister through the heart and scrubbed her face with paint thinner. You've accused Huggins before and they cleared him."

"John Huggins had an affair with Lauren McAllister. She was afraid of him. He changed his name and ran away. He had another affair with a woman in Virginia and she's believed dead, too. Besides, Justin wasn't with her that night. He *wasn't*."

"So he claimed," Victor said, a weary sigh in his voice. "But you're the only one who believes that. You have no proof, Erin."

"What about the picture of Huggins that Lauren drew?"

"It was dismissed as irrelevant—again—just like everything Justin claimed to know about Huggins and Lauren. Look, Erin, this is a stay, not an acquittal. It doesn't mean you won't be here next Thursday night, doing the same thing you're doing now."

Erin closed her eyes. Damn him, he sounded just like David. Giving up without a fight. On the trial, on their marriage, on Justin's life.

Well, *she* wouldn't give up. She couldn't. "Then why the reprieve?"

"The AG's giving authorities a week to talk to the Calloway fellow you found in Ohio and see if he's really Huggins. And to look into the Virginia woman's disappearance."

Erin balled her hands into fists. "Authorities?"

"The sheriff in Hopewell, Ohio—the town where Calloway lives," Victor said, rooting in his breast pocket for a scrap of paper. He unfolded and handed it to her. "Nikolaus Mann. A good German name, probably a no-nonsense kind of guy. He'll determine if Jack Calloway on the Internet is really John Huggins."

"When?"

Victor hedged. "It's the weekend..."

"Justin has seven days," she snapped. "A weekend is a third of his life." Every tendon in her body constricted. She couldn't leave this to the authorities over their precious weekend—

"Erin," Victor said, with a warning in his voice, "don't even think about it. Leave it to Sheriff Mann. Don't forget that Huggins still has a restraining order against you in North Carolina. Let the system do its thing."

"The *system* just tried to kill my brother." Her voice vibrated with emotion, but Victor was unfazed. He was a lawyer; he belonged to the system. Or, she thought—the expression on Victor's face lifting the hairs on the back of her neck—there was something more. Something he wasn't telling her.

"Victor?" she asked.

He dropped his head, then blew out a breath and looked at her. "I'm finished, Erin. If you want to go forward you need to find another lawyer."

"If I want—" Her blood stopped moving. "You don't mean that."

He took her arm, lowering his voice. "Do you know that my secretary was afraid to come to work today? That I found graffiti painted on my car when I left my office this afternoon?" Frustration morphed to something that sounded like true fear. "Damn it, I don't want to be on the wrong side of McAllister anymore."

Erin's bones went cold. She glared in the direction McAllister had gone, anger and powerlessness colliding in her chest. She couldn't believe Victor was bailing. He was a friend; he'd stood up with David at their wedding and stuck by her when even David hadn't. To lose him now, when a sliver of hope glimmered on the horizon...

"One more week, Vict—"

"No," he said, with a finality she knew was real. He glanced around, as if an assailant might be lurking along the dark edges of the prison yard. "I wish you luck, Erin. Really, I do. But I've got a wife, kids. I'm finished."

He turned away and Erin snagged his arm. "Wait," she said. Tears came in a flash. "Did you see him? Did he see you?"

"I saw him, through the one-way window. He didn't see me."

"And?"

"He's thin but strong; his hair's long again. He looks— He looks okay." Victor put up a hand before she could ask more. "Don't picture the details, Erin. It won't help."

He headed for the parking lot and Erin looked at the stone sprawl of buildings that made up the Florida State

Prison, forcing herself to visualize Justin no longer strapped to a gurney with IVs in his veins and witnesses watching through one-way glass. She closed her eyes. Picture him in his cell, no IVs, sitting up. Alive.

She pulled out a copy of the Internet picture she'd given to Victor three days ago. It was too dark to see the details, but they were emblazoned in her memory: a large, scenic inn in rural Ohio, with a folksy Pennsylvania Dutch pineapple stenciled on a sign that said WELCOME TO HILLTOP HOUSE. It did indeed appear to be set on a hill, surrounded by sprawling yew and chesty oak trees, with a whitewashed porch and homey ferns hanging at even intervals. Along the front walkway, ceramic sculptures of a girl and boy waded through beds of coreopsis and snapdragons. And on the front steps of the inn, the proprietor leaned against the porch railing with a caption that read, OWNER: JACK CALLOWAY.

Erin didn't think so. This had to be Huggins. Even if the photo was too distant to see his eye color, even if there were thousands of men of his age and build, even if it were true that everyone had a look-alike somewhere in the world, those two ceramic sculptures in the garden gave it away. Erin would swear Huggins's wife had made those.

The adrenaline that had sustained her for the past three days leaked from her limbs. She tucked away the picture, then put a finger to her lips and breathed a kiss and a promise toward the prison. She started for the parking lot. A security guard muttered, "'Night, miss" as he pushed the various buttons that swung the final gate open and closed behind her. She headed across the pavement toward her car, fifty yards away, and squinted when she glimpsed a straggling figure standing in the far corner of the lot. A woman, she realized, the silhouette of a long, flowing skirt moving as the figure scurried into the darkness.

Mrs. McAllister? She glanced around. The skirt was right, but the senator's entourage was gone. Bitterness rose to Erin's throat: just one more gawker. Executions were good entertainment.

A raindrop hit her cheek and she looked up. A thin smile of moon slipped out from behind a cloud, mocking her, the same moon that looked down just now on John Huggins a thousand miles away. Hopewell, Ohio. A small town with a quaint bed-and-breakfast and a no-nonsense sheriff. Online, it had all the earmarks of a Norman Rockwell painting, a place so peaceful people probably didn't even lock their doors. The perfect haven for a murderer.

Not anymore.

Determination straightened Erin's spine. She did the math: a five-hour drive back to Miami, put her caseload on hold, pack a bag. She could be in Ohio by tomorrow afternoon. Erin knew the way authorities worked. No way would she leave her brother's life to some sheriff who wouldn't care whether he lived or died, and if Victor wasn't going to help her anymore, then she'd do it alone. God knows, she'd learned how to fight her own battles when she was sixteen years old.

An engine turned over. Erin jumped; she hadn't noticed another vehicle. She glanced around. Nothing. Just the hum of an engine somewhere in the darkness.

Her pulse kicked up and she clicked her key fob— twice, three times—but her car was still too far away to read the signal. The engine grew louder and she picked up her pace, her skin pulling into goose bumps. She looked behind her. Darkness, but instinct pushed her to start jogging, her fingers frantically working the key fob to her car.

Finally, her headlights blinked but the phantom engine drew nearer. Two columns of lights swept across her back.

She veered right, running now, the headlights bearing down. She glanced over her shoulder and winced, blinded by the glare. The white disks barreled in, the car coming fast. She lunged for the fence and tried to scream to the guard.

The sound never came.

CHAPTER
2

Thursday, November 8
Hopewell, Ohio
11:58 p.m.

MIDNIGHT, a sliver of moon hanging over the rooftops and a couple of chimneys still breathing into the air. It was a settled neighborhood, the kind grown comfortable with squeaky screen doors and broken sidewalks. The kind that leeched kids into the streets on Saturday mornings and where folks let themselves into the house next door to borrow an egg. The kind whose residents would be seen on tomorrow morning's news, white-faced, saying, "We never thought something like this could happen here..."

The Angelmaker sat in a new Ford F-150, munching saltines, keeping track as the last few night owls turned in. A couple of houses down the street, the Richardsons' front door cracked open to swallow a howling cat. A half-block behind the truck, the lights of Yaeger's television snapped to black. And at the end of the street, where a single light burned in the front window, Rebecca Engel stepped out onto the porch.

The Angelmaker stopped chewing. *Rebecca*. Right there, just yards away, and alone. She was one of the chosen ones—able to see things she shouldn't—yet there she was, oblivious to the fact that she was about to die.

She dropped down the front porch steps, hunching into her coat and throwing a scarf around her face to ward off the sleet. She climbed into an old Camry and headed east, then north out of town. The Angelmaker followed, headlights picking out thin veins of fog. Easy now. No need to hang too close—there was no doubt where she was going. She'd be headed to Ace Holmes's place, twenty miles out on County Road 219, just over the Hopewell County line. The middle of nowhere.

Perfect.

Rebecca's car led the way for fifteen minutes; then the Angelmaker hustled around back roads and jumped ahead, got back on 219 and nosed the big Ford halfway across the double yellow line. Parked and popped the hood to wait. Two minutes after the truck was in position, the Camry's headlights pierced the mist.

Rebecca neared, slowing her car. Blood rushing now, the Angelmaker got out and circled the truck, exhaust fumes rousing a cough. It was a nice touch: a lone driver stranded at night in the cold, hacking up a lung...

The Camry rolled closer, unable to pass, and the driver's side window cracked an inch. The Angelmaker's fingers tightened around a stun gun, a surge of power flooding in. Such a simple device: plastic-cum-mother-of-pearl, one hundred thousand volts, seventy-five bucks on the Internet. It was no bigger than a cell phone, no louder than a whisper, and for twelve years now, all it had ever needed was a couple of three-volt lithium batteries.

"Rebecca." Use her name, take away that edge of natural fear.

Her window slid open a little farther—just a few inches, but enough for the stun gun. The Angelmaker stepped closer. "Rebecca, I need help. I need a phone. Do you have a phone?"

"What?" she said. Cautious, but not overly fearful.

"Rebecca."

"I'm not . . ."

Another cough. "P-please, a phone."

"Hold on." She cranked the car into park and twisted toward the passenger seat to find her phone. The Angelmaker reached in. *Pzzt.* The stun gun sizzled against her shoulder.

Rebecca collapsed.

Now time surged forward, racing as if God had pushed a button on a remote. Move, move. Ditch the car, get the truck turned around and get Rebecca home and into the workshop. So much to do—the transformation, the possession, the preservation—and the clock started running from the first shock of the stun gun.

The Angelmaker opened the driver's side door and Rebecca lolled sideways, hanging half out onto the pavement. A click of the seat belt released her and she tumbled to the ground, a baffled *uhhhh* vibrating in her throat and the scarf dragging from her face. She was a pretty girl, but wore too much makeup. Always caked on like—

The Angelmaker froze. What? The girl's face glowed in the truck's headlights.

Rebecca?

No.

Panic leaked in. This wasn't right; this wasn't right. Who was this girl? Not Rebecca. This girl was a stranger, a nobody. She was *nothing*.

Shock hardened to sheer rage. Stupid, *stupid* girl. God-damn, stupid bitch, pretending to be Rebecca—

Her arm moved, trying to fight the leaden state brought on by the stun gun. *No.* The Angelmaker swallowed back a primordial scream, hooked a foot beneath her rib cage and shoved. Her body rotated half a turn. Again, another half-turn, and again and again, and five kicks later, gravity took over and rolled her into the gully along the road. She groaned and the Angelmaker followed, dropped a knee into the middle of her back and straight-armed her face—that *wrong* face—into the mud, pressing down on the back of her head and neck. The girl who wasn't Rebecca gasped for air, sucking rain and wet clay up into her nostrils. Her sinuses filled with mud and her lungs seized and the Angelmaker held tight, muscles screaming with tension while the girl made a series of wet, rasping sounds, jerked, then went limp.

Bitch. Stupid girl. Wrong girl. How dare she?

The Angelmaker staggered out of the ditch, panting. The wrong girl lay dead in the mud. Not Rebecca. A nobody.

The magnitude of that error clenched inside, and the weight of failure bore down like a hand from heaven, pushing, pushing. The Angelmaker fought the invisible weight, tapping every last ounce of strength, and looked up at the sky.

The sight set every bone to shaking: The moon was smiling.

The dream was the same as always—a three-year-old boy hiding in a cardboard box while his mother lay in a

Dumpster, choking on the fragments of her own hyoid bone—except this time the phone cut in. Nick Mann jolted from bed, reaching for his gun and the phone in one motion, then stood by the bed blinking details of the here-and-now into focus. Thursday night. Friday morning, really. The house was empty, the clock on the nightstand punching red numbers into the darkness: three-sixteen a.m.

The phone rang again and Nick frowned. Eight deputies had the overnight shift. If a call was coming through in the middle of the night—

His gut tightened and he grabbed the phone. "Yeah," he said, trying to holster the gun. No place to put it. He was wearing SpongeBob pajama bottoms.

"Sheriff." The dispatcher's voice vibrated with tension. "Jensen just took a call at LeeAnn Davis's out on Pine Lake Road. There's an intruder in the house."

"Inside? Inside, with her and the kids?"

"Just the kids. LeeAnn's at work."

"Ah, God." The dregs of the nightmare vanished. "I'm on my way."

Pine Lake Road ran due east and west across the south end of Hopewell County, a ten-minute ride outside of town. Nick did it in six, his mind revving as fast as the Tahoe's engine. LeeAnn Davis was a single mom who rented an old farmhouse from a neighbor, Jerry Gaffe. Gaffe ran the rural equivalent of a slumlord's dwellings, but LeeAnn, like his other tenants, couldn't afford any better. A forty-something divorcée, she'd quit college to pay for her husband's dental school, and just about the time the fourth kid was born, he found heaven in the arms of his hygienist. Now LeeAnn worked days at the middle school cafeteria and nights at the 7-Eleven on Gritt Road.

Out of necessity, the kids were largely left to take care of themselves, but as far as Nick could tell, they were pretty good kids.

With an intruder in the house.

He batted back a thump of fear and dumped the SUV in LeeAnn's driveway. Chris Jensen had beaten him there by one minute, his cruiser door hanging open and flashers off. He held a phone pressed to his ear.

"Dispatch put one of the kids through to me," he said to Nick, his breath frosting the air. Another cruiser swerved into the driveway. The troops were rolling in. Two men climbed out and hurried into vests. "It's Kayla," Jensen continued. "She's hiding in the bathtub with the youngest girl."

Toddler hiding in a cardboard box. Mother in a Dumpster, choking . . .

Focus. "Any reports of nearby robberies, escaped prisoners, like that?" Nick asked.

"No, sir. Quiet night, like usual."

Nick took the phone. "Kayla, this is Sheriff Mann. Everything's gonna be all right."

"Someone's h-here," she whispered. "He was on the porch. He came *inside*."

Nick pointed, wordlessly sending the new pair of deputies around to the back. "Was the front door locked?" he asked into the phone.

"I think. . ," Kayla said. "Unless Josh came in that way."

"Are the others locked? Can we get in?"

"Y-yes. No. They're locked. I heard the front door open. It squeaks." The last was issued under her breath, her voice breaking. She was only thirteen years old. Terrified, losing it.

Two more deputies wheeled into the driveway. Bishop and Fruth.

"Kayla," Nick said, "where are the other kids?"

"Lizzie's with me. Josh and Kimmie are asleep, down the ha—Oh, God!" Her voice jumped a notch. "I hear something. H-he's coming, he's coming."

"Hang on, sweetie."

"What happened?" Bishop asked.

Nick traded him the phone for a vest and jammed his arms into it. He pulled out his gun. "Someone may have gone in the front, from the porch. The kids are all upstairs."

"Surround the house?" Jensen asked.

Nick nodded and said, "The front's probably open. Bishop, stay here. Keep Kayla on the phone and keep her where she is. You," he said to Jensen and Fruth, "we're going in."

LeeAnn's screen door lay on its side, propped against the porch rail. Nick flashed a light on it: cobwebs—down a while. But Kayla was right about the wood door. It was open a foot.

Jensen and Fruth flanked Nick and he pressed on the door with an outstretched hand. He stepped inside, leading with his 9 mm and a flashlight, with Jensen coming in behind. The house smelled of firewood and musty curtains, and he blinked to let his eyes adjust. Listened.

Silence.

They stepped into the living room, the hairs on Nick's forearms standing up. It had been a long time since he'd shot anybody—close to seven years. The memory wasn't a bad one.

He tightened his fingers on the gun, then caught a sound from the stairwell. He spun on it, searching. Jensen did, too, but Fruth stayed with the living room, covering the doorways and clearing the other rooms as Nick and Jensen moved toward the place where the sound had been two seconds before. Silent now, but someone was there; Nick could feel it. He skimmed the stairwell with his gun hand, saw nothing in the narrow column of light. He jerked his head to the wall behind Jensen. A light switch right there.

Jensen flipped it but nothing happened. Bulb out. Nick took a step closer, swung the flashlight beam back and forth again, above the landing and lower, then finally low enough. He caught the culprit square in the eyes.

Well, shit.

CHAPTER
3

THE INTRUDER DIDN'T MOVE. For half a second, Nick wanted to fire a round just to release the tension in his body; then he cursed and loosened his fingers on the gun.

He should have known.

"Go on through the rest of the downstairs," he said to Jensen, "but I think this is it."

Nick pinned the intruder in place with the light beam, stepped around him, and climbed the rest of the stairs. He stalked through the upper level of the house, checking closets and under beds, behind the shower curtain in a second bathroom. Kim, about eleven, stirred when Nick swept through her room, then fell back out without really waking. Josh, the fifteen-year-old who lay sprawled across a high bed in the next room, never budged.

Nick called to Kayla as he entered the hall bathroom. "Kayla, it's Sheriff Mann." He tucked his gun away and crooked the shower curtain back with a finger. "You're safe, honey. Come on out."

He picked up the littlest girl and propped her on his hip, then offered a hand to Kayla. She was shaking.

"Did you find him? He's gone?"

"We found him. He's not gone yet; I thought you might wanna meet him."

"What?"

Out in the hallway, Kim had rolled from bed, wearing a Snow White nightgown and rubbing her eyes. "What happened?" she asked, and fell in behind them.

They went to the top of the stairs. Jensen had finally found a working light switch.

"Your intruder," Nick said, gesturing to the possum on the stairs. It hadn't budged. He set down Lizzie and bent to his haunches. "You ever heard the expression 'playing possum'? It's that: frozen like a statue in order to fool someone. No, no," he said, pulling the five-year-old back when she started toward the creature. "They can be nasty." He turned to Kayla, who was finally breathing again. "Have you got a blanket I can use?"

Rodent removal took ten minutes. No, not rodent: marsupial, Nick remembered, as he carried the blanket out the front door. He went fifty yards to the side of the house and dropped the animal on the ground. It stood frozen a minute, then, getting comfortable with the darkness, waddled into the tall grass.

Nick walked back to the house with the empty blanket. Three more cars had arrived and he groaned. One belonged to LeeAnn, who hugged each of her three daughters hard. But the other two cars belonged to Leslie Roach and company. Roach was a reporter for the local newspaper, good enough to freelance for the bigger papers now and then, and ambitious enough to make a story out of anything. Nick thought her name must offend the insect world.

"Sheriff," she said, coming at him with a digital recorder, trailed by a cameraman. "What happened?"

"It was nothing." The irony of that statement sank under his skin like a bee sting. In LeeAnn's front yard were seven vehicles, the county sheriff, five deputies, one reporter, and two photographers. Even as they spoke, Jerry Gaffe's truck bumped into the drive.

Not nothing. Not for Hopewell, Ohio.

A muscle twitched in Nick's cheek. Easy, man. *Someone* has to save the world from dumb, blind marsupials.

"Sheriff," Leslie Roach said, "give me a statement."

"Go away."

"Damn it, Nick. What happened?"

"Nothing happened." He picked up his pace but she jogged along beside him in her heels. Nick placed reporters in a stratum of society just below whale shit. The fact that he'd taken this one to bed before he'd learned she was a reporter had only affirmed his opinion.

"Did anyone get hurt?" she asked.

"Nothing happened."

"The citizens of Hopewell deserve to know what their elected official is doing out here in a single woman's home in the middle of the night."

Nick turned on her, baring his teeth.

"Gotcha," Leslie said, smiling. "Now what happened?"

"Goddamn it. We got a report of an intruder. Turned out to be a fucking possum. Do you want me to spell that for you?"

"I know how to spell 'possum.' Sometimes it starts with O."

"I meant 'fucking.' It's an adjective."

"Nick, Nick, Nick. Do the citizens of Hopewell have to worry about rabies, wild animals encroaching the city limits, anything like that?"

He might have chuckled if it weren't so sad. "Sorry. No

public terror to sell the paper tomorrow. The only thing the citizens of Hopewell have to worry about is making sure their teenage boys shut the front door."

Jerry Gaffe was out of his truck, surveying his property. "What happened?" he asked.

Nick spent the next ten minutes settling Gaffe down—nothing damaged, no one hurt, no lawsuits coming—while Leslie Roach crawled around the scene, interviewing anyone who would talk to her. Finally, it was over. The photography floodlights came down, the patrol cars eased back to the streets, and Roach's entourage rolled out. Just as Nick said good-bye to LeeAnn, fifteen-year-old Josh appeared at the front door he'd left open. He wore polka-dot boxers and an Adio t-shirt, and looked out over his front lawn while scratching a spot on his stomach.

"What happened?" he asked.

Nick followed Jensen back to the office, filed the paperwork on LeeAnn's intruder, then dialed the *Hopewell Daily Gazette*. Got Ralph Winston, the editorial supervisor in the mornings.

"It was nothing," Nick said when Ralph came on the line. "Don't let Roach turn it into a story."

"It got four county cars and newspaper coverage in the middle of the night, cost the taxpayers a little chunk of change. Like it or not, Sheriff, that's a story."

"Damn it, Ralph."

"Tell you what. I'll have McCoy walk over there to get a statement from you, too."

Nick looked at his watch. "Make it fast. I'm leaving town."

"Oh, yeah, November ninth. I forgot."

At the core, Ralph was a newspaper guy. He never

forgot. "I'm going hunting up at the cabin for the weekend."

"Right. You know, Mann, no one believes you go up there to hunt. Wanna know what I think?"

"No."

"I think there's a lover from your past life in the glamour world—Jennifer Lopez, maybe, or Angelina Jolie, or *both*"—he hesitated and Nick thought he heard a faint *Mmm*—"and they meet you there once a year for a weekend of hot, wild sex. Either that or you staff the place with a harem and every November ninth you live out my oldest fantasy."

"Wow, Ralph. That's exactly right."

"Which one?"

"Take your pick. Journalist's prerogative, right?"

"Low blow."

"Keep the story down, Ralph. It was a fucking possum."

"Can you spell that for me?"

And that was the start of his weekend. Nick drove home a little before seven in the morning, his temper illogically frayed, his headlights picking out tacky signs of the season. A pumpkin the size of a beach ball sat at the end of the Myers's drive. Indian corn hung on every fifth or six mailbox, and at those homes lacking corn, a cardboard turkey or pilgrim adorned the front door. Mrs. Piltzecker, whom Nick had always thought was aesthetically challenged, had put a pair of plastic fawns in her dead garden every winter since Nick was old enough to remember. He and his brothers had gotten caught once trying to hoist them onto her roof on Christmas Eve.

He rolled past the timeworn deer and hooked into his

driveway, the thought passing that life here could be a Kodak commercial: festooned yards, affable neighbors, thriving businesses. Hopewell had a respected private college, an active community theater, an historic bed-and-breakfast, and even a sculptor who was a little bit famous. In Hopewell, youth groups caroled door-to-door at Christmas and kids set up lemonade stands for the Fourth of July. In Hopewell, the local rodent population— marsupial—posed the greatest challenge a sheriff would ever face.

Nick forced himself to stop grinding his jaw. This was what he'd wanted: no gangs, no drug warfare, no organized crime. None of the day-in, day-out crises of urban detective work, and except for the likes of Leslie Roach, no relentless buzz of media. All that had been a high for Nick when he was a young, hungry cop in L.A., but now what he wanted was peace and calm. A sanctuary where he could keep the people he cared about safe.

Like Hannah.

He got out of the Tahoe and popped open the back, the urge to get to the cabin gnawing at his bones. Frost hung in the air—not the picturesque kind that would shimmer in a winter calendar photo, but the wet kind that went up your nostrils and opened your sinuses, and clung to your skin like a cold rubber sheet. He zipped his bomber jacket and started loading the truck.

The long guns went in first: a 12-gauge shotgun and scoped Remington rifle. A pair of 45-caliber Hechler & Koch machine pistols followed, guns that made his county-issue 9 mm Glock feel like a toy. Three bottles of tequila were next—the good kind from Mexico, illegal and complete with the worm. Then a Styrofoam cooler with beer and cold cuts. Ten boxes of ammunition.

Ready.

A sickly sun edged over the horizon as he drove out of town, the radio weatherman euphemistically pronouncing the morning "brisk" and promising a break in the sleet and rain. It would turn into a classic November weekend in the Midwest, the voice promised, perfect for playing tag football or raking leaves or roasting marshmallows at a bonfire.

Nick would spend it shooting demons.

He was thinking about that when he pushed the Tahoe to seventy-five, crossed the county line, and ran over a woman.

CHAPTER
4

D LMMP.

The Tahoe pitched, riding up on two left tires. It bounced to four wheels again and Nick stood on the brakes, fishtailed to a stop. His heart thrashed in his chest.

Jesus Christ, he'd just hit a woman. The sound echoed in his ears—*dlmmp*—like when he'd run over a raccoon once, only the coon hadn't bumped his truck nearly off the road. He wrenched the gear shift into PARK and threw open the truck door, grabbed a flashlight and ran back up the road, squinting through the dawn. Hoping, praying he was wrong.

He froze when he saw her.

Ah, God, it *was* a woman, and horror seized him by the throat. She lay partway across the gravel shoulder, twisted half onto her side, stretching up onto the pavement. She looked dead.

Nick tried to think past the terrible drumming in his chest, then said that to himself again: *She looked dead.* Not dead from having just been hit, but an old dead—the stiff, gray dead of having been dead a while. He squatted and touched her neck. She was cold and he nudged one of her fingers. Rigor mortis already coming on.

Okay. Dead, but not from him. His lungs started working again.

He scanned the road for any other traffic, then aimed the flashlight on her body. Her front was coated with mud while her back and one side of her face appeared to have been drizzled on during the night and washed mostly clean. She was young, maybe even a teenager. Her lips had a bluish tint and her eyes, which were open, showed broken blood vessels.

Choked?

Nick's head cleared a fraction and he dialed Dispatch. Asked for Anson Bell, the Carroll County sheriff. While he waited, he spotted the girl's car and climbed down into the ditch to look at it. It was an older-model Camry, dark, with Cuyahoga plates, and the driver's side door stood open. Nick peered inside. Her purse was open and her cell phone half out. There were no food wrappers or half-eaten snacks.

He circled the car. The front bumper barely kissed a tree and Nick's hackles lifted: The slant of the embankment should have caused more impact than that. He looked up to where the girl lay, choked but with no food in sight, and a knot of dread tightened in his chest.

"Anson," he said, when Bell came on the line. Let it go. This one wouldn't belong to him. "This is Nick Mann. I just ran over a dead woman on 219."

"What?"

"Her car's in the ditch. I'm looking at the body."

"What?"

"Eighteen, maybe twenty years old. Jesus, I thought I'd killed her, but she's been dead a while. Probably been out here all night."

"Aw, man." Nick could picture him pushing away his

bacon and eggs, running a hand over his head and mentally forfeiting whatever weekend activities he'd had planned. "You got anyone coming?"

Nick could just make out the sign for the Carroll County line through the mist behind him. The knot of dread loosened just a touch. "Hell, no. This is *your* county."

Bell and three deputies pulled up within minutes.

"I could've lived a long time without another one of these talks with parents," Bell said. He'd been sheriff for thirty years. Had seen more than one young driver in a heap on the road.

Maybe never one that wasn't an accident, though. Nick closed his eyes. Stop it. She'd probably gagged on a piece of chewing gum, pulled off the road, and clambered up the embankment in a panic. An autopsy would find a lump of hard candy or gum in her throat; a search of the car would find the wrapper. Case closed.

One of Bell's deputies produced a driver's license from the purse in the Camry. "Carrie Sitton," he read, "born ten-twelve-ninety-three. From Cleveland." He pushed a button on her cell phone and shook his head. "No calls last night."

Bell walked to the front of the car and looked at the bumper just grazing the tree. His gaze followed a trodden path from there to where Carrie's body now lay. "You hit her right there?" he asked Nick.

"She was out farther in the road, facedown, I'd say, from the way the rain washed off the back of her clothes. My wheels must've bumped her over."

"Looks like she dragged herself up here. But that car couldn't've been going more than five or ten miles an hour when it hit the tree. Why didn't she walk?" Bell stopped at the body. He reached down and fingered her collar back from her throat. Nothing. He tugged a little farther to expose the back of her neck.

Bruises.

Nick's gut tightened. He cursed and walked away, putting space between himself and the dead girl. Not his problem. Nick didn't chase murderers anymore; he chased possums.

Bell took a few more minutes with the scene, then walked over to Nick. He took off his hat. "We don't have murders in Carroll County."

"We don't have murders in Hopewell County, either," Nick said. Time to go. Guns and tequila waiting.

"Whoa. All those years as a bigwig in L.A.," Bell said. "You've worked more murder cases than anyone in this state."

"Past tense. This one's yours, Anson. Are you finished with me?"

"What's your hurry?"

"No hurry, just on my way to my cabin."

Bell hiked his brows, then looked at Nick's truck, where a deputy had been shooting pictures, checking the undercarriage. There was no reason to doubt Nick's story, but there was no reason not to, either. Taking pictures was the right thing to do.

Bell said, "That cabin of yours borders Weaver's Clay Mine to the north, right?"

"Right. On Lake Barrow, about an hour from here."

"So if I were gonna try to reach you—"

"He'll be hunting," the deputy with the camera said, joining them. He shrugged at Nick. "I saw the guns in your truck."

"Right. Hunting," Nick said. "I'll be back on Monday.

By then, you'll either have this all wrapped up or you'll have a helluva lot of questions for me."

Friday, November 9
Bradford Hospital, Starke, FL
10:05 a.m.

Erin woke in a bed, looked around. Her brain felt like damp wool. Everything hurt. She felt like she'd been hit by a—

The previous night rushed in. Justin—alive. The senator and his wife, Lauren's family and friends all appalled by the Attorney General's decision. A stray woman in the parking lot and a car bearing down. A last-second nose-dive toward the fence.

She closed her eyes, putting the pieces of the week back together. John Huggins was in Ohio: She'd raised enough questions about him that the Attorney General had ordered Ohio authorities to follow up. But there wasn't much time.

She looked out the window. It was morning already—she'd been in and out of a daze all night. It was Friday now. The first of Justin's seven days.

Dear God, she had to go.

She pulled the blanket down and sat up, wincing. Pain cut into her hip and she edged the hospital gown back to see. Her body told the tale. She'd landed on her side when she dove from the path of the car and there was an ugly bruise on her hip that felt bone-deep.

She got out of bed and looked in the mirror. Her cheek had an ugly scrape—road burn from playing dodge-car in the dark—but otherwise she seemed okay. She changed into her clothes and a nurse caught her, tried to convince her to stay and wait for a doctor to check her out.

She didn't. She headed straight for the Starke County Sheriff's Department.

"We don't know who was in the car," the investigator told her, around bites of a tuna fish sandwich. "Could've been anyone."

"There had to be cameras," Erin said. "Didn't they catch it?"

"There are, and they did," he said, "but the driver had parked out of camera range until the last minute. The cameras only picked up the car when it came into the frame taking the run at you."

A chill ran down Erin's spine. That didn't sound like a disgruntled protester acting on impulse. It sounded like someone who'd been out there watching, waiting. And when the opportunity was right, he—or she, Erin acknowledged, with an eerie memory of the long-skirted shadow she'd seen—wheeled in, hit the lights, and gunned the gas.

"What was on the cameras?"

The deputy wiped mayonnaise from his chin. "Besides you leaping out of the way like a scalded cat?" He cracked a smile at her, then tossed down his napkin. "It was a dark Hyundai. A rental."

"Rental?"

He put up a hand. "The ID used at the rental agency was bogus. Fake driver's license, fake credit card, fake insurance."

The starch went out of Erin's body. It *was* planned. And the investigation had already hit a dead end.

"We'll keep on it," the deputy said, though Erin doubted it. "We're talking to everyone who attended the execution—er, the almost-execution—and everyone who's been active in the senator's campaign against your brother."

"Even Mrs. McAllister?"

The man stared.

"There was a woman in the parking lot when I left. I could see the silhouette of a skirt, just below the knees, like the one the Senator's wife was wearing."

"Aw, God," he said, wiping his face with a beefy palm. As if he could rub away what she had just said.

"Put it in your report," Erin said.

He jotted down a note. The cynic in Erin made her wonder if it would go into the file or if he'd toss it into the trash the minute she walked out. When he looked back up, his gaze grazed the scrape down her cheek. "Look, miss, this isn't going to go away. It's already in this morning's news and there'll be a lot of hype for the next week, and now you're asking me to look at a U.S. Senator's wife." He shook his head, reminding Erin of a badgered grandfather. "It wouldn't hurt for you to disappear while the sheriff up in Ohio does his thing. Just get out of sight for a bit."

Erin was a step ahead of him. She stood, remembering Sheriff Nikolaus Mann and his quaint little town. "Thanks," she said, gathering her purse. "I think you're right. It *is* a good idea to get away for a while."

She knew exactly where she'd go.

CHAPTER
5

Friday, November 9
Lake Barrow, Ohio
6:00 p.m.

NICK STRAIGHTENED HIS GUN ARM, homed in on the
target, and fired. Staggered backward and almost
fell. That's what happened when you mixed alcohol,
tobacco, and firearms. Mostly alcohol.

He lowered the Hechler & Koch, swayed, and peered
into the woods at the target. Evening now, getting too
dark for this shit. But he could still make out a few man-
shaped pieces of paper hanging on trees, black circles
closing around the centers. The closest one was Malcolm
Hersher, stuck to a tree forty feet away.

Nick took another hit of tequila, aimed, and emptied
the cartridge into the center of Hersher's chest. Wobbled
backward and wondered why he didn't feel any better.
Malcolm Hersher deserved every bullet. The retired math
teacher behind the counter of an L.A. convenience store,
dead from Hersher's sawed-off shotgun, hadn't.

He lit up a cigarette, shoved in a new cartridge, and carried his bottle and gun around the corner of the cabin's deep porch. Took aim at another target hanging on another tree. Darren Hall. Hall was a gangbanger, had stabbed a guy in the name of "initiation" and raped a twenty-four-year-old mother in front of her son. When he was done, he pressed his thumbs into her hyoid bone until it gave, tossed her body into a Dumpster, and left her three-year-old hiding in a cardboard box. Nick chased Hall for two weeks before he collared him on the rape, but a judge sprang him on the claim that the sex was consensual and someone else had killed her afterward. Before they could pull indictments for murder, Hall went underground.

He was one of the ones who got away.

Correction: He was one of the ones Nick had given up on. Moved to Ohio and took up possum patrol, instead.

Boom. Nick nailed Hall in the shoulder. He cursed and squeezed off another shot, a better one, then proceeded around the perimeter of the house, taking out targets until only one remained. Nick glared at it. Bertrand Yost. It didn't matter that Yost wasn't on the streets anymore. It didn't matter that Nick had hunted him down like a dog and fucked him up so bad he spent weeks in a hospital and months in rehab. It didn't matter that Yost eventually wound up in court, and was found guilty.

What mattered was that a battalion of shrinks yanked a jury around until they bought diminished capacity. What mattered was that Bertrand Yost wound up in a cushy mental facility while Nick's wife wound up in the morgue. Seven years ago, on November ninth.

Allison's dead, Nick. Yost got her. And Hannah took a bullet...

He clenched his jaw and took aim but a breeze caught

the ghostlike page of Yost and lifted the edges. No good. Nick staggered out to the tree and jammed the tip of his pocketknife through the bottom, pinning it down. *Hold still, motherfucker. It's our anniversary.*

He ambled back to the front porch of the cabin and traded the Magnum for a Remington 7 mm. A thread of cognition in the back of his mind warned that a rifle at this range would turn the tree to rubble, but the tequila had him now, along with a rage so bitter he could taste it. He propped the barrel of the rifle on the porch rail, folded down to line up the shot and imagined every detail of Yost's features—broad nose, steel-gray eyes, bushy brows.

Boom. The first shot jolted Nick, ripped through Yost, and splintered the trunk of the tree. Nick maneuvered the bolt action of the rifle and pulled off another. *Boom.* Reloaded and kept at it until his ears rang and his shoulder ached, until Yost was confetti and the center of the tree was kindling.

He sank against the porch rail, tipping his face skyward. Sleet caught his cheeks like darts, in spite of the weatherman's promise, and he propped the rifle on end under the eave and closed his eyes. Wondered how long Carrie Sitton had been alive on the road last night, feeling the sleet through the clay caked on her cheek.

Damn it, stop thinking about her; she wasn't his. Nick had some 20,000 residents he'd sworn to protect, including 16,000 in Hopewell proper and another 4,000 who lived in the outer stretches of the county. Carrie Sitton wasn't one of them. Her killer was out of his hands.

Just like Yost and all the others out there in the dark.

Nick unrolled another paper human and walked it out to a tree. He stuck in a tack and pulled a marker from his pocket, the same one with which he'd labeled the others H-A-L-L and H-E-R-S-H-E-R and Y-O-S-T. He stared at the blank target for a long moment, trying to picture the son of a bitch who would leave an eighteen-year-old girl to claw her way to the shoulder of the road and die there in the cold. Finally, he drew a question mark on the target, strode back to the porch, and picked up his rifle.

"For you, Carrie," he said.

Saturday, November 10
Columbus International Airport, Columbus, Ohio
2:40 p.m.

The Angelmaker watched from beneath a hat in a blue vinyl chair, pulse kicking up as a woman walked past just a few feet away. She carried a laptop and purse, and a fat nylon suitcase that would have just barely squeezed into an overhead compartment. Her strides were swift, a woman on a mission.

Erin Sims.

No surprise that she'd come. As soon as the news reported a reprieve for her brother pending an investigation in Ohio, there had been no doubt she'd show up. A little knowledge of her character and a check of the airline schedule was all it took: She would take the first flight she could, no layovers. And since American Airlines flew the only nonstop route between Miami and Columbus, it hadn't been taxing to get comfortable near baggage claim and simply wait her out.

Now she passed nearly within arm's reach of the chair, and the Angelmaker studied her. She hadn't changed much, except that she looked a little worse for wear—like she'd taken a fall or something. But she was still slender and leggy, tall for a woman, and sporting thick waves of shoulder-length hair that could be brown or auburn depending on the light. She wasn't beautiful in the traditional sense; her nose had a faint bend and her jaw was too square. But her lips were full and her eyes resembled green glass—big and bright and fringed with lashes so long there probably wasn't a man alive who could look at her without imagining her on her knees, using her lips and batting those lashes up at him.

No doubt she would bat them at authorities in Ohio just as she had in Miami and Raleigh. Determined to make everyone listen to her lies.

The Angelmaker fell in behind her, sneering. The authorities wouldn't believe her; they never had.

The angels, though, were different. They saw truths they shouldn't. And when they did, they had to die.

Something Erin Sims might want to keep in mind.

She hoisted her bag over her shoulder and walked away from a Hertz kiosk, fingering a new key fob, deep in thought. Busy planning her strategy, no doubt.

Predictable as rain, the Angelmaker thought, and didn't bother following her out of the airport. She wouldn't be hard to keep track of. She'd probably show up at Hilltop before the night was over.

And how far would she get this time? Apparently, there was some sort of new evidence, but the news hadn't said what it was. Enough for authorities to issue a stay of execution for Justin Sims. Enough to bring his dogged big sister to Hopewell on a quest to unearth the truth.

The Angelmaker smiled. *Don't look too closely, Dr. Sims. If you find what you're looking for, it will be the last thing you see. You could be an angel, after all.*

Ohio greeted Erin with open hostility: a sky like steel wool, forty-one degrees and spitting. Two hours after her flight landed, her phone's nav-system had her tooling through sparsely populated cattle pastures and dead corn fields. A couple of gallons of coffee wore off near a town called Tiffin, so she stopped at a gas station for a Mountain Dew and Snickers bar, then drove five miles out of her way to find a Kinkos and bought a ream of bright yellow card stock—just in case. Yellow, advertisers said, was eye-catching.

A mile into Hopewell County, the Chamber of Commerce's welcome station came up, a white building with dark beams that made it look like a German cottage. Erin considered it, then pulled in and looked at the wall of information. Hopewell, the county seat, boasted a population of 16,000. It was the site of Mansfeld College ("home of the 2007 and 2008 National Champion Women's volleyball team"), an annual Oktoberfest, and a "Spring Arts Fling" each May. Next weekend, a kids' soccer league would host regional finals at Blue Limestone Park. And at a newly renovated vaudeville theater called "The Palace," a community group had done the opera *Hansel and Gretel* last weekend.

"Geesh," Erin muttered. "I wonder where Aunt Bea and Andy live."

She found a phone book—the thickness of a magazine—beside an old pay phone and flipped through the scant yellow pages. There it was. SPACIOUS ROOMS, FULLY FURNISHED, HISTORIC ATMOSPHERE. MAKE YOUR STAY THE HILLTOP WAY, CALL 1-800-555-6038. VISIT OUR ART POTTERY GIFT SHOP. OWNED AND OPERATED BY JACK AND MARGARET CALLOWAY, SERVING GUESTS SINCE 2007.

Her heart bumped. The bastard, living his Norman Rockwell existence while Justin sat on Death Row. Well, no longer. This time, she'd make someone listen to what she knew: Lauren McAllister had an affair with Huggins. She'd confided to Justin that he scared her. She'd drawn a picture of him before her death that could only be interpreted as disturbed.

And while none of that had been sufficient to get anyone to look at the case again, Erin's discovery last week was different. Her PI learned that Huggins had fled to Virginia after she chased him from Raleigh, and another young woman—a woman just like Lauren—had an affair with him and then disappeared. She'd been gone for five years now, presumed dead. Erin had spoken with the girl's parents last week, got enough information that the PI traced the lover to Hopewell and found a man who could be John Huggins.

Could be. Erin's own turn of thought drained some of the strength from her limbs. She looked at the ad in the yellow pages. What if the owners of this inn *weren't* John and Maggie Huggins?

Time to find out. She'd dealt with enough indifferent sheriffs over the years to know she wasn't going to leave the job to this one. She wanted to go to Huggins herself, see him with her own eyes and hear his voice. Then, when she was armed with the certainty that she'd found Huggins, she'd bully the sheriff into listening to her.

She checked into a Red Roof Inn, washed her face and added a sweater and denim jacket, then headed to Hilltop House. She tooled up the winding drive and parked the rental car in a gravel lot with three others. She looked around. The main house was huge, in the middle of a spread of outbuildings: an enormous barn, an old-fashioned carriage house, a modern garage. A pickup truck crouched outside the garage, freshly washed and looking out of place among the other vehicles, with undercarriages smattered with slush and salt. The flower beds that had bloomed so colorfully in the online photo were empty now, but the boy and girl sculptures still stood in the garden.

Dead giveaways, Huggins, she thought, eyeing the sculptures. His wife, Maggie, was one of the most drop-dead beautiful women Erin had ever seen. Her sculptures were equally beautiful.

Erin started to get out, then stopped, a thump of fear holding her back. She scanned the area. No cars waiting to run her down.

She cursed. Stupid thought. Whoever had taken a run at her at the prison certainly hadn't followed her to Ohio.

She walked up the wide front porch, through an elegant wood-and-etched-glass door, and into Huggins's lair. She stared. As soon as she'd seen the Internet listing for Hilltop House, she'd given no thought to the inn itself— only to what the discovery of Huggins with a new identity might mean for Justin. Now, standing in a grand foyer with the smell of sweet, spiced cider flaring her nostrils and the sound of a fire crackling nearby, she felt as if the world had tipped sideways.

Not the home of a vicious murderer at all: It was gorgeous. Twelve-foot ceilings with tiered crown molding and wine-red walls, cherry floors splashed with thick rugs. A wide staircase rose to second and third stories and on the wall of the grand foyer hung a set of beautifully decorated clay masks. Mrs. *Calloway,* Erin thought, and couldn't help but be impressed by her talent. There were seven of them—all approximately the same size and shape, like the classic comedy-tragedy masks, but each adorned like a fabulous Mardi Gras mask, with jewels and feathers and designs all crafted from clay. They were stunni—

Her breath caught: Something moved in the hallway at the top of the stairs. She peered into the dimness only to see a shadow slip out of sight. Huggins? No. Huggins sauntered. This person . . . skittered.

She rubbed her hands over the goose bumps on her arms and stepped beneath an archway, looking into a large room. Against the far wall sat a sideboard covered with cheeses, crackers, and bunches of grapes, and a tureen of what must be the hot cider she smelled. The tiny glands beneath her tongue came to life and she realized that except for the Snickers bar, she hadn't eaten since . . . this morning? Last night? She wasn't sure.

She went back through the foyer and through an opposite archway. Another rich, spacious room. In the center burned a fire in a double-sided stone fireplace and on the chimney, a hand-painted sign pointed the way to the gift shop. On either side of the fireplace sat a collection of armchairs, footrests, and lamp tables, perfect for cozying up on a cold winter evening.

Two men had done exactly that. One, an older gentleman with an unlit pipe in one hand and a brandy snifter in the other, sported a graying shock of hair and a magazine on his lap. Back issues of *Field & Stream* sat in a stack at his feet. He lifted his glass when he noticed Erin. The other man, a younger version of the same features and body type, set aside a laptop computer and stood. Erin started to say something to him, then noticed his jaw go slack and heard a *click* behind her. She turned, the hairs on her neck standing up.

John Huggins aimed a shotgun at her chest.

CHAPTER
6

ERIN FLINCHED; then the shotgun faded from view and the only thing in the world was the man behind it. *Huggins.* His eyes struck her first—one green and one blue—both pale and piercing and cold. Then the rest of the details filtered in...six feet tall, well-toned for a man of his age. His waist was a few pounds thicker, his temples a touch grayer, the crow's feet a bit deeper in his skin. But he was the same man.

Dear God, she'd found him. *It's going to be okay, Justin.*

"Misters McCormick," he said, without moving the shotgun even fractionally, "move out of the room, if you please. I don't want anyone to get hurt."

"What the hell?" the older McCormick boomed. "Jack, what are you doing?"

"Move out, Wilson. You too, Evan," he said. "I'm not the marksman the two of you are, and I don't want you getting hurt."

"Son of a bitch," the younger man said. Erin noticed that he saved and shut down his document before closing his laptop, as if more inconvenienced than frightened by the appearance of John Huggins with a shotgun. The two guests moved behind Huggins like lazy dogs being nudged from their evening naps.

"Now, Wilson," Huggins said, once they were safely behind him, "pick up that phone in the foyer and call nine-one-one. Tell Sheriff Mann there's an intruder on my premises."

"Have you lost your mind?" the man asked.

"You might also tell him that this particular intruder is in violation of a restraining order."

Erin thought the older man picked up the phone, but couldn't strip her eyes from John Huggins long enough to be sure. Her body had gone to stone, her mouth so dry she couldn't swallow. She was going to heave the near-nothing in her stomach if she stood in the same room with him any longer. Eleven years. More than a third of Justin's life had been spent in prison because of the man now aiming a gun at her, calmly issuing directives to his guests.

She groped for the name he'd used. "Mr. McCormick?" she said. The man at the phone looked at her, startled. "Did Jack Calloway ever tell you that his real name is John Huggins? Did you know that he was accused of killing a young wo—"

"Wilson McCormick has been coming to Hilltop since we opened and is one of my wife's most loyal patrons," Huggins interrupted. "He's not likely to be bothered by your ranting and raving."

"Listen to me," Erin grated out. She looked at the McCormicks behind him. "You have to understand."

"All they need to understand," Huggins said, "is that you are a poor, misguided woman who believes her brother's lies instead of the facts. I've told you before, Dr. Sims, I didn't murder Lauren McAllister. And I will not let you ruin my reputation or hurt my wife again by spouting your lies."

Erin gritted her teeth. The *bastard,* standing there, pointing a shotgun at her and somehow making himself appear the victim. "So what are you going to do, shoot me right here in front of God and everyone?" She glanced at the younger McCormick, who'd gone wide-eyed, then the elder, who had the phone pressed to his ear and occasionally said something into it. She had to make them listen. Somehow—

"Jack." The front door swung wide. The newcomer stopped short when he saw the standoff. He was forty-something, and looked like he'd just stepped out of the casual section of *Gentleman's Quarterly.* He glanced around, keeping one eye on the gun. "What's going on?"

"I'll tell you," Erin jumped in, but they spoke right over her.

"This is the woman I told you about, Dorian," Huggins said.

"His real name is John Huggins—"

"She's the reason Margaret and I changed names and—"

"He killed a girl and let my brother go to prison for it." Fury carried Erin forward. As if in some sort of out-of-body experience, she realized she was walking toward him, right toward the shotgun. She didn't care; he wouldn't shoot her. That wasn't his style and there were too many witnesses. But they weren't listening to her. No one believed her.

Listen to me, Mom. You have to believe me.

"I want her arrested, Dorian," Huggins said.

"It's you who should be arres—" A hand clamped over her mouth, cutting off her breath. Panic struck and she flailed, then realized it was the younger McCormick who had grabbed her from behind.

"Stop it, lady," he ground against her ear. "He's got a gun."

She writhed, trying to yank free, and everything dragged into slow motion. Sirens whined outside the door. Boots stomped in, voices shouting over one another. A handful of strangers appeared on the stairwell and the man from *GQ* kept talking and wagging a finger and Huggins's wife came in from the back, still strikingly beautiful and standing in front of her masks wringing her hands. Huggins's shotgun finally came down and Erin shook off the hands that held her.

She caught her breath and glanced at a clock over the mantel: six-thirty. Nearly two days gone of Justin's seven, but she was on her way. She'd identified Huggins and the police were here. Next would come the media and soon people would hear the truth and Justin would have another chance. *She* would have another chance. To do what she'd never been able to do before, even when they were children.

To protect him.

"I want to see Sheriff Nikolaus Mann," she said to a deputy who might have been twelve. He had red-blond hair that stuck up like an elf's and had been reaching for his belt when she spoke. For handcuffs, Erin realized.

He seemed startled by her demand but relaxed his hand. "Uh . . . Okay. Come with me."

Huggins intercepted them. "Deputy Jensen, this woman is trespassing, committing slander, and in violation of a restraining order."

"I'll take care of it, Jack," Jensen said, and walked her out, seeming in a hurry to have it over. Erin held Huggins's

gaze as they passed him, and his blue-green eyes bore
into her like daggers.

She shook it off and they stepped into the cold night
air. Erin noticed the two deputies' cars, both with blue
lights flashing. "Where can I find the sheriff?" she asked.

"He'll be back Monday," the young deputy said. His
badge read C. JENSEN. "Come on to headquarters and
we'll write up your complaint. Or, Jack's complaint.
Or..." He stopped. Confused.

Erin steeled her spine.

"This can't wait until Monday. I need to see him now."

"Ma'am, I'm sorry. He's not here." But he'd blinked.
Weakening.

She stuck her hands on her hips. "And does he have a
phone?"

"Yes, ma'am."

"And do you know how to dial his number?"

"Well, yes."

"Then do it."

Somewhere in the distance, funky music played. Nick
stirred, lying on the floor of the cabin. A tequila bottle
lounged in his fingers; cigarette butts littered the hearth of
the fireplace. His brain sloshed at the bottom of his skull.

A minute passed and the music stopped. He climbed
to his feet and humped to a chair—a rickety wooden grab
from a yard sale three years ago. There was a table, too,
also with one leg shorter than the other. "A matched set,"
the seller had said, right before Nick gave him ten dollars
for all three pieces of junk. The third was an old mattress
on the floor in front of the fireplace.

Otherwise, the cabin was empty. Nick had paid a guy
to haul away the Italian leather sofa and chairs, the cherry

dining room set, the king-size bed in the master bedroom and the princess furniture in the adjoining room. A salvage guy had even pulled out the carpet and molding.

The music came again and Nick frowned. It seemed to be coming from his ass. He shifted and it got louder. It *was* coming from his ass.

He pulled the phone from his hip pocket, cursed at the number. Chris Jensen. He opened the phone and snarled into it. "What the hell are you doing, calling me?"

"Sheriff—"

"It's not Monday yet. Leave me alone."

"Sheriff, we have a situation."

"Is Hannah okay?"

"Yes, sir."

"My mom okay?"

"Yes, sir."

"Has Hopewell been attacked by terrorists, burned down, or washed away in a flood?" That long of a speech actually left him dizzy.

"No, sir."

Then Nick remembered, and an instant of sobriety threatened. "Did they find the son of a bitch who killed Carrie Sitton?"

"Uh, no. But there is one thing on that. Turns out she was a friend of Rebecca Engel's."

"Friend?"

"Carrie was on her way home from Rebecca's house when she was murdered. Cleveland cops were down here interviewing Rebecca today."

Aw, hell. Rebecca Engel lived in Hopewell. She was Nick's. Too close, too close.

Jensen went on. "Rebecca didn't know anything about Carrie's plans after she left the house. They met doing some barhopping up in Cleveland and had started hanging out a little. Sheriff Bell is putting two of his men with the Cleveland Robbery-Homicide team. They've got a pretty good group working it."

Uneasiness roiled in Nick's belly and that alone pissed him off. He shouldn't be feeling it. At this advanced stage of this particular weekend, he shouldn't be feeling anything. And yet, after two days of deliberate self-destruction, he'd identified the music in his ass as his phone, formulated coherent sentences, and felt something in his chest that bordered on true emotion.

Not acceptable. It was Saturday night. He still had thirty-six more hours before he was back on duty.

"Sheriff," Jensen said, and a chair creaked in his ear. Nick recognized it as the one at the front desk at the station. "There's a request here for you to check something for a case pending in Florida. It came in yesterday but you were gone already so Valeria left it on your desk. She was afraid to call you."

"Smart woman."

"And now there's someone here insisting that you follow up on it. She says it's urgent. It's about Jack Calloway."

A thread of interest threatened to unravel but Nick stopped it. There wasn't one fucking thing that happened in Hopewell, Ohio, that couldn't wait.

"Will she still be there Monday?"

Jensen hesitated. "Uh, well, sir, I imagine so. She's booked at the Red Roof Inn."

"Well, good. That's just when I'll be home."

"Monday?" Erin bunched her fists on the desk, wincing at echoes of pain in her body. It was nine o'clock at night, and this cherub-faced deputy named Jensen had

spent the past two hours taking her through her story, writing down notes, and reading the online reports related to Justin. Finally, he'd deemed her situation significant enough to phone the almighty, not-to-be-disturbed sheriff.

For all the good it did, she thought, looking around at the sheriff's office. Not exactly a paragon of high-tech law enforcement: a lobby with a couple of large wooden desks and some file cabinets, a set of holding cells down one hallway, a handful of offices Erin couldn't see, and a mysterious miasma of odors. A second deputy had gone searching for someone to open the courthouse across the street on a Saturday night, ostensibly to dig up details about the restraining order against her. Erin had been left to try to convince Deputy Jensen that Huggins should be behind bars and not her.

"Let me talk to him. Call him again," she said.

"Look, Mis—" He caught himself. "Doctor. Technically, I could have you in lockup. Jack wants you charged with trespassing, at the least. I don't think you want Sheriff Mann coming back here until the judge gets a chance to look at the restraining order."

"The judge," she snapped. "The one who's deer hunting?"

"Judge Watkins always goes deer hunting the week after Oktoberfest ends, ever since I was a kid. He'll be back M—"

"Monday," she chorused. She'd heard it all already and dread clawed through her breast. In the hours left before then, how much could John Huggins do? Pack up and get away? If he vanished again, what would that mean for Justin?

Erin closed her eyes. She knew what it meant.

The printer against the wall started spitting out pages again and Jensen got up to collect them. "I'm doing what the sheriff would do, anyway—gathering the information on your brother's case. By the time he gets back, I'll have everything ready for him."

She cursed and rubbed her face, winced. She'd forgotten the scrape. She scrubbed at it again, this time with a nail.

"Oh, damn it," she said, looking at her finger. "I'm bleeding."

Jensen was up in a heartbeat, looking at the side of her face. "Hold on," he said, and started down the hall. Erin felt a pang of guilt. This was a kid, probably living out some childhood fantasy of becoming a deputy, and she was taking advantage of the fact that he was willing to get her a freaking Band-Aid.

Forget it. All's fair in love and war. Her fight to save Justin was all-out war.

Erin gave him five seconds and began rooting through the desk. Address, address…Somewhere, there had to be some indication where the sheriff was. A cabin—that much Jensen had told her—and it couldn't be far. Not when a man went there to hunt for just a weekend.

She pushed papers around, opened those drawers that weren't locked and looked at the computer. No, she didn't dare try getting into that. Keeping one eye on the front door and an ear peeled for Jensen's footsteps behind her, she went to a smaller desk that sat near the door—that of a daytime receptionist, she supposed—and found a Rolodex. A good, old-fashioned Rolodex.

Her pulse skittered and she fingered through…Mann, Mann, Mann. And there it was: *Mann—cabin*.

Erin snatched the card from its file and chanced a

glance down the hall, then pocketed the address just as Jensen came back.

"Here's some antiseptic and—"

"Oh, that's okay," she said. "You know, I think you were right in the first place. There's nothing I can do right now without the sheriff and judge."

His brows drew together a touch but he said, "Right. Go to your motel, so I'll know where to find you. Get some sleep." She turned to pick up her bag and he added, "And listen, you don't have to worry about Sheriff Mann. He'll take care of things."

You're damn right he will, Erin thought, fingering the cabin address in her pocket. *Sooner than you think.*

Just over an hour later, her GPS announced the last turn to Sheriff Mann's cabin, in the middle of nowhere. On her left, strange silhouettes rose in the darkness— mounds that looked like pyramids and huge buildings with security lights. Erin caught the reflection of standing water—ponds?—and just when she'd decided it must be a quarry of some sort, her headlights picked out a sign that said WEAVER'S CLAY MINE.

Maggie Huggins came to mind, evidently a well-known sculptor now. Like her husband, she seemed to have found her niche in life over the past few years. Justin hadn't had the chance to find his.

"You have arrived at your destination," said the mechanical female voice in the phone. Erin slowed, searching for whatever the GPS thought was there. Beyond the clay mine, there was nothing, but on her right, a gravel lane cut into the woods. She turned and followed it, the trees like skeletons with straggly remnants of white stuck to trunks here and there. A hundred childhood fairy

tales rose to mind, all of them leading some poor, unsuspecting girl deep into a cold black forest toward certain doom...

"Stop it," she said aloud, then saw the house. "My God."

The word "cabin" was ill-chosen. The house was enormous, with a deep wraparound porch, French doors, and bay windows. The windows glowed with a faint, flickering light that qualified as downright eerie.

She pulled her Florida-weight jacket tight, then walked up the porch steps by the glow of her headlights, which hadn't turned off yet. At the top of the stairs sat a Styrofoam cooler with a roll of paper on top. A black marker lay on the porch railing. Erin started toward the door and the toe of her shoe kicked something. Small, dark objects were scattered on the floor like dead bugs. She bent to pick one up.

Shell casings.

She swallowed, wishing she could have brought her gun on the plane, then looked at the front door. It stood open an inch—like a dare—and she tamped back a pang of worry. Just do it.

She knocked. Nothing. She knocked again, harder, and the door glided open. She stepped inside.

"Sheriff Mann?" she called. "Sheriff, my name is Erin Sims. I need to talk to you."

Nothing.

She glanced around. The light came from deeper in the house, sputtering as if from a candle or lantern, maybe a fireplace. There was no furniture, no curtains, no heat. No sign of life save for the flicker of light, the Styrofoam cooler outside on the porch, and the open door.

"Sheriff?" Her voice echoed and she realized the floors had been stripped. A row of bare carpet tacks poked up across a threshold, like a strip of tire spikes. She stepped over it and followed the light through an archway down a wide hall, the scent of burning firewood luring her deeper into the house. "Sheriff?"

She rounded a corner and nearly jumped from her skin. A man sat in the center of an empty room—a large black silhouette in a wooden chair with his hands in his lap, the fire glowing behind him. The shape of a giant pistol showed in the dimness, idly pointed in her direction.

"Rumor has it you almost got shot once tonight," he said. "You looking to try again?"

CHAPTER
7

N ICK HEARD THE breath draft from her lungs and wished the light were better. He wanted to see what she looked like—this woman who would barge into Hilltop House with accusations on her lips, lie to a deputy, and steal away in the night to hunt down a sheriff. He wanted to demand that she take back the slander she'd already set rumbling through his town, then put her on a plane back to Miami.

Instead, he sucked on a cigarette until the embers flared red. Blew a stream of sweet nicotine into the air.

"I need to talk to you, Sheriff," she demanded. "You have a man in your town I believe is a murderer. His name is—"

"Jack Calloway."

She stopped, and Nick could almost hear the wheels turning in her mind. "Yes, that's right."

A vein throbbed in Nick's temple. He had a day-and-a-half more numbness coming to him, but had quit drinking an hour ago, after Jensen called and reported that a Miami hurricane named Erin Sims was on her way. It hadn't been enough time to become fully sober or get caught up on what she was whining about. But it had been enough to feel one small section of his brain begin to function. And get good and pissed about it.

He stood, flicking his cigarette onto the stone hearth behind him, keeping his back to the light of the fireplace. He was six-three, broad-shouldered, wholly unkempt, and palming a large Hechler & Koch machine pistol. It pleased him to think he made an imposing silhouette.

"Could you put down the gun?" she snapped. "You're drunk."

So much for imposing. "Not nearly enough, as far as I can tell."

She glanced around. Tequila and beer bottles scattered on the floor. "Well, you can certainly be proud of your effort."

Nick almost smiled. A little chutzpah there. Except for Valeria and Hannah, he wasn't accustomed to being challenged. He was the small-town kid turned big deal, then come home to roost. He wasn't cocky, but like an Old West sheriff, he wasn't often defied.

He exchanged the gun for the lantern and sauntered forward, letting his gaze fall to her feet and back. She was slim, about five-eight, with a mass of dark hair collected with limited success at the back of her head. She wore a denim jacket and jeans, and her arms were crossed over what Nick imagined was a reasonable pair of breasts. A ragged scab scraped down one side of her face.

"What happened?"

"I fell," she said. "Are you sober enough to listen to me now?"

"No. I'm planning to be sober on Monday."

She grabbed his arm, a death grip. "Please. This can't wait." Nick lifted the lantern and looked into her eyes. Mistake. They were green, like the antique bottles his grandfather used to keep on a shelf. Clear and glassy and filled with something Nick had seen before—in the eyes of a woman watching her parents' house burn, the eyes of a man looking at the wreckage of his wife's car, the eyes of a mother watching police drag a river for her son.

In Allison's eyes, on the night she died.

I'm scared, Nick.

Everything's fine, Allison. I've got it covered.

"Sheriff!"

A new voice rang through the house.

"In here," Nick called out. Chris Jensen appeared at the doorway, carrying folders and two cups from a gas station. He shook his head when he saw Sims.

"You're not supposed to be here. You said you would go to your motel."

"*You* said that," she clarified, "not I." He muttered something that, for Jensen, qualified as a curse, and Nick felt a twinge of pride in the young deputy. He'd made a good catch, thinking she'd run out of the station in a hurry and deciding to check up on her. Now he set the folders on the table and held out a cup of coffee to Nick. It was gonna take more than an hour off the bottle and a cup of coffee to get his head cleared up, but it was a start.

He took a swig. Lukewarm. Jensen noticed his grimace and looked around. "Is there someplace I can heat it up?"

"Does it look like there's someplace to heat it up?"

"Uh, no. It looks like no one's been in this place for years. Gee, Sheriff, I thought—"

"Never mind." Nick looked back at the Sims woman, who had dared to interrupt his weekend, upset his town, and allow Jensen a glimpse into the most private part of his life. He set down the cup and propped his butt against the table. "All right, spit it out," he said.

Sims opened her mouth but Jensen spoke over her. "I got a call from Hilltop House about an intruder." He tipped his head toward Sims. "Jack's insisting that we press charges but I—"

"What charges?"

"Trespassing. Disturbing the peace. Slander." He paused. "Violating a restraining order."

Nick looked at her. He was impressed.

"It seems Dr. Sims has a history with Jack Calloway," Jensen said. "She's actually got a rap sheet, if you can believe that."

"A doctor with a rap sheet."

"Psychologist," she said.

That stopped him. Jesus, a shrink. His opinion of her—which had just begun to tiptoe toward interesting—took a nosedive. Psychologists ranked one rung below reporters.

Jensen said, "Jack took out a restraining order against her in Raleigh after they moved there. Tonight, he held her at the tip of his shotgun and demanded that I take her in."

Nick turned to Sims. The haze of two days of tequila had begun to burn into one hell of a headache. "Would you care to elaborate, Doctor?"

She held his eyes. "Jack Calloway is a murderer."

"Then why isn't he in prison?"

"Because police believed him when he blamed someone else." Her eyes—glittering in the light of the lantern and fire—went glassy. "My brother."

Nick winced. He turned to Jensen, who held up one of the folders.

"It's true," he said. "Her brother has been in the Florida State Prison for eleven years, on Death Row for a murder committed almost twelve years ago. His execution was scheduled for the night before last, but a Federal court granted a last-minute stay. One week. The execution is rescheduled for this Thursday, at midnight, pending investigation."

"Investigation of what?"

"John Huggins," Sims said. "You know him as Jack Calloway. He's the man who seduced and murdered a girl named Lauren McAllister. She was the daughter of Senator McAllister of Florida."

Nick's brain stirred. He remembered it, vaguely. "And your brother was convicted."

"Yes."

"Yet, there's a restraining order against *you*. I take it you've accused Huggins before?"

The muscles in her throat convulsed in a swallow. "Yes."

"But weren't able to prove him guilty."

"But he did it. My brother didn't kill anyone."

"Aw, Christ." Nick closed his eyes. A woman wounded and scorned, over something only she believes.

"I know what you're thinking."

He cocked a brow. "Oh?"

"You're thinking I'm some crazy woman with an ax to grind over something I can't prove."

Okay, that was pretty close.

"Look at the case, then," she said. "Prove that I'm wrong."

"That's not the way it works," Nick reminded her, then thought of something. "If his real name is Huggins, how did you find him in Hopewell?"

"Private investigator. Last week, he found that they'd moved to Virginia after they left Raleigh, and from there, tracked him here."

"And you jumped on a plane to Ohio to confront him."

"No," she said, as if insulted by the notion that she'd behaved on impulse. "I jumped in a car to my brother's attorney, then to the Attorney General, then to the prison, then to the hospital, *then* to a plane to Oh—"

"The hospital?" The rest of the sequence made sense.

Jensen stepped in. "On Thursday night, after the execution didn't happen, someone took a run at Dr. Sims in their car. The Starke County Sheriff's Office is investigating, but the car was rented with fake IDs. They came up empty."

Nick's muscles went to steel. *I fell,* she'd said. He eyed the dark scrape down her cheek and caught a flicker of fear in her eyes. She tried to smother it but for one, dangerous heartbeat, she appeared more victim than troublemaker. An innocent woman who'd wound up in the path of a—

Stop it.

"Do you have any idea who was driving?" he asked.

"No," she said. "The sheriff there chalked it up to some death penalty advocate who was upset my brother survived the night. He promised they would investigate." Her tone dripped with doubt.

Nick took a deep breath. If the attack at the prison had been the work of some extremist protester, then she was out of danger now. Still, he didn't like the idea that she'd been targeted. He'd rather be pissed at her than worried.

"What's in the paper?" he asked Jensen.

Jensen tapped the folder. "Everything I could find on a Saturday night. And I sent a bunch of requests for reports that we should get tomorrow or Monday." He scooted the collection of reports toward Nick on the table. "Dr. Sims fingered Jack—John Huggins—for the McAllister girl's murder back in Florida but no charges were ever filed against him. Instead, her brother was tried and convicted, and sentenced to death."

Nick looked at her. "Let me guess. Your brother had never even met the McAllister girl. He was in Nova Scotia at the time of her death with a dozen witnesses and never shot a gun in his life."

Her chin went up. "No. My brother had a crazy crush on her, his semen was found in a condom in her bathroom, and his fingerprints were on the gun that killed her."

Whoa. Nick glanced at Jensen, who shrugged, then looked back at Dr. Sims. She hadn't flinched. Had done this before, he decided. For about twelve years, no doubt.

He rubbed a hand over his face. This had to be bullshit. *Jack Calloway?* He was an upstanding man, a friend. Besides, there were no murderers in Hopewell.

The clay-covered body of Carrie Sitton rose to mind, the taste of bile right behind.

No. That wasn't Hopewell. That case wasn't his.

But this one—he looked at the stack of papers Jensen had brought—this one *was* his. Jack Calloway was his. For the moment, anyway, no matter how much he didn't like the idea, Dr. Erin Sims was his.

"Jensen," he said, picking up the files from the table. "Go back to Hopewell and finish compiling whatever's left. Set up an appointment for me with Jack in the morning and see if Dorian Reinhardt is back—he's been in Georgia visiting relatives with his family."

"He got back today," Jensen said. "Jack called him over to Hilltop when Sims showed up."

"Okay. Then let him know I'm going to talk to Jack." Dorian was Jack's lawyer. He was a prick, but would have to be there. Nick paused, mentally counting out the days until midnight, Thursday. "And call Judge Watkins. Tell him I may need him home."

"Sure," Jensen said, and slid a glance to Sims. "You want me to take her?"

Nick saw her frame tighten. There was plenty of reason to put her in a motel—or cell—for a few hours, not the least of which was to make sure she stayed put. There was no good reason to hear any more ludicrous accusations about Jack Calloway or a murderer lurking in his town.

Except that she was the most interesting thing he'd come across in a long time, in more ways than one. His gaze dipped to her left hand, belatedly enough to know his senses weren't up to speed yet. No wedding ring, just a small silver-and-pearl setting on her right hand.

She was alone in this.

"She can stay," he said, and opened his palms to her. "If she wants to."

"Will you let me tell you about Huggins?" she asked.

"I'll read the files. Since I'm apparently being asked by Florida to look at the case, anyway."

To his surprise, she seemed to take even that much as a triumph. "Then I'll stay."

CHAPTER
8

REBECCA ENGEL CLIMBED onto the sofa from her knees and spat into her bandanna, wiping her face with the back of her hand. She sniffed; that last snort of cocaine had made her nostrils burn.

"Get back here," Ace said. He hauled her onto his lap and dug between her thighs with his fingers. "You like that, don't you, baby?"

"No, it hurts," she said, meaning it. "Stop it, Ace. I'm not in the mood." *I can't stop thinking about Carrie.*

"You barely knew her," Ace grumbled. "Get over it."

Get over it. Rebecca closed her eyes, trying to ignore the ache between her thighs. She couldn't get over it. Carrie was dead. All because Rebecca had told her she could score some crack from Ace. She was murdered on the same road Rebecca always used to come to Ace's house late at night.

Jesus. It could have been her.

Ace made a sound deep in his throat and his fingers dug in.

"Stop," she said. "I have to work the breakfast crowd tomorrow, early. And if I'm late or my mom finds out I was here—"

"You gonna get the money from the cash register?" He twisted her nipple in the fingers of his free hand. Ace's idea of romance. "How do you expect me to take you away from here without money?"

"I will, I will," she said, and a spear of sensation shot from her nipple to her belly. It was more pain than pleasure but heady all the same. Ace was going to take her away; he'd promised. He was going to get her out of this two-bit, stuck-in-the-last-century town and go some-place where no one was breathing down their necks all the time. "I can't go yet. The cops keep wanting to talk to me about Carrie." She shivered. "God, I can't believe she's dead."

Ace came forward. "Forget her," he said, and his fin-gers pushed up between her legs. Rebecca moaned, not with pleasure, but resignation. Nothing short of a SWAT team would stop Ace Holmes when he wanted sex, and besides, sex was what Rebecca Engel was. It was what she had to offer the world: an oversized set of breasts, a soft belly with a gold hoop through her navel, and a pair of naturally bee-stung lips designed for certain tasks.

A girl's gotta be good at something.

She went through the motions until she felt his hips jerk and heard a groan ripped from his chest. Finally, he fell back onto the couch. Used up, at least for now.

She got in her car and headed back to town, the sky pitch black and the road—where Carrie had died—seeming more stark and lonely than ever before. Rebecca steered past the spot where Carrie's car had been pushed off the road, clenching her fingers and trying not to look. A few miles later, she slowed, squinting at something in the road.

A truck. Her heart skipped a beat.

The truck sat at an angle, blocking the road. The shadow of someone trying to wave her down moved in the mist.

Rebecca slowed, chewing her lip. This was Hopewell. People helped one another here. Yet the memory of Carrie on this very road just a few miles north lifted her hackles. Is that what Carrie had done?

Rebecca locked her car doors—something she couldn't remember ever doing before. Got close enough that she could see a figure opening the hood. Something was wrong.

Random attack. That's what they said about Carrie. Police were still looking, but the paper had said authorities thought it was some impulsive act by a stranger passing through. Not someone from Hopewell, stuck on the road with the hood up.

Still, she couldn't seem to settle her heart to a normal beat, and even as her car drifted closer to the stalled truck, the fingers of one hand curled around her phone. For a split second, she had the insane impulse to call home and let her mother know where she was, but she shook it off. She was nineteen—a grown woman. Bad enough that she'd flunked out of college and had nowhere to go but Hopewell. But if her mom found out she'd been with Ace Holmes tonight—and tripping—she'd be a prisoner. She and Ace would never have the chance to get away.

Rebecca took a deep breath and pulled closer to the truck. Don't be a baby, she told herself. For God's sake, this was Hopewell.

Nick threw two logs on the fire, then moved an old radio off the table and adjusted the lantern so he could read. Sims looked around.

"It's not much for creature comforts, but that blanket is clean," he said, nodding to the mattress on the floor.

She went to it, looking a little less confident than just moments before. She was in a cold, empty house in the middle of nowhere, alone at night with a stranger who was half drunk, outweighed her by at least eighty pounds, and wielded a bad temper and a pistol. Nick could see each and every one of those realizations coming to light in her mind.

"I've never attacked a woman before," he assured her.

"But you could make an exception for me?"

He lifted a brow. "You're throwing around some pretty heavy accusations, in a place where you don't know the players."

"I know Jack Calloway."

Nick held her eyes. "So do I."

An impasse. She acknowledged it with a tilt of her head and lowered herself to the mattress so carefully that Nick pulled out the Starke County Sheriff's accident report first: Dr. Sims had suffered a bout of unconsciousness, a couple of bruised ribs, abrasions and contusions. He could see it as she tried to get comfortable—the careful movements, the wince. He made a mental note to call Starke County first thing in the morning.

"I could tell you in a nutshell," she offered, but Nick didn't want the emotional-sister version. He wanted the facts.

"I'd rather read it in detail," he said.

She leaned back against the wall to wait, crossing her arms over her rib cage. Nick knew about bruised ribs. They hurt like a son of a bitch.

Read.

Lauren McAllister: She'd been a promising art student

with a love for cocaine, and the only child of a two-term senator who had, according to some, won his third term on a sympathy vote. Lauren's body had been found when early morning bird-watchers saw something floating in the Everglades. Authorities got to her before the alligators and determined that she'd been dead since the night before, though she hadn't been in the water very long. The bullet that killed her, point blank into the heart, came from a .38 with Justin Sims's prints, which turned up in the swamp. She'd been tripping: cocaine in her blood.

Interesting, but not unusual. Pretty run-of-the-mill, as murders go. There was evidence that pointed straight to Justin Sims, with nothing to distinguish this case from a hundred other murd—

Nick blinked, and the hairs on his arms stood up. He reread a passage: *traces of paint thinner on face.*

He glanced up and caught Sims looking at him.

Paint thinner? Jack Calloway was a skilled carpenter. Paint thinner would be a staple in his workshop. And Nick had seen Margaret, a sculptor, use it to clean up clay.

He blew out a breath. Sims was a shrink, and he could see it coming. "I imagine you have a theory about the paint thinner?" he asked. "Some psychological profile you've concocted and applied to Jack Calloway. Let's see . . . His wife is drop-dead gorgeous without makeup so he can't bear to have it on his lovers?"

"A little cliché, don't you think?"

"His mother used to scrub his face with paint thinner and lye, until he bled."

"Better," she said. "It's always about the mother, after all, isn't it?"

Fucking shrinks. They were the reason Bertrand Yost wasn't in a real jail serving real time. The reason Nick's career had gone to hell. "No," he said. "It's usually about money or sex or vengeance, and hardly ever about psychological mumbo jumbo. Jails need bars, not couches."

"Look, I'll be the first to say I don't know why Lauren's murderer cleaned off her face with paint thinner, but I do know there's a reason. Something that would explain his actions." She squared her shoulders. "Why don't you ask Calloway what it is?"

Nick suppressed a scowl. He tried to paint Jack Calloway with the brush of a psycho-murderer—someone with some weird compulsion to shoot a woman and leave her fresh-faced, then dump her for gators. It wouldn't work. Aside from the simple weirdness of it, Jack was a good man, successful, and devoutly religious. He was married to one of the most attractive women Nick had ever laid eyes on; even now, at nearly fifty, Margaret's features were put together in a way that made men of all ages catch themselves staring, and she wore them naturally and without arrogance, with a slim figure and thick dark hair attractively threaded with silver. She never wore a speck of makeup yet—

Christ.

Nick cursed beneath his breath. This was the problem with shrinks: They could take a man apart and put the pieces back together in a way that created a different man altogether, something that wasn't real.

Detective Mann, isn't it a fact that you went there with the intention *of killing Bertrand Yost? Isn't it a fact that you* enjoyed *beating the hell out of him?*

Nick bit back a curse. Focus. This is about Lauren McAllister. Not Allison, not Yost.

He slid a finger beneath the portrait of Lauren provided by her family and held it beside the ME's headshot of her in death: a Marilyn Monroe look-alike, complete with the mole above the left corner of her lip, heavy makeup, and a come-fuck-me look in her eyes. Typical nineteen-year-old these days, Nick thought, feeling his age, then remembered that this shot was actually twelve years old.

It was an old case. A closed case. A case in which the murderer had already been identified, tried, and convicted. Justin Sims.

He pulled out another folder: Sims. Justin and Erin were the children of Marla Gordon and Chuck Sims. Sims died in a boating accident when Justin was a baby and Erin was six, and her mother remarried Jeffrey Collins, a successful Realtor in South Florida. By all accounts, the family was respected and privileged, and though the marriage ended in divorce several years before the murder, there were no indications that teenage Justin was on any sort of bad track at the time. His mother attended his trial but was noticeably absent from her daughter's efforts to defend him afterward; Jeffrey Collins disappeared after the divorce. Similarly, there was a husband in there for at least a little while. David Cox was a law student Erin Sims married a year before the murder. He testified for the defense, claiming Justin didn't own a gun, but after that, he, too, stopped showing up in reports.

Nick looked across the room at Sims, at the empty left ring finger. She *was* alone. Even the rest of her family seemed to have accepted Justin's fate and, one by one, had abandoned the cause. Jensen had a whole stack of pages here that showed ten years of visits to police departments, the FBI, journalists, and a string of private investigators—none of them mentioning anyone but Dr. Sims.

A twinge of admiration threatened and Nick bullied it back. No matter how much she believed in her brother's innocence, her methods couldn't be condoned. When Justin was convicted, she went after Huggins—publicly and with a vengeance. Police didn't listen, but everyone else did. Eventually, Huggins's neighbors shunned him, contractors fired him, and his own pastor asked him to leave the church for the sake of the congregation. His wife's classes in sculpture emptied of what few pupils she had left. Sixteen months after Justin's trial had ended, John and Maggie Huggins moved to Raleigh, North Carolina, to try to start over.

Erin Sims followed. Within weeks, she had papered the city with posters declaring him a sexual predator, drug dealer, and murderer; gotten herself interviewed on TV; and published an editorial in the paper. For John and Maggie, life in Raleigh never got off the ground. Sims found herself at the hard end of a slander suit and a restraining order but neither fazed her. For the next ten years, while Justin lost one appeal after another, she hired private investigators and hounded police departments, but no one took her seriously. In the margin of one report, Nick found a note scrawled from one cop to another: *JD—don't waste your time. A loose screw.*

Loose screw or not, Erin Sims earned a doctorate during those ten years, becoming a victims' advocate for the Dade County court system. She had a reputation there as a pit bull, but continued to work on Justin's case on the side.

Nick switched to the file Valeria had tagged for him. It was from the Florida Attorney General's office: a citation of a court-ordered stay of execution and a request for Nick to confirm the identity of one Jack Calloway.

He tipped his chair onto two legs, closing his eyes on an ache that swelled in his brain. Jack was a town leader, a prominent businessman, and a loyal churchgoer. His work to renovate the run-down Hilltop property into an historic bed-and-breakfast had been a boon to the area, and between the inn and his wife's artwork, Hopewell had become somewhat of a tourist trap. Margaret Calloway was a little bit famous. She taught art classes, hosted sculpting *Elderhostels*, and mined her own clay right here at Weaver's. Nick knew she'd been featured in at least one trade magazine and had a handful of pieces in museums. With the help of her nephew, Rodney—whom she and Jack had raised from childhood—and a couple of employees, they kept Hilltop House in peak condition. And if Jack and Margaret had come to Hopewell to escape something from the past, well, Nick could hardly blame them.

He'd done it, too.

Until now. Now there was some media-hungry rabble-rouser from Miami handing Nick the very things he'd gone two thousand miles to avoid. Murder, drugs, illicit affairs, rumors. Christ, he didn't want Hopewell to face that kind of shit, but by now the whole town had probably heard the accusations against Jack. The local media were probably having a field day.

His hands fisted and he looked at Erin Sims. No one knew better than Nick what destructive sensationalism could do to a man. No one had worked harder than he to create a refuge from that sort of destruction.

And no one—no matter how pretty and sad-eyed—was gonna come into his haven and fuck it up.

CHAPTER
9

W HAT A FUCK-UP.
　　The Angelmaker slid into the front entrance of Hilltop House, inched the door shut, and held still for the space of several seconds. Listened.

The inn was asleep. No one to notice the truck missing, no one to question being out so late.

Except the angels. *They keep watch. They see the truth.*

Fucking angels. Always watching. Well, not anymore. Not all of them, anyway. The first seven had been neutralized. They were harmless now—deaf, dumb, and blind. After twelve years, only three angels remained. Rebecca, the eighth, was next. Soon she'd join the others.

But she was being difficult. Bitch.

Tonight's failure rolled in on a wave of anger. Rebecca had been inches from pulling up to the truck, seconds from falling into the trap meant for her in the first place. Then, for no reason at all, she'd slammed on her brakes, wheeled around, and rushed off into the distance at about seventy miles an hour.

She *saw.*

The Angelmaker took a deep breath, nerves dancing. Rebecca couldn't become like the last one—Shelly Quinn. Shelly had proved herself as an angel and then disappeared. Kept watching, watching until it wasn't possible to *breathe* without feeling her eyes. The months waiting to kill her had been a nightmare, and when she was finally dead, the weight of the universe had lifted.

No way would the Angelmaker let Rebecca's destruction drag out like that. She had to die, before she became dangerous.

Still, there was no room for panic. Panic caused mistakes; just ask Justin Sims—or his sister. For a moment, not for the first time, the Angelmaker wondered if Erin Sims would emerge as an angel. She was brazen enough, but in all these years, she'd never seen the truth. There was no reason to think she would now.

Unless Nick Mann climbed onto her bandwagon.

The Angelmaker drew a breath, thinking about that. Nick was more blind than anyone. Blind and pigheaded and so protective of his good citizens in his good town that he'd never believe anything damning about the Calloway family. Nick wouldn't be an issue, unless Erin Sims worked her way under his skin. He wasn't a player, but he was no monk. It wasn't inconceivable that she could get him thinking with something other than his head.

Have to keep an eye out for that.

The Angelmaker tiptoed through the lobby, dropped the keys to the Ford into the drawer of a cherry secretary, and cocked an ear toward the stairs. Still nothing. Just a few more steps, and tonight's fiasco would be over. No one would ever know how Rebecca had slipped from his grasp.

A spread of gooseflesh prickled to life and the Angelmaker looked up at the masks on the foyer wall. Hollow eyes, sealed lips, and no ears at all. Harmless now. They might as well be monkeys on display: *See no evil, speak no evil, hear no evil.*

Words for the wise, Dr. Sims.

At four-thirty in the morning, Erin pulled into the city parking lot behind the sheriff's Tahoe. Mann met her at her car door with an expression like thunder.

"I told you to follow me to your motel exit," he said, but Erin didn't care. He'd spent a couple hours at the cabin reading files—barely talking—then told her to follow him back to Hopewell. When she hadn't stopped at the motel, she could almost *feel* his anger stretching from his car to hers, but she'd be damned if she was going to leave until she knew he was taking what he'd read seriously.

Less than five days left.

"Not until we talk," she said.

He bent a forearm onto the roof of the Aveo and it sagged beneath his weight. In the wash of security lights, the details of his face were visible—strong Germanic features with deep grooves on either side of his mouth, a white crescent scar bisecting one eyebrow, and a dent marring the left side of his chin. Combined with the weekend's beard and debauchery, he had a haggard, beat-up look that seemed out of place for Mayberry.

"I read the reports," he said. "I know enough to do what I need to."

"You know about the other woman?"

He might have stopped breathing. "Other woman?"

"That's what I thought," Erin said. "Her name was Sara Daniels. She was a twenty-one-year-old bartender who went missing from Hampton, Virginia, in April 2008. Twenty miles from where John Huggins lived."

"No," he admitted, "there was nothing about a second woman." Then he cocked his head, his gaze taking aim at her. "Why is that? Could it be her case has nothing to do with Jack Calloway?"

"John Huggins. His name is John Huggins," she ground out, and stepped around him. She slammed her car door, not caring that he barely snatched his fingers out of the way. "Sara Daniels was just like Lauren McAllister. Lonely, lost. Vulnerable to a handsome older man with a little sex appeal and plenty of money for cocaine. Do you have any women like that here in Hopewell?" He winced and Erin knew she was getting to him. "Then maybe you shouldn't be trying to keep me quiet. Maybe you should get a bullhorn and alert the newspaper reporters and TV anchors and help warn people, instead of protecting a man—"

"Who is *presumed innocent*." His voice vibrated with anger. "Lady, I don't know why you're so sure Jack Calloway is a beast, but there's one thing I do know: No one is gonna come in my town and destroy a man with no cause—"

"No cause?"

"No cause." His voice ricocheted off concrete like a bullet. Erin was actually tempted to cower.

But she didn't. "My, my," she said, with deliberate calm. "We do have anger issues, don't we?"

He ground out an inventive curse. "Understand something, *Doctor* Sims: Jack and Margaret Calloway are a valued part of this town. They run a respectable business and art studio and have a nephew who needs them. If you try pulling that media shit around here that you pulled in those other places, I'll throw your ass in jail without a second thought. *Then* where will your brother be?"

The threat hit its mark. Justin. Dear God, this sheriff was turning into one more like all the others. He'd already decided that Justin was rightly condemned.

"Dead," she said, her voice like chipped ice. "If you do that, he'll be dead."

"Ah, Christ." He blew out a breath. Turned, and started walking.

"So, you'll talk to Calloway?"

He unlocked the door to the sheriff's office and gestured her inside. "Sure. I have a report due to the Florida Attorney General, anyway. With any luck, you can hand-carry it there."

Just after sunrise, a deputy pushed his way through the Sunday morning crowd that had gathered outside the sheriff's office. Jack Calloway was with him.

"Get in here," Nick said. He held the door with one hand, ignoring the ill-mannered shouts of reporters. He was wiped out. He'd left Dr. Sims dozing on a vinyl sofa at the station two hours ago. He'd run by his mother's house and stretched out on top of the covers next to a sluggish Hannah for twenty minutes, then scraped a razor over his face. After that, he hit the phones—the judge, the mayor, the county commissioner—and once back in the office, paused just long enough to skim a series of newspaper articles that had appeared over the weekend and turned LeeAnn's possum into a world event. Something about wasting the county money answering "911 calls of nature."

That fucking Roach.

But he'd deal with her later. Right now he had a Florida whistle-blower in the break room and a respected citizen needing armed escort to get through the reporters on his stoop.

Quentin Vaega was the armed escort. He banged the door shut behind them.

"Holy hell," he said, shaking the rain from his jacket. Water splattered everything in a six-foot radius. Samoan by blood, Quentin weighed two-forty and had spent eight years as a Cleveland Browns' defensive back. He wasn't often seen ducking and hiding like a child. "I haven't been tackled like that since I left the Dog Pound."

"Valeria," Nick said, crossing to a desk in an annex of the lobby, where the department receptionist sat working the phone. "If you start getting calls from the media, I want to know."

"*Si*, Sheriff." She said "Sher-eef." Nick suspected she worked hard at the accent; she was from Michigan. "Sheriff?"

"What?"

"I start getting calls from the media since I come in at six." *Seex*.

"Well, shit," Nick said. Sims hadn't even been here for twenty-four hours yet, and already the Leslie Roaches of the world were in his face like vultures.

Detective Mann, your father-in-law has accused you of having multiple affairs during your marriage...

Detective Mann, how do you answer the accusation that you hired Bertrand Yost to murder your wife?

Detective Mann, is it true that you now stand to inherit a large fortune?

Nick shook it off and herded Calloway to the largest interview room. He looked as if he hadn't had much sleep, either. "You holding up?" Nick asked.

"I thought this was over," Jack said. "Why is that woman doing this to me?"

"She thinks her brother's about to die in your place."

Jack slumped. He was a good-looking man in middle age, six feet tall and still basically fit, a little gray at the temples. If you looked hard enough, you'd notice that one iris was blue and the other green.

"You know what she's done to me, right?" Jack asked. "You understand why I changed our names and moved here?"

"Listen, Jack," Nick said, "this is probably all bullshit, but I can't let an accusation like this hang over the town without looking at it. Besides which, I have a State Attorney General's order to fulfill."

"To do what?"

"To see if the Jack Calloway in my town is really John Huggins."

"Why does that matter?"

It was a good question. The only reason Nick could think of was that if the Virginia case wound up holding water, the AG wanted to know where Huggins was in a hurry. "I'm guessing the Florida AG is just lining up ducks and locating the players."

Jack narrowed his eyes: He knew better. "Should I call Dorian?"

Dorian Reinhardt was the type of lawyer who would revel in a case like this. Murder, a senator, multiple states, the death penalty. Christ, Nick was surprised Dorian hadn't shown up yet for the photo op.

The prick.

"You don't need him yet," Nick said. "But he was at Hilltop last night, wasn't he?"

"I called him when I saw Sims. He thinks she'll blow this up big."

And if she doesn't, Dorian will.

"We need to give something to the press, Nick," Quent said. He'd been looking out the window.

"Give them the truth." Not that the truth ever mattered to newsmakers. "Tell them a local citizen is being questioned in a Florida case and say the Sheriff's office is doing everything it can to cooperate with Federal officials, ya-da ya-da."

"What about the name change?" Jack asked. "Won't it make me look as if I had something to hide?"

"People are fond of you, Jack; you won't be tarred and feathered for looking for a new start in life. But," he said, "I'm going to ask you point-blank, man-to-man: Did you kill Lauren McAllister?"

"No."

"But you knew her?"

"I'd met her." Jack's eyes flicked down and left. *Lie,* Nick thought, and a coil of doubt began to twist in his gut. "She was in one of Margaret's sculpture classes. I saw her around."

"And?"

"And, nothing. I saw her around."

"What about Sara Daniels?"

Jack blinked, and Nick had to admit the bewilderment looked real.

"In Virginia. She was a bartender who disappeared in 2008, while you and Margaret lived in Lawrenceville."

"I don't understand."

"Apparently, the court's looking into that, too."

Bewilderment turned to shock. Jack shook his head. "I can't believe this—"

"Sheriff?" Valeria stuck her head in the door. "The commissioner is on the phone."

"Tell him to go fuck himself."

"*Sí,* sir," she said, and ducked out.

Quentin looked at Nick. "Better stop her, man. She'll do it."

Christ. Nick looked at Jack: He had to ask. "Where were you on Friday night?"

Jack frowned at him. "Excuse me?"

"You heard me."

"Is this about that Sitton girl?" he asked, getting angry now. "Erin Sims comes to town and suddenly I'm a suspect for every—"

"Where were you, Jack?"

His Adam's apple bobbed. "At Hilltop. Playing cards with the McCormicks until twelve-thirty or so. After that I was in bed, like any normal person."

Nick nodded. The ME had put Carrie's death between 12:00 and 2:00. But then, this wasn't about Carrie. Her case was for the Carroll County sheriff and the Cleveland guys.

He turned to Quent. "Get the newsmakers off my front stoop, and take a formal statement from Jack. Jack, go home."

"What about Sims?"

It was a new voice. They all turned to see Dorian Reinhardt standing in the doorway.

"Sheriff, are you talking to my client without his attorney present?" He strutted in wearing a gray silk suit with a pink Volare necktie, which he petted and twisted so everyone could see the designer tag on the back.

Prick.

"Since Jack isn't charged with anything," Nick said, "an attorney seemed irrelevant."

Dorian puffed up. "I just talked to Judge Watkins. We're filing a new restraining order. He wants to see Sims in chambers."

"This morning? It's Sunday."

"You're the one who called him back from his hunting trip."

Not exactly, Nick thought, but closed his eyes, realizing that he wasn't going to be able to head this thing off at the pass. Hopewell was about to be on the morning news; Jack would be under a microscope. And it was going to take more than a restraining order and a warning from an old judge to blow Erin Sims out of town.

Nick turned to Jack. "Like I said. Go home. Don't talk to anybody but Margaret and Rodney. Let me clean this mess up."

Dorian's lip curled. "Already done, Sheriff," he said, picking up his briefcase. "Be sure to get Sims to the courthouse at nine."

CHAPTER
10

JACK PUSHED THROUGH the reporters with Dorian saying, "He's innocent, he's innocent..." and heard Deputy Vaega offer to answer questions behind him. He got into his truck and headed toward Hilltop House, grateful when the reporters stayed behind to hear Vaega.

Damn Erin Sims. Just when life had evened out. The inn was thriving; Margaret's notoriety as a sculptor was growing. She was happy. Even their nephew Rodney had settled in—he had his own place and made an honest living working at Hilltop House. With Justin Sims's prison term close to an end, Jack had finally begun to believe the horror of Lauren McAllister's death was behind them.

Not anymore.

The weather was cold and abysmal, but Jack was sweating by the time he got home. A reporter had camped out in the parking lot and he waved her away, walking through the inn and outside to the barn. When he'd bought the place, he'd turned the barn into a studio for Margaret—a huge space filled with tables and counters, all piled with clays and glazes and sculptures and tools. At the far end, an enclosed porch held two medium-sized kilns, and at the back, Jack had built an additional vented room for an industrial-model kiln she used for her largest sculptures. She'd since gotten rid of that beast and now focused on smaller pieces like her masks.

"Maggie?" he called, and stopped short. Something moved behind a table.

He looked and let out a breath. "Calvin," he said. "I didn't know you were there."

Calvin rose from the floor, a collection of lean gangly limbs and scraggly facial hair. He and his mother, who worked for Margaret as a breakfast cook and maid, lived in an apartment in the second story of the barn. He shook his head at brain-rattling speed.

"Broke, broke, broke," he said. "Pieces."

Jack looked down. Shards of clay lay scattered on the floor. He bent down to pick them up. Calvin was capable but would obsess over the cleanup. He was autistic and little things could send his mind in circles. He was also a savant. He sometimes spoke in times and temperatures and dates—a strange quirk of neurology that allowed him to recite accurate dates and temperatures from weeks or even years ago.

"Where's Margaret?" Jack asked.

Calvin nodded to the porch. "Nine-hundred-and-fifty degrees Fahrenheit, eight-twenty-six a.m., November eleventh, two-thousand-twelve. Nine-hundred-and-fifty degrees Fahrenheit, eight-twenty-six . . ."

He started repeating himself, but Jack understood: It was 8:26 on November 11, and Margaret was on the porch firing pottery. At 950 degrees.

"You better get going," Jack said. "Your mom will want you in church."

"Pieces, pieces, pieces . . ." Calvin hauled his backpack

over his shoulder and left in a string of repeated words, and Jack went into the back room. Margaret was stacking the cones at a kiln, the digital temperature display reading 950°F and flashing the word HOLD. A set of unfired vases choked with clay vines sat on the counter, awaiting their turn in the fire.

"Maggie."

She turned, her skirt swirling around her calves and her eyes meeting his. Sometimes his heart still stuttered when he looked at her. She was beyond beautiful—dark, soulful eyes and soft lashes, porcelain skin that had only gained character with the fine creases of age, delicate cheekbones and a soft, slender jaw. Indeed, there had been only one other woman in the world who matched her in physical beauty: her twin, Rodney's mother.

"You haven't called me that in a long time," she said, her voice low.

Jack sighed. No, he hadn't. "We need to talk."

"I heard. Lauren McAllister, again."

"And there's more," Jack said. "A woman disappeared from Virginia a few years ago."

"Sara Daniels."

He flinched, then shook his head. Of course, the news was out already.

"We were there, John," she said, her eyes dark with shadows. "We lived only forty minutes away."

Jack stared. "For God's sake, Maggie. You can't think I killed Sara Daniels."

"But you slept with her, didn't you?"

He cursed. Sara was nothing. A one-night stand he hadn't even tried to keep going.

"A little discretion would go a long way, John."

He closed his eyes. Not really much to say to that.

Maggie was gifted at keeping up impressions; she'd had a lifetime of practice. She expected that same scrupulous secrecy of him.

He started to leave but as he reached the door, a thought popped in the back of his mind like a kernel of hot corn.

"Wait." He turned back to her, almost afraid to ask. "So, you knew about me and Sara Daniels? Even back then?"

Maggie looked up from her vases, and the look in her eyes seeped into Jack's veins like poison. A glint of steel there. Not just sadness. "Of course," she said. "I've known about every one of them."

Erin stood in judge's chambers beside a big Hawaiian-looking deputy named Vaega, fighting to keep her eyes open. Judge Watkins read some papers. He was an old, bearded man who wasn't happy about cutting his hunting trip short. Dorian Reinhardt, on the other hand—Huggins's attorney—fairly beamed. Erin had worked with lawyers like him before. Smug, greedy, and more interested in publicity than justice. Here he stood arguing for a restraining order against her. For God's sake, *she* wasn't the one who'd wielded a shotgun.

Erin wanted to scream. Justin's life was ticking away, and she was stuck here—

The door opened and a security guard gestured in the sheriff. Erin did a double take. He looked different than he had in the exhausted, wee hours of this morning or on his weekend bender. The shadowy beard was gone, the dark hair combed. He wore jeans with a sports coat and dark shirt, and his big hand smoothed down a tie speckled with a design Erin couldn't make out. He moved behind her and the scents of soap and aftershave touched the air.

She shifted, aware of her own tired clothing and straggles of hair. For a second, her mind wandered to a hot shower and a warm bed, maybe a cool pillow against her cheek—

"Dr. Sims." Judge Watkins's voice. Erin snapped back to attention. "By court of law, you are hereby forbidden to have contact with Mr. Calloway, directly within fifty feet or indirectly, via any means including letters, e-mail, phone calls, Facebook and other social media, or through the use of a third party..."

It was over. She turned and Mann was right there. Little roadrunners speckling his tie, aftershave lingering.

"Come on," he said, picking up her computer bag from the floor where she'd let it drop. He slipped a hand beneath her elbow and hurried her out a side door, down a hall.

"Personal escort, Sheriff?"

"I'm taking you out the back. You might need help getting by the reporters."

"You mean I might need help making sure I don't stop and talk to any of them."

He turned on her so quickly she nearly lost her balance. "Don't even think it," he warned, catching her by the shoulders. For a second he looked as if he wanted to wring her neck but an instant later his gaze trekked down her body. Erin flushed, her head gone light.

"When was the last time you ate?" he asked.

She looked up at him. He'd been so drunk or angry or harried that concern for her basic needs was the last thing she expected. "I had a Snickers bar yesterday on my way here. And a jelly donut before I left Miami."

"Jesus," he said. "What are you, some kind of health nut?"

He pushed the door open and a melee of media

exploded: shouting and shoving, boom mikes prodding and bulbs flashing. Mann hunched over her and barreled through, saying, "No comment, no comment," as they worked their way through the parking lot and to her car.

When she got in, he said, "Wait here until I pull my car around. Follow me to your motel and I'll point you to a place you can eat."

She did, and when they got to the Red Roof Inn, she wheeled around to the back corner of the motel. They got out and the sheriff walked her to #231. Erin slid the key card in and pressed open the door.

She froze. "Oh, my God."

CHAPTER
11

"S ON OF A BITCH," Mann said. He drew her back with one hand and pulled out his gun with the other, then entered the room. Erin staggered against the railing outside, her heart thrashing against her breastbone. She waited a minute and heard him pick up the phone and bark some orders into it; then she took a deep breath and stepped into the doorway.

"Don't come in," he said, hanging up. But she did, and reached out to the wall to touch the sticky red substance splattered all around the room. She rubbed it between her thumb and forefinger and sniffed. Paint.

Thank God.

But the impression someone had meant to convey wasn't erased by that knowledge. The room looked as if a murder had taken place there, the walls and bed and floor all splashed with red, like a crime scene in one of those creepy reality shows on TV.

Only this wasn't TV. It was Erin's motel room.

She took one more step, just enough to see into the bathroom. *GO HOME.* The words marched across the mirror, awkward black letters with an oval face outlined below. A downturned line for the mouth and two dots of paint for eyes, the red of one dribbling down the glass like something on the cover of a horror novel.

A wave of cold fear washed down Erin's spine. In the back of her mind, an engine roared to life, tires squealing and headlights bearing down—

"Hey." Mann's voice. He was standing inches away, and touched her chin. "Come back."

The memory rippled away. Yes, come back. Don't be stupid.

"John Huggins did this," she said. "He's trying to scare me away. He—" She stopped, realizing what she'd just said. "Where was he on Thursday night?"

Mann shook his hand. "He isn't the one who took a run at you at the prison."

"It was a rental ca—"

"I checked it already. He was here, not in Florida."

She stared. He'd checked it already. So he hadn't blown her off. He didn't believe Jack Calloway was a murderer, but he hadn't blown her off.

"Come on," he said, guiding her out. "Deputies are on their way."

They went outside, and Erin was astounded at the emotion weakening her limbs. She was used to feeling anger and determination. Her job called for those things in spades. But this—this chilling sensation that turned her bones to jelly—she hadn't felt this since she was sixteen years old.

She leaned back, letting the wall take her weight. The sheriff paced a couple of steps, rubbed a hand over his face, and paced some more. Belatedly, Erin realized he was as shaken as she.

"I take it you don't see this sort of thing in Hopewell very often?" she asked.

"I think we can safely assume you brought it with you."

"Oh, so it's my fault—"

"I didn't mean that," he said, but that was all. A black sedan pulled up, lights flashing, and he went to meet his men. Erin followed.

Vaega rolled out of the driver's side and an older man, leathered and bony, climbed from the passenger seat. Both went to the room and looked inside. When they came back out, the older deputy stopped in front of Erin. His badge said HOGUE and he scowled at her. "What'd you do," he asked, "pay some teenager to do this, so ever'body'd think you weren't full of shit?"

Erin sprang but Sheriff Mann grabbed her. He snarled at the deputy. "Do your job, Wart. Secure the scene. Canvass the area and take statements from anyone who has access to a key."

"That would be about a hundred people," Vaega said. "Jimmy Fowler works the front desk. He leaves it unattended most of the time, plays video games in the back."

"Then get about a hundred statements." Mann looked down at Erin, his hand still seizing her arm, then blew out a breath. He didn't like whatever he was about to say. "If you need me, Dr. Sims and I will be at Engel's."

Engel's Eatery was a Pennsylvania Dutch diner on Main Street, with the daily specials written in German on a chalkboard. It always smelled of yeast rolls and cinnamon, and in the winter it was famous for hot white chocolate with vanilla-bean whipped cream.

And at every time of year, it was a hangout for the locals. Nick frowned at the idea of courting the public but knew it was the right thing to do. Someone was threatening Sims. No place like Engel's to make sure folks knew the Miami visitor was under his watch.

He held the door for her and waved at Leni Engel, who was wiping off the pie counter. She was a big woman with wire glasses and a conservative bun at the back of her head. She might have been mistaken for Amish but for the fact that she always showed some cleavage.

"Hey there, Sheriff," she called out. "Rebecca will be right out."

He murmured to Sims, "That's the owner, Leni Engel. You'll like her food—not a fruit or vegetable in sight."

Rebecca appeared, wearing a too-tight blouse and overdone makeup. Her fingers were tipped in black nail polish and a rhinestone stud winked in her nostril.

"Sheriff," she said, giving Sims a once-over. "Back booth?"

"Maybe you and I should have a talk first."

She shot a glance to the cash register. Her mom, Leni, was watching. "I haven't seen him," Rebecca said, without moving her lips.

"I wasn't talking about Ace. I was talking about your friend, Carrie Sitton. Pretty scary stuff. You got anything you wanna tell me?"

"I told that other sheriff and the Cleveland cops. Everything I could think of."

"Okay. But I don't mind hearing it, too. Whenever you wanna talk." Then he wagged his finger at her. "And stay away from Ace Holmes."

"I told you, I haven't seen him."

"But you're lying."

He let it go—nothing he could do about her hanging out with Holmes—and they followed her to a booth in the back. Nick tipped greetings to wide-eyed patrons on the way, but didn't stop to chat.

Let 'em look.

But when he saw the man seated at the back corner booth, he cursed. He hadn't counted on *that*.

He waited for Dr. Sims to slide into her seat, then said, "I'll be back," and went to the corner, where Rodney Devilas sat drinking coffee. Rodney was Margaret Calloway's nephew. She and Jack had raised him after his mother committed suicide. He was legally blind, and though thirty, had a shock of white hair that was rumored to have lost its pigment when he was a child, in the months after he found his mother dead. Nick had heard stories of trauma doing that to people, but until meeting Rodney, never knew it was real.

"Sheriff?" Rodney said, and Nick shook his outstretched hand.

"How did you know it was me?"

"The silence when you walked in was deafening. I take it you aren't alone?"

Nick heard the accusation in his voice. "Erin Sims and I are having a talk. That's what I came to tell you. I didn't want you to hear it from somebody else." He paused, searching for the right words. There was no good way to tell a man that you were about to investigate his uncle for murder. "Look, Rodney. About Jack. I'm going to try to do this right. I want you to know I'm not going to let this turn into a circus."

"So noted," Rodney said, but Nick wasn't feeling the love. Rodney had a protective streak, particularly for Margaret. Nick had always wondered if it was because Margaret and Rodney's mom had been identical twins. That had to be strange for a kid, even a blind one.

Nick went back to where Erin Sims waited.

"Rodney Devilas," she said.

"Yes. He can make out shadows and shapes, but wouldn't have been able to identify you. That didn't seem...right."

"Always protecting your citizens. Even the ones who don't deserve it."

"Rodney's been through enough in his life. The least we can do is try to keep him out of it while you tear apart the only family he has."

Sims flushed. "My brother is about to die, Sheriff. Forgive me if my top priority isn't the emotional welfare of Huggins's nephew."

"Okay, easy," he said, but understood.

Rebecca came back and Nick said, "Two coffees, two orange juices, and *brötchen*." He looked at Sims. "A standard breakfast okay?"

Sims nodded and Rebecca left with the order. The same breakfast nine out of ten patrons ordered every morning. Nick leaned onto his forearms and got down to business. "I want the truth: Did you vandalize your own motel room?"

Sims looked at him like he was out of his mind. "How would I have done that? I've been with you since last night."

"Deputy Hogue was right. You could've hired it done when you got to town."

"Oh, for the love of God. I barely had time to check in to the motel and get over to Hilltop House, let alone scout out a hired thug. Check my flight time if you don't believe me."

"I will," he promised, but he did believe her. Wished he didn't. It would be easier if she were the bad guy. He leaned back. "Okay, I've read all the paper we could get over a weekend. Now I want to know what's *not* there. Start with your brother."

Her eyes widened—emerald green in this light—and he realized she hadn't expected him to ask. She'd assumed he wouldn't bother.

"Justin was a senior in high school," she began. "He lived with my husband and me."

"Why? Were there problems at home?"

"Of course not. Everything was fine," she said, but it came out a little too rushed to sound sincere. "Our mother moved and Justin wanted to stay in the same school, that's all. David and I had room."

"Okay." Could be.

"Justin had a part-time job at a community center, setting up for conferences and banquets and things. Lauren McAllister was part of an event there. She had some artwork on display for a show and Justin got this crazy crush. He was seventeen and she was nineteen."

"He admitted to sleeping with her."

"They dated a little. And before you point it out, he also admitted to having an argument with her the day she was killed."

"Over another man."

"Over John Huggins."

"Over an *unidentified* man," Nick insisted. "From what I read, there was no proof it was Huggins. Hell, he would have been almost twenty years older than Lauren. And married."

"Right," Sims said, with an edge that could have cut diamonds. "Married, middle-aged men never have affairs with younger women."

They both leaned back while Rebecca piled food on the table. When she was gone, Nick went on. "Why are you so convinced Lauren's lover was John Huggins?"

She reached into her purse, handed a page across the table. Nick set down his fork and unfolded it.

"Holy shit," he said. It was a pencil sketch of a male figure, all angles and planes and broken lines, with the distinct feeling of angst. Disjointed arms and legs, an oversized penis, eyes contorted and angry. The only hints of color in the picture were two dabs of watercolor bleeding over the lines around the irises: one blue, one green.

"Did you give this to the police?"

"Yes. And to the DA and to Justin's attorney. But there were dozens of other pictures. Lauren was an aspiring artist and these were all products of an artist's imagination. They said that even if this *was* John Huggins, she could have just known him from his wife's art studio, and that even if she'd had an affair with him, it didn't mean he'd shot her."

"All good points." Nick gestured for her to eat. "Did you ever consider that Justin could have done it?"

"He didn't."

"That's not what I asked. I asked if you ever, just for one minute, thought he *could* have done it."

"Of course not. Never. I'm his sister. Why would I think that?"

Nick eyed her over his food and Shakespeare came to mind. *The lady doth protest too much.* He took another stab at it. "In the trial transcripts, there's reference to testimony from a court-appointed counselor, but the judge ordered it suppressed. What was that?"

Sims bristled and a flicker of emotion crossed her features. "It was irrelevant. That's why it was suppressed."

Nick watched her eyes, trying to put a name on what he saw there. It was the same expression she'd smothered at his cabin when they talked about the car that had tried to run her down. The same look he'd seen in the doorway of her motel room an hour ago.

Fear. She may have tried to disguise it with something bolder, but it was fear, nonetheless. And it was justified. Some son of a bitch had threatened her. Not just in Florida but also in Hopewell.

Nick rubbed a hand over his face, forcing himself to take a step back. Dangerous waters, here. Erin Sims was earnestness and fire, but the hint of vulnerability that whispered above it all caught him off guard. She was probably wrong about her brother's innocence, but she wasn't lying: She believed everything she said. And no matter how much Nick would have liked to pin the motel room vandalism on her and send her back to Miami, every instinct told him she'd had nothing to do with that. The cold fear in her eyes couldn't be faked.

Not here. Not on my watch.

A wave of protectiveness washed over him. And another wave of something not nearly so noble. His blood altered its course and against all sane judgment, he tapped her naked ring finger. "What happened to the husband?"

She blinked. "David? He had dreams of a political career. He was hobnobbing with bigwigs, eating caviar..." She pulled a face. "Having a wife out leading an ugly public crusade against a senator was bad for his image."

"You mean he didn't stay around to support you and Justin."

She winced and something tugged in Nick's chest. A man was supposed to be there when his wife needed him, not leave her to handle things herself. God knows, he'd made that mistake once, too, but it wasn't because he'd been promoting his career.

Well, yes. It was exactly that.

The taste of tequila rose in his throat. Christ, he was just getting ready to make crazy promises to Erin Sims, and yet he was the last person she should depend on. Just ask Allison.

That thought was the one that cleared his brain. He had enough responsibility. He had Hannah to think about, not to mention a town counting on him. Erin Sims was trouble, and she'd be even more trouble if Nick let his libido enter the picture or let things get personal. He'd send the required information to Florida; he'd find out who vandalized her motel room. He'd confirm for himself what everyone else already knew—that Jack Calloway was innocent—and then he'd send Erin Sims home to Florida and get back to busting town drunks and shoplifters.

They finished their food and Nick tossed down a tip. "Come on," he said, holding out a hand to help her slide from the booth.

"Where to?" she asked.

"Somewhere out of the way, where I don't have to worry about you."

"You can't push me aside just so you don't have to deal with me. This is my brother we're talking ab—"

"I meant where I don't have to worry that someone's going to break into your motel room or try to run you down in a car."

Her face lost its color. "Oh, that."

"Yeah," he said. "That."

CHAPTER
12

Out of the way was a private motel outside of Hopewell but still in the county, where Nick knew the manager and would have a deputy passing by every thirty minutes. He checked her in, moved her bags, and while he made a couple calls to touch base with Quentin and the office, she unpacked her computer bag. Laptop, portable printer, and bright yellow paper.

Damn her. This was her MO. The minute he walked out of this room, she was going to launch a full-blown assault on Jack. She'd print fliers, start crusading, and the hounds of paranoia and sensationalism would take over Hopewell, just like they had in L.A.

Detective Mann, is it true that you became acquainted with Bertrand Yost two years ago when you arrested him for possession?

Detective Mann, what about reports that an LAPD psychologist has recommended your dismissal?

"Have you got a picture of John Huggins on that thing?" he asked, pointing at the laptop.

A lie stirred behind her eyes. "Of course," she said, and Nick was surprised how relieved he felt that she chose the truth.

"And you brought your printer with you from Florida and a whole ream of bright paper."

She shrugged and Nick closed the distance between them. Close enough to catch a whiff of spearmint on her breath.

"Let me give you a little warning about an ordinance in Hopewell that prohibits posters from being placed on public property."

She grew an inch. "You mean like 'Found: black Labrador' or 'Ice Cream Social, 3:00 Saturday'—you mean posters like that?"

"And things like 'Jack Calloway is a murderer' and 'Save my brother'—posters like that."

Her chin jutted out. "You said your parents lived here. Does that mean you've been here all your life?"

He almost chuckled. "You mean, have I spent my career breaking up barroom brawls and making sure the town's dogs are on a leash, or have I ever dealt with *real* crimes?"

She had the grace to look embarrassed, even as she crossed her arms again.

"I grew up here," he answered. "But you'll be relieved to know I went to college in California and spent seventeen years on the LAPD."

She looked impressed; he liked that.

"What brought you back?" she asked. "I mean, it seems like this is a totally different life than in L.A."

Oh, yes. "You want the gory details, try Google. You won't have any trouble finding dirt about me." She looked surprised, but said nothing. "Suffice it to say Hopewell *isn't* like L.A. and I'll be damned if I'm gonna let you make it that way."

The threat hit its mark. "I didn't come here to ruin your paradise," she said. "I came here to free my brother."

Nick's heart took a twist. She tried to sound harsh but her eyes glittered with tears and dragged his mind places it didn't often go. He didn't mean to sex—like men everywhere, Nick's mind wandered to sex about every six seconds. This was a different place. A place of compassion, admiration. For her chutzpah and doggedness and passion.

For the fact that she was alone and frightened and counting on him.

He stood thinking about that for five seconds. On the sixth, he thought about sex.

"I've gotta go," he said. Christ, there was no time for an affair with this woman. "I'll have someone driving by here this afternoon, keeping an eye out for our vandal."

"What am I supposed to do?"

"Wait. Just for a little while until I can get some traction on the case. I'll call you."

She scoffed, a bitter sound. "I've heard that before." She started to turn, and Nick snagged her arm.

"Not from me, you haven't."

She searched his eyes, probing them, he thought, for something she could dare to believe.

"I'll call you," Nick promised. "Be here when I do."

Maggie Huggins had never gotten used to being called Margaret Calloway. She had accepted the change of names as a necessary fact of life, but never liked it. Calloway was nothing more than a dart thrown at a list of names in a phone book, and Margaret was the name her father had called her. It always sounded full of derision.

The names wouldn't matter anymore, of course: No more secrets. Everybody knew about their former names and former lives. It had been on the local noon news and trailers were already running for more stories on the six o'clock news. Tonight, it would headline the eleven o'clock news and start again on the morning shows, then spread to regional news at noon and six and eleven, day after day until the public grew bored with it.

Or until Erin Sims was gone. Maggie slapped a brick of clay onto the worktable, scooped it up and slammed it down again, working out the air bubbles and digging the backs of her knuckles into the cold lump. Just when their lives had seemed almost serene, Erin Sims was back, spreading her lies and—

Spreading some truths, too.

"Maggie." A knock pounded on the door. "Margaret?"

Rodney. Maggie started to slip from her stool to let him in, then stopped herself. Thirty years old, a grown man.

"Come in," she said. He did and she got up and pushed a stray chair under the ledge of a table. "Okay. Coast is clear. I'm at the back table."

Rodney drew a finger along the tabletops, feeling his way through the room. He'd been born with an illness that affected his corneas, and transplants when he was eighteen had been a heartbreaking failure. But his blindness wasn't the greatest loss he'd suffered. His mother, Maggie's twin sister, Claire, had been mercilessly scarred in a car accident when he was nine. A year later, unable to cope with the reality of what had once been striking beauty, Claire had committed suicide. Ten-year-old Rodney found her lifeless body, sat with it for two days, then finally wandered down the block in New Orleans to a cathedral.

Since then, he'd been Maggie's. Much to her father's chagrin. As far as Rodney's grandfather was concerned, Claire had been the angel of the family—and Maggie mortally flawed. From the moment he learned that Maggie had filed for custody, he'd waged war against her. He took everything Claire and Rodney had owned, right down to the angel collection that had meant so much to Claire, and went to his grave trying to keep his precious, blind grandson from Maggie's depravity.

Bastard.

She threw the clay against the table to give Rodney sound to follow, an old habit he didn't really need. He was nearly as independent as any sighted man. He lived in what had once been a hunting cabin about a mile from Hilltop and during daylight could drive his three-wheeler on a paved path between the inn and the cabin, and around town. He worked in the office at Hilltop, attended concerts and theater and baseball games, and occasionally even dated. More than once over the years, Maggie had envisioned her sister looking down on them from the heavens, and hoped she was pleased.

"Simpson?" Rodney's voice snapped her back.

Simpson. Oh, yes. Maggie had been commissioned to make a pair of masks for a Connecticut collector, Elijah Simpson. In the art world, he was big enough that his interest in her masks would be a boon to Maggie's career.

"Work, as usual, huh?" he asked.

She gave a little snort. "What else should I do? Go after Erin Sims with a shotgun?" She pressed the heels of her hands into the clay, spread it and rolled it onto itself, then tossed it onto the table again.

"Be careful what you say. Sheriff Mann's got her back."

Maggie put her shoulders into the work. He was right: Be careful. More than once, a stray comment had, rightly or wrongly, led a man to prison.

She muscled the brick of clay into a ball, worked it with her fingers until it warmed and came alive.

"Have you got a form?" Rodney asked.

"They're on the counter to your left. I haven't picked one yet."

He felt his way to the counter and fingered a few clay facial forms, molded on wig blocks or mannequin heads to become the bases for her masks. He turned a couple of them over in his hands, studying the contours with his fingers.

"This one," he said, and brought one over to her. "Where's Jack?"

"I don't know. He went to see Nick Mann this morning, and Dorian, then came home and went out again. I don't know where."

"Church?"

"Maybe." Maggie frowned. *Church.* Probably. Unburdening his soul to Reverend Whitmore? Oh, dear. She'd have to think about that.

Rodney felt for a stool and pulled it beneath him. "Mann was with Erin Sims a little while ago. At Engel's."

Maggie stopped working and looked at him. "Did she talk to you?"

"No. And even if she had, I'm not that fragile. I can handle it."

"She has no right to ruin us just because your uncle—"

"Fucks everything in a skirt?"

"Stop it," she snapped. Rodney didn't understand. As perceptive as he was, there were some things he couldn't see.

"Look at you, Maggie," he said. "You're talented, you're successful, you're still beautif—" He stopped, his eyes aimed in her general direction. "Aren't you?"

Maggie's heart melted. He remembered how she and Claire had been, though he'd never seen it with his own eyes. They'd been blessed by some quirk of genetics that combined with the laws of symmetry and societal standards and made them breathtakingly beautiful in the eyes of the world. When he was little, he used to play a game—climb onto her lap and explore the contours of her face with his fingers, then pop over to Claire's lap to try to find a difference. There was none, not until after Claire's accident.

Maggie didn't obsess over her looks but she knew, even now, she drew stares from men. The occasional woman, too.

"I'm not bad for an old fart," she said.

Rodney shook his head. "He doesn't deserve you, Maggie. He never did."

"I don't want to talk about it."

"Right," he said, letting it go. They'd been through it before. "I should get back to the office, anyway; I shouldn't leave the phones unattended."

He meant, *I'd better go field the cancellations*. When word spread that the owner of Hilltop House was accused of murder, it was bound to happen.

He left and Maggie went back to her clay, urging it to life in her fingers. The artwork was her solace—it always had been. She reached for the facial mold Rodney had selected and began pushing fresh clay over the surface, smoothing the silky mud over the curve of a cheek.

But all the while, even as the mask began to take shape, a question pricked at her brain like a fish hook: Was John telling Reverend Whitmore the truth?

CHAPTER
13

NICK PREPARED THE appropriate paperwork for the
Florida AG: The Jack Calloway residing in Hopewell
was the man who had gone by John Huggins prior to
2007.

Done, Nick thought, tossing his pen on the desk. His
role was finished.

Except that Erin Sims was still in town and her brother
was still facing death. And except for the fact that some
son of a bitch had deliberately scared the living hell out of
her at her motel, right under Nick's nose.

Jack? It seemed unlikely that Jack would believe a little
paint in her motel room would get rid of her. On the other
hand, he didn't need to get rid of her entirely. He only
needed a stall tactic: delay her for five more days and it
would be too late to save her brother. Lauren McAllister's
murder would be laid to rest along with Justin.

Nick propped his feet on the desk and laid a forearm
over his brow. Even at the height of his detective days, he'd
never worked a case this old. When a murder was fresh,
solving it was a matter of tracking down real live people
in real time, handling evidence as quickly as possible, and

rushing around in several different directions trying not to let any one of multiple trails cool off. When a murder was twelve years old, solving it was a matter of reading age-old reports, mentally re-creating relationships and situations so they could be studied. It didn't have the sense of urgency a current case did.

Except that this time, a man was about to die. The urgency was there, but the people, the relationships, the situations weren't. And there was nothing Nick could do about that.

Except one relationship—the one between Erin Sims and whoever wanted her gone—did exist today. Here, in real time, in Hopewell. That's the one Nick had to unravel. Because whoever was at the other end of it knew something about Lauren's murder.

Nick pulled his feet from his desk and arranged to meet Quentin at Hilltop House. For the next two hours, they talked to anyone who had information about the confrontation between Jack and Erin. Jack and Margaret, of course. Dorian. The McCormicks and another pair of guests who'd heard the commotion and wandered in on it. Rodney, who'd gone home to his cabin just before Sims arrived, and Rosa, who worked at the inn in the mornings and lived with her son in an apartment in the second story of the barn. Finally, there was only one person left. Calvin, Rosa's fifteen-year-old son.

"Bad woman," Calvin said, twisting his hands. "Margaret cry, cry, cry."

Nick looked at him. "What do you mean?"

The boy shook his head but his eyes didn't move from a spot on the carpet. Calvin's peers considered him a freak, but Nick had always thought that his brain was just over-run with data. It wouldn't surprise him if, somewhere in there, Calvin was calculating equations that could solve the energy crisis or build a nuclear bomb.

"Where were you last night? Did you see Dr. Sims here?" Quentin asked.

"Guns. Shotgun. Gunsgunsguns."

"Guns?" Rosa asked. She stuck her hands on her hips. Nick recognized the expression and the pose: Rosa was Valeria's daughter and he'd been at the dangerous end of Valeria's no-nonsense glare more than once. "Calvin, were you into Jack's guns again?" she asked.

He shook his head faster. Not to argue, Nick realized, just to move. "Seven-eighteen p.m., November tenth, two-thousand-twelve. Seven-eighteen p.m., November tenth, two-thous—"

He started going in circles with the time and date Erin Sims had been there, and Rosa looked at Nick. "He likes the guns. Jack has said it's okay. They aren't loaded. Calvin takes them apart, puts them back together."

Nick nodded. At the top of the main stairway from the lobby stood a gun cabinet with several nice weapons. He'd admired them more than once. They were just for show; Jack was neither a hunter nor a marksman.

"So you were looking at the guns when Dr. Sims was here," Nick said. "That's fine, Calvin. You're not in trouble for that. But you said Margaret was crying. Why?"

"Bad woman. Go homehomehomehome."

Nick straightened. He glanced at Quentin and Rosa caught it. She took a step forward.

"What's the matter?"

"Calvin," Nick said, "did you get mad at Dr. Sims for coming here?"

"Wait a minute," Rosa said. "What's going on?"

Nick hesitated, but had to tell her. "Someone vandalized

Dr. Sims's motel room early this morning. Left her a message to go home."

Rosa stared. "You think Calvin did it? He was here this morning. How would he even get there?"

Nick refrained from pointing out the obvious: Calvin may not have a license, but he could drive. He often did odd jobs around Hilltop. Nick had seen him drive the van Margaret used to transport sculptures and carry supplies, as well as use Jack's work truck on the property. Not to mention Rodney's scooter.

Nick said, "Rosa, you come over here to cook pretty early in the morning, don't you?"

"I come at 4:30," she admitted.

Leaving Calvin asleep in the apartment.

Just how angry had Calvin been when he stood by the gun case watching Erin throw accusations at Jack? Angry enough to try to scare her home?

Nick stood. "Rosa, we'd like to look around in the barn."

Her eyes blazed. "You won't find anything."

"Then we could move on," he said gently.

She worried it for a few seconds, then said, "Come on."

The Calloway property consisted of forty acres and three main structures: the big house, which included the gift shop and all the guest rooms; a carriage house now used as a garage; and a barn, which included Margaret's studio, classroom, and the apartment in which Calvin and Rosa lived.

Rosa and Calvin had moved in three years ago, when Hilltop's business picked up to the point that the Calloways needed full-time help. Hell, Nick thought, passing through Margaret's workshop to the back stairs of the barn. Just about everyone in town had worked at Hilltop House at one time or another, including him. A decade earlier, the abandoned Hilltop area had all the earmarks of an up-and-coming drug haven that posed a threat to Hopewell's Norman Rockwell existence. Nick and Jack had arrived about the same time—about five years ago—and when Nick's first act as sheriff was to clean the area up, the Calloways bought it and secured a grant from the Historical Society to refurbish the buildings and grounds. The County annexed the three hundred acres surrounding it, and now, instead of sprouting meth houses and trash, the land surrounding Jack's forty acres was surrounded by parks, historical markers, and a reservoir. Nick had even initiated an ongoing work-release program for jail inmates to keep up the county property.

Rosa led them upstairs and entered the apartment without a key. Calvin ducked in ahead of them.

"Go," she snapped, and Nick and Quent walked around, sticking their heads into a bath and looping through the kitchenette. It was a small apartment, with exposed beams and rough-hewn walls, calico curtains on the two windows and matching chair covers. A Realtor would call it "quaint."

And there were photos everywhere: a wedding picture of Rosa and Calvin's father, a picture of him in uniform, and several shots of Calvin at various ages. The most recent showed him and his dad just a few months ago, when he'd shipped out to Afghanistan.

"How much longer?" Nick asked.

"His tour ends in three months."

Nick nodded, sympathetic. He knew about single parenting. He pointed at a closed door. "Calvin's?" he asked.

Rosa nodded and Nick rapped his knuckle against it. When there was no answer, Rosa opened the door.

Calvin sat on his bed, a set of headphones in his ears and an MP3 player in hand. His head moved back and forth. If he noticed them, he didn't show it. Nick looked around: a few books and DVDs on a shelf, a small TV and stereo on a nightstand, and an armoire against one wall. The room was neat, obsessively so, and Nick wondered if the compulsion for order came with Calvin's condition. There were no pictures on the desk or posters on the walls, no piles of junk or containers sitting out, filled with spare change or paperclips or old erasers. No calendar or baseball trophies or keepsakes. No dirty socks on the floor.

Nick found himself stricken. This wasn't like any fifteen-year-old kid he knew. As autism went, Calvin was highly functional. But he would never be fully independent, would never quite fit in, and might never have a career—no matter how much brilliance was trapped inside.

A wave of gratitude washed over Nick. It could have been Hannah. There had been a few days after a bullet struck her head when brain damage had been a possibility. Christ, they were lucky.

Nick buried that thought and peeked under the bed, looked out the window, pulled open some drawers. Last, he stepped over to an old armoire.

"Sticks," Calvin said, to no one in particular. "Sticks-sticks-sticks."

Nick pulled on the door of the armoire. It stuck. So, Calvin *was* paying attention. He turned back to the armoire and gave it a tug, then another, and the door came open.

And there it was.

CHAPTER
14

RUMOR TRAVELED LIKE WILDFIRE. By afternoon, only a few hours after the sheriff was seen sharing *brötchen* with Sims, the possibility that Jack Calloway had a secret past was the talk of the town. Rebecca Engel told everyone who walked in, and everyone who walked out carried it to someone else. Countywide, the reaction was the same: *Jack Calloway? Couldn't be.*

Stupid, blind fools. People believed what they wanted to believe. They made it easy to keep up an image.

Except Rebecca Engel. She was dangerous now, and the weight of that knowledge was like a cement block pressing down. She'd *seen*. She *knew*. She didn't know the significance of what she knew yet, but it was only a matter of time. The longer she was out there, the more dangerous she became. The Angelmaker could *feel* her watching.

And someone else. Strange, in all the years, there had never been more than one angel at a time. Sometimes, months and even years passed without feeling the weight of their censure. But now, the Angelmaker had to face the fact that it wasn't just Rebecca.

Erin Sims? Nick Mann? The minister at church?

Maybe. Or maybe it was the scrutiny of the town, in general. Everybody involved in everybody's business.

Have to think about that. Whoever it was, the Angelmaker had to be ready.

See no evil, hear no evil, speak no evil.

The Angelmaker would make sure of it.

Rosa gasped. Nick pulled a gallon container of red paint from the floor of Calvin's armoire.

"Calvin?" Rosa said, her voice a study in confusion. She walked over to the bed and snatched the headphones from his ears. "Calvin, what is that paint doing in here?"

"Rosa," Nick said, "don't do that. Don't ask him anything here. Not without a lawyer."

Her eyes filled with betrayal and Nick felt as if he was tearing off his own limb. Still, there was no choice.

They took Calvin to headquarters for questioning. Pastor Carl Whitmore was waiting there. He started toward Nick the minute he walked in, but Valeria saw her daughter and grandson and barged in front of him.

"What's this?" she asked.

Rosa leaned in and spoke in Spanish. Valeria turned to Nick with horror in her eyes.

"No puede ser. No."

"I'm sorry, Valer—"

"I need to talk to you, Sheriff." Whitmore. His hand was on Nick's arm.

"Go ahead, Nick," Quent said. "I'll take care of Calvin."

Nick snapped his fingers. "Attorney."

"Of course." Quent gestured for Calvin and Rosa to precede him down the hall. Valeria glared at Nick, and he nodded.

"You too," he said, then saw the Post-it note stuck to her fingers. "Is that for me?"

It took a second; then she remembered and held out the note. "A call for you." Nick took it and looked at the name: Luke.

"Goddamn it," Nick said, then glanced at Whitmore. "Oh, sorry." He fired Luke's note into a trash can. "Come on, Reverend."

Whitmore looked relieved not to be put off. He'd been the pastor at Ebenezer Lutheran Church for fifteen or twenty years. Nick didn't know him well. Nick's parents had belonged to a Methodist congregation to which they'd hauled the Mann kids, but it didn't stick. Church was one of the few places in town Nick didn't frequent.

Still, as reputations went, Whitmore was an okay guy. Just now, he looked like Job.

In his office, Nick said, "Something on your mind, Pastor?"

"Jack Calloway is a parishioner at Ebenezer."

"I know."

"This is awkward, Sheriff, but in light of the accusations that were made last night, I thought you should know." Whitmore wrung his hands. "Jack is a good man."

He tithes generously, Nick thought. "But . . . ?"

"But he *is* a man, and he has certain needs."

"Ah," Nick said, as if he understood. He didn't.

"Sex isn't a sin, Sheriff. It's the way God created man."

Nick resisted the impulse to shout "Hallelujah." Instead, he propped a hip on his desk, watching Whitmore pace. "What's this about, Reverend?"

"It's about Margaret."

"Margaret?"

"The marital relationship comes with certain duties.

Among them is a wife's duty to share her husband's bed. The Bible is clear on that."

"Ah, Jes—criminy."

"Margaret doesn't fulfill those duties. She hasn't been in Jack's bed in years. And so, he's found other, uh, venues."

Nick's antenna went up. "You're telling me he's had affairs."

Whitmore nodded.

"Reverend, did Jack confess something illegal to you?"

"No." He gave a sad smile. "Ironic, isn't it? If he had, I wouldn't be able to share this with you. I would have to hold it in confidence. But since he didn't"—he spread his hands—"I can ruin his life without betraying my ethics."

"A girl is dead, Reverend," Nick said, losing patience, "and a man is about to be put to death for her murder. If you know something—"

"That's why I'm here." The pastor closed his eyes. When he opened them again, they were the eyes of a tired hound. "Drugs."

Nick's blood picked up speed, but he kept his mouth shut. Let him talk.

"One of the outreaches we do at Ebenezer is a regional program involving several congregations. We go into downtown Cleveland to feed and clothe, and to witness. I've been to the shelter there on the river dozens of times and had the occasion to learn that Jack Calloway is known to a drug dealer there." He held up a hand. "No, I will not tell you how. Confidentiality is part of the program. All I can say is that I became convinced Jack had bought drugs on the waterfront there. More than once."

"What kind?"

"Cocaine, mostly."

"Did you ask Jack about it?"

"I tried. I told him what I had come to believe, but couldn't speak in bald terms because confidentiality—"

"Is part of the program."

"I offered him counsel and spiritual guidance. He denied using drugs. But in my heart, I have always thought he lied to me that day. I have always prayed he didn't."

"Holy sh—cow."

Nick stood. This was getting interesting. Disturbing, rather. He gave his brain a shake and made the distinction. "Did you ever hear the name Lauren McAllister before today, Reverend?"

"No."

"What about Sara Daniels?"

"The other woman Erin Sims is ranting about? No."

"So you don't know whether Jack had affairs with them?"

"No."

"But the idea doesn't shock you."

"It takes a great deal to shock me anymore, Sheriff. But, no, imagining Jack with a pretty young woman? That is not difficult."

Nick stood, considering what to do with this knowledge. Jack was married to one of the most beautiful women in the world, who didn't share his bed. He *had* committed adultery, apparently more than once. With Lauren McAllister? Could be, except the other authorities who had dismissed Erin Sims were right: Even if that were true, it didn't mean he'd killed her.

And Jack had bought cocaine. At least, that's what Whitmore thought, and Nick didn't think the pastor would rat out a generous congregant if there was a chance in hell he was wrong.

Cocaine had been Lauren's drug of choice. What about

Sara Daniels? Something to check. And in a hurry. Sunday was nearly gone.

Nick handed a legal pad and pen to the minister. "Write out what you told me, Reverend—as many details as you can about the drugs. And about the affairs. Sign it."

Whitmore looked up at him. "What about Margaret? Finding out about his affairs . . . this would destroy her."

Margaret. Nick took a deep breath, turned the thought over a few times. "I'll be careful what I say to her," he promised, and meant it. "In my experience, though, the wife is usually the first to know."

"Yes," Whitmore said. "Mine, too."

Jack sat on a pew in the center of the chapel, elbows on knees, head bent. He'd never had much interest in praying, despite what Carl Whitmore believed. Could recall only a handful of times in his life when he'd actually done it . . . After the car accident that nearly killed Claire. After Rodney went into surgery for his eyes. After he'd been accused of Lauren's death.

It occurred to him now that he ought to have spared a prayer for Lauren herself.

Lauren. Sara. And how many others?

I knew about every one of them. Oh, Maggie.

And Rodney. Jack didn't know what to do about Rodney. Maggie meant the world to him.

He left the church in the late afternoon, but found he didn't want to go home. He drove. He drove for an hour up County Road 219—past the place where Carrie Sitton's tragic demise had occurred—his knuckles growing white on the steering wheel and his mind tangling with worries. He drove without noticing direction or landscape or speed, and with anger dripping slowly into his veins.

Erin Sims. This was her fault.

A horn screamed through his brain and he swerved, just missing an oncoming car. He pulled over, dumping the car on the shoulder, panting for breath. God Almighty, he was going to kill someone if he wasn't careful. Hadn't he done enough of that already?

He might have sat in the car for ten minutes or an hour; he wasn't sure. When he blinked back to the present, he knew what he had to do.

Money. Fake credit cards. Fake IDs. He'd had the stash for years, ready to go, though he'd hoped to never need them. Now there was no choice. Nick Mann was going to get to the bottom of this. Their reprieve in Hopewell had come to an end.

So it was finally time: He had to face Maggie with the truth. And make sure no one else ever learned it.

CHAPTER
15

S HERIFF, I NEED TO CONFER with my client. Surely you
wouldn't deny him that right."

Dorian. Prick.

Nick glanced at Calvin—who wasn't making sense
anyway—then nodded to Quentin and surrendered the
room. Outside, Jensen was just entering the lobby.

"Did Jack do anything interesting?" Nick asked.

"Nope," Jensen said. "He left the chapel a little before
five, then just drove around."

"Where to?"

"Nowhere. Out on Route 219 a ways, just about caused
an accident, then pulled over to the side of the road a
while—like he was thinking. Then he came back to town,
picked up Chinese food, and went home. Looked to me
like he was tucking in for the night, but I can keep watching him if you want."

"Nah," Nick said. There was no good reason to watch
him in the first place. Whitmore had gotten the wheels
turning, that's all.

Jensen pointed at the interrogation room. "I heard you
brought in Calvin Lee for the vandalism against Dr. Sims."

"We found a bucket of red paint in his closet," Nick said. "It looks like the same stuff in the motel room. But he says he didn't know it was there."

"Do you believe him?"

"I don't know. Calvin's a hard read, and as soon as Dorian Reinhardt got hold of him, he went into time-and-temperatures mode. Plus, Calvin used that paint around the barn. He painted the wheelbarrow handles yesterday."

"Who paints wheelbarrow handles?" Jensen asked.

"They were getting old, giving splinters," Quentin said. "Calvin sanded them down and put a couple coats of paint on top. And," he added, before Jensen could ask, "I looked: The wheelbarrow handles are freshly sanded and painted red."

"Hmp." Jensen ran a hand through his hair, leaving rusty spikes sticking out. "So why is Dorian Reinhardt handling it?"

"What do you mean?" Nick asked.

"I never knew Reinhardt to take on someone who can't pay, that's all. Rosa's not rich."

Nick hadn't thought of that. "Favor to Jack, probably," he suggested. But Jensen was right: Defending indigents was out of Dorian's character.

And threatening a woman was out of Calvin's. Nick couldn't quite wrap his mind around the idea of Calvin figuring out where Erin Sims was staying, stealing a car, and coming to town in the wee hours of the morning while his mother cooked breakfast for guests. He couldn't fathom Calvin slinging red paint all over a motel room. Calvin may be unusual and may have a deep sense of protectiveness for Jack and Margaret, but he wasn't violent. Plus, someone would have noticed him. He wasn't the type of kid people didn't notice.

Nick walked over to a desk and dialed the cell number Sims had given him. It rang five times before she picked up. "We have a suspect for your vandal," he said. "If he's the one, it's just a kid acting out. He wasn't really trying to hurt you."

"Will his arrest free my brother?" she asked.

"No."

"Then there's still work to do. Did you look into the other case?"

"I said I would, didn't I?"

"Forgive me, Sheriff, but I've heard those platitudes before. It's what police say when they still believe I'll go away."

"I don't do platitudes. I made some calls." Of course, none of those calls had been answered. In the first place, it was the weekend, and in the second, the Florida court order had frozen the files on the Virginia woman. Tonight, he'd have to call in some favors and see what he could find out. Tonight, when he was supposed to be playing a rousing game of Dinosaur-Monopoly with Hannah. Sunday night was their standard game night, and except for this morning when she'd been asleep, he hadn't seen her in three days.

Nick closed his eyes, then looked at his watch. Six o'clock, Sunday. Justin Sims's execution was set for four days and six hours from now.

"Okay," he said into the phone. "I'm sending a deputy over to bring you to my place. We'll go through the files on Sara Daniels that came in this afternoon. You can catch me up." *And then you can go back to Florida.*

"Really?" She sounded dubious.

"The sooner I check it out, the sooner things can get back to normal, for both of us."

He hung up and dialed his mother's number. Hannah answered, and the grime of the day washed away with the sound of her voice.

"Daddy!" she squealed. "I knew it was you."

"Because you're psychic?"

"Because I looked at caller ID," she said.

"Ah. How was your weekend?"

"Okay. Jake Snell got in-school suspension on Friday."

"For what?"

"He called Mrs. Schmedden *eine alte Scharteke*."

Nick smiled. Mrs. Schmedden *was* kind of an old hag.

"And Leah Reinhardt says she's getting a kitten for her tenth birthday, but I don't believe her. She's a big fat liar."

Dislike of Reinhardts was genetic.

"I missed you, Daddy. Did you get any work done remodeling the cabin? Grandma says you just go there to think about Mommy."

Christ. Forty years old and his mother still catching the lies. "I do think about your mom when I'm there."

"Do you ever cry 'cause she isn't there?"

"Sometimes."

"Me too. Sometimes." She sighed. "Daddy, are you coming home soon?"

"I want to, sugar, but I've got a situation here."

"You mean that woman who says Mr. Calloway is a murderer?"

News spreads. "That's the one."

"You'll fix it."

His heart skipped a beat. Nothing like pure, unadulterated confidence to make a man feel like a hero. Or scare the shit out of him.

There's nothing to worry about, Allison...I've got it covered.

"Say, squirt, I was thinking. Since I have to do some work tonight, and you want to play some games, and everybody has to eat supper, what do you say we do all three at once?"

"Okay," she said with exuberance. "How do we do that?"

Nick pictured her screwing her brow into a frown, the scar on her forehead disappearing into a crease. He'd brought her to Hopewell to keep her safe and just now, he wanted to chase every hint of danger back to Miami and hold Hannah next to his heart. "Why don't we invite the Vaegas over for dinner? You and I can cook up a meal, and then you can play with Tyler and Marissa while Uncle Quent and I figure a few things out."

"Okay." Her delight reached right through the phone lines. Then, "Dad, did you remember this is a school night?"

Nick smiled. "Wild, huh?"

Quent was next.

"Hey, man," Nick said into the phone. "Can you convince your wife to bring the kids over for dinner tonight?"

"It's a school night, you know."

"Jesus." Nick dropped his forehead in his hand.

"You cooking or are we ordering Domino's?"

"When was the last time we ordered Domino's at my house?"

"Right. Iron Chef Mann. We're working?"

"Yeah, with Sims. Can you swing it? School night and all."

"Are you kidding? My wife considers your place a five-star dining experience."

"As well she should."

• • •

A deputy escorted Erin as far as the sheriff's drive. A Chrysler minivan with a Cleveland Browns bumper sticker sat in the turnaround, and when she got out, the smell of dried leaves and charcoal touched her nostrils. The house, a cedar two-story with skylights across the front, was trimmed with shutters and flower beds and a birdbath in the front yard.

Not at all what she would have expected of Sheriff Nick Mann, had she bothered to expect anything at all. Of course, she hadn't. Maybe there was a wife inside, and a passel of five or six kids—

The front door burst open and a dog the size of a moose bounded out. Three children pushed past each other onto the porch, while the canine skidded to a halt in front of Erin.

"Daddy, she's here," cried a voice, and then, "DeeDee, come on. Here, baby, here!"

DeeDee? Baby?

A whistle broke through and the beast bounded away.

"Take the dog inside, sweet pea," the sheriff said, emerging from the garage. He wore jeans and a Buckeyes sweatshirt, a dish towel slung over one shoulder. In his left hand were tongs the size of a big-game rifle.

"Sorry about that," he said. "DeeDee's harmless."

"Yeah, forget the dog," Vaega said, joining him from behind. "Beware of the kids."

Erin glanced to the front porch, where all three children and the dog disappeared back inside. In retrospect, it registered that two of the children were dark-skinned with curly, jet-black hair—the deputy's kids. The third... *Daddy, she's here.* Erin stared at Sheriff Mann.

"I guess I should've warned you we wouldn't be alone.

Come on," he said, inviting her through the garage. "I was just firing up the grill."

"You're grilling?" she asked. "It's about ten degrees outside."

He smiled—for the first time since she'd met him—and it about knocked Erin off her feet. "Wuss," he said. "It's almost forty."

They passed through a garage that housed the sheriff's Tahoe, a motorcycle, and a riding lawnmower, plus a bicycle with purple tassels hanging from the handles, a pair of Barbie Rollerblades, and two pairs of ice skates. A couple of sleds and a toboggan hung on the wall.

When they passed into the backyard, Erin actually gasped.

Deputy Vaega said, "Yeah. That's what we all said when he built it. Ten months a year, no one ever goes inside the house."

It was incredible, like something on the cover of *Better Homes and Gardens.* A massive, two-tiered deck, slate patio, and a built-in stone grill that would have made Bobby Flay green with envy.

The sheriff checked his flame, closed the lid, and turned to Erin. "You like chicken?"

"Sure. This is something."

"My dad and I built it a few years ago, just before he died. It was a great house, but the kitchen and deck left a lot to be desired."

"Not anymore," Erin said, looking around. Deputy Vaega sipped a Corona with a wedge of lime inside. Something told her a lot of beers had been shared on this patio, a lot of stories, and—to the extent a town like Hopewell could have many crime-solving challenges—a lot of cases. She looked out into the backyard, where she could just make out a tree house perched sixteen or eighteen feet up, with a spiral staircase winding down a tree trunk.

"Did you build the tree house, too?"

His big shoulders lifted. "Hannah wanted one."

"Hannah?"

"Come on," he said, opening one of the French doors. "You might as well meet the crew."

CHAPTER
16

THE CREW WAS on the floor in a great room, fighting with the dog over a big stuffed snake from one of those game booths at a fair.

"You're not afraid she's going to kill them?" Erin said, watching the dog.

"She's a he," he corrected.

"DeeDee?"

"*D. D. Deputy Dog.* I found him at a drug raid over in Crawford County." He bent closer. "The kids think he helped me catch the bad guys, so don't blow it for them. The truth is the mutt almost got me killed."

Erin smiled, felt the warmth of his fingers on her arm, and let him usher her past the ruckus and into a kitchen the size of her apartment. Butcher-block island, black granite countertops, oversized stainless steel appliances—the works.

A woman stood at the island, laying freshly washed asparagus out on a towel. She wore dreadlocks pulled back into a thick rubber band and a tie-dye shirt. A giant diamond winked from her left hand.

"Dana," the sheriff said, lifting his voice over the noise in the family room, "that's Hannah's job."

"Oh, shut up, Nick." She laid paper towels over the vegetables and held out a hand to Erin. "I'm Dana, Quent's wife. The babysitter, so you guys can get some work done."

Erin felt a wave of hope: The sheriff hadn't been blowing smoke. He was planning to work on Justin's case tonight. She caught his eyes and saw the message there: *Told you.* Her cheeks prickled. Gratitude swelled inside.

The dog raced into the kitchen with the snake in his mouth, the kids trailing after. The sheriff snagged the first child. "Dr. Sims, this is my daughter, Hannah."

"Hi, Dr. Sims," the girl said, putting on her manners. They lasted as long as it took for the other girl to poke her in the ribs; then Hannah whirled, slapped at her, and wiped her hair from her face. Erin wasn't sure, but thought there was a pretty big scar on her forehead.

"Hi, Hannah," Erin said.

"And the girl antagonizing Hannah is Marissa, and the boy pulling Marissa's pigtails is her brother, Tyler."

Dana yanked her son away from his sister, who was just lifting a foot to go for Tyler's instep. The sheriff pointed a long finger at them. "You two, put on your coats and take this hound outside. Stay in the back where your dad can see you—no going to the pond. And you," he said, turning to his daughter, "have asparagus to make."

"Oh, yeah." She turned to Erin, beaming. "I saw this recipe on the Food Network. Asparagus wrapped in phyllo. Do you know what asparagus is?"

"Do I know what it is?" she repeated.

"Daddy said you didn't know what a vegetable was. That you probably can't name the four major food groups."

Erin cocked a brow at the sheriff and held up a hand,

ticking each group off on her fingers. "Frozen, drive-
through, takeout, and canned."

Again, that rugged—surprising—smile. Something
fluttered in Erin's belly, but the sheriff only shook his
head and pulled a couple of Ziploc baggies from the
fridge. He disappeared out back.

"Get the salt and pepper, Aunt Dana," Hannah said.
Dana produced a pepper grinder and a small stone crock.
"What else, Chef?"

"Parmesan. In the fridge."

"I'll get it," Erin said.

She went to the refrigerator, searched the shelves, the door,
the drawers. The sheriff, having come back inside with the
empty baggies, threw them away and came up behind her.

"What did she send you in here for?"

"Parmesan," Erin whispered.

He reached past her shoulder, the cool, November air
clinging to him with the scent of charcoal, and pulled out
a blond wedge of cheese.

"Oh," Erin said. "I thought it came in a green can."

"Bite your tongue." He handed her a long grater. "Here.
Grate a pile and take it over there to the food Nazi."

Erin couldn't help but smile. Daughter, friends, dog.
Casual dinner in a great house. It was what Erin might
have thought she and David were going to have someday,
but she'd been sadly mistaken about that.

She dragged her mind back. "Hannah really seems
to know what she's doing," she said, watching her slice
through layers of paper-thin dough.

"We cook together all the time. It was one of the things
that helped get us through her mother's death."

Erin's heart stumbled. She looked up at the sheriff.
"I'm sorry. How long ago was that?"

"Seven years." He cocked a brow. "You mean you haven't Googled me yet?"

"I started to." God. He'd raised his daughter alone most of her life. A seedling of compassion threatened to sprout. "I just didn't get around to it yet."

"Hmph," he said, heading back out to the deck. "I think I'm insulted."

Jack had a couple of brandies, then three, then four, but the truth was still there, haunting him. He staggered to Maggie's room, tossed back the last gulp, and knocked.

Nothing.

He opened the door. She'd turned in early, her narrow form curved beneath the quilt and lashes in soft crescents on her cheeks. As beautiful now as she'd been twenty years ago, the spitting image of the twin she'd lost—twice. First, to the car accident that had left Claire a brutally scarred recluse. And then, a year later, to Claire's suicide.

The guilt pressed down, and it surprised him. He thought he'd gotten over that. Not his fault, the suicide. He'd tried to be there for Claire but she wouldn't have it. The accident was different, though: He'd been driving the car. And the problems since then, the ones that grew from the affairs he'd had over the years...*I knew about every one of them*.

Jack closed the door, a stone in his chest. There was no choice now. Too many secrets, and because of Erin Sims, too many people now working to ferret those secrets out. He knew Sims. And he knew Nick Mann. They wouldn't stop until every skeleton was unearthed.

God Almighty, Jack was sorry it had come to this.

He padded down the long flight of stairs to the second

level of the house. The rented rooms were all on the first and second floors—empty now, thanks to Sims—and at the head of the main stairwell leading downstairs to the foyer, a wide oak cabinet displayed his guns. For a man who was neither a hunter nor collector, it was an impressive parade of weapons. Ambience for a country inn—that's all the collection had ever been.

Until now.

His chest grew tight as he walked through the wide hallway toward the gun cabinet. He'd never thought it could come to something like this. Not with Lauren McAllister all those years ago, or Sara Daniels, or... For a moment he hesitated, realizing there had been a dozen or more. Young women who craved the attentions of an older, well-established man who was still handsome and had plenty of money, who could indulge their need for cocaine and let them fly.

But he'd never meant for it to come to this.

There was no choice. The threads were going to unravel. The truth was going to come out. He couldn't let that happen.

He approached the cabinet, a lump of granite forming in his throat. He reached out to open the glass door, stopped.

It was unlocked.

Jack frowned, and a second later something cold touched his neck. He turned, and in the split second it took to catch his breath, he realized everything he'd come to believe was wrong.

A second too late.

CHAPTER
17

THE SHERIFF'S DEN was modest by comparison to his kitchen, and after a sumptuous dinner, he folded into a chair behind his desk and pushed a couple of buttons on his computer. Erin and Deputy Vaega settled into two visitor's chairs facing the desk, the dog flopping down between them.

"We're holding a boy named Calvin Lee for vandalizing your motel room," Mann said without preamble. Erin guessed a gourmet meal had been preamble enough. She couldn't remember the last time she'd eaten anything that didn't come in a bun or couldn't be microwaved.

"Boy?" Erin asked. "Who is he? Why would he threaten me?"

Calvin Lee, it turned out, was the wraith she'd seen skulking around the second story at Hilltop House, a teenager who lived on the premises with his mother. Apparently, he'd taken issue with her accusations against Jack.

"We found red paint in his apartment; it looks like what was used in your room."

"That sounds certain."

"Not really. He did odd jobs around Hilltop House, and

had used it there. His lawyer will claim that's why he took the paint into the apartment. I expect Judge Watkins to spring him in the morning."

A shiver brushed over Erin's skin. "What about the motel owner? Certainly he's going to press charges."

"Probably not."

"What?"

"Calvin's a cousin of his. And everyone knows he isn't . . . Well, Calvin's not quite all there."

"All the more reason to lock him up."

"He is locked up, damn it, and if I find out he's guilty, he'll stay that way. Meanwhile, though, I can't imagine that chasing a troubled teenager through the court system will serve your purpose."

"Will it get into the local newspaper?"

A muscle twitched in his cheek. "Yes."

"Then it will serve my purpose."

In the space of one heartbeat, Mann's expression grew dark. "Don't do that," he said.

"Then lock up John Huggins before he runs away and changes his name again." Erin came to the edge of her seat. "You have a murderer in this town, right under your nose. Why is that so hard for you to accept?"

The door flew open and Hannah bounded in, Marissa and Tyler right behind. "Aunt Dana's making us go upstairs for bedtime stories. We're reading *Grimm's Fairy Tales* for school."

Mann held out his arm and drew his daughter into a squeeze, planting a kiss on her head. Deputy Vaega hugged his own kids.

"Night, pumpkin," Mann said, and watched them charge back into the hall. He turned that pale gaze on Erin. "That's why," he said.

Erin didn't know what to say but it didn't matter. The sheriff moved on, picking up a file. "Sara Daniels," he said. "I only know the bare bones of her case. Tell me the rest."

Erin took a deep breath. It was more interest than anyone had shown in a long time. "April twelfth, 2008. Sara was walking her dog in the park down the street from her house. She vanished. The dog was found wandering the park on its leash the next morning."

"What makes you think Huggins had any connection to her?" Vaega asked.

"I talked to her mother."

Mann came forward in his chair. "You what?"

"Sara's mother told me that Sara had been in a bad place. Insecure, lonely, looking for love. Doing cocaine." Erin looked at both Vaega and Mann. "And she'd started dating a married man, older. He lived somewhere not too far away, but not in her town. Sara was very secretive about him."

"You could tell a similar story about any number of young women," Mann said.

"Yes. But this young woman vanished. And the Hugginses moved shortly after, and changed their names."

Vaega said, "Maybe she ran away. With the mystery lover."

"No. She's dead," Erin said.

"How do you know?"

"Because John Huggins killed her. Just—"

"Like Lauren." Mann glared at her.

"Sheriff, Sara Daniels *was* just like Lauren. She was the same girl." Erin scooted forward on her seat. "Huggins has a type. He goes for young women on the edge, who are having trouble at school or at work, dabbling with drugs and experimenting with their sexuality. Looking for love. They're the type of women who would easily fall prey to an older man with a little money and a little charm, the type you have right here in Hopewell. You even introduced me to one this morning. Rebecca Engel."

The sheriff's spine stiffened, but the phone rang. He answered with a curt, "Mann."

Erin watched him as he listened to the caller. He'd be a helluva poker player, except for that tiny nerve that twitched in his cheek. He said, "Jesus," then tapped on the computer keyboard, watched the screen, and tapped a few keys more. "It's right here. Okay, thanks."

"Anything?" Vaega asked.

"Maybe," he said, and got his printer spitting out pages.

Erin looked back and forth between the two of them and realized they had no intention of explaining anything.

"What is it? Tell me."

"No," Mann said.

"Oh, for God's sake." She popped up and made a beeline to his printer, but he stood and cut her off. When he spoke, his voice was low.

"There's nothing besides geography that connects Jack Calloway with Sara Daniels. She may not even be dead. There's nothing but Lauren's pottery classes and a hunch from you that connects him to her."

"And the picture Lauren drew and Justin's word."

"And that," he conceded. "But even if Huggins and McAllister knew each other—or had an affair—it doesn't mean he cleaned off her face and killed her. He did pass a lie detector test."

Erin's teeth ground. "A true sociopath can lie without betraying himself to a machine."

He looked at her, his eyes seeming to search for something more. Lunacy? Lies? She'd been accused of both by Senator McAllister. Hell, she'd been accused of them long before—by her own mother. *You've got to believe me, Mom...*

The dog jumped up and barked, and a split second later, the doorbell rang.

Mann looked at his watch. "After ten o'clock," he said. He and Vaega went to the front door. Erin stood back while the deputy positioned himself in front of her.

"Shit," the sheriff said when he looked out the window.

He opened the door. It was the woman from Engel's restaurant, crying.

"Sheriff," she sobbed, "Rebecca's gone."

CHAPTER
18

ALARMS WENT OFF in Nick's mind—one after another and each more terrifying than the last. *Ace Holmes? Carrie Sitton's murderer? Jack Calloway?* Erin's words replayed in his ears...Calloway's type of women: *The type you have right here in Hopewell. You even introduced me to one this morning...*

God, no.

"She's probably hanging out with Ace, not answering her cell phone," Quent said, doing his best to be the voice of reason. "Leni said Rebecca threatened running off with him."

They piled into the Tahoe and a knot of fear clogged Nick's throat. Pray, God, Quent was right.

They raced through town and stopped at the restaurant first—the last place Rebecca had been seen. The cash register had been emptied of bills.

Thank God. But even as a twinge of relief plucked at Nick, the realization that he was thanking God that Rebecca had probably stolen money and run off with Holmes hit him between the eyes. In the old days—last week—that would have been a horrible thing in Hopewell.

Now, in the scheme of what Erin Sims was claiming, finding out that Becca had run away with an asshole boyfriend would rate as good news.

He closed his eyes, and the message he'd just printed at home rose up to haunt him. He'd grabbed it on his way out so as not to let Erin see it, and handed it to Quent as he drove. It was from the FBI.

Quent read it, then looked at Nick. "Man. You think Sims is bullshitting us?"

"Maybe. All in all, that report doesn't make her appear very credible. But I gotta tell ya, Quent, there's something else that's been rolling around in my head all day." Nick swallowed, but the knot in his throat didn't go away. "What if she's not bullshitting us? What if she's right and Jack Calloway's been screwing girls and killing them, right under my nose for the past five years?"

Quent thought about it for a full minute. "Holy God," he finally said, almost under his breath. "I hope not."

John was gone, the son of a bitch. Well, almost. *Pzzt.* He dropped where he stood in front of his own gun cabinet.

The Angelmaker secured a plastic bag over John's head to keep the blood from spreading, dragged him out the back in the hall rug, and piled him into the shiny new Ford. Hit him with a few strips of duct tape just in case, then went back inside and carefully replaced the rug. On the way back through the foyer, the Angelmaker paused to look at the masks. A thrill surged deep inside.

John would go right *there,* to the left of Lauren McAllister and a little bit lower. An angel, after all.

The Angelmaker went back outside, zapped John again and bound him with more duct tape. Hauled him to the

workshop and wrestled the deadweight of his body onto
the table.

Ready.

Now the preparation. The plastic on his head could go;
it wasn't necessary anymore. Then the duct tape—yards
and yards of it—spiraling over John's body and under the
table, round and round, making them one. When he began
to stir again, it wouldn't matter; he was immobile. For his
head, there was a *technique*: one strip of duct tape across
the top of his brow just dipping beneath the roots of the
hairline and another strip, longer, looped beneath the chin
and up over the ears like a horseshoe. It was a practice
perfected years ago. One that held the head as still as a
mannequin, yet left the face completely exposed.

Ready. Well, almost. Better do the lips. Not much possibility anything could be heard outside this workshop,
but it would be a few hours before the job was finished.
No sense in taking chances.

The Angelmaker picked up a tube of Super Glue,
wiped the tip with a cloth, then dragged a single bead of
the clear liquid across the crease of John's lips. Pressed
them together for five seconds.

Now John was ready.

The Angelmaker walked around the dim space and lit
seven candles—one for each angel so far—then added an
eighth for John. A shame he had turned out to be one of
them, though it had probably always been just a matter of
time.

Time. It was moving quickly now, getting harder to
keep things in hand. So much to juggle.

The Angelmaker got to business, turned on the CD
player and let the strains of an angel choir float into the air.
Regina coeli, Regina coeli, semper angelis conservabor...

Now for the clay. It was warm, moving like silk in hand, and when the first smear touched John's face, he came to just enough that his brow wrinkled and his eyelids flickered. He tried to say something but his voice came out *mmmm* and his lips worked against the glue, muscles tightening with panic and the sounds in his throat rising to a feverish pitch. A second later, his eyes—pupils wide and dilated—lit on the Angelmaker.

The truth leaked into John's eyes like drops of poison. The Angelmaker smiled, gazing into the mismatched orbs. Those piercing, all-seeing eyes that would soon be rendered harmless.

"Well, good," the Angelmaker said, "you're awake. Just in time to watch yourself die."

Ace Holmes lived a stone's throw over the Carroll County line, out of Nick's jurisdiction. Nick thought about calling in Anson Bell, then decided to fuck jurisdictions and fall on Holmes himself. Bell had enough going on with Carrie Sitton's murder.

Besides, Nick was pumped. Rebecca was probably just falling under Ace's bad influence and giving her mom hell, but God help him: He was *pumped*.

Holmes's place was exactly what he'd envisioned: a run-down house suffering from long-term neglect, sitting on a plot that would have looked right in an old trailer park. Scrap metal, splintered wood, and discarded containers of antifreeze and motor oil were piled against one wall. Several bags of garbage had been raided by coons or dogs; Holmes's Chevy pickup sat in a gravel turnaround, along with a beater-Dodge with expired plates. Nick laid a hand on the hood of one vehicle, then the other. Both engines were cool.

He freed the clip on his 9 mm holster, saw Quentin do the same. Without a word, they flanked the front door, and Nick reached to his side and knocked.

Holmes peeked out. "Aw, fuck you," he said, and Nick strong-armed the door.

"Aren't you gonna invite us in, Ace?" he asked. The smell of cooked onions oozed onto the porch. Sleazy music—boinky synthesizers and whining electric guitars—came from the TV inside, punctuated by the exuberant "unh, unh" of a woman being pounded by too large a dick.

"Get outta here, man. I didn't do nothin'. I didn't even know that Carrie girl."

"Then you've got nothing to worry about," Nick said. Holmes backed off, stepping from the door and rubbing a hand over his close-shaved head. Nick repeated: "I said, 'Aren't you going to invite us in?' Because out here on the porch, I think I smell some pot. Do you smell pot, Deputy Vaega?"

Quent made a show of sniffing the air. "Smells like top-grade grass to me."

Holmes swore, then hit the front of the TV with a fist. The woman's grunts died along with the music. "Assholes," he said, but didn't shut the door.

Invitation enough. Ace Holmes had done time for possession and had a couple of raps for robbery. He was sunk if they decided they had sufficient grounds to search the place. Suspicion of marijuana use constituted sufficient grounds.

Nick stepped inside.

"She ain't here," Holmes said.

"Who?" asked Quent.

"Shit. You know. I know. Everyone knows. She ain't here."

Quentin had eased closer to Holmes while Nick circled around the living room, pausing at a door. "This the bedroom, Ace?"

"She ain't here."

Nick pressed the door wide and peered in. A rumpled mattress, piles of dirty clothes on the floor, beer cans. The smell of sex and sweat.

"Where is she, then?" Nick asked, checking the bathroom. Quent had moved to where he could see into the kitchen, and shook his head.

"Probably out hitchhikin'."

Holmes was built like a tub: six foot, bulky, solid as porcelain. But he didn't put up any show as Nick stepped close. "Why would she do that?" Nick asked.

"Bitch has a temper. What can I say?"

Nick grabbed his shirt and shoved him against the wall.

"Hey, hey, hey," Holmes complained. His hands flailed, as if he wanted to fight but knew better. "Let go, man."

"You're telling me you're out here in the middle of fucking nowhere, close to where a girl was murdered just three nights ago, and you let your girlfriend leave, alone in the dark, on foot, and it's less than forty degrees outside?"

"I'm not the controlling type."

Nick let his fist fly, into Holmes's left jaw. He caught him and hauled him back up against the wall.

Holmes groaned. "I ain't shittin' you. She took off outta here, mad."

"About what?"

He spit blood. "Money. She brought me a gift, ya know?"

"Where did it come from?"

"A puss gives you money, you don't ask questions. You take it and fuck her brains out."

Nick slammed him against the wall. "Where were you when you did her?"

"What?" Holmes was confused.

"Did you do her in your truck?"

"Yeah, I did her in my truck," he said, showing a slash of bloody teeth. "The *first* time."

Nick tightened his grip. Holmes was too stupid to realize what he'd just said. "So she was mad at you but let you have her, anyway; is that what you're telling me?" Nick pressed. "You didn't have to do any...convincing?"

"Becca likes it rough. Being *convinced*"—he tried to waggle his eyebrows—"it gets her dripping."

This time Quent caught him. Nick threw the punch, watched him stumble into Quent's arms, and took a step back to rub his knuckles.

Quent deposited Holmes on the sofa. "Wake up, you son of a bitch," he said, and dumped the remainder of a beer over his head.

"Jesus," Holmes sputtered. "What do you want from me?"

Nick, in his face again. "I want your filthy hands *off* any girl in my county. And I want Leni Engel's money back."

"Free country," Holmes snapped.

"Yeah. That's what all the guys in the state pen said." Nick stood up. To Quentin: "I'll send you a car. I'm gonna go look for Becca."

"Fine. Ace, here," Quent said, patting Holmes's shoulder like an old buddy, "is gonna help me look around for that money."

Nick called in three cars—one for Quent and two to help him search for Rebecca. His heart pounded like a jackhammer. He stuck to County Road 219, the most direct route from town to Holmes. *Dlmmp.* The sound of his tires thumping over Carrie Sitton's body echoed in his ears. The image of her pale, muddy face in his mind's eye, Erin Sims's accusations in his head...

Nick cursed. *No. Not on my turf, not on my watch.*

He found her twenty minutes later, not hitchhiking, but walking along a two-lane road, her hands shoved into her pockets and her head scrunched below her collar. Relief poured into his chest and he piled her into the front seat of his Tahoe and cranked the heat to full blast. "I oughta turn you over my knee, then lock you in a cell until you're thirty," he growled. "What the hell are you thinking, walking home alone at night like this?"

"H-he said he loved m-me," she said through the clickety-clack of chattering teeth. The tears were right behind.

"Ah, jeez." Nick kept his eyes on the road. "Someone a lot better than that is gonna love you someday, Becca."

He felt her look at him. "You think?"

"Yeah. I think."

She dropped her head, wringing her fingers on her lap. "I used to think that, too, but I don't know anymore. I feel kinda used up."

Nick pulled to the side of the road and parked, angling toward her. "Not yet. But you gotta quit going like this, save a little something for later. You have a long life ahead of you."

"He said if we had enough money, he'd take me way. Then, when I brought it and wanted to leave, he got mad..."

Nick flipped on the interior light. "Did he hurt you? Anything that happened in the truck would have been in my county. I'll take him in if he hurt you."

"Well, it always—" She stopped, confused. "I think it's just how it is."

Emotion got Nick in the chest. "It isn't supposed to hurt, honey."

She looked at him like she didn't believe him. "But I— I *let* him..."

"You let him do this?" Nick used a finger to push her hair back. Fresh bruises blossomed along her jawline, and the cold finger of rage touched his heart.

She swallowed and pulled her hair back down. "Are you gonna call my mom?"

"Not yet."

"Are you gonna take me home?"

"Not yet."

She about came out of her skin when she realized where he *was* taking her.

"You can't make me go in there," she said, as Nick pulled into a slot marked AUTHORIZED VEHICLES ONLY. It was the closest he could get to the doors without blocking the ambulance parking. "I won't do it," she said.

"Yes. You will."

"Ace'll...God. He'll be so mad."

"I'll handle Ace."

She went silent, chewing her lip. Nick wanted to comfort her, even bring her into his arms, but didn't. "Rebecca, it's going to be hard. They'll have to examine you inside and out, and they'll ask a lot of embarrassing questions and take pictures. But in the end, you'll give us something to lock him up. And," he added as an afterthought that just might matter to her, "we can get your mom's money back."

She looked up and Nick was stricken by how much of

a child she really was. The idea that she might have been taken by Jack—as Erin kept suggesting—gnawed at his soul. He'd gotten lucky this time; Jack wasn't involved.

But what if Erin was right?

Rebecca sucked in a shaky breath and looked at the hospital door. "Do you think you should call my mom now?" she asked.

"Absolutely."

The mask was finished; now the clay just needed to dry. It would take a few hours, and John's breathing had already grown raspy and labored. Even with a tiny hole in each nostril to keep him alive, he'd breathed clay up his nose. It was just one of those things that couldn't be helped. Not a perfect system.

But good enough. He'd be dead by the time the Angel-maker got back. And then all that would be left was getting rid of the body. Easy.

It was over.

Now to set up a trail for Mann. A little drive in Jack's truck, be sure to leave some tire tracks outside Sims's hotel, or make sure someone sees the Ford there. Mann thought moving her to an out-of-the-way motel was safer, but it just made things easier. It had been a simple matter to follow him there—he wasn't hiding and even had cruisers passing by the place all day. So it ought to be easy for someone to see Jack's truck there tonight.

Tonight, that was important. Jack needed to be noticed.

CHAPTER
19

L ENI GOT A PHONE CALL from the sheriff and ran off like a shot. It was almost two in the morning. Apparently, Rebecca was at the hospital, okay, but asking for her mom. Dana tucked Leni's coat over her shoulders and shut the door behind her.

"Lord," she said, "it scares me to death to think of my Marissa getting old enough for that sort of thing." She looked at Erin. "I guess in your line of work you get used to it."

"Not really."

"Come on," Dana said, tugging her dreadlocks into a ponytail. "Nick's gotta have some decaf tea somewhere."

Erin was wired, too. Sitting late into the night with Rebecca's mother had been a nightmare. All she could think about were things Leni Engel didn't know to even worry about: Lauren McAllister and Sara Daniels. Rebecca *was* similar. A prime target for a man like Huggins.

But then Rebecca had been found, Erin reminded herself. Not entirely safe, perhaps, but at least together enough that she'd be going home later tonight. That was as much as Erin had gotten out of one end of the phone conversation before Leni rushed out.

Dana found tea bags in the first cupboard she tried.

"You must know the sheriff pretty well," Erin said.

Dana turned up a flame under the teakettle. "He and Quent played football together in high school. By the time Quent and I got together, Nick already lived in L.A.—he went to USC when Quentin went to Ohio State—but he's been back now for a few years." She plopped two tea bags into a couple of empty mugs. "I just hang out with them so Nick will rub off on me and I'll turn into a culinary genius."

"It worked with Hannah."

An easy smile appeared. "Hannah's amazing. Most kids come home from school and turn on cartoons. Hannah turns on cooking shows. The Manns' idea of a great Saturday night lineup is a marathon of *Top Chef* episodes."

Erin couldn't help but smile. "I would've never guessed it when I met him. When I found him at that empty house in the middle of the night, I thought he was something out of the back woods."

"He was coming off his hell-weekend. At least, that's what Quentin calls it."

"Hell-weekend?"

"Years ago, when they still lived in California, Nick and his wife bought that piece of land up at the clay mine. Nick wanted a place where they could vacation near his folks, but then Allison died. Now he goes there every year on the anniversary of her death. Spends a weekend alone doing God-knows-what, and looking like hell when he returns. *That's* where he was when you arrived in town."

Well, that explained some things. Not others.

"He wants me to leave," Erin said.

Dana looked into her cup. "Maybe we all do."

Erin frowned. "You'd rather live with your heads in the sand?"

"Jack Calloway, a serial killer? That kind of thing doesn't happen here."

"Forgive me, but wasn't there a woman murdered here just a few days ago?"

Dana tightened up. "I don't know what to think about that. Quent won't talk about it—departmental policy. If there's one thing Nick Mann hates, it's rumor."

"I thought it was shrinks. And the media."

"There's a list." She seemed to have more to say but the teakettle whistled and she poured steaming water into each mug. Erin used a favorite trick of counselors: She waited.

"You've seen the scar on Hannah's forehead?" Dana finally asked, into the silence.

"Yes, I saw it."

"That was from the gun that killed Nick's wife."

"Oh, God," Erin said. "What happened?"

"Nick had been working on a big case for months—involving L.A.'s organized crime ring. They were supposed to attend a big birthday gala for Allison's dad—he was pretty famous—but the case was going down that night so Nick couldn't go. Allison didn't want to go without him; she was afraid of the fallout from his case. But he told her to go. He swore that he had everything covered, that she'd be fine. He was so tied up making arrests he didn't know what happened until it was over."

"What happened?"

"She and Hannah were waiting for her father outside the restaurant when a man named Bertrand Yost drove up and opened fire."

"On *her*, specifically?"

Dana nodded. "The bust had happened an hour earlier. Yost slipped the net. He couldn't get to Nick, so he went for Allison. She died instantly. And another bullet hit Hannah."

Erin couldn't think of anything to say. She was imagining a three-year-old girl in a spray of bullets, watching her mother die. "What a nightmare."

"Yes. And after the nightmare ended, the hell began. Nick tracked down Bertrand Yost. Yost came at him, armed, and when Nick got the upper hand in the fight, he didn't stop. He was beating the hell out of Yost when his brother, Luke, pulled him off. Nick was suspended from duty and required to do therapy with some quack psychologist from Internal Affairs."

"Dear God," Erin said. A few more things fell into place about him.

"Allison's parents wanted Hannah and they used Nick's outrage against Yost to get her away from him. They accused him of affairs and violence against Allison—which was all bull, of course, but once the press got into it, the media uproar was amazing. There were rumors that Nick planned his wife's death, that he hired Yost to do the killing."

"Where did all that come from?"

"It's what happens when the murder victim is an heiress and her husband is the LAPD's star detective."

Erin choked on her tea. "Heiress?"

"Allison Taylor, the daughter of Jessup Taylor."

Jessup Taylor, Jessup Taylor. "The real estate guy. The one who's always talking about trumping the Trump?"

"In California, he's a household name. He makes *People* magazine about every three months, not to mention the business magazines. By association, Nick and Allison were constantly in the spotlight. They were hounded by the press, mostly because her father had never made any bones about how he felt when his daughter married a common cop. L.A. loves the rich and the famous, loves a juicy story, and loved its local über cop. This story had everything: Jessup Taylor's daughter and granddaughter, the L.A. mob, a vengeful cop husband, and eighteen million dollars in Allison's trust."

"Eighteen—" She couldn't say it.

"Nick's never spent a dime of it. This house...it was a fixer-upper. He laid every tile and hammered every nail himself, with his dad." Dana canted her head in thought for a moment, then said, "He would have rather stayed in L.A. and cleared his name. But the media was bad for the department and vicious for Hannah. She asked Nick once if it was true he'd paid Yost to kill her mother."

"Oh, my. Does she still remember the shooting?"

"She still has nightmares. That's why Nick left L.A. and came back here."

"To Mayberry."

"That may be what he was trying for, but he didn't get it. Hopewell had changed since he'd been gone. There were drugs here and everything that comes with them. Hilltop was a meth house and the old sheriff got killed there. Nick was a natural to finish his term. No one around here, not even the older deputies like Wart Hogue—who should have been a shoo-in—had the type of experience he did. He didn't want to do it at first, but Quentin was a cop in Cleveland, and we were looking to get the kids into a smaller town. A safer place. They decided to work together. And then Jack Calloway came."

"In May of 2007," Erin said. Huggins's history wasn't news to her.

"He wanted to buy the Hilltop property and set up shop for his wife. Nick knew the renovation would help Hopewell. He supported Jack all the way, and got just about everyone in town working on Hilltop. He even got the commissioner to put prisoners out there doing the county stuff—the roads, easements, electricity. Nick whipped Hopewell into shape and when the election came up, no one ran against him. You know what his campaign motto was?"

Erin shook her head.

" 'Not on Nick's watch.' It wasn't something he came up with; it was just what everyone said about him."

Frustration knotted in Erin's chest. "Look, I'm not the one who brought crime to Nick Mann's watch. Huggins is."

"I underst—"

"No, you don't. No one here does." Erin pushed from the island. "You all believe that there are places in the world where bad things don't happen. Well, let me tell you: Bad things happen everywhere. In big dirty cities and in quaint little towns. In trailer parks and hospitals and alleys and in nice, expensive homes behind closed bedroom doors and—"

She stopped, memories clambering to the surface. She clutched her arms around herself, tamping down the emotion that threatened.

Dana stared at her.

"I have to go," Erin said. "Tell the sheriff I'll talk to him tomorrow."

She was shaking as she drove away. And no matter how much she scrubbed at her eyes, they kept filling.

Not here, on Mann's watch.

Fools. Blind, ignorant jerks. The whole damn town had their heads in the sand. And while people here were refusing to look at John Huggins—really *look*—Justin had inched one night closer to death.

Erin drove with her hands clenched on the steering wheel, fear squeezing her heart. She had to stop it from happening somehow. This couldn't be the end of the fight. There had to be a way to—

The headlights came from nowhere. Erin winced. Bright beams, closing in on her rearview mirror so fast and so close she had to squint and turn away. Her heart dropped to her stomach and she swerved to avoid being rear-ended. A horn blasted in her ears and the headlights swung out around her. She tried to move over, but there was no shoulder, and her eyes watered from tears and the glare of the headlights. The truck came up beside her from behind, too close, then even closer, then—

Impact. The car careened. She hit grass and gravel and wrestled the tires back onto the road, but the dark beast of the truck was right there. Metal crunched in her ears and the Aveo jumped, the pavement spinning beneath her. The world swirled for two seconds, then lurched.

Then faded.

CHAPTER
20

THE ANGELMAKER SAW Erin Sims's car wheel off the road, a gush of excitement spilling out in laughter. Holy Mother of God, how perfect.

Who's watching now, Jack?

Now keep driving, don't look back. The extent of her injuries—whatever it was—couldn't be changed, and it was too risky to stop. If anyone saw this truck now, with the damage from having just hit her car, it would be over.

So, go on. With any luck, Sims was dead, though the chances of that were slim. The plan had just been to be sure someone would know Jack's truck had been outside Sims's motel; having her come tooling along in the middle of the night had been sheer luck. It would be interesting to know where she'd been at such a late hour, but then again, there was no need to question fate.

Now get out of town. It wouldn't take long for someone to find her, even in the middle of the night. When they did, Jack's truck needed to be long gone.

An hour and two county lines passed before the turn-off came into view, the truck's headlights leading the way through a cut in the chain-link fence. The Angelmaker climbed out of the Ford, looked out into the pitch-black acreage surrounding the quarry, and peered into the sky. It was cold—dangerously so. Just thirty-eight degrees, said the thermometer on the dashboard. But it wasn't predicted to drop much more and there was a seventy percent chance of rain, so the plan should work.

But what if it didn't? What if it got colder and stayed that way until morning, or didn't rain?

Forget it. Just do it.

The Angelmaker went to the back of the Ford and unhitched the ramp, maneuvering a small motorcycle to the ground. It was an old 150 that leaked oil, but it had only cost a hundred dollars, was easy to conceal and easy to handle. Like the stun gun: Sometimes the simplest things were the best.

The Angelmaker slipped back into the driver's seat and inched the truck forward, riding the brake, heart drumming as the distance between the front tires and the overhang to the quarry grew shorter and shorter. Good that it was dark; it had been scary enough in the daylight to be this close to the edge, and able to see the depth of the quarry pit below. Now only the two columns of headlights were visible, disappearing into darkness that seemed infinite.

The truck rolled another few feet down the slope and the Angelmaker stopped, pressing down the parking brake. Now for the ice. Warmer would be better, but with a little rain, it should melt soon enough. Still, it was nerve-wracking having to leave everything here and not know exactly *when* it would happen.

The Angelmaker pulled the plastic off the first ice block and wedged it beneath the front left tire, then walked around the front of the truck to do the same on the other side. Stood for a minute and worried about the setup. What if the blocks didn't hold when the brake was released, and the truck went careening over the edge right now?

Relax. Ultimately, it didn't matter. If it happened now, even if the truck burst into flames, no one would see it. This quarry was in the middle of nowhere and had been abandoned for years.

So, get on with it. It was getting late and there was still more to do back in town. Busy night.

Gently, gently, the Angelmaker opened the driver's side door to reach the gear shift. Easy, now. Not *neutral*— that would be a dead giveaway—but *drive*. The gear shift moved without resistance, and the parking brake held. With one leg hanging from the open driver's side door, the Angelmaker leaned out as far as possible, ready to jump if need be, then took a deep breath and released the brake.

The truck lurched—a couple of inches, that's all. The Angelmaker's breath caught. The ice blocks held.

Relief rushed in. This was it; it would work. Jack was finished and his demise would waylay Erin Sims even if her own accident didn't. Nick Mann's head would spin.

The Angelmaker sucked in a cold lungful of air, the power a heady sensation. The end was near. There was only one thing Jack had left standing in the way: Reverend Carl Whitmore.

Erin's eyes burned. Lights. Too many lights, glaring in the night. And voices, one of them calling, "Lady, lady," and the other more distant, speaking in code. *Needs assistance… Eleven-eighty on Holcomb Bridge Road one mile south of Tulle, request an ambulance, code 3…*

Erin dragged to the surface and might have groaned. Her rib cage was on fire. Her rental car seemed to be at an angle in the ditch. A deputy had his upper body halfway through the passenger side door, reaching for her.

"Dr. Sims, look at me. Dr. Sims."

She turned to the voice but tears blocked her vision. She wiped at them and her fingers came away sticky. Not tears. Blood.

"It's just a scratch," the deputy said. "Don't worry about that." At the same time he said it, he pressed a thick pad against her forehead. "Dr. Sims, where are you from? Tell me your phone number, say your name. Jesus, say *something* that tells me you know who you are and what's going on."

"Jack Calloway tried to kill me."

The deputy blinked. "That'll do."

Nick took the call from Fruth as he and Quent pulled into his driveway. He sent a pair of deputies to Hilltop House to pick up Jack and confiscate his truck, checked in with Dana for thirty seconds, then headed to Holcomb Bridge Road at the speed of sound.

Two-thirty in the morning. Apparently, Erin had left Nick's house to go to her motel and wound up in a ditch. She was claiming to deputies that a dark pickup truck had purposely run her off the road.

Jack had a dark pickup truck.

"So do about two thousand other Hopewell residents," Quentin reminded him.

Sims was at the hospital getting patched up. Nick and Quent poked around the accident site for ten minutes; then Quentin caught a ride back to Nick's house while Nick headed to the hospital.

"You're full of surprises," he said, walking into a

curtained-off section of the emergency room. She sat at the foot of a gurney, working the buttons on her blouse.

"Jack Calloway ran me off the road," she said.

"I heard."

Her face was the color of soap. Her eyes, normally a vibrant green, looked gray. The buttons wouldn't cooperate with her fingers. The doctor had said she was lucky: Her car had been stopped by a rise in the ground before it spun out of control and she had suffered only cuts and bruises. She'd be fine.

But he wasn't sure he would be. She was on his turf now, at his *house,* for God's sake, and some son of a bitch—Jack?—had tried to hurt her. She might very well have been killed. The weight of that knowledge rode on Nick's chest like a boulder.

"Did you go get him?" she asked.

"Of course. He's not home."

Her eyes widened. "See? What have I been telling you? It's the middle of the night. Where is he?"

"We're looking for him. For the record, there are 1,946 dark pickup trucks registered to residents in this county. Are you sure you can't pinpoint the make?"

"What make does Calloway drive?"

"That's not helping," he said, then homed in on her face. Six stitches crept along her hairline where her head had struck the window. A bruise rose near her temple, just above the scrape she'd picked up in Florida.

He took her chin, angling her face for a better look, and the fear in her eyes settled in his gut. She probably didn't think it showed; hell, she probably didn't even know it was there, buried beneath all that bravado. But it *was* there, and a parade of images marched through his mind: a wife afraid to attend a party, a daughter terrified of nightmares, and now, a woman putting up a tough front for her brother. Nick had always considered himself a capable man, but fear was his downfall. It was beyond his control. It was insidious and untouchable. It rendered him as useless as an empty gun.

He dropped his hand, stepping back before he did something stupid—like pull her into his arms, or murmur a promise he couldn't keep. *Everything will be all right... I've got it covered.*

"There's no need to get dressed," he said. "They're checking you in 'til morning."

"I don't need to stay until morning." She eased herself off the bed. "I need to get on with things."

"Things?"

"Public persecution. The ruination of storybook villages. You know."

His jaw ground. He took her by the shoulders; she winced. "I'm sorry, I didn't mean to hurt you. But you need to lay low. Take a day or two to heal, give me some time to figure this thing out." *Let me keep you safe.*

"Justin doesn't have a day or two."

She picked up her jacket from the bed, started to slip an arm into the sleeve before the pain made her think better of it. Nick bullied down the impulse to help and watched her lay the jacket carefully over her arm rather than putting it on. She started for the door.

"Where do you think you're going?"

"You have cabs in Hopewell, I presume."

"Erin, for Christ's sake," he started, then saw by the tilt of her chin that he wasn't going to win. Her brother's life was ticking away. She had a battle to fight. But no matter how hyped she felt right now, when the shock and adrenaline wore off, she was going to crash.

And he wanted to be there when she did.

Nick chose not to examine that fleeting notion; he just took her elbow. "Mann's Taxi, at your service."

Dana met them at his kitchen door. "I sent Quentin to bed in the guest room. And the kids are all lined up in your bed, Nick. They wanted to sleep together and I didn't know at the time it would be all night."

"That's fine," Nick said. "Thanks."

She turned to Erin. "Are you all right?"

"Yes. Sheriff Mann refuses to take me back to my motel room, that's all."

"Good," Dana said, and disappeared up the stairs.

Erin waited, uncertain what should happen next, as the sheriff took off his jacket and dropped his holster over a chair. He pulled out the gun and checked the safety, then slid it onto the top shelf of a cabinet—a father accustomed to having guns in the house. For the first time since he'd left to go after Rebecca, Erin really studied him. His short hair was a mess and the knuckles of his right hand were bruised. He looked ragged and rough and exhausted, insanely handsome, with an air of protectiveness that clung to him like a scent. For Rebecca, for his town.

For her. The idea was so foreign, Erin didn't know what to do with it. She'd never had someone watching out for her before. That was *her* job.

She took a deep breath and regretted it halfway through.

"Did they give you anything for pain?" Mann asked.

"They told me to take ibuprofen and try not to sneeze."

He went away and when he came back, ran a glass of water and held out four pills. "Don't be a hero."

Erin was no dummy. The night was getting to her. She swallowed the pills and wondered about Justin's night.

Did he lie awake in order to make the nights pass by more slowly? Did he have any idea how hard she was trying?

And where had Huggins gone after he left her in the ditch? Was he running away again? Buying drugs and picking out his next victim?

"We have to find him," she said, though she knew it was an empty thing to say. "What do we do to find him?"

Mann's gaze settled on her face. "We find a couple of pillows and blankets and get a few hours of sleep." He held up a finger when she started to interrupt him. "We're running a check on all dark pickup trucks in the area, and I put out an APB specifically on Jack's. Everyone in fifteen counties is looking for him or a truck with damage."

"What about the women?"

"What women?"

"The ones he may be trying to seduce right now, or killing. He could be out trolling for someone, right this minute while we're standing here doing nothing. There could be another woman who just disappears or he could decide to run where I'll never find him or he could wait a little while and then come back for m—"

"Erin." The sheriff cupped her upper arms, his strength a palpable thing. A wave of something she didn't recognize threatened to buckle her knees. "No one can hurt you here."

"It's not that."

"It is that. Someone hit your motel room and has taken two swipes at you in a car. You're afraid. There's nothing wrong with that."

Afraid? Erin? Erin was a warrior, not a victim. She was the unflinching sentinel who fought for her clients and the tireless soldier who fought for Justin. Fear wasn't in her constitution.

And yet, for no good reason, her knees began to shake and a chill prickled her skin and—

The tears took her by surprise, but Mann seemed to have been waiting for them. He thumbed them away, saying nothing, then pulled her against his body and held her. Gently, as if she were made of blown glass.

Erin sank into the embrace, his sheer tenderness wreaking havoc in her brain. For a fleeting moment she had the sensation that anyone in the circle of Nick Mann's arms had to be safe from the evils of the world. He was hard and powerful and resilient. There must be nothing he couldn't fight and win—

Dana's story poured back in. *Beating the hell out of Yost...suspended from duty...accused of setting up the murder...*

Erin shifted. Mann opened his arms and took a good long look at her.

"Ah. So you got the scoop on me, huh?"

Lord, she might have been staring at him. She looked down. "Dana," she said, then jumped to defend her. "She wasn't gossiping, really, just—"

"There wasn't anything I was trying to hide. I told you to Google me. Dana just saved you the trouble."

Right. As if Googling him weren't the first thing she'd been planning to do when she got back to the motel. It's just that she never got there.

He crossed his arms over his chest. "So, knowing what you do now, are you afraid to stay here? Afraid I might have hired someone to shoot my wife and daughter?"

"No, of course not." And it was the absolute truth. "I wasn't thinking that."

"Hmm," he said, and his gaze dropped to her lips. Made her aware that she'd just moistened them with her tongue. "Then maybe you're thinking about letting me hold you again, letting me kiss you."

Heat flooded Erin's belly. Dear God, she did want to sink back into his arms. The mere idea made her joints turn to butter. And the thought of kissing him...She almost swayed.

Mann ran his hands down her arms. "I'd like to think being with me makes you weak-kneed," he said, with the ghost of a smile, "but I'm afraid this is normal. Your limbs feel like they're turning into Jell-O. Pretty soon your head will be weightless; then it'll hurt like a bastard. Adrenaline rushes are great while they last, but afterward, it's hell."

Oh. Yes, that's what it was. "You've been here before," she managed.

"A time or two." A feral glint came to his eyes. "But I won't let it happen to you again."

He swore to Allison that he had everything covered, that she'd be fine. Erin looked up into those colorless eyes, surprised by the desire to console him. It must be tiring lugging that kind of guilt around.

His hand tightened on her arm and she realized he was right. Her head was suddenly weightless. "I'm okay," she said. "I can take care of myself."

"Uh-huh," he said, with utter insincerity. He ushered her to the sofa and reached into a blanket chest by the hearth. Came up with a fluffy blue pillow and a down-filled throw. "Lie down, get some sleep. You'll still be sore in a few hours, but your nerves will be calm again. I'll be in the den, since the kids are in my bed." He tossed one last look in her direction as he walked out. "In case you need anything."

CHAPTER
21

CARL WHITMORE WAS an early riser. Most days, he had breakfast around five; he was ashamed to admit that since his wife had died his standard fare was a bowl of Cap'n Crunch and a glass of prune juice. By six, he was usually sitting at his office computer, working on sermons. He liked to do that before the church office opened at ten. Ideas were fresh in the mornings, and there were no interruptions.

Today, the church office wouldn't open at all. The church secretary, Eloise, had taken a personal day to go visit an ailing relative in Toledo. Carl would have the whole day free. He'd work on sermons in the morning, fit in a hospital visit, then maybe go home early and rake some leaves. Yet another task his wife had usually done.

So with an entire day to himself planned out, he was surprised to see Margaret Calloway's Saturn pull into the church parking lot. He closed his eyes and lifted his face in prayer. He hoped the sheriff hadn't openly accused Jack of anything. Jack was one of his flock, and Carl had betrayed him. Not legally, and not to the letter of ethics,

quite—since Jack had never formally confided in him—
but nonetheless, Carl had felt the strings of guilt strum-
ming ever since he'd gone to Sheriff Mann. Jack Calloway
was a good man with a dark side, that's all. People, by and
large, would be surprised to know how many of the loyal
parishioners had a dark side. Not to mention that Jack
pledged twenty thousand dollars a year to Ebenezer.

Carl shook off that unholy thought and closed his document; he hadn't had any good ideas yet, anyway. Maybe
a sermon on sins of the flesh was in order, or one about the
dangers of vigilantism in place of God's justice. His con-
gregants would likely appreciate that these days, given
the actions of Erin Sims. *Thy Father's Will,* he thought
and jotted the title down.

He was still scrolling through ideas in his head when
he got to the lobby, but no one was there. Carl walked to
the annex. *In God's Hands, Not Ours.* He kind of liked
the sound of that one—

He stopped, hearing the front door open behind
him. He turned, saw the gun, and Carl Whitmore's last
thought before his head exploded was, *Oh, Jack, now I
understand.*

Erin slept until after six, awakening to sounds she
couldn't identify. Grunts, almost, or growls. She looked
around for the dog, but didn't see him.

In the hallway, the sounds became clearer outside the
den. The sheriff. Working out?

The door stood slightly open and D.D. lumbered over,
nudging it the rest of the way. Erin dropped a hand to the
dog's head and peered inside. The long form of the sheriff
sprawled across a leather sofa, one arm thrown above his
head, his legs twitching, a grimace twisting his face.

He was dreaming. And not about something pleasant. Erin watched, hesitant to intrude yet torn by the basic human desire to stop someone from suffering. She eased into the den and crouched beside the sofa, feeling the reminders of the accident with every tiny move. She laid a palm against the sheriff's cheek. "Shhh. Sheriff," she crooned, "you're having a nightmare. It's okay."

He winced at the initial contact, then moaned. She stroked his forehead and murmured to him. A moment later, he shifted and was out again.

Erin held still, listening to his breathing, watching the sculpted contours of his chest move beneath a t-shirt. She wasn't a woman who sought out affairs or one-night stands. The occasional man had interested her in the years since David, but there had been nothing meaningful. She was self-aware enough to know that was her own doing: Meaningful meant being willing to lean on someone, willing to trust. Erin wasn't.

The thought cleared her head. She shouldn't even be thinking about Nick Mann in that way; she shouldn't be remembering how it had felt to be held by him. It would be dangerous to get used to that. Or to want it.

And it would be disastrous to be lured into counting on him to save Justin. An entire day had slipped by in Mann's hands. Erin should have known better than to depend on someone other than herself. Some things, she'd learned one night in her bedroom when she was sixteen, had to be faced alone.

So, move on. No matter how nice it had felt to lean into the sheriff's strong arms, last night's moment of weakness was over. In the light of day, she was back to being smart again. Back to counting on herself.

She pushed to her feet and went to the kitchen, found

Vaega just getting ready to leave and bummed a ride to her motel. There, she bought an Almond Joy from a machine in the lobby, a bottle of Advil from the desk clerk, and asked about a package she had been expecting. The desk clerk gave it to her. It had been delivered at 6:38 the night before.

She took it all to her room, popped some of the Advil and got into the package.

Her pistol. She probably wouldn't need it, but old habits died hard. And given the warm welcomes she'd received since coming here, she was glad she'd had it shipped.

She jammed in the cartridge and stuck it in her bag, then stood in the shower for fifteen minutes, letting the hot streams of water do their best to melt down the pain. She brushed her teeth, slowly, and dressed in jeans and tennis shoes. Wriggling into a tank top got her popping an extra Advil; then she put a blouse on top and added a sweater. God, it was cold in Ohio.

She spent some time on her computer, filed away all that she read, and headed into town in a cab. First stop: Engel's.

An impressive breakfast crowd was scattered about the diner. Erin wondered if business was always this good or if diners had turned out for the morning's gossip special. The stitches along her hairline were likely to be dessert.

"I didn't know if you'd be here this morning," she said to Leni.

"No choice. The breakfast/brunch crowd is my lifeline, especially on weekdays. Weekends, people go to Hilltop House." Her brows drew together. "What happened to you?"

"I left the sheriff's house last night a little while after you did. Jack Calloway ran my car off the road."

Leni's eyes widened. Erin felt the people in a close

radius pay attention. "No one could ever claim I was a fan of the Calloways," Leni said, "but that's hard to believe. Mind, I'm not saying it isn't true. Just hard to believe." She paused. "You want coffee?"

"No," she said, "I can't stay long." *Just long enough to make sure people know about Calloway.* "I came by to see how Rebecca's doing."

"Who knows?" said a new voice. "She won't talk to anyone."

Erin did a double take, looking at the girl with a coffeepot who'd jumped in on the conversation. She was rounder than Rebecca, younger, and had none of the dramatic makeup. But she had to be the sister.

"This is Katie," Leni said, "my second."

"Hi," Erin said. "Rebecca's not talking?"

"And not working and not going to school."

"Katie," Leni scolded. She looked at Erin. "I didn't know what to do. I mean, Ace is in jail—they're holding him for assault—but she didn't want to come to work today. I told her it was okay."

Erin looked at Katie. "Your sister was hurt last night. It's going to take some time to feel okay again."

"Sure," she said, but she sounded more angry than concerned. Something there, Erin thought, but it wasn't her business. Katie eyed her stitches. "So, where is Calloway? I mean, if he ran you off the road."

"He's disappeared," Erin said. "In fact, I'm on my way to the sheriff's office, to see if they have any leads."

Katie started to untie her apron. "Gosh, Mom, I forgot. I have to get to school early. My social studies group is meeting to work on our project."

"Okay." Leni passed Katie's backpack over to her, trading it for the apron. "Have a good day, sweetie."

The sheriff almost bowled Katie down as she left. Erin saw him barrel through the door and felt a little rush of anticipation, like a schoolgirl with a crush, then noticed that he looked ready to kill someone.

Her.

"Come with me," he said, ignoring Leni and everyone else.

Erin's pulse kicked up. "Did you find him?"

"Come with me."

CHAPTER
22

NICK SEETHED. He ushered Erin into his truck without explanation, took her to his office through the back door, and dropped the blinds. He reached for a cigarette on his ear but there wasn't one. Checked his drawer—nothing.

Damn Valeria. She'd thrown them out again.

He leveled a glare on Erin. "Let me have it," he said.

"Have what?"

"The gun."

She blinked, and her hand moved across the zipper of her purse. "Why?"

"*'Why?'*" he repeated. He was incredulous. She'd brought her fucking gun to town, had it shipped by special courier. As if she didn't have troubles enough. "Because the state of Ohio has restrictions on firearms and guess who's responsible for enforcing them?"

"Oh. You mean, you'd like to see my carry permit? Well, Florida and Ohio have a reciprocity agreement, so there shouldn't be any prob—"

"Damn it, Erin."

"How did you know?"

"The motel clerk. He had to sign for it, saw the declaration and insurance for the package. He got to thinking about it and decided I should know."

"There's nothing illegal about it. If there's paperwork to do on this end just let me know—"

"That's not the point."

"What is the point, then?"

The point is I don't want to see you get hurt. The point is I couldn't bear it if something else happens to you in my town... "Sit down," he said, and she stiffened. Nick could see her deciding whether or not to defy him.

"I don't have time to do this."

He caught her arm. "You don't have time *not* to do this." He could feel the tension rippling beneath his hand. "We need to come to an agreement."

"I agree to shut up and not tarnish your precious town, and you agree to let me. Is that it?"

"No."

She opened her mouth but shut it when the single syllable registered. *No.* Not the answer she'd expected. She frowned, her gaze searching his face as if looking for the catch. Always waiting for him to disappoint her, expecting the worst. It's what she'd gotten from everyone else.

"Are you ready to listen?" he asked.

"Let go of me first."

"I don't think so. You'll bolt." Not to mention that he liked having her in his hands. Like hanging on to fire.

"What's the agreement?"

"I'll tell the AG in Florida that we're onto something. Support the stay."

Her breath caught—an instant of hope and joy—then the skepticism came on. "What's my part?"

"You have to lay low. You have to trust me to take care of things." *You have to let me keep you safe.*

She blinked, as if trusting him were the most ludicrous notion in the world. Nick's heart sprang a leak. After she'd curled up on his sofa last night, he'd spent the next hour reading and rereading the file that had come before he'd gone looking for Rebecca. What he learned had ripped at his heart. "Erin, I promise to find out the truth about Jack Calloway. But you have to let me handle the media, let me handle the search for Jack, let me handle the FBI."

"FBI?" Her bones got a shot of steel. "You called the FBI?"

He swallowed; not exactly. They'd called him.

"They won't listen," Erin said. "They'll tell you I'm a loon."

"Crackpot."

"What?"

"They told me you were a crackpot, not a loon. Two entirely different things."

She stared. She couldn't seem to decide if he was teasing or not, if she should keep fighting or not. Nick wondered if she *could* stop fighting. Like the fight might be the only reason she got up in the mornings.

"But you don't think I am?" she asked. "A crackpot or loon?"

And there, Nick thought, was the crux of the issue. *JD—don't waste your time. A loose screw.*

And from the FBI: *History of mental illness. Unreliable accounts. Heavy medications.*

No one had given her the time of day for ten years.

Nick had always been a sucker for a good mystery. Now he found himself even more a sucker for this brittle, dogged woman who had battled the system alone for more than a decade. A woman who, despite her self-reliance, had leaned into his arms almost as if she needed him, and then brushed her fingers over his forehead when Bertrand Yost haunted his dreams.

By morning, Nick had come up with a few better ideas for how they might spend the nights together.

Of course, Erin wasn't thinking of such things. She was engaged in some inner battle that tempered her spine and made her eyes hard as glass, a battle that made her momentary fragility last night a distant memory. Nick reached out and ran his knuckles across her cheek, wanting to recapture that fleeting moment of trust. He cupped her chin and offered her the one thing no one else ever had. "I'll listen to you, Erin. I'll believe you."

The muscles in her throat convulsed. As if she could hardly swallow the idea. "You mean it? You'll talk to the Florida AG?"

"I already called. He'll get my message first thing when he walks in."

Hope filled her eyes and something in Nick's chest went *thmp*. He kind of liked being her hero. It held a lot more possibilities than being her nemesis.

"Deal?" he asked.

She stood, then threw her arms around him. "Deal."

Maggie headed out to the workshop, early. Seven-thirty-one a.m., forty degrees Fahrenheit, Calvin would say. Except Calvin wasn't here. He was still being held on charges of vandalism.

A car pulled up. Maggie looked out the window and watched the driver get out and look around. The Engel girl. Not that slut Rebecca, but the younger one. The straight-A student, the hard worker. A little chunky, a little on the shy side. Sweet sixteen and never been kissed? The same could not be said of her sister.

What was she doing here?

The girl stared at the house from the parking lot, then walked toward the barn, peeked in a window, and came back up the path. She did the same at the carriage house, looking nervous, fiddling with a small piece of paper in her hand as she walked. Looking for someone? That's what it seemed like, but Maggie couldn't imagine why.

She stepped outside. "Good morning." Rebecca's little sister turned at the sound. "What are you doing out here in the cold?"

The girl froze in her tracks.

"Darling?" Maggie asked, pulling her coat around her shoulders. "Was there something you wanted?"

The girl shook her head and darted across the path and ran to the parking lot. Got in an old Honda Civic and peeled out, leaving behind the smell of burnt oil in the exhaust. Maggie watched her go, then crossed the driveway and picked up the piece of paper the girl had dropped. She unfolded the scrap and began to read.

Rage filled her chest and she crumpled up the note.

Dear Lord, Jack. Where does it end?

A half hour after Nick pulled Erin from Engel's, they were in—of all places—the local radio/television station, in time for a segment on the morning news shows. With a bitter taste in his mouth, Nick summarized the allegations Erin Sims was making, gave a statement about her "accident" last night, and announced the APB on a dark truck with probable damage to the front right side. He let the vultures get a couple of pictures of Erin's new stitches.

Didn't like using the media but couldn't afford not to. He had to find Jack.

They went back to the sheriff's office and Quentin slapped a note on Nick's desk. "The commissioner called. That makes about ten times. He wants to talk to you."

"About Calloway or a possum?"

"I don't know. Maybe you can ask when you *call him back*. And Luke called again. And your mother, telling you that Luke's trying to reach you."

"Shit," Nick said, then saw Valeria rushing toward him. She still wore her coat, had her gloves on, and held an envelope in hand.

A sliver of worry pricked Nick's skin. "What is it?"

"This," she said. She held up the envelope. A piece of folded paper stuck out of it. "It was on my car this morning, under the windshield wiper."

Nick took the envelope, opened the page. A name: Shelly Quinn. It was typed.

Shelly Quinn, Shelly Quinn. Nick couldn't place it. "Do you know who this is?" Valeria shook her head. "Or who left it on your car?"

"No."

Nick tried not to let the sliver cut any deeper. He handed the note to Quentin. "Find out," he said, then looked at the clock. Monday morning, and here he was, just starting to wade into years of information authorities had blown off. Sorting it out in four days' time—soon enough to matter to Justin—was going to take a miracle.

But not if they used what Erin already knew.

"Valeria," he said, "set Dr. Sims up with a printer." He looked at Erin and pointed at her laptop. "I presume you have information on that thing?"

"Years of it."

"Print it out. Then I want you to sit down with Jensen and organize it."

The look on her face was filled with such gratitude it nicked his soul. He hoped he could live up to it.

She followed Valeria out and when they were gone, Quent said, "So, you're buying it now? That Jack's a murderer?"

Nick closed his eyes. "All I know is that Erin Sims could have been waving irrefutable evidence around all these years and no one would have listened to her."

"She isn't waving irrefutable evidence."

"No. But the fact is that someone doesn't like what she *is* waving. Reason enough to dig in."

The computer on his desk *ding*ed and Nick hit the button, recognized the address in the e-mail header. The skin on the back of his neck tightened. "It's from the FBI," he said.

Quentin came around the desk to look at the monitor, and Nick typed in his security code. The message came up and his heart turned to stone.

"Jesus Christ," Quent said beneath his breath. "You were right."

CHAPTER
23

THE ANGELMAKER SAT in the workshop with Jack's face in hand, sanding, sanding. The finest grade sandpaper, smoothing every edge and curve. It had to be perfect to go with the others.

Finally it was finished. Jack was gone. Burning in hell now with the other fallen angels.

The Angelmaker walked to the shelf behind the stairs and eyed the porcelain figurines. Once there had been ten. Angels, one and all, each a little different but each fulfilling the same promise: *They watch over you.*

No, they didn't. The Angelmaker was seeing to that. One at a time, each one became deaf, dumb, and blind.

Three left. The Angelmaker picked up the third to last figurine—with an oval base and big, knowing eyes—held it high overhead and let it drop to the concrete below. It smashed into pieces, and a rush of power swelled up inside.

Eight down, two to go.

Nick sank into his chair, looking at the message on his computer. Horror washed over him. There *was* a person from Hopewell on the FBI's missing persons list.

Shelly Quinn.

Quent took over the mouse and read from the computer screen. "She was a student at Mansfeld College. Disappeared in 2008, during her freshman year."

Nick bullied his brow with his fingers. He'd been here in 2008. He collected the memory in bits and pieces. "She quit college, moved back to her hometown."

"Right," Quentin said. "And then she went missing. That's why we didn't get into it. She was already back home living in Pittsburgh."

That's why Nick didn't remember it in detail. It was an abduction in Pittsburgh. It had barely touched Hopewell.

"They never found her?" Nick asked.

"Nope. Gone."

"How hard did they look here?"

Quent scrolled down. "A field agent from Pittsburgh drove over here once, asked some questions." Nick nodded; he remembered that. "The college administration told the FBI she was no longer enrolled. There's a couple of interviews here—her girlfriends, or roommates, I guess. Elizabeth Kunkle and Shea Blaurock. They said they didn't know her that well. Her midterm grades were mostly Fs and she was living on kegs and drugs. No close friends, no dates." He straightened. "There was no one to keep up with her after she left."

Nick closed his eyes. *He has a type . . . Lost, lonely, experimenting with drugs . . .*

He stood. Jesus. A college student gone and he'd never even known it. The implications of that stabbed him in the gut. He looked at Quentin. "Fucker could've taken a bunch that way and we'd've never raised an eyebrow."

"Naw," Quentin said, "not a bunch."

"But more than Shelly Quinn." Fear nibbled at the edges of his brain. "Jesus, Quent. What if there's more?"

Quentin picked up his jacket. "I'll get over to the college."

Nick read through the file on Shelly Quinn twice, then called a guy named Feldman in the FBI field office in Pittsburgh. Missing persons almost always went to the Feds.

"There was nothing," said Agent Feldman, crunching on something that might have been a carrot. "Her parents said Shelly was wild and spent her time at bars, coming home drunk. They thought she might've been doing some drugs, too. One night, she went out and just didn't come home."

"And there was no boyfriend."

"If there was, no one knew about him. Martinez— he's retired now—came with me to Ohio and we poked around your campus a little."

"I remember."

"There was nothing. She didn't really make friends there, and it was fall of her freshman year. She'd only been there a couple of months. No one stayed connected with her after she left."

"Anyone hunt for a dealer? Where was she getting her shit?"

"Walk down any street, man."

In Pittsburgh, maybe. Not here. Here, she'd have to have a way to get it.

"Hey, you know what I do remember?" Feldman asked.

"What?"

"I remember thinking the boyfriend thing was weird. Quinn was beautiful. You know, CoverGirl beautiful. And she dressed for sex. I always thought it was weird she didn't have studly frat boys crawling all over her, inviting her to all the parties."

"You remember her pretty clearly."

"Sure," Feldman said, and his voice took on a weary note. "You always remember the ones you don't catch."

The ones you don't catch. Nick chased the thought away and dug in his drawer for a cigarette. Valeria appeared at the door and he jumped her. "For God's sake, stop taking my cigarettes."

"You ever decide to light one, I'll buy you a pack. But you won't, because you're the only parent your daughter has, so stop grumping at me." She handed him a note. "Dispatch called. They just took a 911 call from Ray Cod. The aliens are back, in his barn. Dispatch wants to know what to do."

Nick gaped at her. "What do you mean, they want to know what to do? What are they fucking supposed to do when a resident calls 911?"

"But the commissioner . . . after the possum incident . . ."

"Fuck the commissioner. Send someone to Cod's. We don't assume false alarms. Not even for aliens."

"Yes, sir." Happy with that. But not moving.

"Is there more?" he asked.

"Calvin didn't do those things."

Nick closed his eyes. Calvin had been sprung this morning by Dorian. Not before Nick had gone to see him and put the fear of God into him. "I don't know, Valeria. I just don't know."

She wagged a finger at him. "You'll see."

"I hope you're right," he said, and meant it.

She snapped back to business. "Milner is doing traffic near Ray Cod's. I'll send him."

"That'll do." Milner wasn't the brightest candle on the cake, but then again, these were aliens. Nick sighed. He had a full-time staff of twenty-five deputies. Enough to handle traffic issues, ward off aliens and deal with the occasional robbery, brawl, overturned truck, or possum. Enough to carry out the various court orders for which the sheriff's department was responsible. Enough to handle all that and still look into Lauren McAllister's murder and her possible connection to Jack Calloway.

But Shelly Quinn, too? Others?

The question should have dropped him to his chair, but instead Nick felt a surge of excitement shiver through his bones. God damn, what kind of asshole was he, to get a kick of adrenaline from a missing college student? But Christ, it had been a long time since he felt useful. Seven years.

Jensen stuck his head in, waving a piece of paper. "You told us to check clinics and hospitals where Lauren McAllister and Sara Daniels went missing?" he said. "I faxed warrants to all the ones within an easy drive from each of the girls' homes. I just got this back from a clinic outside Miami. An hour from McAllister's home."

"What?"

"Lauren McAllister had an abortion a month before she disappeared."

Nick snatched the page from Jensen. Southeast Regional Women's Center letterhead, from Milton, Florida. "Jesus," he said, flipping through the pages. "Is a father's name listed?"

"Page three. Signed consent."

Nick found the page, drew his finger down to a man's angular scrawl: *John Huggins.*

CHAPTER
24

H E PHONED QUENT at Mansfeld College.

"Give me a break, Nick. I just got here."

"Leave someone there to compile the list," Nick said.

"The registrar says it'll be a couple hundred names. Maybe more."

Couple *hundred*? "That many girls dropped out of college in the past five years?"

"Yup."

"So have them fax the names ten at a time so we can start tracking them down. Right now I need you to meet me at Hilltop House."

"Something happen?"

"Lauren McAllister aborted Jack's kid just before she disappeared."

Silence, then Quentin said, "Whoa."

"We gotta talk to Margaret."

"She already told us she doesn't know where he is. She doesn't even know when he left."

"I know. But the son of a bitch lied to us about Lauren. I bet Margaret can tell us about that."

"And may know the name Shelly Quinn?"

"We'll find out."

"Jack is represented by counsel. A wife can't be forced to speak against her husband. Want me to call Dorian?"

"Who?" Nick pulled the phone halfway from his face. "You're breaking up, I can't hear you..."

Nick left Jensen with Erin, to compare her information with what they had collected, and had Valeria call in two office assistants to man the phones. "Track down every name on the list," he said. "Find every girl who quit college at Mansfeld."

The list was coming ten at a time: girls who had, for whatever reason, left Mansfeld. The college administration would be able to narrow it some—transfer students and those who took some time off then came back later— but there would be a pretty long list of others who left college to get a job, get married, go back home, or whatever. Nick wanted to account for each and every one of them.

A second list was from the FBI: women reported missing and never found, from all over the country. If a name showed up on both lists... God willing, Shelly Quinn would be the only one.

"And find Kunkle and Blaurock," Nick said, then spelled out the names for Jensen.

"Who are they?"

"They were roommates of Shelly Quinn. They'd be seniors now, maybe still here. Wherever they are, I wanna talk to both of them."

He pulled up the drive to Hilltop House and Quent swung in right behind him. "Let's go," Nick said, but Quent put a hand on his sleeve.

"This is the kind of shit that ruins marriages."

And breaks up families and destroys careers and

causes custody battles. Nick remembered all too well. "This isn't rumor, Quent. We have Jack's signature."

"Right. But you can't go in there the way you are. You're vibrating."

"I am not." Nick took a deep breath. "I'm nothing but calm and relaxed."

"Calm like an earthquake. You're a textbook for plate tectonics."

"I'm cool."

"You don't look cool."

"I'm cool, God damn it."

Margaret was in the kitchen, stirring a mulled cider concoction that smelled of cloves and cinnamon and orange zest. Rosa walked in with a load of folded towels from the laundry room and a couple dangling from her fingers. She shot Nick a glare. "A couple of these won't come clean," she said to Margaret. "Mud, I think. Do we have another set like this?"

"Check the linen closet outside Room 6," Margaret said.

Rosa marched past Nick, deliberately snubbing him. Still mad about Calvin. Nick couldn't blame her, but didn't know what else to do. Christ, the paint had been right there.

"Margaret," he said, "we need to talk to you."

She closed her fingers around a silver pendant between her breasts. "I don't know where he is. I told the deputy that hours ago."

"It's not about that." Nick took a deep breath and pulled out a piece of paper. It had only one thing on it. "Does this look like Jack's signature?"

She took the page, then looked back up at Nick. "Yes. When he used to go by his real name. Why?"

"Margaret, I'm sorry about this." And he was. "This is a copy of Jack's signature at a clinic. Jack *was* having an affair with Lauren McAllister. He went with her to abort a baby." Her eyes widened, then slid away. *The wife is usually the first to know.*

"You already knew that, didn't you?" he asked. "Jack *was* having an affair with Lauren."

She didn't look at either Nick or Quent, but moved to the sink.

"You lied to authorities in Florida," Nick said, then just waited. Chances were good she was about to start leaking. Men would stick to a lie no matter how stupid it was. Women, when they felt the truth closing in, started explaining.

"I wasn't sure," she said, "but always wondered. Lauren McAllister was in one of my pottery classes. She was... loose, as my father would have said."

"If Jack was angry enough—like over a pregnancy or abortion—could he have killed her?"

She turned on him and Nick expected that tears weren't far behind. He was surprised when her eyes turned fierce instead. "Of all the people in the world, you ought to know how it feels to have horrible rumors spread about you. You ought to know, Nick."

Yes, he knew. It didn't matter now. "Has Jack ever stayed out all night before?"

Margaret closed her eyes, fondling the pendant. "Occasionally."

"But you don't have any idea where he might be."

"No."

Finally, she opened her eyes, seeming to notice the pendant in her hand for the first time. She swallowed and opened it up.

"Could I see?" Nick asked, when he realized it was a locket.

Her hands trembled as she held it out to him. Two young women; identical twins. Utterly beautiful.

"You and your sister?" he asked, wondering why he'd never seen her wear it before.

She nodded and touched one of the faces in the tiny frame. "You know, I married John to help get custody of Rodney. I just wanted to take care of Claire's son. Did you know that?"

No, he hadn't, and felt a pang of regret for such a marriage. He didn't think he was noble enough to have settled for a sexless marriage, under any circumstances. "Margaret, did Jack also have an affair with Sara Daniels? Were there others? A girl named Shelly Quinn?"

Her lips tightened and she looked down. Answer enough.

"We'll need a list," he said gently. "And we'd like to take another look around. You okay with that?"

She met his eyes, a little steel in them. "Does it matter?"

Earlier in the morning, deputies had searched the inn and the outbuildings for clues as to where Jack might have gone. Now Nick and Quent found nothing more.

"Did anyone question Rodney yet?" Nick asked.

"Fruth rooted him out of bed this morning. Rodney didn't even know Jack was gone."

"We still gotta talk to him about Jack's affairs. He may remember something."

They took the Tahoe, bumping along the narrow stretch of road to the cabin. "Rodney," Nick called, knocking. He could hear music going inside. "It's Nick Mann."

"I'm coming. Hold on."

A minute later, the music died and the door opened. Rodney wore brown corduroys and a blue flannel shirt. His dark glasses. "Sheriff? Did you find Jack?"

"No, not yet," he said. "Deputy Vaega's here, too. Mind if we come in?"

"Come ahead."

The cabin had been here for as long as Nick could remember, a good fit for a man who was almost entirely independent, yet who needed to be able to walk or drive a three-wheeler to work. Nick looked around. It was neat in the way a blind person would keep house: everything in its place. The furniture was sparse but functional, the floors pine planks with one woven rug stretched out beneath a sofa and sticking out from under the coffee table. The walls were empty, and there were no shelves of knickknacks or clutter except for one, above a peninsula that divided the kitchen from the living area. Nick strolled past it, taking a look at Rodney's keepsakes: an old Mardi Gras mask decorated with fake jewels and feathers, and a bowl containing plastic beads, also from Mardi Gras. Nick remembered that Rodney had lived in New Orleans as a child, before coming to live with Margaret and Jack. He didn't seem to have much else in the way of keepsakes from that part of his life.

On the back wall of the living room stood a unit with a TV and sound system, a couple dozen CDs, a number of books in Braille and several that weren't. A high-powered magnifying glass sat on the coffee table near a copy of the *Gazette,* and a desk in the corner held a large-screen laptop. It had Braille keys but Nick knew Rodney didn't need them. He handled the computer at Hilltop all the time, just enlarged the type and adjusted the brightness, and leaned close or used a magnifier—

"Don't talk, don't talk, don't talk."

Nick swiveled toward the kitchen. "Calvin," he said. "What are you doing here?"

"Don't talk, don't talk—"

"Rosa let him stay home from school today," Rodney said. "I told him he could hang here."

"Don't talk, don't talk."

Rodney looked in Nick's direction. "Dorian told him to keep his mouth shut around you."

Of course.

"I'm not here to interrogate you, Calvin," Nick said, but the kid backed up against the countertop in the kitchen, incoherent words passing his lips at record speed. Nick had greeted him this morning with a tour of the jail. Showed him the slots where food trays were shoved to inmates, the toilets sitting out in the open with cameras in the ceilings. The place he'd be living if Nick found out he'd committed the vandalism at the motel and didn't confess. If he confessed—and here Nick had shrugged— he'd probably be spared some hard time at juvey.

He hadn't, but Nick knew he understood every word.

"Don't talk, don't talk," Calvin said, rocking on his feet. The muttering began. "Forty-six degrees Fahrenheit, ten-twenty-eight a.m., November twelfth, two-thousand-twelve..."

"Sheriff, is there any word on Jack?" Rodney asked, drawing a hand along the back of the sofa to find his way around it.

"We were hoping you might know where he is."

"I don't," he said. A little bitterness there. "I already told you people that."

"Could he be with a woman?"

Rodney shrugged, but his expression, even behind the

dark glasses, betrayed the casual gesture. "Could be. Has been before. I guess you know that or you wouldn't be here."

"We know he did have an affair with Lauren McAllister, though all three of you are on record denying that."

"We didn't know then. And it doesn't mean he killed her."

"And Sara Daniels?" Quent asked.

"I don't know anything about her. Except...except that he was pretty shaken up when he heard that she was missing."

Nick frowned. He'd gotten the same impression the first time he mentioned her to Jack. "What makes you say that?" he asked.

"Jack came back to Hilltop after talking to you yesterday morning and looked up news about Sara Daniels's disappearance. I followed the history on his computer when he left."

"You saw him leave?" Nick asked.

"To the extent that I see anything. He was upset. I could tell by his voice."

"Did you ever hear the name Shelly Quinn?" Quentin asked, and Rodney shook his head.

"What about drugs? Did you ever see Jack with cocaine?"

"No." Rodney's jaw tightened. "But I never saw him fucking women behind Maggie's back, either, and it doesn't mean he didn't do it."

Nick winced and glanced at Calvin, who stood whispering numbers, then went back to Rodney. "You're mad at Jack? He's been like a father to you."

Even without seeing Rodney's eyes, Nick could sense the cold glare. "What's he been to Maggie?"

• • •

On the way back to Hilltop, Quentin said, "It's gotta suck when your wife and kid—or nephew—both hate you."

"Yeah," Nick said.

"You think he bailed? Saw the sky about to fall and decided to just take off?"

"I don't know." Nick looked around, trying to *feel* Jack here. The air was too still. So still he actually jumped when his phone rang. "Yes," he said, answering. It was Dispatch.

"Rawling County just called," the dispatcher told him. "They have a truck that went into a quarry bed sometime early this morning, burned up pretty good. It belongs to Jack Calloway."

CHAPTER
25

NICK WALKED TO within a few feet of the ledge of the quarry, his heart jammed in his throat. Jack's truck was snagged on a ridge fifty yards down, a charred black tangle of metal clinging to the side of the steep gully, tingeing the air with the scents of smoke and gasoline. Thirty feet farther down sat a pool of water. A couple of rescue workers climbed around the wreckage, having rappelled down the side of the quarry bed; they looked like orange-clad ants crawling around the remnants of a Tonka toy.

"Truck got caught on the way down," the Rawling County sheriff told Nick. "The license plate was all melted but the guys called up a partial VIN number. We found twenty-eight trucks registered in the state of Ohio with that partial, but you're the only one of the twenty-eight who was actually looking for one."

Nick nodded. Rawling's sheriff was about fifteen years older than he, a round man who would never have to worry about hair loss. His eyebrows were as bushy as his head. He might've been taken for a bumpkin except for his eyes, which were two keen spots of intelligence.

"How long 'til we can haul it up outta there?" Nick asked.

A firefighter—the chief, said his emblems—came over. "A couple of hours, maybe. Gotta give the guys a chance to process the scene. They still had hot pockets until an hour ago."

"And no body?" Nick said, though he knew.

"Nope." The sheriff handed Nick a pair of high-powered binoculars. Nick took two steps closer to the edge and peered down. Jesus. There was nothing left. A couple of thin scraps of metal jutted out from the front left of the wreckage. "Driver's side door was open. He bounced out along the way?"

The sheriff nodded. "Could be. Or he got out and ran when the fire started. We'll start dragging the quarry as soon as we can get a team together. Wanna get the truck up first. It's too teetery for me to put men under it right now."

"Okay," Nick said. It was the right sequence of events. "How did it get reported?"

"There's a private airstrip thirty miles south of here. The pilot of a Cessna that took off this morning spotted the end of the fire, called it in."

Nick used the binoculars to scan the whole path down the gully—imagined Jack, battered but alive, climbing up from under a rock—but knew that wasn't going to happen. He lowered the binoculars and looked behind the tape that marked off about thirty square yards. "Anything up there, where the car went over?"

"Silt. Anything that might have been there got rained out overnight. We may never know if the car went over trying to skid to a stop or at sixty miles an hour." He noticed Nick's grimace and added, hastily, "But we'll process the

whole thing good. If there's anything foul, we'll find it."
The sheriff paused, stroking his chin. "You suspect some-
thing foul? I mean, I've been hearing a little news about
Calloway. Sounded like the guy had his troubles."

"Yeah," Nick said, and a pulse of anger tapped at his
chest. *Damn you, Erin Sims, bringing this shit to my
town. Damn you, Jack, for being part of it.*

He handed the binoculars to the Rawling County guy
and started back up the slope. "I'm gonna send one of my
men out here with you today, okay? His name is Hogue,
and he's already on his way. I'd like to stay close." He
didn't say *just in case you guys fuck it up*, but everyone
understood the game.

"No problem. An extra set of eyes is always welcome."

Nick stuck out his hand, and they shook. "Do me a
favor," Nick said. "Check the truck for damage on the
right side. It might have hit another car before it went
over."

The older sheriff whistled. "We'll check," but Nick
knew what he was thinking. No way any evidence like
that would show up now.

Nick started back to his Tahoe.

"Hey, Mann?"

Nick turned, lifted a brow.

"This guy a friend of yours?"

"Yeah." Nick swallowed. "He was."

Back to Margaret. Nick called Valeria and asked her to
put in a call to Reverend Whitmore: Margaret was going
to need him. He didn't tell her why; the media would have
it soon enough. Then he asked about Erin and found she'd
moved from talking to Jensen to working the phones,
helping track down Mansfeld dropouts.

Good girl.

"Leni Engel called," Valeria told Nick. "She's pretty upset."

"What happened?"

"Carroll County let Ace Holmes out. Rebecca won't press charges."

Nick ran a hand over his face. "Ah, shit." He sat in the front seat of his truck feeling as if the threads of the life he'd built here were slipping through his fingers. He blew out a breath and asked for Erin.

"Erin," he said, and knew how much he was asking. "I need a favor."

"What is it?"

He told her about Rebecca. "Oh, no," she said, sounding like a shrink. "Do you think Holmes got to her?"

"Or Holmes's lawyer." Either would be enough to scare a woman away from testifying. "Things are moving with Calloway, I promise. Do you think you could—"

"Go talk to Rebecca?" Erin asked.

He could hear her thinking about it, pictured her rubbing her temple. "I'll go. But only if you get someone to cover my phone and keep working the college list."

"You got it." And then he added: "Make sure a deputy drives you over."

At Hilltop House, Margaret met him in the front lobby, her hand shaking on a piece of paper.

"What's this?" Nick asked.

"I found it after you left, inside my pillowcase," she said, her voice breaking. "I went to make the bed and—"

Nick unfolded the page. A few lines, computer-printed: *Maggie, forgive me. Reverend, forgive me. God, forgive me.*

"Ah, jeez," Nick said.

She looked at him with hollow eyes. "He's gone, isn't he? That's why you're here."

"We're not sure, Margaret."

"But no one knows where he is, and you're back again. And...a gun is gone."

"What?"

"From the cabinet upstairs."

"Show me."

She took Nick through the foyer, past her display of masks, and up the stairs. She stopped at the oak cabinet on the wall in the hallway.

"Right there," she said.

Nick saw the empty spot. "A .38?" he asked, of the missing gun.

"I don't know...I don't know guns. They scare me. I've never handled them. I don't even like to clean this cabinet..." Starting to babble.

Nick took her shoulders. "Look at me, Margaret. Did Jack keep ammunition around?"

"In the bedroom, not here. Too many guests, strangers. And Calvin liked to handle them."

"Go check. See if anything's gone."

She came back in two minutes, holding a box of .38-caliber hollow points. It was open. Missing ten rounds.

"Dear God," Margaret said, staring at the bullets. "He shot himself, didn't he? Is that what you came to tell me?"

"No," Nick said, taking her arm. She was beginning to tremble. "We still haven't found Jack. Come on, let's find a place to sit down."

And passing back beneath the masks to the front sitting room, Nick looked down at the box of hollow points and thought, *Helluva thing to do before you drive your car off a ledge.*

The Angelmaker tooled past Rebecca's house, dressed so commonly no one would notice the incongruity of it. Fools. Yet another example of how easily manipulated people were. And another example of the Angelmaker's superior skill.

No one was home; at least, that's what Rebecca seemed to want people to believe. The younger sister would be at school and Leni at the restaurant. That left Rebecca. Holing up with all the curtains closed, pretending to be innocent and untouchable, yet all the while watching. *Knowing.*

Anger rushed in. Need a plan. Need to get her. As soon as she comes out, be ready with a pl—

A sheriff's cruiser pulled around the corner. The Angelmaker froze. What? It rolled in front of Rebecca's house, Chris Jensen at the wheel.

Erin Sims got out. Jensen walked her to the door and knocked. Knocked again and again, and finally, the door opened.

Rebecca.

They spoke for a couple minutes; then Rebecca walked away, leaving the door wide open. Erin patted Chris Jensen on the arm and he left, and then she went inside with Rebecca. Shut the door behind her.

Oh, dear. *This* was a problem.

Erin gave Rebecca some space, paged through a *People* magazine about ten times, then slapped it down on the table. Rebecca had been holed up in her bedroom for twenty minutes. She refused to press charges for rape. Ace hadn't meant to hurt her, she claimed. He *loved* her.

Erin couldn't count the number of times she'd seen it. She'd never gotten used to it.

A rattle sounded at the door, like someone working the lock. Erin froze.

Katie stepped in. "Whoa," she said, drawing up short. "God, you scared me."

"Sorry. You scared me a little, too." A lot, maybe. Erin's heart was racing.

Katie glanced around. "Where's Mom?"

"She's still at the restaurant. I'm here because I was hoping to talk to Rebecca. But she wasn't interested. I thought I'd wait a little while and try again."

"Oh." Katie deposited her backpack and jacket on a hook in the mudroom, then toed off her shoes and put them in a basket beside the door. On the way to the kitchen, she bent to pick up a piece of leaf someone's shoes had left on the carpet, tossed it into the trashcan.

Erin followed, careful not to invade her space. "How was your social studies meeting this morning?"

"My what?" Katie pulled a glass from the cupboard and dropped in some ice.

"Your group project."

For a split second, her hands stopped moving. Then, "Oh, yeah. Uhh, it turns out we didn't meet. Joey couldn't come."

Erin's antenna went up. Katie—the sweet younger sister and perfect student—was lying. She hadn't had a group meeting this morning.

She got a glass of water, then stuck her glass in the dishwasher. "So, where's Becca?"

"In her room," Erin answered. "She wasn't very happy about having me here."

"Sorry." Katie got a dishcloth and toweled off a couple

drops of water that had spilled onto the counter. "She's not always like that."

Erin thought it likely that she was. "She's been through a lot lately."

"She'll be okay," Katie said, scrubbing the counter more fervently. "Everything's okay. We're fine."

Erin's heart slipped. *Everything's okay.* She wondered how many times she had said those words when she was Katie's age, trying to make it so.

"Katie," she said, "you don't have to pretend anything with me."

"What have I got to pretend? I'm not the one Ace Holmes raped."

"Maybe not, but my guess is you're the one trying to make the family okay. I bet you'd do anything to help your sister."

Katie looked at her, maybe getting ready to say something, but the side door flew open and Leni rushed in. Her face was flushed.

"Ace is out of jail," she said, her voice quaking with anger. "And—" She looked at Erin. "Jack Calloway is dead."

CHAPTER
26

Erin watched it on TV, disbelieving. She stood in Leni's living room with her arms wrapped around her midsection like a tourniquet, trying not to shake.

Sheriff's departments from two counties spent the day clearing the wreckage of a truck fire at an abandoned quarry in Rawling County. Police have been looking for the owner of the vehicle, Jack Calloway. Channel Eight Eyewitness Account has learned that authorities in Hopewell County now believe he might have been involved in an accident just before his truck ran over the ledge. A suicide note was found by his wife. More on that from Leslie Roach, who is live, near Hilltop House...

The shot morphed to the reporter, her breath coming out in frostclouds, and Hilltop House looming as a backdrop.

Erin could hardly make sense of what she was hearing. She heard her name and the words "accuser" and "slander" and "injured." A token attempt to be unbiased reared up when a county official said something about the need to investigate whether there was any truth to the accusations, but the slant was clear: The Florida woman with a vendetta against Jack Calloway had finally pushed him over the edge—literally.

He was dead. Suicide. Dear God.

Justin.

Pounding. There was a terrible pounding on the motel room door.

Erin stood up. Television running in the background, phone on hold. She was trying to reach Victor Santos. The Starke County sheriff's department. The Florida Attorney General's office.

No one would talk to her. Justin's only hope was dead. She might as well have pushed him into the quarry herself. Might as well have held the needle for Justin.

She opened the door. Sheriff Mann.

He took one look at her and kicked the door closed with his foot. Turned off the TV.

"Get your bags. You're coming with me."

"Where?" she asked.

"Where they won't find you."

By "they," he meant the media. He stood in the lobby of the motel and made some phone calls, checking her into another motel across town, carefully spelling her name into the phone. He called Dispatch, also from the lobby, and did it all in a voice a bit too loud. "Make sure we have a deputy outside Dr. Sims's motel tonight—the new one, over at the Riverview Inn on Knight Road. That's right." When he finished, he looked at the man and woman working the check-in counter: "Don't spread it around," he warned.

But instead of going to the Riverview Inn, he took Erin to his house.

"I don't understand," Erin said, clutching her jacket

around her body as he pulled into his driveway. She couldn't seem to get warm in this god-awful state. "The other motel was a decoy?"

"I don't want them hounding you yet."

Yet.

"It won't give us much time, but maybe the night." The words were brusque. Erin realized he was coiled like a spring. "I imagine the employees working the lobby have spread the word over half the town by now that you're at the Riverview."

"This can't be over," she said, shivering. "I have to save Justin. It can't be over."

He pulled the keys out of the ignition and looked at her across the front seat of the truck. "It isn't over, hóney. It's just beginning."

Hannah was at his mother's house; D.D. was, too. After the call from Rawling County, Nick hadn't been sure he'd get home at all tonight, so he'd made those arrangements earlier. Now he carried Erin's bags inside and dropped them in the kitchen. Part of him wanted to strangle her for bringing this shit to Hopewell, even though his head told him it was Jack who'd brought it. Another part of him wanted to take her in his arms and shield her from the hell she was about to face.

"Come on," he said. She followed him to the great room and he got a fire going. He unlocked a liquor cabinet, poured a glass of the good stuff, and handed it to her. "Brandy. It will warm you up."

She took a sip and coughed; Nick waited for that dependable slither of heat to unravel in her gut. She was going to need it. It was only a matter of time before the accusations started.

Nick drew a deep breath, thinking, *No way*. No way Erin Sims killed Jack and staged his suicide; it wasn't in her. Murder might be in her, but the hypocrisy necessary to cover it up wasn't. If Erin Sims were going to kill Jack Calloway, she'd march up to him, blow his brains out, and damn the consequences.

Besides, she needed Calloway alive. To take the fall for Justin.

Still, if Jack was dead—a substantial if—either he'd committed suicide or someone who *did* have the capacity for hypocrisy had killed him. Either way, he was gone and Erin Sims was standing in Nick's great room struggling to wrap her mind around the consequences for her brother. Brandy wasn't the answer. She needed comfort. A friend.

He gave her more brandy.

"I didn't mean for him to do that," she said, staring into the fire. "Damn him, how could he do that? How could he leave Justin—?"

The trembling started but Nick didn't think she realized it. By the time he got her glass out of her hand, bone-deep tremors rattled her from the inside out. He opened his arms and let her cry, trying not to think about how relieved he was to know that Jack's death had come as a surprise to her.

Trying not to notice how sweet she felt against his body.

He held her while five seconds passed, several times over. That sixth was always a killer.

She pushed away and touched her cheeks. "God," she said, "twice in two days."

"Go sit in front of the fire. You're still shivering."

He pulled himself together enough to think; for a minute there, it had been touch and go. But simple attraction wasn't the reason he'd brought her here. Not you-woman, me-man. More like me-sheriff, you...suspect. At least, that's how it would appear to everyone else.

Fuck 'em.

He went to the kitchen for something to put in her stomach besides brandy. He cut up an apple and sliced some good white cheddar, grabbed a package of whole wheat crackers and took it all back to the great room. She was a little more composed now, had stopped trembling and taken off her jacket. Flames played over her face as he set down the food.

She slanted him a look. "So you're *not* trying to get me drunk and take advantage of me in my stupor."

"Crossed my mind," he said, honestly. "Too easy."

"That's what you think," she said, but blushed. She rotated the plate of food in front of her. "Sheriff?"

"Nick. Once a woman has eaten my cooking, slept in my house, and cried in my arms, the rules say to go by first names."

A tiny smile turned up the corners of her mouth. "Nick?" She held up a slice of apple. "Do you have a Three Musketeers bar or something?"

"Eat it," Nick ordered, and when she had, he replaced the brandy with water. He needed for her to be clear-headed.

He sat down on the coffee table, facing her. "There's something we need to talk about." She looked up at him and Nick's heart squeezed. She'd entrusted the better part of a day to him, when a few days were all Justin had. And now Justin was worse off than ever. "Jack Calloway wasn't found in the truck that went into the quarry."

She blinked. "You mean...Oh, God, he's still alive?"

"Maybe. More likely, he killed himself and his body

will float up sometime next month. Or, someone murdered him and then pushed his car off the ledge." He paused, looking her square in the eyes. "Where were you this morning before I picked you up at Engel's?"

It took a minute; then she glared. "You aren't serious. You can't be serious. You can't really think—"

"I don't, honey. God help me, I don't. But unless we find a body with a lot of answers, the press is gonna float two stories: one, that Jack staged his suicide to run away from the murder charges you threatened. And two, that someone killed him and set up the truck to look like an accident, or suicide. In either case, you're the first person everyone wants to talk to."

"I didn't kill him. He can't take the blame for Lauren's murder if he's dead. And I was here most of the night, you know that."

"Jack's car went over the ledge early this morning."

"Then I was at the motel. Deputy Vaega took me straight there. I showered. I ate an Almond Joy. Maybe someone saw me get it out of the machine in the lobby. I logged on to Wi-Fi and Googled you, like you said. Wouldn't my computer history show what times I was online? You can check it."

"I will," he said, "and that's good. All that will help. Does anyone know you have that gun?"

"Besides the motel clerk who called you?" she asked. "Not that I know of."

"Good."

"Would you like to confiscate it, Sheriff?"

"How well can you shoot it?"

"Better than most of your deputies, I imagine."

"Keep it," he said. His nerves might have settled except for the small sound that caught his attention while she spoke. He waited, expecting D.D. to bark, then remembered D.D. wasn't here.

"I'll be right back," he said, and went to the kitchen. He heard it again when he got there: a scraping sound at the French doors onto the patio. A bump.

Jesus. Someone was working the lock.

He stepped back, drew his pistol. He glanced to the great room—*stay there,* he thought—and inched toward the French door, his back against the wall. Six feet away, four. The door opened and the intruder was right there.

"*Freeze,*" Nick said. "Don't move."

He hit the light switch with one hand. Blinked when the patio lit up.

"Son of a bitch," Nick said, breathing hard. His heart pounded like the devil. "Son of a bitch," he said again, and angled his 9 mm toward the sky. "What the fuck are you doing?"

"Breaking into your house." Luke held up a key between two fingers. "Mom didn't tell me the lock stuck."

Nick vented another oath. Luke was his brother, younger by two years, distant by thousands of miles and a history that hung between them like a toxic cloud.

He looked like hell. Scraggly hair and beard, cold features. The kind of hard look that comes from a life in the underworld of a drug cartel.

"What are you doing here?" Nick snarled.

"You didn't return my calls."

Nick made a crude sound, walking around the island. An eight-foot slab of granite between them seemed a good thing. "There's a message in that somewhere."

"You've got a woman named Erin Sims running around pissing off a U.S. Senator."

Nick peered at him. "What's it to you? The Rojàs cartel is into U.S. politics now?"

Luke's expression gave away nothing. "This chick, Sims. She might be telling the truth about Jack Calloway."

"Believing doesn't make it so. Besides, odds are that Jack Calloway is dead now, so it doesn't much matter anymore."

Luke looked genuinely startled. "It matters to Justin Sims. And maybe to the families of Sara Daniels, Shelly Quinn. You're pretty fucking nonchalant about having a serial killer in your town."

Every muscle in Nick's body turned to stone.

"Ah, so that's it," Luke drawled. "A criminal, right here in little old Hopewell—"

"Shut up."

"Under the nose of the mighty superhero, Nikolaus Mann—"

Nick sprang. He smashed Luke against the cabinets, Luke steeling himself but not fighting back, grating his words through clenched teeth. "Go ahead, beat the shit out of me like you did Allison's killer. That'll make it all better."

Nick braced a forearm high across Luke's chest, not quite crushing his windpipe. "What the fuck are you doing here?"

"I thought you might wanna know what the FBI has to say about Erin Sims."

"I already know what they say, damn it. They say she's a mental case."

"And you didn't wonder why?" Luke's voice was gravel, his fingers digging into Nick's sleeves, but for a man on the verge of being choked to death he was illogically calm. Of course, they both knew Nick wouldn't strangle him. They were equally matched in size and strength; they had a lifetime of fights between them as practice and two careers spent honing the skills. If Nick did decide to hurt him, there would be one helluva brawl before either one of them went down. "Don't you want to know *why* the FBI says she's mental, or why they care?" Luke asked.

"*I* do," came a thin voice.

Nick turned, his weight still braced against Luke. Erin stood under the archway to the kitchen, a hand on the doorjamb and her face sheet white.

"*I* want to know," she said.

And Nick thought, *Shit*.

CHAPTER
27

ERIN, go back to the great room. Luke and I need to talk."

The man named Luke choked on a chuckle. "This is Nick and I, having a talk."

Nick gave him a shove and backed off. "Leave us alone, Erin."

"This is about me," she said. Her courage grew now that it looked like no one was going to die. "When it's about me, the rules say I get to hear it."

She turned to Luke. A big man, like the sheriff, but his hair was shaggy and his eyes like ice.

"Who are you?" she asked.

"Nick's brother."

"No shit," she said. "That's clear from a mile away. What do you want with me?"

He reached beneath his coat and pulled out an envelope. "I have some information for you, courtesy of the FBI."

Erin went for the envelope but Nick grabbed it first and squared off to his brother—two big dogs establishing rank. Luke tipped his head to Erin. "Nick didn't tell you he had a brother on the dark side."

Nick hadn't told her much of anything, Erin realized all of a sudden. "No," she said. "He didn't."

"That's no surprise. He likes to pretend I don't exist."

"Stop it, Luke," Nick said.

"Both of you stop it," Erin said. The two big dogs had degenerated to surly ten-year-olds. "I want to know what's in that envelope."

Luke leaned back against the counter. "It tells why you hit a brick wall every time you went to the police about John Huggins. It's because Senator McAllister wanted it that way."

A cold rage gathered inside. "What?"

"The FBI has a file on you, claiming you're nuts." Luke winced. "That's probably not the clinical term for it. But you get the picture."

"That son of a bitch," she said. From the corner of her eye, she noticed Nick skimming a page, his brow furrowing. Luke went on.

"Your medical history arrives at a police department as soon as you start screaming about Huggins. Paranoid schizophrenia. Delusions. Manic episodes. Medications."

Erin's jaw unhinged. "I never took meds for...I was never—"

Luke put his hands up. "The cops don't know that. They hear you ranting about your brother's innocence, they combine that with the report from the FBI, and think you're a little cooked. Anyone who decides to check up on you comes across it."

She looked at Nick. The idea that he had seen that sort of file on her made her want to explode. "You told me you were looking into Justin's case, not doing a background check on *me*."

"I did both," he said, with infuriating calm.

"You had no right."

"I had every reason."

"You were just looking for a way to discredit me, like all the rest—"

"Damn it, I was looking for a reason to *believe* you—"

"Whoa, whoa," Luke said, making a T with his hands. "Nick, shut up. And you," he said, pointing at Erin, "calm down. Nick only did what any cynical bastard would do: He looked you up."

"But none of that is true."

"Could be, but McAllister's career will end if it turns out he's wrong about your brother. When it became clear that you weren't going to let the verdict rest, he decided not to take any chances."

Erin stared. "His career. For Justin's *life*?"

"He's not going to let a simple case of 'Oops, I killed the wrong man' ruin him."

"But Justin hasn't been killed. McAllister could still come forward."

"And risk someone finding out that he paid off a cop before the trial?"

"Christ." Nick tipped back his head, rubbing a hand over his face.

Erin was flabbergasted. "No."

"Yes. McAllister and the police helped the case along. For example, the fingerprints on the gun were too smeared to be identified for certain. Someone lied."

"So, the Senator knows Justin didn't kill his daughter?"

Luke shook his head. "The truth is, he probably believed Justin was guilty. He may still. But it does look like he went above and beyond to make sure Justin got convicted. If you uncover that, he's finished."

Erin stood, started pacing, and tried to contain the

emotion prickling every fiber of her body. All these years, she'd blamed herself. For confirming to police that the picture they were showing her was the girl Justin had been seeing. And yet it was McAllister who'd provided the final nail for his coffin.

Your medical history arrives at a police department as soon as you start screaming about Huggins.

A ribbon of nausea slipped into her gut. She remembered sitting in Nick's den and his refusal to let her see the printout arriving on his computer. She turned to Nick: "You had this information, too?"

He shrugged. "Bunch of bullshit."

Her breath went shallow. One heartbeat at a time, she realized she didn't have to convince him of anything. "Why did you believe me?"

Those pale eyes met hers. "I didn't wanna have the hots for a loon."

A thrill shivered through her belly. Erin didn't know what to do with it. She didn't know how to handle faith. Not to mention the blatantly sexual suggestion that accompanied it. She felt like a teenager, being handed a note in gym class: *Nikolaus Mann likes you.* It was a heady sensation.

She pushed it aside and stood, batting down the physical sensations in her body and trying to focus on what this meant for Justin. "What do we do now?" she asked.

Nick looked at her with an expression that brooked no argument. "I go find Jack. You go through that FBI report. Find me a reason to confront a U.S. Senator."

CHAPTER
28

NICK WATCHED ERIN carry the file into the great room to read: If she could finger McAllister, Florida authorities would have no choice but to reexamine Justin's case, and they'd do it in a hurry. Meanwhile, Nick had work to do.

He reholstered his gun, picked up his jacket. Luke was oddly silent.

"How did you get that report?" Nick asked.

"When you contacted the FBI for info about Shelly Quinn, you tripped a wire. A friend called me."

"So you came running home to help your big brother. And here I haven't even thanked you for the last time."

"You'll never forgive me for stopping you, will you?"

"The fucker's in a hospital. Fresh sheets and soft pillows, three meals a day. My wife's underground."

"Putting Yost there too wouldn't have changed what happened to Allison. It would only have changed what happened to you."

Nick scoffed. "I could handle it."

"Hannah couldn't. Mom couldn't. Ask that lady out there what it's like to have a brother in prison. I don't think I would have liked it much, either."

"And what about you being here? I've got enough to worry about without thinking Manuel Rojàs might decide to send you a message through a family member."

"Jesus, Nick. You don't think I know how to cover my tracks?"

Nick studied him. Yes, a man who'd spent years under-cover wrestling his own demons knew how to cover his tracks. Besides, Nick couldn't think about Luke now. He had to think about Jack Calloway and Justin Sims, Erin, his town...

Nick started out, then turned. "Did you see Hannah?"

"She was sleeping. She's gotten big. Pretty. She looks like—" He stopped, a faint smile on his lips, then stepped to Nick and lowered his voice. "This thing with Sims is bigger than you know. It's a good time to swallow your pride and accept some help."

"Yours?"

"And Alayna's. I were you, I'd give her a call."

"I already did. She's on her way to Florida."

"A regular family affair," Luke quipped.

"Listen, Erin has attracted some threats," he said, and let Luke fill in the rest.

"I'll watch her. She's not hard to look at."

Nick shot him a glare that could freeze an ocean. "Touch her and I'll kill you."

Luke chuckled. "There's something new."

Coffee brewed at the office, filling the air with the prom-ise of false energy. Hogue, Jensen, and Quentin perched on the edges of desks and a chair. Roger Schaberg stood against a wall reading a file. He was a dick to his wife—chased anything in a skirt—but he was a smart investiga-tor. Nick had specifically called him back from vacation.

Nick caught them up. First, he told them about the bogus FBI reports about Erin. Second, about Carl Whitmore's concerns about Jack. Third, about Lauren McAllister's abortion. And fourth, about the disappearance of Shelly Quinn.

The fourth scared the shit out of each and every one of them.

"Suicide note," Nick said, reading from a list.

"It didn't come from Jack's computer," Schaberg said. "Maybe he didn't want Maggie to stumble on it, wrote it someplace else, or maybe someone else wrote it."

Jensen asked, "So who wanted Jack dead?"

Wart Hogue scoffed. "How much time have you got?"

"Who's on your list?" Nick said, and Wart took a deep breath. He pulled out a rumpled piece of paper and a two-inch pencil whittled to a dull point by a jackknife. "Erin Sims—not much question about that one. Calvin Lee—he's just a kid, but he'd just been in jail, and Rosa said Jack came down on him hard about the paint. Mighta snapped. Margaret Calloway—gotta look at the spouse, especially when her husband was diddlin' everyone but her."

Quentin said, "Margaret told us she never loved Jack. I don't think she cared enough about his affairs to kill him."

Wart shrugged. "Maybe." He touched another name with his pencil. "Leni Engel."

"Leni?" Nick asked. "Why?"

"A few years back, Jack's business at Hilltop nearly put her place under. Ain't no secret she's never liked the Calloways."

Nick closed his eyes. Christ.

"And last," Wart said, folding up the paper, "Dorian Reinhardt. He defended Jack, helped him with the name change and all that. Was mad as hell when he found out Jack had lied to him about having an affair with Lauren."

"Since when has a defense attorney ever cared about his client lying?" Schaberg asked.

Nick shook his head. If Jack was dead and it wasn't suicide, it seemed the pool of suspects could include half the county.

Jensen said, "The truck went over the cliff between four and nine a.m. It's almost an hour away. Who does that keep on the list?"

Everyone stared at Nick, who'd gotten up to pour a cup of coffee. Wart was the only one with the guts to ask: "Where was your girl this morning, Sheriff?"

"She's off the list."

Everyone looked at Quentin. He could say things to Nick no one else could. "We'll take you at your word. But what do we tell the media?"

"Fuck the media. I don't run investigations for their amusement. Fuck the media," he said again, but then he cursed and handed Erin's black bag to Schaberg. "This is Dr. Sims's laptop. She was at my place until early this morning, when Quentin took her to her motel. She says she was on the motel Wi-Fi during the morning hours. Check it. And check with the clerk in the lobby to see if anyone remembers her getting a candy bar from the snack machine before seven-thirty. After that, we can put her at Engel's, and then with me."

"Got it."

Nick looked at his watch. "It's twelve-thirty in the morning." Justin's life was down to less than three days. "Go home, get a few hours of sleep. First thing tomorrow, we do this: Jensen, keep the phone team going locating girls who left Mansfeld College. Schaberg, go see Dorian.

Make sure he wasn't so pissed at Jack that he might've killed him. I'll take Margaret. I'll also take Calvin again, but I'll want one of you to take him after me. You, Chris. I'll strong-arm him, then you play nice."

"Calvin," Jensen whispered, shaking his head. "I don't think he's got the brains to set up something like this."

Nick said, "Calvin *does* have the brains. In fact, his brain might be superior to any of ours. But even if he's Erin's vandal or Jack's killer, he has nothing to do with murdered women starting back twelve years." He turned to Jensen. "Check in with Reverend Whitmore. Did Valeria ask him to go see Margaret?"

"She had to leave a message. The church office was closed today and he wasn't home."

"Okay. Go run him through his story again, see if he gives up anything else now that Jack is gone. Make sure he's taking care of Margaret. Oh, and, Roger, get with the Cleveland narcs and see if you can get a lead on someone who might've dealt to Jack."

"What about Leni Engel?" Quentin asked. "She really on the list?"

Nick pressed the heels of his hands to his eyes. "I don't know, but I need to talk to Becca anyway, so I'll talk to Leni."

Before they broke up, Quentin said, "We've still got a note to figure out. Someone pointed us at Shelly Quinn."

Nick thought about it. He didn't like it, but couldn't help the direction his mind was going. "That sounds like a scorned wife to me. First thing in the morning, she's the one I'll talk to."

Schaberg looked surprised. "You're gonna go jack up a grieving widow? You're a cold son of a bitch, Mann."

"I'm a pissed son of a bitch. Someone's fucking with my town."

• • •

Erin could hardly see the words anymore. They blurred on the page. From fury, from fatigue. The Senator had composed every detail, right down to dosages of medicines and the root of her supposed psychoses. She closed her eyes and tipped her head back against the pillow on the guest bed, trying to color the blow-offs of the past decade with that knowledge.

"It doesn't help, does it?" Nick's voice. No, it was Luke. They sounded alike.

"What doesn't?"

He propped a shoulder against the door frame. "Knowing that there's a reason no one listened to you. It doesn't get your brother off Death Row."

Erin marveled at how clearly he'd read her mind. "The week's not over yet."

"He's a lucky man, your brother."

"Hardly."

"No, he is. Most people would have written him off by now."

"That's what Nick tried to tell me," she said, looking down at the stack of reports. "But it doesn't feel that way."

Luke nodded, then cocked his head. "Are you sleeping with Nick?"

Erin stared. She couldn't seem to form a response.

"Okay," he said. "Not yet. But soon."

A nervous laugh popped out. She would have liked to think of some smart and sassy retort, but all she could come up with was, "How could that possibly be any of your business?"

Luke smiled. "Just making sure I know the rules. My brother has a caretaker complex. If you're the one at the other end, well . . ." He made a hands-off gesture.

"He has Hannah to take care of."

"Sweetheart, go look in the mirror. There's a helluva big difference between taking care of you and taking care of Hannah."

"I don't need for Nick to take care of me."

"Good."

She blinked. Must have misunderstood. "I thought—"

"Everyone needs Nick. Allison needed him. Hannah needs him. Our mother needs him. This whole fucking county needs him."

"I don't understand."

"*Want* him," Luke said. "That's what he needs."

The distinction took a moment; then Erin's skin shrank a size. The idea of *wanting* Nick Mann sent a purely sexual rush through her body. "You're jumping to conclusions," she said, trying to ignore that unexpected wave of sensation. "Nick and I barely know each other. We've never been on a date or held hands or kissed or anyth—"

Nick walked in. Erin stopped mid-sentence. "God." She buried her face in her hands.

"Hey," Luke said, when Nick stopped behind him. Erin inched her cheeks from her hands and Luke smiled. "I got her thinking about sex for you."

"Get out," Nick said.

"You're welcome," Luke said, and disappeared down the stairs.

Erin forced herself to look at Nick, who leaned a shoulder against the door frame, filling the doorway. She knew her cheeks were the color of raspberries; they felt hot and flushed. She noticed the dip of his eyes to her breasts and wished she hadn't taken off her sweater. Her nipples came to tight peaks.

Nick crossed to the bed. "Never kissed, huh?"

"Well, I—"

He bent down, and in the next breath his lips were on hers, hands pulling her up and dragging her into his arms. The lingering soreness in her bones dissolved in a rush of sheer sexual pleasure as his lips worked hers, stoking a flame that spread through her veins like fever. She opened her mouth and invited him in, sharing breath in a tangle of tongues and colliding heartbeats. One of his hands got under the tank, smoothed around her rib cage and found a nipple, and Erin arched into his arms as he rolled it between a calloused thumb and forefinger.

A moment later, he pushed her away. Hunger burned in his eyes and his breath was ragged, but he stood back from the bed and shook his head as if trying to flick something off. When he spoke, his voice was hoarse.

"High time I got that out of the way," he said, and left.

CHAPTER
29

FIVE IN THE MORNING. Tuesday. Big day. Today, Rebecca would become the ninth angel.

At long last.

The Angelmaker moved about on tiptoe, though no one was around. Only the kitchen was awake at Hilltop House. Rosa was making her cinnamon rolls, getting the coffee and spiced cider going. Leaving Calvin asleep in their apartment.

The barn was silent as a tomb, the only light spilling in from a security bulb for the parking lot outside. The Angelmaker climbed the stairwell and entered Rosa's apartment, stopped and listened, then slipped into Calvin's room like a wraith. A pendulum clock ticked off the seconds beside his bed—*tick-tock, tick-tock*—a reminder that this morning, timing was everything. Engel's Eatery opened at six and Rebecca worked the early shift. She'd be going to work—walking eight blocks in the still-dark morning—within the next half hour.

The Angelmaker would catch her on the way. No mistake this time.

And Calvin would provide the alibi.

A faint touch of his arm and Calvin came from sleep like a shot. "What?"

"Calvin, it's me. I'm sorry to wake you, but I need yo—*Ahgh!* Ah, Calvin. My head, my head."

"Wakeupwakeupwakeup." One word.

"Yes, wake up. Please." The Angelmaker reached to the nightstand and turned on the light. Calvin wore a gray polo shirt with plaid flannel pants, and the creases of a wrinkled pillow marked his face. He looked dazed. "Five-oh-two a.m., five-oh-two, five-oh—"

"I know. I'm sorry. But I need help."

Calvin was waking up. "What-what?" he said.

"I can't stand this pain, this headache." Eyes squeezed closed. "I bought my pills...I must have..."

"What-what? Five-oh-two..." He was concerned now. He'd never seen this kind of pain.

"I need my pills, Calvin. My head..."

"Pills-pills-pills."

"I bought them, but I threw away the bag on my way from the store. Outside, in the trash can on the sidewalk. Oh, Calvin, I must have thrown the pills away."

Calvin frowned, his eyes never settling in one place.

"Ahh...Calvin, please. Can you ride over there and find them? You can go before school."

"Five-oh-three, Tuesday, November thirteenth, two-thousand-twelve. Pills."

"Oh, thank you. *Ahh*..." A spasm of pain. "At the Kroger on Shallowford. You know the one?"

Calvin nodded, his face a mask of concern. He'd probably never seen a person having a migraine before. "Find pills."

"No, don't go through the trash. Someone will think

you're crazy. Just bring the whole bag from the can outside the door. I'll go through it here."

"Trash bag, trash bag...Five-oh-three..." He was
starting to panic, worry getting to him.

"Hurry, Calvin," the Angelmaker pleaded, and knew
he would.

Rebecca tied her tennis shoes in double knots and kept
to the left of the stairs: the boards on the right creaked like
an old woman. The whole stupid house made noises—the
door hinges squeaked, the banister groaned, and if you
turned on the fluorescent light in the kitchen, a thin *buzz*
rattled in the ceiling. Becca had never understood how
such small sounds could awaken her mother in the middle
of the night, but they did. And if her mother didn't hear
them, little Miss Prissy-Perfect-Katie did. Becca had been
caught more than once slipping out for the night.

But she wasn't a kid anymore. She'd graduated high
school, lived away from home. All right, she was back for
now, but still, she should be able to make her own rules,
do her own thing. She shouldn't be reduced to sneaking
around her own house like a rat. Her mom didn't see it
that way, though. *As long as you're living in my house,
young lady, no matter how old you are, you'll follow my
rules...*

Sure.

She skirted the creaking boards without touching the
banister, and didn't turn on the kitchen light. Got her
purse off the pie safe. Ace would meet her down the
block. He'd promised. This thing with Carrie had scared
him a little—cops from Cleveland all on his case and
Sheriff Mann busting his balls just as a matter of course,
getting the Crawford County sheriff to join in. Ace wasn't

any Prince Charming or anything, but he had wheels and knew a guy in Buffalo who owned a club where she could get work, and he didn't have anyone trying to tell him what to do every minute.

And, he loved her. He'd told her that. *Ah, baby, don't press charges. I didn't mean to hurt you...I just needed you so bad...*

She used the side door instead of the front, and glanced at the clock on the way out. Five-twenty. Ace had said five-thirty.

Better hurry.

The clock was a worry. Kroger was less than a ten-minute drive, but it would take Calvin longer on a bike. What if the timing was off? What if Calvin changed his mind, or stopped to talk to someone? What if his mother left her cinnamon rolls in the oven and came back to the apartment and found him gone?

No. Relax. There was no reason to doubt that Calvin would do exactly what he was asked to. He would need about twenty minutes to get to Kroger—just long enough. And when he came back, he'd hand over the trash bag from the can outside. Alibi-in-a-bag.

The Angelmaker walked through the empty spot in the garage where Jack's truck used to sit and climbed into the Saturn, setting the box that would serve as bait in the backseat and heading into town. At the restaurant, two cars were parked out back, but neither one was Rebecca's. She usually walked.

Five-eighteen, the dash clock said. Should be soon.

The Angelmaker rolled past Engel's Eatery and drove onto the residential streets a few blocks east, into the neighborhood where kids had lemonade stands in the summer and went trick-or-treating in the fall. Kept an eye out for Rebecca along the way, then pulled past her house and circled the block, searching the dark streets, peering down every lane—

And there she was. On the corner two blocks away. But she wasn't walking to work. She was just standing.

The Angelmaker pulled around the corner, parked facing the wrong direction and watched in the rearview mirror. What was she doing?

She had a suitcase.

Laughter bubbled up. Unbelievable. The girl was waiting for someone. Running away? There she stood, alone on the corner, just waiting.

Perfect.

The Angelmaker nudged the headlights to bright, pulled around several yards behind her and bumped the front tire of the Saturn against the curb. Moved into the passenger seat while the glare was in Rebecca's eyes and rolled down the window. The faux mother-of-pearl handle of the stun gun nestled in hand, like the touch of a lover.

"Rebecca."

She turned toward the voice; recognized it. Would she *know*? Better move fast, don't give her time to think it through.

She walked up to the car, squinting into the headlights. Glanced around. She probably hadn't counted on anyone seeing her. "What are you doing here?"

The box. Get the box. "I can't believe we ran into you. We were just taking this sculpture to the restaurant before it opened." Make her think someone else was in the car. Hold out the box. "Your mom asked for it. Here."

"What?" Rebecca asked. It was weird, but not so weird

as to be dangerous. She reached to the passenger side window for the box.

Pzzt—the stun gun sizzled against her hand. Rebecca dropped.

The Angelmaker's spirit soared to the sky. At long last. Finally. Rebecca wouldn't be watching anymore.

CHAPTER 30

SHORT NIGHT. Nick woke Tuesday before dawn, keenly aware that Justin Sims's life had slipped closer to ending and that saving it had taken on new significance. It wasn't only that Justin may well be innocent of Lauren McAllister's murder. It was also that Justin's sister had gotten under Nick's skin. Deep.

He showered, shaved, and dressed in jeans and boots with a long-sleeved shirt, then added a puppy paw-print tie Hannah had given him. Decided he looked pretty good except for the shadows under his eyes and some noticeable shots of silver at his temples. Okay, gray. He paused, thinking about getting older and yet feeling vital for the first time in seven years. Nothing like a murder or two to pull a man out of a slump. The hand of guilt started to press down and Nick pushed it away. "Fuck it," he said aloud. He was *alive*.

He paused outside the guest room, listened, and opened the door. Erin lay curled beneath the quilt with one hand tucked under the pillow. Something bumped in his chest and he smiled, remembering the heady sensation of having her pressed against him, their tongues tangling together.

His body stirred. Damn, he'd have to do that again soon, but finish the job this time. He wasn't interested in a repeat of last night—pulling away and leaving her fully clothed, his hands tingling with the warmth of her flesh, his body straining to be inside her.

Yes, he definitely had to finish that soon.

He ran by his mom's house and had breakfast with Hannah, drove her to school, then called Alayna on his way to pick up Quentin. True to form, she'd jumped at the chance to get involved in an underdog's case, hopped on a plane, and started eating her way up the food chain of the Justice Department to get access to Justin.

"McAllister's lawyer didn't give you any trouble?" Nick asked.

"McAllister's lawyer is suddenly the model of obsequiousness. They don't want anything to happen that could be construed as a lack of cooperation or that might lead to the appearance that Sims's rights have been compromised. That could hold up the execution."

"So you've seen him."

"I've seen him," she said, as Nick headed south on Frankfurt Drive. "But he won't talk to me about Lauren McAllister or the case. He only talked about his sister. He wants her to leave the case alone and let it go. Leave Ohio."

"What?"

"Interesting, huh?"

"Son of a bitch," Nick said. Erin had spent years working to free her brother and the bastard wanted her to leave the case alone.

Nick spared a thought to realize that it had only been a few days since he'd wanted the same thing. And he spared another thought to acknowledge that Justin's actions were

possibly the actions of a man who was, indeed, guilty
and had accepted his fate. The notion twisted in Nick's
heart—for Erin. "Do you need Justin in order to get to the
AG?" he asked.

"Maybe not. I'm on the assistant AG's schedule for
three-thirty. I'll push it."

"Thanks."

"Hey," she said, before he hung up. "This sister of
Justin's . . . Did you know she sleeps with a gun under her
pillow?"

Something in Nick shifted. "No."

"I asked Justin if it was because she'd been threatened
by McAllister's camp, and he shook his head. Said she'd
learned it long before McAllister came along."

A dark, uneasy feeling took hold but there was no time
to deal with it. Quentin's ranch house came into view,
Quentin standing in the driveway waiting for him.

"I gotta go," he said to Layna. "Call me when you
know something."

They disconnected and Quentin piled into the Tahoe
with a thermos of coffee. They headed to Hilltop and
found Maggie in her workshop, on a tall stool etching a
design into a sculpture with a tool that looked like a cro-
chet needle. A handful of raw clay masks sat on the table
beside her.

"Working," Quent murmured, while they were still out
of earshot. "While her world is crashing in."

But Nick wasn't surprised. He'd seen more than one
survivor of death or violence dig into a project as a cop-
ing mechanism. Hell, it was the reason he had a gourmet
kitchen and deck.

She kept her face down as they talked, but behind that
serene beauty was exhaustion. She hadn't had much sleep.

"I don't know what else I can tell you," she said. Nick had seated himself on one of the tall stools beside the worktable, and Quentin remained standing. "Of course he was upset. Erin Sims said such terrible things. But I never dreamed he would..." She stopped, closed her eyes.

"Margaret," Nick said, "we need to look at the possibility that maybe Jack *didn't* take his own life."

Her hands went still. "Did the coroner find something?"

"The coroner isn't involved—there's still no body. We always take a second look at a suicide, that's all," Nick said, only half a lie. "And," he said, in a tone that was carefully neutral, "we always go to the spouse."

Her eyes flared. "You're looking at *me*?" She squared her shoulders. "If Jack didn't take his own life, you know who did."

Nick wagged his head. "She was at her motel. The night clerk verifies that she picked up a package and a custodian saw her go to the vending machines. Her computer also shows that she was hooked up to the motel's Internet during the hours when Jack's car went over that ledge."

"Computers can be fixed. That's not a good alibi, is it?"

"It's good enough to make us look at other possibilities," Nick said. "So think of someone else. Who was around in the past couple days giving him a hard time?"

Her pupils darted away and Nick closed in a little. He could see the tension in her spine, but she kept fingering the clay, smearing away the etching she'd just done and starting over, molding on a ridge along the outer perimeter of the mask's left cheekbone. "I'm not trying to be hard on you, Margaret," he said. "But you have to know something like this looks bad. You told us yourself that your marriage was lacking. We know you and Jack—"

"Look around, Nick," she snapped. "I'm here, with this

huge house and business and my own business, too, and you're standing there insinuating that I want to handle it all alone. That's crazy, do you know that?"

"You two weren't intimate," Nick said.

"No," she admitted. "But we were pretty good business partners."

"Lauren McAllister wasn't—"

"The only lover he had?" Nick's brows went up and she laughed—a nasty sound. "So you think that after all these years, I suddenly realized he'd been unfaithful and I killed him. Is that it? Sheriff, I lived with that man for twenty years. For most of it, he got his sex elsewhere."

Nick tried not to be superficial. But looking at Margaret, with her startling beauty, and imagining that beauty in her younger years, he couldn't fathom any husband of hers seeking other women. "If you knew Jack was cheating on you, why did you stay with him?"

She met Nick's eyes. "I told you I didn't love him. But I didn't kill him. I don't know where the gun is. I don't know where Jack is. I only know where his truck is because you told me."

"Then give me something else," Nick pressed. "Something, anything, that's been unusual the past day or two. Any guests who were unhappy, anyone who called and harassed you, anyone who came by just to be a curious spectator."

Her brows drew together.

"What?" Nick asked.

She shook her head, as if whatever she remembered didn't make sense. "The Engel girl."

Quent straightened. "What?"

"She came here, early yesterday morning."

"Why?" Nick asked.

"I don't know. When I called to her, she ran off. But..." Margaret dug into the pocket of her apron, came up with a scrap of paper. "She dropped this."

Nick took it, found a scrawl of words in ballpoint pen: *Rebecca, meet me. I have something for you. 8:00. J.*

Nick felt like he'd been hit with a brick. He looked at Quent and fury pulsed through his veins. "Jack was screwing Rebecca Engel?"

"I don't know," Margaret said, without emotion. "If he was, I didn't know it."

"Christ, Margaret, why didn't you show us this yesterday?"

"Yesterday, you weren't looking for suspects in his murder."

"What time did she leave?"

"Around seven-thirty, I think."

"Okay," Nick said. Something horrible took root in his brain. *Huggins has a type... You even introduced me to one this morning. Rebecca Engel.* He caught Quentin's eye and knew he was thinking much the same, then pushed from the worktable and grasped at one last desperate thought.

"Margaret, how big of a stretch would it be for you to imagine that Jack staged his death himself? That he's still out there?"

She thought for only a second. "Not too much of a stretch, I'm afraid."

The Angelmaker stepped to the window, watching Nick Mann leave skid marks on the drive. *Scrambling.* Like a gerbil in a maze, hitting a new wall at every turn.

A thrill vibrated in the air and the Angelmaker nearly laughed aloud. The sheriff of Hopewell was smarter than the average bear, but had no idea what he was looking at. He couldn't see a thing.

Mann's car sped down the road. Poor guy, trying to find Jack. Jack was history.

Of course, as soon as Nick learned that Rebecca Engel was missing, things would pick up. For the moment, no one even knew yet that Rebecca was gone or where she was: All trussed up with nowhere to go.

Another smile. Everything had gone like clockwork this morning. Not a single light on Rebecca's street as the Angelmaker popped the trunk and loaded her in, then zapped her again and carried her to the workshop. Now she lay on the worktable, faceup, wrapped in duct tape with her lips sealed tight.

Ready.

A shame to have left her there, but it might have seemed odd to Rosa not to come by the kitchen in the morning. No need to raise any eyebrows by doing anything out of the ordinary. Rosa hadn't said a word about Calvin, which meant Calvin hadn't said anything about his early morning outing, but the Angelmaker hadn't expected that he would. Now with Nick gone again, the only thing left was to go through the trash bag Calvin had brought and find a receipt for something, anything, that would make sense to buy so early in the morning.

Then, get to the clay. An angel was waiting.

Nick dropped Quentin off at headquarters and stopped by the Eatery to tell Leni he wanted to see Rebecca. He didn't need Leni's permission; Rebecca wasn't a minor. But it was one of the concessions to courtesy he made living in a small town. Nick had a theory about big cities and crime: Anonymity mattered. In a place like L.A., you could spend an entire day out and about with near certainty you'd see no one you recognized. But in towns like Hopewell, no one was anonymous. You never flipped off the driver behind you because it might be your preacher, your English teacher, your father-in-law. Keeping up those relationships was key, and going behind a mother's back to talk to her daughter—even a grown daughter—would have been an unnecessary power play.

Of course, he didn't let on to Leni that this talk wasn't about Ace.

"She's not working this morning," Leni told him, untying her apron behind her back. "I'll come with you."

Nick gave her a lift to the house. He frowned when he saw Luke in the driveway, leaning against his car.

Leni gave Luke a hug—they'd been in the same class at school—then Nick said, "What are you doing here?"

"Erin wanted a ride here."

"What's going on?" Leni asked.

"Your daughter called the sheriff's office and tracked Erin down, wanting to talk," Luke said.

Leni's face lit up. "I was hoping Becca would come around and talk to Erin."

Luke's brow wrinkled. "Okay. But it wasn't Becca who called. It was Katie."

Katie? Nick's brain stumbled on that. He followed Leni inside, with Luke trailing behind. Katie and Erin sat at the kitchen table.

Leni said, "Katie, why aren't you in school?"

Katie rolled her eyes. "Geez, Mom. You never cared when *Becca* used to skip school."

"Where is she?" Nick asked.

"I don't know," Katie snapped, and Nick wondered if

he'd ever heard her snap before. She was usually peaches and cream. "In bed, probably."

Nick spoke to Leni, low. "Go check."

She blinked, and the color poured from her face. She raced up the stairs.

The air stood still and a moment later she came back and grasped the stairwell. "She isn't there," she said, her voice shaking. "Oh, God, Becca isn't there."

Dread slammed into Nick. He pulled out his cell phone and found Wart Hogue. "Get in touch with Crawford County," he said. "Find out where Ace Holmes is."

Leni nearly wailed. "I told you this would happen. Why couldn't you have kept him locked up? He's a monst—"

"Leni," Erin said. "Come sit down."

Nick turned to Katie. "Honey, do you know if your sister went over to the Calloways' yesterday morning? Early, between seven and eight."

Katie swallowed. "No," she said. "But I did."

CHAPTER
31

Nᴵᴄᴋ'ꜱ ꜰᴀᴄᴇ ɢʀᴇᴡ thunderous. Erin put a hand on his arm.

"I was just getting ready to call you, Nick. Katie has something to tell you." She glanced at Leni. "It's pretty bad."

"What is it? Where's Becca?"

Luke leaned in to Nick. "I'm gonna to get going."

"Wait," Nick said. Luke stopped, and Nick seemed to be struggling with something. "You got some free time?"

"What do you need?"

"I wanna know where Ace Holmes is. *Un*officially."

Luke flashed a cold smile. "I'll call you," he said, and left.

Erin waited while Leni and Nick each took a seat at the kitchen table. The silence was thick, except for a steady buzz from the fluorescent lights overhead. Katie manhandled a mug of hot chocolate.

"Sweetie." Nick touched Katie's hand and Erin's skin tightened. He was big and he was rough, and he was more often a seething storm trooper than comforting caretaker, but when he did that teddy bear thing, it messed with Erin's heart. "Do you have something to tell me?"

Katie took a breath. "I went to Hilltop House yesterday."

Nick didn't react—just waited, studying her, his long, square-tipped fingers laced together on the table. "Why?"

Katie studied her hot chocolate and Erin said, "Would it be easier if I told them?"

A nod.

Erin looked at Nick. He wasn't going to like this. "Katie believes that Jack Calloway and Rebecca..." She let silence finish it.

Leni gasped. "Oh, God."

"Why do you think that, Katie?" Nick asked.

"She told me. One time when she was mad at me, calling me a nerd and a Goody-Two-shoes... She said she was going over to Hilltop House to give a little"—she drew up short and looked at her mother—"pussy."

Leni quailed.

"But she didn't go, Mom. Well, at least not that time."

"Why not?" Nick asked.

"Ace called. She went with him instead. I think she only started in with Mr. Calloway to make Ace jealous."

"I don't believe this," Leni said.

"When did this happen, Katie?" Nick asked. He sounded calm, but Erin knew better. A cold rage was building inside.

"June." That was Leni, and everyone looked at her. Her face was blank as a stone. "Right after she moved back home. She said she wanted to go take pottery classes. It wasn't like her. Oh, God, I should have known. I should have known..."

Nick said, "Why did you go to Hilltop House yesterday, Katie?"

"I wanted to get him in trouble. I had proof and wanted to show his wife—"

"What kind of proof?"

"A note to Becca. From Mr. Calloway."

"You thought a man who's accused of murder was sleeping with your sister, and instead of telling me, you went to *him*?" Leni was losing it. "Are you crazy?"

"Okay, okay," Nick said. "Listen, Becca's probably fine. She could be anywhere." To Leni: "When was the last time you saw her?"

"This morning. When I left for the restaurant, I peeked in her room. She was still in bed. It was four-thirty."

"Jack Calloway died *yesterday* morning. That means if Becca was here in bed a few hours ago, he didn't hurt her."

"Unless he's not dead," Leni said. "They haven't found his body."

"Mom, Becca's always talked about running away with Ace. She probably went with him."

Nick said, "Go check Becca's things. See if there's anything missing."

Leni spun on her heel and dashed up the stairs. A minute later, she was back. "A suitcase is gone. She packed."

"Okay," he said. "That's good, then. Wherever she is, she went willingly." He turned to Katie. "What happened yesterday when you got to Hilltop?"

Katie sniffled. "I looked around, at the inn and the garage—or carriage house—or whatever they call it. Then Mrs. Calloway came out."

"From where?"

"She was in the barn, in her workshop, I guess. She had clay on her apron."

"What time was it when you got there?"

"About seven-thirty. I drove there from the restaurant

and left pretty soon after. I missed homeroom, but I made it in time for first period."

"Okay," Nick said, and Erin wondered what was going through his mind. For damn sure, he was focused on something. "You said something about a note. Where is it?"

"I stuck it—" She looked around, saw her purse sitting on a pie safe, and went to get it. Dug around in the outside pocket, getting agitated. "I had it. I had it in my hand when I saw Mrs. Calloway."

"What did it say? Were there names in it?"

"Just Rebecca's. It was like, 'Rebecca, come meet me. I have something for you.' Signed with a J." She paused and looked at Leni. "He meant coke, Mom. Becca got it from him all the time."

Leni dropped her head. Erin had been here before, watching a mother learn her child's painful secrets.

She'd often wondered why her own mother hadn't bothered learning hers.

"So," Nick continued with Katie, "you were going to confront Mrs. Calloway."

Leni's head popped up. "And you didn't think Jack might have been there, that he might have hurt *you*? Are you cra—"

"Dr. Sims had just told me he'd disappeared, at the restaurant," Katie shot back. "Besides, I had your gun. I'm not stupid, Mom."

"Gun?" Nick looked astonished.

"I . . . Well, I took Mom's gun from the back room of the—"

"Stop," Nick said. His voice was so sharp, Katie jerked back. "Don't say another word."

Nick went still for ten seconds, then pushed from the table. He raked his hand through his hair.

"I wasn't going to *use* it," Katie said, "I just want—"

"I said, *stop*." Nick held a long finger in front of her face, his expression frightening. He turned to Leni. "Come with me," he said, and they disappeared into the next room.

Erin reached across the table and took Katie's hand. "It's okay. You had to tell."

"Am I in trouble?" Katie asked.

"Not if you tell the truth." What a crock.

"The truth is that I went to see Mr. Calloway with a gun and a couple hours later, they found out he was dead." Not a stupid child.

"Yes, but they think it was suicide. And we don't know what time he disappeared. Maybe it was before you went there. Sheriff Mann knows you didn't kill him. You can trust him." And that, Erin thought, with a fair amount of surprise, didn't feel like a crock.

Leni came back, Nick right behind her. He crooked a finger at Erin and when she joined him, said, "A public defender for Katie will meet us at the station. Until Calloway's body shows up without any bullet holes, we need to cover her ass. And I'm calling in a counselor to work on her, get the story straight and make sure she has whatever emotional help she needs. Leni agreed. The court-appointed guy is named Andrew Bak—"

"I'm a counselor," Erin snapped, "and she asked to talk to me."

He looked at her like she was nuts. "Jesus, Erin. This girl's sister is gone and she had an affair with a man you've been chasing for years. You're not exactly unbiased."

Now she was pissed. "You think I'm *leading* Katie—"

"Oh, for Christ's sake."

"I do this for a living. I didn't put words in her mouth.

I didn't *lead* Katie to suggest that Rebecca had been with Calloway."

His eyes flared. "And do you think Dorian Reinhardt is gonna buy that? With your brother on Death Row and your history against Jack, do you think there's any court in the country that will believe anything *you* milked from that child about Calloway?"

"I didn't *milk* her." Seething now. "I came over here when *she* called *me*. Then I called you."

"Not quite," he reminded her.

"Well, I was going to. You just showed up first."

"Right."

"It's the truth."

"*Truth.*" He laughed, a raucous sound that held no humor at all. "How did you get so naïve, Doctor, spouting about truth?" His eyes were cold. "This is going public, Erin. From here on out, it will have nothing to do with truth."

Eloise Farmer was sixty-two years old, had her silver-blue hair set once a week at Amy's Salon on Heritage Farms Road, and drove her late husband's 1972 Cadillac. It got nine miles to the gallon. She was a dyed-in-the-wool Republican who tithed generously, but didn't turn away the six-thousand-dollar-per-year salary Ebenezer paid her to work part-time in the church office. Her tithing was a tax deduction, of course, and the salary a nice little addition to her Social Security check, which she drank, religiously, every week. Vodka, usually—she liked vodka mixed with just about any fruit juice—but sometimes she splurged and drank the fruity champagnes. And lately, she'd discovered fruit liqueurs. Pricey, but they went down nice. You didn't need to mix them with anything.

242   KATE BRADY

Eloise arrived at the church on Tuesdays and Fridays at ten o'clock, and parked by the side door. This morning, Carl's car was in the parking lot—he was an early bird; he liked to work on his sermons in the mornings before the phone started ringing and people started coming and going. She went inside, warbled her normal greeting, and unlocked the top drawer of her desk. Took out the empty bottle, replaced it with a full one.

She pushed the power button on the Xerox machine—it took a few minutes to warm up. Warbled to Carl again.

No response. Restroom, maybe. She picked up the phone and took down the messages that had come yesterday while she was in Toledo. Her uncle, bless his heart, hadn't even known she was there. God getting ready to take him, Eloise thought, her sadness tinged with the knowledge that it was time. He was ninety-two. Rich. She would inherit.

Yes, it was time.

The phone rang the second she set down the receiver. Deputy Jensen. He was a sweet young thing, and a *deputy*. Ah, if she were thirty years younger... All right, forty.

"Just a moment, Deputy, I'll transfer you to his office."

The light on the phone flashed and she watched, knowing Carl might still be in the restroom. After a suitable amount of time, she picked up again. "He's not answering right now, but his car is here. Why don't you let me go find him and he'll call you back? Yes, okay."

She dropped the phone on the receiver and got up, decided to take a shot of that *good* raspberry liqueur first, smacked her lips, and walked down the hall. The church was unusually quiet, what with Carl not answering. Not that they often chatted while he was working, but when he was in the building there was a *vibration*—a hippie sort of word, but the only thing she could think of to describe it. She'd come into the church alone only once before, to pick up the bulletin to copy at Kinko's when their Xerox had broken down, and noticed then that she didn't like being alone in the building. The silence, the lack of *vibration*, had given her the willies.

She passed through the annex, calling for Carl, the willies tickling the hairs on the back of her neck. She wrung her hands, peeking around corners before she stepped past. By the time she reached the front entrance, she felt like Miss Marple, more than half convinced she'd find a dead body sprawled at her feet. So convinced, in fact, that when she actually *did* find a dead body sprawled at her feet, she stopped, studied the hole in the bridge of the nose for the space of a full breath, and said, "Oh, my, that's a mess."

Then she passed out.

CHAPTER
32

Nick's phone rang before he was finished with Leni. He ignored it, trying to account for Leni's whereabouts during the hours in question without quite accusing *her* of killing Jack. The newsmakers hadn't gotten on the murder bandwagon yet—too busy watching Rawling County officials drag the quarry—so the public, by and large, still thought he'd committed suicide. Leni was beginning to suspect something more.

"Nick, for God's sake," she said. "I never left the restaurant yesterday morning and there are probably fifty people who will tell you that. But let me tell you something else: I wish now I had. I wish I'd known what that bastard was doing with Rebecca, and I wish I'd gone over there and killed him with my bare hands—"

"Jesus, Leni, don't say that," he said, his phone ringing again. This time he picked up. It was Valeria.

"Sheriff, Sheriff," she said, and there was no accent. She wasn't thinking about it. "Chris Jensen found Reverend Whitmore at the church. He's dead."

• • •

Carl Whitmore had been standing at the front door of the main entrance to Ebenezer, apparently greeting his killer. The .38 slug punched through the top of his nose and into his brain, and exited into an easel holding a poster that announced a Bible study session for Thursday night and a chili cook-off for Friday.

Nick looked at the body and rage nearly choked him. "Who found him?"

"Eloise Farmer," Jensen said. He was pale. Shaken. "She's in the office. That's where she was when I got here. She was supposed to have Carl call me, and when he didn't, I came out. I found her sitting at her desk, drinking raspberry liqueur."

"Okay." The forensics unit was filing in. Martin Gamble, the supervisor, swiveled his head, taking in the scene with a faint twitch of his nostrils, like a prairie dog surveying the landscape. His usual alertness turned to sadness. He was a member of Ebenezer.

"Carl told me once he wanted to find a way to get you to church, Sheriff," he said, looking at the gray body. "Don't think this was what he had in mind."

Predictably, Eloise Farmer was no help. Besides the fact that she was only half-sober, she'd been in Toledo when the murder happened, early yesterday morning. As far as they could tell, with the office closed, no one but Carl had been at the church.

Except for the murderer.

Reverend, forgive me . . .

Nick phoned one of Eloise's old friends to come and get her, and wandered back through the front lobby of the church. He waited, his pulse throbbing in his temples, until Martin and his team had finished the preliminaries. "Can you match to a specific gun?" he asked.

"I don't know," Martin said, tweezing remnants of the bullet from the wood frame of the easel. "Hollow-points don't hold up very well going through bone, wood. This one went through both. It's pretty messed up."

"How close?"

"Inches. Nitrates all over his face. I'd say he just opened the door and *pop*. Probably didn't have time to be scared."

"Someone he knew, then."

"A stranger wouldn't get that close. Not unless this is some sort of freaky execution."

Nick stayed until the crime scene guys were ready to flip the body, watched, felt his gut lurch, and saw nothing that changed his mind about what had happened. Martin announced that rigor mortis had already set in and was on its way out, which would make pinning the exact time of death harder.

"Early yesterday?" Nick pressed.

"Could have been."

"Before nine?" He meant, *Before Jack's truck went into the quarry?* And, *When Katie Engel was out running around scared with a .38?*

"Could have been."

Rebecca had wet herself; the odor of urine rose from the table.

"Not pretty," the Angelmaker said, but it happened. In fact, it happened more often than not. It was a lengthy process, silencing an angel. On the road, in particular, finding a viable workspace for long enough to make a mask was difficult to manage. With Lauren, all those years ago, the studio van had sufficed, though it had taken some extra sanding to get the mask suitable for an art piece. And once, in Minnesota, there had been a fishing shack handy. But in those days, there had still always been the challenge of disposing of the body, and making sure it was clean just in case it was found.

Not anymore.

Here, in recent years, Hilltop had provided plenty of workspace, plenty of privacy. And easy disposal of the body when the work was done.

Rebecca's eyes grew wide when the Angelmaker neared, her body tensing in the elaborate webbing of duct tape. Her nostrils flared, trying to suck in air. The fools never understood that once their lips were sealed, crying wasn't smart. It made them sniffly and stuffy, and they had trouble breathing through their noses. Rebecca had become downright hysterical when she finally became aware what was happening, but by then there'd been no use trying to fight or scream. She was already bound to the table with spiraling yards of duct tape, her breasts hiked up by the tape like an ad for a push-up bra, and lips held tight with the glue.

A ready mold.

The Angelmaker lit nine candles, drew in a deep breath of vanilla, and looked Rebecca up and down. The wild terror in her eyes was unimpressive; the Angelmaker had gotten used to that years ago. The first time, with Lauren, had been horrifying—her death had been an act of impulse. Their eyes had met by chance when the Angelmaker had been caught eyeing her artwork at an exhibit—a fleeting look, but one that made everything clear. She *knew*. And she would tell. Panicked, the Angelmaker lured her outside and killed her, hiding the body in the back of the work van.

It was then, in the moments after her death, that reality set in: She was gone, but still watching—like the angel figurines. Her body was there in the work van—filled with supplies—so the Angelmaker set to work, transforming Lauren to an empty shell. Left her there for hours in fear someone might find her and went home to face the angels. One was dead. So the Angelmaker picked up the first figurine and smashed it into pieces, and for the first time in memory, a heady sense of freedom rushed in. Power. Picking up the pieces had been sheer joy—an arm, a wing, a face. They all went in a bucket.

They'll keep watch.

Not that one. Not anymore.

The terror lifted; the Angelmaker had been born. For the first time, the angels were powerless. The Angelmaker went back and took the mask from Lauren's face, cleaned her off, and drove her body to the Everglades. Lived on the rush of that kill for years, until another angel came along.

"Mmmm." Rebecca strained through her lips. Superglue was good stuff.

"Stop that. You'll only rip your own skin off. Robin Weelkes did that when it was his turn." The Angelmaker remembered, sharing aloud. "He was a firefighter, a big burly man, and just about ripped his lips to shreds, waiting for his mask. I thought I'd never get him sanded smooth."

"Mmm Mmmm."

A tear slipped from the corner of her eye, leaving a black trail of mascara down her temple. The Angelmaker toweled it away. "Stop that. Clean and dry. The mold must be clean and dry."

She tried to shake her head but couldn't—the tape. She tried to scream but couldn't—the superglue. She tried to fight but couldn't—her long-awaited destiny.

The Angelmaker straightened and began removing the hoops in Rebecca's eyebrows. Four of them, all in the left brow. The stud in her nose wouldn't matter—the clay would go right over that—and finally, she was perfect: Clean and quiet and utterly still.

The Angelmaker turned down the lights to let the candle glow take over, stepped to a boom box and pushed a button. *Regina coeli...Semper angelis conservabor....*

CHAPTER
33

"VALERIA," NICK SAID, "set up a press conference."
"What time?"

Nick took a deep breath. It was four in the afternoon.
He'd stuck around the church until the murder scene
had been fully processed, talked to Carl's relatives and
friends, and gotten yet another investigation moving. At
last count, there were two dozen members of the media
swarming the church, and another half dozen here at the
station. They would take what little they thought they
knew and put it on the air by six o'clock. "Half an hour, in
time to make the news."

Valeria flattened both hands on her desk. "You *want* to
make the evening news? Who are you and what have you
done with the real sheriff?"

"At least this way, they'll have accurate information,
whether they choose to use it or not." But that wasn't the
main reason he needed to go on TV. Rebecca was gone
and so was Ace Holmes. If they were together, maybe
Nick could reach out to her before she got too far. Maybe
she'd call or sneak out on Ace. Something.

A thought: *Rebecca uses Mom's gun to kill ex-lover,*

then pushes his car off a ledge. The next morning, she kills minister who knew too much, and runs away.

Jesus.

"Is Sims in the back?" Nick asked, but knew she would be. Leni had dropped her off at headquarters when she brought Katie over to the courthouse.

"*Sí.* With Deputy Fruth."

Erin turned when he entered, her hands clenched. Fruth shot Nick a look that said, *She's all yours, buddy,* and made a hasty exit. As soon as he was gone, Erin opened her mouth.

"Don't start," Nick said, before she managed to get a word out. "It was a fucking crime scene. You didn't belong there. And I know helping get Katie and Rebecca through the system is right up your alley, but I swear, Erin, you have to stay as far away from those girls and their connections to Huggins as possible."

She snapped her mouth closed on a curse, then said, "I know. I get it. I just can't stand being on the sidelines watching Justin's hours tick by."

"I'm moving as fast as I can. I have a press conference in a little while and I want you to know what I'm going to say."

Her fingers loosened a touch and he propped his hips against the edge of the desk. "I think you're right that Jack Calloway may have been involved in the death of Lauren McAllister."

Erin lifted a brow. "You're willing to say that to the press? Confirm the word of a crackpot?"

"Stop it," he snapped, and crossed his arms. "There's more than your word. We have confirmation that Jack had affairs with both Lauren and now Rebecca, and Margaret Calloway says there were others."

"Sara Daniels?"

"I'm not sure of her yet. But in addition to Rebecca Engel there's a college student named Shelly Quinn who might have known him. She fits the mold—"

"So let's go talk to her."

"We can't." He could tell by the look in her eyes that she knew why.

"She's gone," she breathed. "Oh, God. Just like Rebecca."

"Rebecca may have slept with Jack, but she was in her bed this morning twenty hours after Jack disappeared."

"That doesn't mean he couldn't get to her. If he's still alive."

"I know," he conceded. "Still, chances are better she's with Ace Holmes. It's what Rebecca said they were going to do and she packed a bag."

"But he raped her."

"Not if she says he didn't."

Erin cursed. "This Andrew Baker," she said, "the therapist who's going to work with Katie...Is he any good? Will he be able to help Rebecca?"

He's a sixty-four-year-old chauvinist asshole, counting the months until retirement. "He'll probably contend that both girls have a great big case of penis envy."

"You're kidding."

Nick put up a hand. "Sweetheart, these girls aren't your clients. They're off-limits. Andrew Baker's on his way; he's gonna debrief Katie so we can be sure what we're getting about Rebecca is right, that she's not—"

"Being an overzealous sister begging to be heard."

Nick looked at her. Bright, courageous, and christened an overzealous sister begging to be heard. No longer. Nick had heard. "The bottom line is that whether Jack is dead or alive, we know he had an affair with Rebecca. It's one more straw to add to the camel's back. Straws may be all we ever get."

"How much do you think Huggins might still be out there?"

Nick closed his eyes. "I don't know." He told her about the missing gun and Jack's note asking for forgiveness. Finally, he handed her the letterhead from the Southeast Regional Women's Clinic in Florida.

"What's this?"

"Lauren had an abortion a few weeks before she disappeared."

"What?"

"John Huggins signed as the father of the baby."

She gaped at him. He could see her mind travel back twelve years, trying to fit that in with Justin's relationship, then saw the *mea culpas* start rolling through her mind... *Why didn't I know that? How could I have missed it?*

"That would have changed everything," she said. "Why didn't I think to check something like that?"

"You're a psychologist, not a detective."

"I should have thought of it."

"The detectives investigating the case should have thought of it. And I wouldn't doubt that they did."

She looked at him. "You're thinking the Senator kept it secret."

"I don't know that. But I can see that it wouldn't have been good for his career, or for their case against Justin."

She stood, vibrating with tension. "We have to report this to the AG. We have—"

"I already did. And . . ." He swallowed, startled by how much he wanted to get the case against Justin dismissed. Save the day for Erin. Redeem himself.

Stop it. There's no redemption for getting the mother

of your child killed. This wasn't about being attracted to Erin, or even loving Allison. It was about Justin.

He walked over to her. "And, I sent a lawyer to Florida. Someone who can handle the evidence we're turning up. She met with Justin, and is probably with the assistant AG right now."

"What?"

"My sister, Layna. She's an attorney. And she's a sucker for an underdog."

"She saw Justin?"

Yes. And told Nick things he couldn't shake from his mind. "She owes me a few favors—you know, for busting up her dates with loser boys all through high school."

Erin looked shocked but within seconds, the look in her eyes gave way to hope. And gratitude. Nick's chest went *thmp*.

"Somehow I doubt your sister feels that way," she said.

"That's her problem. As far as I'm concern—"

Erin kissed him. Grabbed his shirt, pulled him down and met him with lips that were warm and mobile and exuberant. Nick didn't question it—he deepened the kiss and closed his arms around her, running his hands up her back, into her hair. He kissed her back with everything he had, startled by the depth of his desire and the need to protect her from pain.

A knock broke it up. Erin stepped back and touched her lips with a finger; Nick cleared his voice. "Come in."

Valeria. "Four-thirty, Sheriff. The vultures are hungry." She looked at Erin sideways. "You staying here?"

Erin straightened, like a fighter shaking off a hard right hook. "No. I have to go to the press conference."

Nick turned to her. "Don't speak, Erin. No matter how much the bastards try to make you. Let me handle it."

It was a plea not an order, and Nick realized it required a degree of trust he didn't think she had. Chemistry was one thing, gratitude another. Trust was far beyond.

Erin brushed her hands down her sweater. "All right," she said.

The sheriff didn't take any questions. Looking straight into the camera—at the Angelmaker?—Mann announced Carl Whitmore's murder and ran through details regarding Jack's disappearance. He stated that new evidence suggested that Jack Calloway had indeed been involved with at least three women who were either dead or whose fates were in question, including Lauren McAllister. With a muscle twitching in his jaw, he asserted that reports emerging about Sims's instability were unfounded. And he shared that authorities were consulting with the FBI and the college on the possibility that there were other young women who might have been victims—including revisiting Carrie Sitton's murder to see if it was somehow related. Finally, he announced that authorities would like to question Rebecca Engel and Ace Holmes, with whom they believed she had left town. If anyone had knowledge of their whereabouts...

The Angelmaker watched, a pulse of fear colliding with anger. Mann wasn't onto Rebecca yet, but the FBI? Other college students? Carrie Sitton?

No one had ever looked so closely before. No one had ever threatened to connect the angels together.

The Angelmaker shifted, sweat beading up. Mann? Number Ten? As blind as that man had been all his life, it didn't seem likely. Still, he was looking too closely, and at too many things.

Oh, Sheriff. That's a grave error on your part.

• • •

After the press conference, Nick and Erin went back to his office. They found Luke leaning against the desk looking up at the television.

"You look old on TV," he said, turning it off. "And ten pounds heavier."

"Go to hell," Nick shot. "What did you find out?"

"Ace Holmes's place is half empty, and the half he left behind is shit. His truck's gone, though he left an old Dodge there—no plates—and his personal items are gone. His friends, if you can call them that, don't know where he is, but say he'd been talking about blowing town with Rebecca. If he did blow town, from what I've heard, Buffalo is a good bet. I've got some names."

Nick blew out a breath, glancing at Erin. He never dreamed he'd *hope* Rebecca Engel would run off with Ace Holmes, but just now, that would be good news.

Nick turned to Quent, who was just walking in. "What happened with Katie while we were out there with the press?"

Quent said, "Sam Fulton, her defense attorney, finished with her and turned her over to the shrink. Fulton puffed his chest out and told me the sheriff's department has no case against his client and he dares you—no, he *double-*dares you—to try to charge her with Jack's murder..."

"Aw, Jesus."

"Bluster. The media was there, so he hit me with both barrels."

"That's how public defenders get hard-ons," Luke said.

Quent went on. "Sam lost his a minute later when I told him we don't really think Katie has done anything wrong. That we just want her protected until we know what happened to Jack. We already grabbed her mom's gun and it doesn't look like it's been fired. We just need time for the lab to confirm that."

"Did Leni take her home?" Nick asked.

"Yeah," Quentin said. "We released her into her mother's custody, but that's another thing: Leslie Roach wants to know why we didn't charge her."

"Fuck Leslie Roach," Nick said.

"You, maybe," Quent said, with a shiver, "not me. The point is, Katie's sealed up tight. No way we can talk to her again, not without Sam Fulton, and I don't think Leni would go for it. She's pretty pissed at us. Andrew Baker's going over later this evening."

"To accuse her of penis envy?" Erin snapped.

Nick cursed. If Andrew Baker could get something out of Katie that would help find Becca, or help explain Becca's relationship with Jack, then by God, let him take a crack at it. But it was Becca they really needed to talk to. Damn, he wished he could've gotten through to that girl. "Any word on Shelly Quinn's roommates?"

"Yeah," Quentin said, and unfolded a piece of paper. "They're still here, seniors, and they still room together. They live off campus at the Town Lake Apartments on Perry Street. I checked their schedules with neighbors. They should be home after eight o'clock."

One little break. Nick closed his eyes. Labs under way, Katie with her defense attorney and counselor, the list of Mansfeld girls being checked by a group on the phones. Rawling County was doing the quarry and Jack's truck; Layna getting some attention in Florida. Everybody to talk to already talked to.

It was a waiting game now. He didn't know what else to do. But Justin couldn't wait much longer.

"There's nothing," Quentin said, following his thoughts.

"Things are going like they should, and a lot of people are working it. What you need now is something to eat, touch base with your kid. Me too."

"Yeah." He'd go talk to Shelly's roommates at eight, two hours from now. He looked at Erin, and realized that she'd never actually checked in to the motel he'd booked for her. Realized he didn't want her to.

She slept with a gun under her pillow...a long time before Huggins.

He found Luke watching him. "I think I'll take Erin to get some dinner," Luke said. "Is that steak house out on Route 9 still open—The Texas Star, or whatever?"

"Steaks at that place taste like leather," Nick said. "They serve salad dressings by Wishbone."

"So, what are you saying?" Quent asked. "You're cooking again?"

"Good idea," Luke said. "It'll smooth you out, give you a chance to get your brain in order."

"Ah, man," Quentin whined. "Don't cook for me. I gotta go home and be a dad for a little while. Eat beanies and weenies and read stories from the Brothers Grimm."

"Your life sucks," Luke said, as Quentin put on his jacket. "Beautiful wife, adoring kids, wide-screen HDTV with surround sound..."

"Beanies and weenies," Quentin said, going down the hall.

Nick looked at Luke. Said a whole lot without saying anything at all.

Luke said, "So, why don't you start dinner and I'll run to Mom's? I'll bring Hannah back and meet you at your place."

"Gee, I never would've thought of that," Nick said.

Luke went out the same way as Quentin. "Real smooth, Nick..."

CHAPTER
34

Y OU DON'T HAVE to babysit me," Erin said, walking beside Nick to his SUV. "You have a daughter who doesn't need a stranger hanging around."

"Hannah loves company." He opened the truck's passenger door and Erin slid halfway onto the seat. Nick braced a forearm on the roof above her, his big body shielding her from a gust of November wind that lifted his shirt collar. "She'll make her favorite salad, with raspberries and arugula and goat cheese."

"You're just worried I'll go to the motel and have a Three Musketeers bar for supper."

"Ah, jeez, don't even talk like that."

She couldn't help but chuckle, then caught him staring. A second later his thumb stroked the curve of her jaw and a shiver having nothing to do with the wind raced over Erin's skin.

"You should do that more often," Nick said. "Smile. It's enough to knock a man off his feet."

Her heart did a flip-flop. His eyes followed the path of his thumb, passing over her lips, leaving a trail of fire. Want him, Luke had said. Dear God, she couldn't remember the last time she'd *wanted* a man. The suggestion trickled through her belly and settled at the apex of her thighs.

This was crazy. She'd never been a slave to her libido, or tempted into bed with someone for a short-lived affair. She was a psychologist, wired for relationships, not flings. And she hadn't had the time or energy necessary for a relationship since Justin had—

Her brain came to a halt. Justin. Here she was, stricken by lust while her brother counted down the final days and hours of his life. How could she even think about a fling with Nick right now?

"Had enough?"

His voice brought her back. "Enough what?" she asked.

"Analysis. Doubt. Guilt."

Her cheeks prickled. "What are you, some kind of shrink?"

"Erin, look at me," he said, and cupped her face between his hands. "There's nothing else to do right now. Trust me. You've done it all. *We've* done it all."

"It can't be all."

"It is, just for this moment. Just for a little while." He swallowed, his voice sounding like sandpaper. "I want you."

She looked up, feeling small and fragile as he cradled her cheeks. And she realized that in all the years since Justin's trial, she'd never come close to freeing Justin until Nick had taken up the gauntlet.

Dear God, she'd been as useless protecting Justin in the past twelve years as she'd been when they were children.

That realization shuddered through her. Her eyes grew hot with tears.

Nick leaned back. "What is it?"

"Do you know the last time I saw him?" she whispered.

"When?"

"Eleven years ago, in court. At the sentencing."

Nick cocked his head. "You didn't visit him in prison?"

"I did. Every month. On the second Tuesday at ten-thirty." The tears began to spill. "But he wouldn't see me. Never once."

"Why?"

"When the police came, I confirmed their photo was the girl he'd been seeing. I'm the reason they went after him."

"No, sweetheart, you're not," Nick said. "They would have found out. They would have gone after him, anyway."

"I've never been able to protect him. I tried so hard but—" She jerked herself to a halt. "Oh, God. I'm tired. I'm so tired of fighting."

Nick traced the outline of her face with his fingers, his gaze following, and he nudged her chin up to face him. "So stop fighting. Just for a little while." He held her eyes for a long moment; then his gaze fell to her lips and lingered. They homed in on her eyes again, leaving her lips alive and tingling as if he'd already ravished them. A promise of something yet to come. "Be with me, Erin," he said, brushing his hand down her rib cage like a feather. "I won't hurt you. Just say yes."

She wasn't afraid of his hurting her; all she could feel was heat swirling in her belly. She reached up to his hard cheek, wanting nothing more than to let him take her away for a little while. Wanting to let him feed the hot embers burning deep inside her body.

But then his phone rang. He cursed, but his face changed when he saw the caller ID. "My sister," he said, and answered.

Erin listened, watching his face. Something good? She found herself crossing her fingers.

"That's great, kid," he said. "Go get 'em."

He disconnected, looking at Erin with a glint in his eyes. "Layna's in. She saw the assistant AG and sees the judge and the AG in the morning."

A wave of relief spilled into joy. Erin threw herself against his chest, her arms looping his neck. He held her that way for a long minute; then his hand cupped the back of her head and he tipped back her face with a fistful of hair. "Can I take that as a 'yes'?" he asked, his voice ragged.

"Yes," she whispered.

He was on her when they got out of the truck at his house, a gentle mauling as they stumbled through the kitchen and great room. Erin caught sight of a princess book bag by the sofa and pulled away. "What about Hannah?" she rasped. "And Luke."

"Luke's not an idiot. We have time."

"You mean, he knows?"

"Jesus, Erin." Nick let her go and tipped his face skyward, sheer frustration in his voice. "Yes, Luke knows. Valeria knows. Everyone knows. Hell, the deputies have a pool going. If I nail you tonight, Chris Jensen wins; wait 'til tomorrow and Wart's got it, the pot doubles—"

"Nail me tonight?"

A grin crossed his face. "Why, thank you. I think I will."

Despite the crass turn of phrase, there was nothing crass about the way Nick made love. He was hungry and controlling, handling her, angling her face to his liking and molding her lips to his, but with a touch that was almost reverent. His arm slid around her back and beneath her shirt, heat flaring as his knuckles brushed her spine and her bra fell loose. Erin gasped and his hand came to the front, her breast straining to fill it, and when his fingers found her nipple, bolts of sensation shot through her body. She quivered at the contact and knew, no matter how crazy this was, she wasn't going to stop him.

She wanted this. She wanted him.

He lifted her into his arms and carried her upstairs, and there Erin marveled at how his touch soothed her nerves and transformed lingering soreness to sheer desire. He caressed her and cherished her, chasing every quiver of response as if he knew, if pursued, it would blossom and spread into an all-consuming wave of pleasure. In Nick's bed, the trials of life slipped away, fear dissolved to nothing. Her limbs quaked and her flesh came to life, pleasure eddying between her thighs and swirling inside. And when he finally entered her, it was she who bucked and writhed, pushing their pace and their rhythm beyond all pain to a place where nothing existed but raw hunger and passion. She drew back her knees, urging him deeper, until the pleasure was too much to bear and she came apart in his hands, pulling him over the edge with her.

"Jesus," he said, his breathing ragged. He shifted to drag his weight from her. "Did I hurt you? Are you all right?"

She was way past "all right." "I think you broke three ribs—"

"Ah, Christ—"

"I'm kidding," she said, laughing at him. "I'm fine." She touched her torso. "But laughing hurts. God, don't make me laugh."

His eyes went dark, and he dropped his head to her nipple. "All right. No more laughing."

She fell back under his spell, too immersed in passion to laugh or talk or do anything but hang on for the ride. When they finished, she lay in a boneless stupor, listening to her own heartbeat, until at last she corralled enough brain cells to form a thought.

"So, who won?" she asked.

His eyebrow moved.

"The pool," she said. "Now that you...nailed me, who won?"

A faint smile curved his lips. "I did."

The Angelmaker Xed out of the website, went to Internet Options, and deleted the computer's history. Five minutes and a few clicks provided instructions that were easy enough: glass bottle, rag, gasoline. Any idiot could do that. But more thorough research showed that there were risks. Surprisingly, as often as not, the bottle wouldn't break. And apparently, gasoline was so thin that, depending where the bottle landed, the flame might simply surge in its place and burn out without catching onto too much else.

Didn't want that. That sort of thing probably had the cops chuckling over beers at such amateurish moves.

But the Angelmaker was smarter than that. This bottle would break. This fire would spread. And give Mann something new to focus on.

Nick cracked one eye open at the clock. Time ticking. He could hear Erin moving around in the bathroom. A little while being coddled and pampered and treated the way she deserved, and she was up again, ready to fight the world.

I'm so tired of fighting.

He got out of bed and met her when she came out, holding a sheet around her like a toga. She smiled and ran a hand up his chest. He caught it.

"It's time," Nick said. "Time to tell me what you've been fighting all your life."

She gave him a cockeyed look. "Justin."

"No. I mean before that."

"Befor—" She went still, and he could almost feel the inner guards taking up arms. Anger started to well up— that she would let him fight for Justin and make love to her, but when it came to whatever was eating her up on the inside, he was still an outsider.

"Nick," she said, but he stopped her. He'd had enough of the walls.

"Why do you sleep with a gun under your pillow?" he asked.

The look in her eyes nearly brought him to his knees. Caught without anger to front for it, he could see the emotion for what it was: sheer, unadulterated terror. Her body turned to steel and he had to force himself not to pull her in and try to kiss the fear away.

"How did you know that?" she asked, dumbfounded.

"It doesn't matter. Tell me."

She closed her eyes and one breath at a time, the fight drained out of her. "You remember asking me about the court counselor's testimony, the part that got buried by the judge?"

Nick nodded.

"My stepfather—Jeffrey Collins—used to beat the shit out of Justin. The defense wanted to use that to paint a history of violent behavior, but the judge wouldn't allow—"

"Where was your mother?"

She scoffed. "In her room, drinking, and planning which jewelry to wear to her next ladies' outing."

The bitterness in her voice took him by surprise. *It's always about the mother.* For the first time Nick could remember, he wanted to delve into a psyche, root out all the hurt. Replace it with pleasure.

"She wasn't—isn't—a strong person. She was blind to what Jeffrey was doing."

And she left Erin to cope with it. Nick had the fleeting urge to wring her mother's neck. "And you never told anyone?"

"Sure, I did. I told Mom, but she couldn't stay sober long enough to remember a night that had already passed. I went to the school counselor, who called in Jeffrey and fell for whatever lies he told her. And once—when Jeffrey threw Justin against the hearth and broke his arm—I went to the police. Would you like to know how interested the authorities are in accusing a wealthy, upstanding citizen of a violent crime, when he denies it? Oh, wait. I guess I don't have to tell you that."

"Now, hold on—"

"I'm sorry." Her cheeks flushed. "You didn't deserve that."

No, he didn't. But that didn't matter right now. "What about you?"

"Me?" she asked, and a shimmer of tears came to her eyes. "I tried to protect Justin. But I wasn't strong enough."

"You were a kid. You did your best." But her best hadn't been enough. He could see it in her eyes. And more.

Nick's hands fisted. "Did Collins beat you, too?"

"No. I was older. And I was a gir—" Erin stopped, and something at the core of Nick's body iced over.

"Jesus, Erin. What did he do to you?"

"Nothing," she said, and stepped from Nick's hands. "Not really."

"I don't believe you."

"He only threatened." She turned her back to him, crossing her arms tight over her middle. "He negotiated with me, to leave Justin alone."

"Negotiated."

"At first, when I was twelve or thirteen, it was little things. He wanted me to sit with him on the couch and watch TV or come to the basement to watch him work out. Then it got bigger. He'd want a goodnight kiss, or want me to wear a certain outfit he bought for me. If I didn't, he'd take it out on Justin. If I hesitated, all he had to do was go toward Justin's room and I'd give in. Then, when I turned sixteen, he came into my bedroom and laid down with me in my bed. My mother was out." She began to tremble, her voice fraying like a thin strand of silk. "He touched me. I said, 'no.' And he said, 'No? Is that really your answer?' And when I didn't give in, he left my room and dragged Justin out of bed. He was ten. Jeffrey beat him unconscious while I listened from behind the locked door."

"Holy Christ."

"He said that if I told anyone, he'd kill Mom and Justin and have me to himself whenever he wanted. And that he would never, ever take 'no' for an answer."

Nick tasted bile. He tried to swallow it back and walked up behind her. He was afraid to touch her, afraid she might shatter like blown glass and that he wouldn't be allowed to hear anymore. But then she turned around, the sheet knotted tight between her breasts and her eyes hard as emeralds.

"The next day I took my mother's gun. It was this little pearl-handled Derringer she carried in her purse for show. A fashion item," she quipped, but there was nothing light-hearted in the tone of her voice. Nothing fragile, either. "When he came into my room that night, he asked if I'd changed my mind. We talked about what he'd done to Justin and he said he'd do it again. I gave in. I let him get in bed with me."

Dread congealed in Nick's chest. And rage and fear and the overwhelming desire to hunt down Jeffrey Collins and make him pay.

"And when he was settled in bed beside me, I drove the pistol into his balls and told him if he ever came near me or touched Justin again, I would shoot them off, one at a time. And I pointed under the desk to the cassette tape player that had recorded everything."

Pride washed over Nick.

Erin let out a shaky breath. "He left. I mean, really left. He left my mother and never came back. A year later, he filed for divorce."

"Where is he now?"

"The last we heard, he'd remarried. In Bismarck, North Dakota, where he was developing a new mall."

Bismarck. Nick had never been there. Soon enough, he vowed, he would go.

He brushed a hand down Erin's cheek. "And you slept with the gun under your pillow after that."

She closed her eyes. "I was afraid he'd come back. I jimmied the lock on Justin's door so it wouldn't latch. For weeks, at night I would sit with my back against my bed-room door and the gun in my hand, listening for his car to come in the drive, or for the front door to open. When I went to bed, I'd lie there thinking every sound was his footsteps. Sometimes I'd wake and my hand would be cramped from holding the gun so tight."

She rubbed at her hand and Nick took it in his, unfolded her fingers and kissed her palm, first one hand, then the other. "No more," he murmured into her hands, and the combination of her strength and vulnerability shook loose a promise from his lips. "I'll protect you now." He abandoned her hands and trailed kisses down her arms, backing her up until her ass hit the dresser. He cleared the surface with a sweep of her hand, then took her by the waist and set her butt on the dresser. Unfastened the knot of the sheet.

"Do you know how proud I am, you crazy little fool?" he asked, lowering his lips to her neck. He watched in the mirror behind her as her back arched in pleasure and her hands shot out against the dresser like buttresses. He pressed her knees open with his body and clasped one ass cheek in each hand.

"No," she said, on a breath that was almost a sigh. "Show me."

CHAPTER 35

LATER, THE FRONT DOOR opened with an excessive amount of clatter. D.D. trotted in first, sent in as a scout, Nick supposed, and Hannah followed a long minute later. She ran into the kitchen, sniffing the air. "Rosemary potatoes," she said. "What else? I'm starving. Uncle Luke and Grandma just kept talking and talking and talking..."

Nick looked at his brother. Luke was making it hard to nurse a grudge.

"You're just in time to do the salad," Nick said, plopping Hannah on a barstool at the island. "Here's the goat cheese. I already pureed the raspberries for the dressing."

"Yum, my favorite. You have to reach the red wine vinegar for me," she said, and he did. "Did you toast the macadamia nuts?"

"Oh, shi— I forgot."

"That's a quarter," Hannah said. She looked at Erin. "I charge him a quarter every time he cusses."

"You must have a thriving college fund by now," Luke said.

"He owes me thirty-eight dollars and twenty-five cents," Hannah said. "Fifty cents, now."

"Like hell I do..."

"Seventy-five. Daddy, how could you forget to toast the macadamia nuts?"

"I've been busy," he said, with a glance to Erin.

Luke caught it and Erin's cheeks flamed red. "Come on, Chef Hannah," Luke said. "Show me what goes in this raspberry stuff. I'm hungry."

Nick stifled a growl but felt great. He couldn't remember the last time he and Luke had had an exchange that was beyond civil, couldn't remember the last time his body had been used so thoroughly and yet straining for more. Having Erin in his world—in the kitchen with his family—seemed right.

So right he could almost forget it scared the shit out of him. She was his now, to keep safe.

He dumped a bag of macadamia nuts into a dry skillet and caught Erin eyeing Luke. "You two both know your way around a kitchen, don't you?"

Luke said, " *'Der* Mann *Jungs...'* "

"Will cook,' " Nick finished for him. Our mother's credo. I can drive a sewing machine, too."

Erin's eyes popped. "You cannot."

"Is that a challenge I hear?"

Hannah chimed in, "Grandma says he flunked sewing."

"No one asked you," Nick said.

Eight o'clock came too soon. Dinner done, Hannah giving Erin a lesson in herbs, Nick's stomach pleasantly full while his body and mind both existed in a state of flux: exhausted from a distinct shortage of sleep and a few mind-blowing orgasms; charged by the chase and the case and the mystery Erin had brought to Hopewell.

He grimaced. Thought he might have a topic for the

next time he had to do staff development. *A Cop's Guide to Kicking Tobacco and Emotional Gratification: Serial Murder.*

The shrink in L.A. had accused him of possessing a twisted need for intensity, to handle the worst cases and go beyond what was fair and orthodox to nail the bastards of the world.

"Detective Mann, how does it make you feel to know that Bertrand Yost will never walk again as a result of your actions?" she had asked.

And Nick was supposed to say, *"I feel torn and guilty."* Instead, he'd looked her in the eye and said, *"I wish he would never breathe again."*

Twice a week for ten months Nick sat in her designer office rehashing the fate of the man who had murdered his wife and wounded his daughter—not to mention the list of crimes that had set Nick's task force after him and his boss in the first place. At the end, the shrink reported that Nick's "fervency bordering on obsession puts not only the targets of his investigations in danger, but also has the potential to pull the entire department and even the city's innocent citizens into the cyclone of vengeance Nick Mann calls justice."

His phone rang, and Nick realized his hands were fisted. He shook them out and answered. Dispatch.

"Sheriff, we just took a call from police in Elyria. They got Ace Holmes in a bar picking a fight."

His heart kicked up. "Rebecca Engel with him?"

"I don't know. Do you want to talk to them?"

"Patch me through." She did, and a couple of clicks later a husky voice came on.

"Sheriff Mann? This is Gavin Stone. I'm a patrol officer with the Elyria City Police Department." Elyria was a suburb of Cleveland, about an hour and a half from Hopewell. "You wanted to talk to Ace Holmes?"

"Absolutely," Nick said. "What's going on?"

"He's drunk, sitting in a bar up here and owing the manager a couple hundred dollars in damages."

"You know what we've got going down here?"

"Yes, sir. And I asked him about Rebecca Engel. He says he hasn't seen her."

A sliver of fear slid under Nick's skin. *Ah, Christ, Rebecca, where are you?* "Is he telling the truth?"

"I don't know. He's pretty messed up. Hard to tell when they're like that."

"I need him. Sober him up and hold him until one of my guys gets there. If he doesn't cooperate, bust his ass for something and lock him up."

"We can do that."

"And search his truck. I'm looking for any sign of Rebecca Engel."

"Will do."

Nick punched out and looked at Luke. "Ace Holmes is drunk near Cleveland. Rebecca's not with him."

"Uh-oh," Luke said.

Nick walked back in to where Erin and Hannah were talking.

"Honey," he said. They both looked up and something in Nick's chest went *thmp*. "I have to go out for a little while."

"Daddy," Hannah whined, "do I have to sleep at Grandma's again?"

"Nope." Nick shook his head. "I won't be long. I'm just going out to talk to a couple college students. Uncle Luke can stay with you."

"Actually, I was thinking I'd tag along," Luke said

from behind him, "if Erin doesn't mind staying with Hannah. That okay?"

Erin looked between Nick and Hannah, considering. Trust, again. It was always a matter of trust.

"Okay," she said, in the end. "So long as you tell me what you find out."

Nick stepped into the hall where Hannah wouldn't hear and asked for Fruth to come keep an eye on the house. Looked at Luke and wondered when it had started to feel good to have him around. He'd harbored a grudge against him for sparing Yost for all these years, and now had a feeling his warmer attitude had nothing to do with a change in Luke's character, and everything to do with a change in Nick's. He wasn't sure when that had happened either, but if he stopped to analyze it, he wagered he'd find Erin Sims in there somewhere.

He went back and kissed Hannah on the head, gave in to the urge to plant a very different sort of kiss on Erin, and pointed a finger at Hannah. "In bed by nine-thirty."

"Okay," she grumped, but her eyes twinkled.

The Angelmaker drove by Mann's house. Found a deputy parked there.

"Shit." A shot of anger rose up—this wasn't what Mann was supposed to do. Getting an extra pair of eyes to keep watch? But a moment later, the Angelmaker laughed. *All right, Sheriff. Two can play this game.* If anything would be more enjoyable than sending his house into a ball of fire, it would be doing it under the nose of a deputy.

The Angelmaker veered a block out of the way and headed back home, thinking about the cheap, simple things in life. Like a seventy-five-dollar stun gun and a hundred-dollar motorcycle.

CHAPTER
36

ELIZABETH KUNKLE WAS a slim twenty-two-year-old with blond hair and inch-long dark roots. She wore a tank top with no bra and indecently cut jeans that displayed a gold loop through her belly. When she bent over to clear junk off the sofa, the tattoo above her butt was like a slap in the face. Nick had the urge to cover her with a blanket, then run home and go through Hannah's closet and trash anything more revealing than sweats.

Getting old, he thought. Luke was eyeing the tattoo.

Shea Blaurock was Elizabeth's opposite. Chunky, with wine-colored stripes in black hair, wearing tight leggings and a baggy sweater that she probably thought disguised her size. She had a nervous habit of pushing her glasses up even when they hadn't slipped, and Nick decided she wore them to hide the stupor in her eyes.

"Go ahead and sit down," Elizabeth said, dropping a stack of magazines to the floor. "Sorry, it's kind of a mess."

"It's fine," Nick said, sitting down. Something poked his butt and he scooted over a little, making room for Luke on the sofa. A couple of candles burned on the end table, but the smell of vanilla spice didn't quite mask the odor of marijuana that oozed from the upholstery.

"You said on the phone you wanted to know about Shelly . . . ," Elizabeth said, dropping into a bean bag chair. Shea sank into a fuzzy Walmart-brand mushroom chair, hot pink. "We never really knew her that well," Elizabeth continued. "I mean, we lived together for a couple of months, but she was..." She looked at Shea—no help there—and concluded, "...weird."

"How do you mean?" Nick asked. Elizabeth's nipples puckered under her shirt. Too chilly in November for a tank top with nothing over it. He glanced around for that blanket.

"She wanted to be a music major—voice. Music people have their own worlds. She never wanted to rush or anything—I mean, go Greek."

"I know what 'rush' means."

"She went out some, but she never said much about where she was or what she was doing. We didn't really know who she hung out with."

"Did she ever go to Hilltop House?"

Elizabeth's brow wrinkled. Then she got it and her eyes grew big. This was exciting. "Omigod. Did that Calloway freak get her?"

"Why would you ask that?" Luke said.

"I've seen the news."

Nick said, "We don't have any reason to believe that. But it turns out that she never was found. She's still missing."

The two girls gawked for a minute—Elizabeth gaping in earnest and Shea seeming to have trouble wrapping her mind around anything.

Luke prompted, "So did she? Ever have any connection to Hilltop House?"

Elizabeth shook her head. "Not that I kn—"

"Yes." Shea.

"She did?" Elizabeth asked.

"She applied for a job there. Said she wanted to work the night desk or gift shop or something, get a little cash for—" She stopped. Oops.

"Drugs," Luke said.

"Maybe."

Nick felt a tingle. "Are you sure? I mean about going for a job at Hilltop House."

"Yeah. One of the other girls on our floor worked there, helping out with breakfasts on weekends. That's what gave Shelly the idea. But I don't think she ever worked there. She just...inquired."

Luke said, "Did you mention that to the agents you spoke with? Two FBI guys came from Pittsburgh and interviewed you."

"I don't think so," Shea said. "I mean, you two asked specifically about Hilltop House. They didn't."

"Did Shelly meet Jack Calloway?" Nick asked. "Did she say anything about him?"

That question seemed to give Shea a headache. "Geesh...I don't know. Not that I remember. I think she just talked to Mrs. Calloway."

"Listen, girls," Nick said, and got the feeling Elizabeth was insulted by the characterization. She stuck out her boobs a little. "You gotta think about this hard. Could Shelly have struck up a relationship with Jack Calloway around that time? Did she have something sexual going on with him?"

Elizabeth grimaced. "Ick. He's like, old."

"Did she?"

The roommates looked at each other, clearly baffled.

"I don't think so," Elizabeth finally said. "I mean, Shelly was a lesbo."

Nick blinked. *Whoa*.

He and Luke poked around a little longer but in the end, the only thing the roommates seemed sure of was that Shelly *hadn't* had an affair with Jack. "*With his* wife *she might've...Not with* him..."

Nick stood, pocketing the find from the sofa, and looked down at Shea in the gaudy mushroom chair. "I want you to come downtown tomorrow morning and give a statement about Shelly going to Hilltop House. Can you do that?"

She hauled herself out of the chair. "I guess so."

"No," Nick said, putting a little edge in his voice. "I mean, can you do that *straight*?"

Caught. She swallowed. "I'm...okay."

"Bullshit." Nick got in her face, wagged a finger. "Don't touch another joint or drink before you come to my office tomorrow. Do you understand? I want you clear. If you're hazy, or if you don't show up at all, I'm coming back here and I'm gonna bust you both for possession and anything else I can think of. Fuck up your senior year."

"There's nothing here..."

"Oh, for God's sake," Nick said. He held up the baggie of grass he'd pulled out from between the couch cushions. It was the pipe that had poked him in the hip. "You might've at least put it in the freezer, down your bra or something."

Elizabeth shrugged. "I don't wear one," and Shea pouted, "Okay, okay, I'll be there..."

Nick hit the office, waiting for Schaberg to bring in Ace Holmes, and called Pittsburgh. He woke up Louis

Feldman to confirm that Shelly Quinn had been a lesbian. If so, then she probably hadn't been a lover of Jack's.

"Well, could be, maybe," Feldman said, groggy. "She was getting high with men and women alike. But I always did wonder why there was no boyfriend. She was a looker."

CHAPTER
37

WHERE ARE THE

Erin and Hannah formed little chunks of dough into balls, then rolled them in a bowl of cinnamon sugar and set them a couple of inches apart on a cookie sheet. "Dad's not gonna believe this," Hannah said. "He doesn't think you know how to cook anything."

"I can do cookies," Erin said, though if she thought about it, she hadn't done any in...about twelve years. "These were my brother's favorites. Snickerdoodles. He didn't like fancy cookies with lots of stuff in them like chocolate chips or nuts or anything. Just liked plain old sugar cookies with cinnamon."

And when the first batch came out of the oven, Erin poured two glasses of milk and they ate snickerdoodles and talked about cooking and school and Hannah's grandparents, and eventually, her mom.

"She was really pretty. Daddy says he can see her in me."

"I don't doubt it. You're awfully pretty yourself."

"No, I'm not. I've got these crooked teeth right here..." She bared her teeth and poked her finger at them.

"All ten-year-olds have crooked teeth. They come in wacky. If they don't straighten, then you get braces for a while, and poof. Straight teeth."

"Did you have braces?"

"Sure. 'Cause all these right here"—she rubbed a finger over all her front teeth—"were like this." She cocked her finger sideways in her mouth and they were both giggling when the phone rang. Hannah picked it up, talked for two minutes, and hung up. She frowned. "Dad. He says I have to go to bed."

Erin looked at the clock. Just after ten. "Uh-oh. We're caught. You'll be wiped out tomorrow if you don't get some sleep."

"I guess."

"Do you need a bath, or shower?"

"I do it in the mornings. But..." She hesitated, mulling something over.

"What?"

"We're reading these stupid stories in Ms. Moran's class...It's a unit on fairy tales, because The Ritz did *Hansel and Gretel* and we went to see it as a field trip, and I was wondering...Would you read a couple to me? I mean, I can read and everything, but sometimes Daddy still reads to me and I like it."

"Sure, come on," Erin said, amazed at how much the request touched her. "I like fairy tales."

"You do?" Hannah's eyes got huge, like she couldn't believe that. "Have you ever actually *read* any?"

Erin chuckled. "Well, not for a long time, I guess."

"That explains it," she said, trotting up the stairs. "The Grimm Brothers were psychos."

Ace Holmes was mostly sober but feeling like shit when he came in with Roger Schaberg. Schaberg had already interrogated the hell out of him.

"He was gonna meet Rebecca at five-thirty this morning, a block from her house. They were going to Buffalo."

"Buffalo. Why Buffalo?" Nick asked.

Holmes said, "I got a cousin there, owns a bar. Becca could work there."

Schaberg went on: "Ace says he went to pick her up, but she wasn't there."

"At five-thirty?" Nick asked.

"I mighta been a little late."

"How late?"

"Ten, fifteen minutes. Not more."

"So," Schaberg continued, "since Ace was packed up and all, and Becca didn't show, he decided to just go ahead without her. Thought she might've changed her mind and be pressing a rape charge. Then he got sidetracked in Elyria and couldn't keep his temper in check. The cops up there wouldn't't've tagged him if he hadn't been fighting."

Nick said, "Thanks, Roger. You can go now."

Schaberg lifted his eyebrows, catching on. He shifted his feet. "Uh, listen, Nick...," he said just under his breath. "I already got everything Ace kno—"

"I said, you can go." Nick didn't take his eyes off Ace Holmes as he said it. Roger gave a very believable impression of a man who was truly concerned, shot a worried look at Holmes, then sort of backed out of the room. Later, Nick would have to commend him for the performance.

When he was gone, Nick braced his hands on the arms of Holmes's chair. "Now it's just you and me, Ace," he said, his voice barely above a whisper. "You, and me, and not a camera or tape recorder in sight. Do you know what I think should happen to men who kidnap girls?"

"I didn't fuckin' kidnap her." Holmes was an asshole

and a bully, but he was a stupid son of a bitch, too. The idea of tangling with a psycho cop alone and off the record scared the shit out of him. Too much TV. "She wanted to go," he said. "She's been beggin' me to go. Jesus fuckin' Christ, man. I didn't kidnap that cunt."

His sincerity was almost believable. A boulder of fear dropped on Nick's chest. "Then where is she?"

"Well, shit, you're the cop. You figure it out."

She wanted to go...She's been beggin' me to go...I didn't fuckin' kidnap her...

Ace was lying. He had to be.

Ten, fifteen minutes late. Not more...

You're lying, Holmes. Where is she?

You're the cops...You figure it out...

Twenty more minutes with Holmes, and Nick stormed from the interview room, reeling. Ace *wasn't* lying. If Becca hadn't met Ace, then she'd been missing since early this morning. Nineteen hours ago.

The rage jumped him. *Blind.* That's what Erin had said of her mother and he was no better. Couldn't see what was right under his nose, not even when Erin was screaming and pointing a finger at it.

Or *wouldn't* see it. That was worse.

He yanked open his desk drawer. Cigarette. They were there, a brand-new pack, and Nick slammed the drawer shut again. Didn't want one. Bad habit gone by the wayside. All it had taken was two men dead and a missing woman, a nice, juicy mystery to unravel and a first-rate villain to chase. Nick was in his element now. Hell, if another one or two of his charges got murdered, he could stop drinking tequila and shooting at demons.

What a sick son of a bitch.

He curled his fingers into fists, then forced himself to move. He found Luke firing up a fresh pot of coffee.

"I figured you were about to call a meeting," Luke said.

"How soon can you get me some Feds?" Nick asked.

"Let's find out."

Luke left and Nick got on the phone. He sent four deputies to start searching the block where Rebecca had been planning to meet Ace and warned them the FBI would be joining them. To his office, he called in the core crew: Quentin, Schaberg, Hogue, and Jensen. Not Fruth; Fruth was posted at his house. Meeting in forty-five minutes, he told them. Come prepared for the duration.

No one would be going home again until Rebecca was found.

While he waited for the team to arrive, Nick made a quick run home. He wanted to see Hannah, and clutch her against his heart. Wanted to see Erin, and do more than that.

No time.

He stepped into his kitchen, and the aroma of hot baked cinnamon curled around him. A pile of cookies sat on a plate and another batch had been set out on a rack to cool. He dropped his jacket over a kitchen chair and popped a cookie into his mouth. Sweet, on the verge of gooey but not quite, and the delight of chewing it in his warm, safe kitchen brought a shudder of fear for Rebecca. Cold night, and she was out there somewhere, *not* running away with her boyfriend...

He left his jacket but not his gun or wallet. He wouldn't be here long.

He went upstairs, planning to check in on Hannah and make sure Erin was willing to stay put until morning.

He paused in the hallway to shake off the tension. Didn't want either one of them to see how worried he was.

Erin's voice drifted to his ears first. "...the old woman had only pretended to be so kind; she was in reality a wicked witch, who lay in wait for children, and had only built the little house of bread in order to entice them there. When a child fell into her power, she killed it, threw it in an oven and cooked and ate it, and that was a feast day with her. Witches have red eyes, and cannot see far, but they have a keen scent like the beasts, and are aware when human beings draw near...."

"Nice," Nick said, and Erin about jumped out of her skin. "You're reading horror stories to my daughter before bed."

"Daddy!" Hannah jumped to her knees on the bed, and D.D., who'd been lying across her feet, pumped his tail against the bed.

"Some watchdog you are," Nick said, patting the dog with one hand. With the other, he hugged Hannah close. Hard.

D.D. got jealous, nudged them apart, and tried to lick Nick across the face.

"Yech," he said to the dog. "You smell like cinnamon."

D.D. seemed pleased with that, and plopped back down on the bed. Nick looked at Erin, cozied up in the rocking chair in his daughter's room, a book in her lap, and a tiny smear of cinnamon on her chin.

Thmp.

"Hannah told me she's supposed to read these for school," Erin said, defending herself.

"Psycho tales," Hannah said.

"What the hell—"

"Quarter," Hannah said, but Erin held up the book to show him.

"Oh, the fairy tales," Nick said. "Quent was griping about Marissa reading those. Which one is that?"

"*Hansel and Gretel.* You know, Dad, if they made movies out of these, they'd be rated like double R or something. Witches with red eyes, moms who dump their kids in the forest so they don't have to feed them, cats who pretend to be friends with mice and then eat them..."

"I don't remember a cat in *Hansel and Gretel.*"

"That was another one," Erin said. "This is our fourth."

He grunted. "Obviously I wasn't specific enough when I called and said, 'Go to bed.' I meant, 'Go to sleep.'"

He kissed Hannah and turned off her light, followed Erin down to the kitchen. He knew he should tell her to get lost. He knew he should make her understand that someday she might decide to go to a restaurant and some bastard who hated him would pop her in the chest. He knew he should make her understand that he couldn't keep her safe. Not even in Hopewell.

Instead, he pushed her back against the sink and kissed her. Thoroughly, desperately. A deep, turbulent kiss that turned her liquid in his arms and left him aching to possess her and protect her the way a man should.

"Okay, okay," she said, pulling back. She was gasping for air. "I agree, wholeheartedly. But maybe we should wait until Hannah's asleep."

"I can't," he said. "I have to get back."

She blinked. "Oh. Uh-oh. What happened? Something about Shelly?"

"No," he said, still trying to shake off the effects of the kiss. Not damned likely. "Shelly didn't have an affair with Jack," he said. "She was a lesbian."

Erin's eyes got big. "Then he wouldn't have killed her. She's not one of the victims."

"That's our hope."

"Oh, my God, that's wonderful. That's..." She rose on her tiptoes and kissed him, her arms looping around his neck. Nick cupped her ass and lifted her onto the counter, mouths open and bodies straining to come together through their clothes.

He groaned and ripped away. "Ah, God, Erin," he said, his heart drumming like a timpani. "I can't do this right now. I can't—"

She stiffened. "What happened?"

"Things are moving. I just came back to see Hannah, and ask...Would you stay with her the rest of tonight? Deputy Fruth is parked out front, watching the house. But I have to get back."

She was taking a minute to process things. Thinking about letting him take care of Justin while she babysat Hannah. "Nick, what happened?"

"We found Ace Holmes. Becca isn't with him."

Her face drained of color. "Oh, God, Calloway's out there, isn't he? He's got Becca—"

"I don't know, sweetheart. But Ace has me ninety percent convinced he hasn't seen her, and Jack *could* still be alive. All I know right now is that Becca's missing. And she's in trouble."

Erin pushed off the counter and looked up at him. Laid a hand on his cheek. "Then you'd better go find her."

The Angelmaker watched the sheriff leave his house. Wait, now. Don't be in a hurry. Wouldn't want to emerge from the backyard tree house too soon and find out that Mann forgot something and came back. Just wait back here in the woods.

The night was young.

CHAPTER
38

A REPEAT OF THE NIGHT BEFORE: late meeting in Nick's office. The difference was the addition of a murdered minister and a missing woman. And two days of dragging the quarry. Divers had quit looking for Calloway's body.

The mood was different, too. No one was sitting down scratching his head in contemplation over Jack's *suicide*. Now a minister was shot and a nineteen-year-old woman was gone. And while it had been easy to believe Rebecca might have gone willingly with Ace Holmes, no one believed that if Jack Calloway was still alive, she'd have gone willingly with him. To a man, they were bouncing on the balls of their feet.

Nick said, "We'll tap the FBI. This is the kind of shit they do."

"Suits," Wart grumbled.

"Suits, maybe," Nick said, "but we'll have to scour the whole neighborhood around Rebecca's house—people, sidewalks, Dumpsters, buildings, everything—and that'll take manpower. And put Rebecca's picture on the news, every half hour. Like an Amber Alert."

"We'll get the Feds to monitor a tips line while we

pound the pavement. People will talk to us better. But sooner or later"—Quent looked around, all of them an hour past exhaustion, running on adrenaline and caffeine and now fear—"we're gonna need some sleep. A few Feds could keep things rolling."

"Tell you what," Nick said. "I've worked a few task forces with the Feds. Some things, they're good at. And I don't wanna be the one telling Leni Engel that we're not calling in the big guns because we don't work and play well with others. Everyone got that?"

They did.

"Jensen," Nick said, "put together pictures of Rebecca and get them all over the media along with the details of where she disappeared. I want at least four more of us canvassing Becca's neighborhood. There has to be something there."

"Gonna scare this town half to death," Schaberg said.

"They need to be scared." Nick smothered the thought and turned to the wall where he'd hung a large whiteboard. A matrix of thoughts webbed the board, scribbles he'd used over the past few days to organize ideas, brainstorm, try to tie things together. One side worked the case as if Jack were alive, the other side as if he weren't. On the second side, where Jack was dead, one arm considered him the victim of murder, the other the victim of suicide.

Too many unknowns. And the only constant in every scenario was . . . Margaret.

"Gotta consider it," Quentin said. They all knew Nick was looking at her name. "If we buy into the idea that Lauren McAllister, Sara Daniels, *maybe* Shelly Quinn, and now Rebecca Engel have disappeared from the face of the earth, and accept that Jack didn't do it—at least not

Rebecca and probably not Shelly Quinn—then there are only two other people in the same orbit."

"Margaret and who? Rodney?" Schaberg snorted. "The minister's bullet wound was a pretty good shot for a blind man."

"Besides which," Jensen said, "he can't drive. The killer would have to have a car to manage the distances and times of these murders. No way Rodney could have done them. Not here, not in Florida."

"Unless he had help," Hogue said. "A driver."

Which led them back to Margaret again.

Always gotta look at the spouse. Beneath Margaret's name, three lines sprawled out with ideas jotted on each: *betrayed wife, motive, opportunity.* Similar lines dropped down from Jack's name, but at least where Rebecca Engel was concerned, Jack supposedly lacked the third quality: opportunity.

Supposedly. Then again, what better way to allay suspicion of committing a crime than to be thought dead when the crime occurs?

Nick added a new line from Margaret: *afraid of minister?*

"God," Jensen said, shaking his head.

Quent said, "Margaret knew Carl Whitmore came in here and talked to Nick. She knew Jack had spent the day at the chapel. If she did something to those women and thought Jack knew it, it makes sense that she'd worry about Carl having too much information."

Nick turned to Jensen. "Dig up some background on Margaret; her maiden name is Devilas, like Rodney's mother. Find out if there's something there that no one knows."

"Wife rage? Split personality?"

"Whatever." Too much talk. Time to move. "Roger, get out with the search team. Jensen, keep with the phones, the list of college girls. Stay with Shelly Quinn until you find her."

"Shelly Quinn doesn't fit the pattern. She never had an affair with Jack."

"Sounds like she might have met Margaret, though," said Quentin. "Margaret wouldn't be the first woman to knock off another one out of jealousy."

"Or two, or five?" Wart said.

Schaberg: "So where was she at five-fifteen this morning?"

"Tucked in bed alone, probably," Jensen said. "An alibi that makes sense, but can't be verified."

"Find out," Nick said, then clapped his hands. "Let's go. Wherever Becca is, she doesn't have time for us to sit on our asses."

Glances bounced around the room. No one was sitting.

The room started to clear, but Chris Jensen stopped. "Hey, uh, Sheriff? Dr. Sims isn't at the motel. Where is she?"

Nick scowled, and Jensen smiled.

"Son of a bitch," said Roger. "You won the pool, didn't you, Jensen? Nick, you SOB . . ."

"I'm rich," Jensen said, as Nick's desk phone rang.

"Fuck you all," he said, and picked it up.

It was Dispatch. "Sheriff, we just got a nine-one-one call. Your house is on fire."

CHAPTER
39

WE FOUND ACE HOLMES. Becca isn't with him...

Erin wandered the great room, looking at nothing, feeling the walls closing in around her. She wanted to help. She wanted to be with Nick, searching for Rebecca, talking to neighbors, giving interviews for TV—doing *something*. But she knew Nick was doing everything that could be done. For the first time in twelve years, someone had listened and taken on the fight with her.

And she loved being here in the circle of warmth and love and safety Nick had created for Hannah. Wouldn't mind being in that circle tomorrow, and the next day—

CRASH.

Erin jumped. Glass shattered at the back of the house, and something hit the floor. D.D. flew down the stairs from Hannah's room, barking. Erin, heart in her throat, followed him toward the great room.

And saw flames. Huge, bright gold flames climbing the drapes, *whooshing* up the side of the wall and spilling across the carpet.

Erin called for D.D., who backed away but kept barking. She raced for a phone, realized she didn't know where one was, then remembered the one in Nick's office. She grabbed it and ran up the stairs, dialing and trying to dig in her purse for her gun at the same time, screaming for Hannah.

Hannah came out of bed, wide-eyed but only half-awake. "Get up," Erin yelled. "Fire."

The nine-one-one operator came on while they were running down the stairs. Hannah screamed for D.D. and Erin pushed her ahead and said, "Go," then veered to the back of the house and peered into the darkness outside. Something moved. She grabbed her gun and fired a shot, watched the movement and fired another one. Then the hot tongues of the flames licked too close and she dashed out after Hannah, trying to come up with the address for the house, and in the end just shouting, "The sheriff's house is on fire; the sheriff's house is on fire."

Nick almost beat the fire trucks to his house, but not quite. When he got there, he saw water running like a giant fountain, a fire truck in his drive along with a smaller Emergency Response Team truck, and Luke, who had been on his way back to the house when the call came in.

Nick jumped out of the Tahoe, his heart squeezing like a fist. Luke jogged to meet him.

"It's good, man, it's good. No one's hurt," he said, putting a hand on Nick's chest to slow him down. It didn't work and Luke grabbed him by the shirt. "Stop!" he shouted. "You're gonna scare Hannah to death. Calm down."

The words finally penetrated. "No one's hurt?" Nick asked, blowing like a winded racehorse.

"No one's hurt. Your house didn't even get much damage.

Just one room. Erin called it in the second it happened. It's cool, man. Relax."

"Where's Hannah?"

Luke slapped him on the back a couple times: Everything okay. "Over there," he said, pointing at the ERT truck. "She's sitting in the back."

Hannah unwound her arms from the dog's neck and ran to Nick. He held her, squeezing, swaying, and pressed her face against his neck.

She squeaked. "I can't . . . breathe, Daddy."

"Okay, okay," Nick said, and loosened his grip. The dog circled his knees.

"Pet D.D.," Hannah ordered. "He's scared, too."

Nick hiked her onto his hip like he'd done when she was little, and dangled a hand to the dog. He looked at the back of the ERT truck, where Erin stood watching them.

Nick, I'm scared.

I've got it covered, Allison. Let me handle it.

A wave of grief washed over him—for what he was about to lose. He couldn't say for sure whether loving Erin would have saved his sorry soul from the life he'd made for himself, but he'd never know now. A woman loved by Nick Mann might as well wear a target on her back. He couldn't do anything about Hannah belonging to him. But he could sure as hell keep Erin away.

A shout went up and the water fountain died, a couple of firefighters dragging on the hose. Nick stripped his gaze from Erin and saw Quentin and Luke take flashlights around to the back of the house, walking through the running puddles of water and ash. He put Hannah down.

"Stay here," he commanded, and followed. The picture window off the deck was broken; the sofa and curtains just inside totally destroyed, and the carpet burned in a design Nick had seen before. He glanced around, looking for the bottle shards, and saw them almost right away.

"Molotov cocktail," Luke said. "From the back. Must have come in on foot."

"Had to," Nick said. "I had a deputy out front."

Quentin said, "We'll get some floodlights out here and search the yard, figure out which way this motherfucker came in." No sense in focusing here, where the hoses had already washed away the evidence.

"Start a canvass on Birch Street." Birch was the closest street running *behind* Nick's house.

Fruth walked in. "Where did Dr. Sims come up with a gun?" he asked Nick.

"What?"

"She fired two rounds out the back just before she and Hannah came running out. Five seconds after the flames started."

Nick looked at Quentin. "Find those bullets. They'll be .22s from a Derringer. I want to know if one's missing."

"Think she hit him?"

"On the run, through flames, in the dark with a .22? Doubtful." But they could hope.

They looked at the carnage for another minute and Luke shook his head. "If they'd been asleep, if Erin hadn't been awake and walking around downstairs when it came in..."

He didn't need to finish. Nick looked at him. "I want you with Hannah and Mom."

Luke nodded. "I was just thinking that."

They talked for five minutes; then Nick went back to Hannah, wanting to die inside, but presenting a strong front. Luke would take her and they'd go root Grandma out of bed. Take a little spontaneous vacation.

Hannah didn't fall for it. "You just want me out of the way."

"Never," Nick said. "But I want you safe. And Grandma, too. So we're gonna let Uncle Luke be your personal bodyguard."

"What about Erin? Doesn't she need a bodyguard, too?"

Nick looked past Hannah to where Erin stood, stiff as a nutcracker soldier. "Erin's going away, too."

Hannah frowned, then leaned in close. "I don't think she'll want to."

"It doesn't matter a damn what she wants."

"Quarter. Are you two going to have a fight?"

"Probably," Nick said darkly.

"Who's going to win?"

"I am."

"I wish I was allowed to fight with you like that."

"Well, you're not," Nick said, giving her one last kiss. "So get the hell out of here."

"Quarter," Hannah said, and trotted off to Luke.

"Goddamn it."

He made a beeline to Erin, whose spine grew taller with every step he took.

"No," she said, before he even got to her.

Half of Hopewell's emergency response team members stood in the cold night, studying their toes and scrupulously not watching. Nick clasped her arm and pulled her into the garage.

She felt brittle and small and if someone hurt her, he'd be responsible for it. He should have heeded the warning bells going off in his head when he came home to the aroma of snickerdoodles. Should have remembered that for a woman, being in his life was the kiss of death. Like trusting him.

Allison had learned that. So had Rebecca Engel.

His heart wrenched with a knowledge he held in his bones but hadn't yet muttered in conscious realms: Rebecca was dead and that was on him. If he'd only opened his eyes and accepted what Erin had known all along: *Yes, here. Yes, on your watch.* Instead, he'd accepted a notion better-suited to Hopewell—that Becca had run off with her boyfriend.

I'm scared, Nick.

I'll handle it... It's okay.

Not this time.

He got into the garage and seized her arms. "I want you out of here. Out of Hopewell."

"No."

"Damn it, Erin."

"What about Justin? Have you forgotten about him?"

Nick stepped back. Christ. He *had* forgotten about him. For Nick, it was all about Becca now. And Jack Calloway and Carl Whitmore and the girls on a list. It was all about Hopewell.

Yes. He'd forgotten about Justin.

"I can help," Erin said.

"How?" he snapped. "By getting killed?"

"Katie. If Becca's not with Ace, then Katie is the key. She knows something, even if she doesn't know what it is."

"Baker is working with—"

"She won't talk to that Baker quack, and you know it. But she'll talk to me. You need me."

"I don't need you."

"Then you want me." She said it with such hopeful conviction that he stared at her. Jesus, yes, he wanted her. And that very fact made her a target.

"I wanted you," he said, stiffening his resolve. He dropped his hands. "I wanted you for a tumble and it was great. But it's too inconvenient to keep you around for just that. By the way, Jensen won the pool."

She looked like she'd been slapped. Nick felt a chunk of his heart fall away. He steeled himself against it and turned away. He didn't want to see the shudder of pain that rippled through her.

But instead of shuddering with pain, she came around to face him, squaring her shoulders. "Liar," she said.

"Excuse me?"

"You don't get to throw me out of town because you're afraid of caring for me."

He was taken aback.

"You're a coward," she said. "If you want to get rid of me, okay. But at least be honest about your motives. It isn't because all we had was a tumble. It's because we had more. So much more, it scares you."

"Don't shrink me, Doctor. You won't like what you find."

"I already know what I'll find. I'll find a man who's spent five years pretending he's happy chasing shoplifters and arresting drunks. I'll find a man who's been punishing himself, one cigarette at a time, for giving up on the big cases. A man who's trying to live with the fact that the criminals he once chased are still out there killing people, while he's hiding here in Hopewell. So he goes to his wife's woods once a year and takes out his frustrations on pieces of paper—"

"I don't have time for this," Nick growled.

"I'll find a man who says he wants peace and quiet in his town, but who hasn't felt so alive in the past five years as he has in the past five days."

He glared at her. "I don't *enjoy* having my town terrorized, damn you."

"No, of course you don't. But don't you see, Nick? This is big. Life and death. It's okay to want to be a hero. It's not just what you do. It's who you are."

"Are you finished? Because Deputy Hogue is waiting to take you to a—"

"It's too late to get rid of me. I mean, you *can,* physically. You can have me removed and I can't stop you because you have an army of deputies to carry out any order you give."

"Then go peacefully so I won't have to waste manpower. We're spread a little thin right now."

"And what about Katie? Are you going to let Rebecca die out there while Andrew Baker drugs Katie and drives her into a hole?"

Rebecca's already dead. The thought squeezed his heart.

"Maybe it's too late for Rebecca," Erin said, reading his mind. She spoke through gritted teeth. "But it's not too late for Justin. There's still two more days. Please, Nick. It's still my fight, and for the first time ever, I feel like I may win. Because I have you fighting with me."

Nick gazed down at her and saw what she must have been fifteen years ago—a terrified girl with a pistol, trying to keep her and her brother safe. She'd been fighting monsters all her life. Alone.

"You can do the cop things," she said. "But I think I can get through to Katie. You just have to let me."

"She's right, Nick."

Quentin. His voice was quiet, his expression resolved.

Nick grimaced. Tension reached down his neck through his shoulders and arms and curled his hands into fists. Tension, and maybe something else. Fear.

He looked at Erin for a full ten seconds, then grabbed her by the jacket. He pulled her up and kissed her, hard. When he was finished, he glared at Quentin. "Put someone on her," he ordered. "All the time."

CHAPTER
40

Back to headquarters, in the wee hours of the morning. The fire had cost him more time in the hunt for Rebecca: working the scene, talking to Mrs. Piltzecker and other neighbors, processing. He thought about the delay. If this were a cop movie, that's what the fire would be—the murderer trying to distract them, tie them up while something else was happening.

But it didn't feel like that. It felt like someone had gone after Erin. And the fact that Hannah was in the way... Jesus.

Bishop met him at the office. "Geez, Sheriff. Is everyone okay?"

Nick gave him a *Reader's Digest* version of the fire, then said, "I want you to talk to Margaret Calloway. I wanna know where she was when Rebecca Engel disappeared, between five-fifteen and five-forty-five this morning."

Bishop looked at his watch. "You mean yesterday morning."

"Yeah," Nick said, with the razor edge of guilt cutting in. Wednesday morning now. Justin's execution was scheduled for midnight Thursday. "Push her. Scare her if you need to." He thought about the Molotov cocktail. An easy enough weapon. Anyone who could log onto the Internet could make one. "And find out if she went anywhere late tonight."

"Okay." Bishop held out his hand. An envelope. "This was on the front door just now."

Nick took it. "You see who left it?"

"No, sir. Nobody around."

Nick opened the envelope. It was typewritten and sent ice through his veins.

                      ROBIN WEELKES

He dropped the note as if it burned him. "Don't touch that," he said, and shot out the front door. Bishop followed him outside, following instinct. They picked up Quentin on the sidewalk.

"Looking for the person who left a note on the door," Nick said.

The three of them scattered, scouring the street, the parking lot, the area around the courthouse and jail. Spent fifteen minutes looking.

No one. One in the morning. No one.

They jogged back together, convening on the lawn of the courthouse. Nick was still catching his breath. "The note wasn't here when I left."

Bishop said, "Maybe someone was out late, saw something. I'll keep looking."

Nick blew out a breath. "Goddamn it."

Quent was panting, but didn't know why. "I'm lost. What note?"

Nick told him, then shook his head. He couldn't seem to get his heart to settle down.

"Ah, man," Quent said. "Someone's giving us clues."

But Nick didn't think so. It felt more to him like someone was pulling their strings, watching them dance. Manipulating them and enjoying the show.

"So, who's Robin Weelkes?" Quentin asked.

"I don't know," Nick said. "But I'd bet my left nut it's the name of a missing woman."

"Weelkes."

An office clerk named Brendan Madigan, a stout Irishman with a tendency to break into tenor arias when he got drunk, scanned the master list of names. He'd become the lead on a four-person team trying to locate missing students from the past five years.

"Not here. We've been going alphabetically so I thought maybe we just hadn't gotten to her yet. But Weelkes isn't here at all."

"Find her."

Madigan rubbed a hand over his face, but didn't say the obvious. Middle of the night didn't seem to matter to the sheriff anymore.

Nick walked across the street to the lab. Martin Gamble's prairie-dog eyes had the look of a sleep-deprived mouse.

"Couldn't this have happened during the daytime?" he griped. He held up the envelope, now stuck inside a plastic bag. "Yours, Sheriff. No one else's prints anywhere on the note. I haven't checked the envelope yet, but the note itself was handled by someone wearing gloves. Someone being careful."

"What about the typeface, the lettering?"

He shook his head. "Courier font, 10-point. Every computer in the state can do it. And the paper is standard white Georgia-Pacific; I buy it ten reams at a time at—"

"Ink?"

"Give me a little while and I could determine the type of cartridge, maybe..."

"Give me *something*."

Gamble hummed a note. "Find me a printer."

Nick's brows went up.

"Printers are almost like fingerprints. They have a specific pattern to their lettering—heavier ink in the upper right corner of a line, for example, or a little less weight to the 'Q,' like that. If you bring me the suspect's printer, chances are good I can tell you whether or not that printer did this note."

"Suspect?" Nick said. "What fucking suspect?"

But on the way out, he had a thought: "How fast could you tell me if that note was printed on the same machine that printed Jack's suicide note?"

Martin rubbed his chin, then pulled a copy of Jack's suicide note from a file. He eyeballed both notes through a magnifying glass. "I can tell you right now. It wasn't."

Bad to worse. Six investigators went to the street where Becca lived. Nick sent two pairs block to block, on foot, scouting with high-powered flashlights, checking everything they could find, including trash. While they got started, he knocked on Leni's door, with Erin in tow.

"Did you find her?" Leni asked, through a stuffy nose. Her eyes were red-rimmed.

"Not yet," Nick said.

"Then go to hell." She slammed the door but Nick stuck his boot in the corner. "Leni. I need to talk to you."

"So you can put the daughter I have left in jail?"

"Honey, you know that isn't what I'm about. Let us in."

There were too many years between them, too much

friendship, and Leni was too beat-up to fight him. "Sam Fulton will have my hide," she said, naming Katie's public defender.

"So call him if you want to. But I swear to you, Leni, we're not trying to pin anything on Katie. I don't think she killed Jack or Carl Whitmore. Neither does anybody else. By tomorrow, we'll know for certain that your gun wasn't fired, and Katie's part in this will be over. But before that, we've got to know what was going on with Becca. Katie's the one who may know." He stepped back, touched the small of Erin's back to move her forward. "I don't care about protocol anymore, Leni. You want Erin with Katie, you got her."

Leni thought about it, then backed up. The look in her eyes sent a wave of horror through Nick. What if it were Hannah, gone, into the dust?

Stop it.

"Listen, Leni," Nick said. "Ace Holmes swears Becca wasn't with him. I believe him."

A split second of disbelief, then the panic took over. "He's lying. The bastard's lying..."

"I don't think so."

"Let *me* talk to him." She started past Nick, hysteria moving her toward the door, and Nick caught her, bullied her into his arms. She wailed and slapped at him, and he held her and fielded her panic until it faded, then took her by both arms and pushed her back a step. He wanted to say that he'd find Becca and everything would be all right, but the words jammed in his throat. In the end, all Nick could manage to say to her mother was, "God, I'm sorry."

Erin stepped in. "Leni, I think Katie will talk to me."

"No," she said, and when Nick opened his mouth, she added, "Not because I don't want her to, but because she's asleep. Baker gave her a sleeping pill." She looked at Erin. "That damned Dr. Baker, he drove her into a shell. He accused her of being jealous because Becca had the boys. Katie just clammed up." Tears came. "I'm afraid I'll never get either one of my girls back."

Erin touched Leni's arm. "I'll get Katie back."

Nick caught Erin's eye; this was her element—dealing with victims. He had no business putting her back with the Engel family, but he was going to do it anyway. "Okay. In the morning, then. Fulton can be here if you want. Put Erin with Katie as soon as she wakes up."

Leni nodded and looked at Erin. "You can try. But I don't know if she's in there anymore."

Erin stayed with Leni, and Nick waited until a deputy showed up to watch the house. It was almost two o'clock in the morning. He had just shut the door behind him when his radio burped.

"Sheriff." It was a deputy named Cutter. "We're on North Franklin Street, across from the back of Woode's place, with Lud Ferguson. You better come."

CHAPTER
41

WOODE'S WAS AN ANCIENT neighborhood grocery in a depressed section of Hopewell, a couple of miles off the main drag. It had survived the era of twenty-four-hour Krogers and SuperWalmarts out of sheer stubbornness. Chuck Woode would hack up a side of beef for a customer any way they wanted, and because he was that kind of a guy, he'd take the time to wipe his hands on his apron before he sliced a hunk of cheese to go with it.

The back of Woode's was precisely what you'd expect: a Dumpster, a bunch of cardboard boxes and crates, a truck that had rusted there since the '60s, a whole lot of trash. For a five-block stretch, the streets were lined with bars, a couple of low-end sandwich shops, and Hopewell's only tattoo parlor. If Hopewell had a slum, this was it. Eighty percent of the crimes Nick dealt with, though mostly petty, came from this area.

Lud Ferguson—short for Ludwig—was a drunk. He'd spent a number of nights in temporary lockup, usually for his own safety. As far as Nick knew, he'd never hurt anyone, but neither had he ever worked except for the odd hour or two of chores here and there, and he was at least

occasionally influenced by voices in his head. Lud lived
on the kindness of neighbors and his ailing social security checks, which he gambled away in the back room of
Hank's each month.

Which was why Deputy Cutter had thought to ask the
question: What was Lud Ferguson doing with a brand-
new iPod?

When Nick and Quent arrived, Cutter and his partner, Browning, had Lud seated on the front stoop of a bar
under a sign reading HECK'S CASH D HERE—with an unnecessary apostrophe. Music leaked from ill-fitting windows
and the air smelled of onion rings and beer under a thin
layer of urine. The drizzle had stopped earlier in the day,
but the sharp edge of November cut through, men talking
through puffs of breath and hunched into their jackets.

"Lud," Nick asked. "I hear you got some new music."

"What's it to ya?" Lud asked, and Nick frowned. One
thing about hometown drunks—they were unusually
good-natured. Most of the occasions on which Lud had
been taken into custody, he'd gone in smiling: gonna get
a warm bed for the night and hot breakfast the next day, a
friendly deputy to chat with.

"Where'd you get it?" Nick asked.

"Uh... Someone give it t' me."

Nick held out his hand, and Cutter handed over the
iPod, in a clear plastic bag. "You listen to it?"

Cutter said, "Lud's developed a fondness for Crystal
Bowersox."

"Huh," Nick said. Quentin moved in on the other
side. Lud wasn't usually stupid enough to try to outrun
the authorities; then again, Lud wasn't usually found in
possession of a missing woman's iPod. Nick propped a

booted foot on the step beside him, and bent down. "Let me tell you what's about to happen here, Lud, 'cause I'm just guessing you haven't heard."

Now a spark of worry flickered in the dull eyes. "Heard what?"

"That Rebecca Engel was kidnapped from a street near her house yesterday morning. We figure anyone who might have happened to, say, come across any of her belongings might be able to help us find her."

"Don't know no Rebecca Engel." His tongue flicked out like a lizard's. "Is that *Engel,* like in the rest'rent downtown?"

"You know what *Engel* it is," Nick countered. "Now let me tell you the rest of it. The rest of it is this, Lud: Anybody who did come across this girl's belongings but *doesn't* tell us about it, well he'd pretty much go straight to the top of our list for suspects in her kidnapping. We'd probably be inclined to think he'd done something to her. Murder, rape . . . Who knows?"

"I didn't murder no one." Getting nervous now, his eyes showing the whites.

"Then where did you get her iPod?"

"Found it. Just found it."

Nick's hand shot out. He curled Lud's shirt in his fist. "Don't lie to me, fucker, or if that girl's dead, I'll throw your ass in front of a jury for murder. With your priors, no one'll doubt it, and you know what? Even if they do doubt it, the jury'll say, 'Well, he might not've done the woman, but he's no good. Oughta be in jail for *something . . .*' That's what they'll say, Lud."

"I found it; it's *mine,*" he whined. The Wino's Code of Ownership.

Nick dropped him to the cement step. "Take him in,"

he said to Browning and Cutter. "Charge him with the kidnapping of Rebecca Engel, and don't waste a holding cell on him. Take him across the street to the jail."

"Whoa-whoa-whoa...," Lud sputtered, but Nick gave him his back. Three steps out, Lud said, "Wait. I'll tell ya, I'll tell ya..."

Nick turned, watching the weird hues of a Budweiser sign flash on Lud's face. "Tell me what?"

"In the Dumpster." He tipped his head toward the back lot of Woode's. "The Dumpster."

Nick froze. He glanced at Quentin, whose expression had gone to horror. They all turned and looked toward the Dumpster. "Ah, God, no," Nick said, but even as he strode the thirty yards across the cement, he was thinking about it, preparing himself for the sight of Rebecca's pale limbs bent on top of each other. He'd seen a woman in a Dumpster once before and the picture never went away. Tossed in like a rag doll, the killer apparently had held her by an ankle and a wrist, and when she'd landed, her lower back had hit the edge of an old window frame sticking up, folding her backward. Nick had hoisted himself over the Dumpster rim and seen her belly first, her spine broken over the edge of the window, her head and feet buried in the garbage people had thrown on her all day long....

The memory climbed on top of him and he stopped five yards from the Dumpster, swallowing back bile. Some ingrained habit from years gone by made him breathe through his mouth in preparation for the stench. Without speaking, Quentin laced his hands together and Nick stepped onto them, pushing his body above the rim. He swiveled to balance his butt on the corner of the Dumpster and took a flashlight from Quentin, swung the beam back and forth until he found it.

"Ah, Jesus," he said, and closed his eyes. Nick tilted his face skyward, muttering something that might have been a prayer. He took a minute to recover, then pushed off the ledge to the ground. "We better talk to Lud some more."

They were doing that when a car rolled up, slowed, and pulled on past, the silhouette of the driver showing a cell phone. Ten minutes later, Leslie Roach appeared with her band of photographers and bright white lights.

"Don't you ever sleep?" Nick asked, walking away from Lud, who had begun to chatter like a chipmunk once they emptied the Dumpster. "Or do you feed at night?"

The characterization seemed to please her. She smiled. "What happened?"

Nick walked past her. "Go to hell."

"I love it when you talk rough with me."

Nick stuck out his elbow to block her, not quite catching her in the face, but close enough that she backed off a step. He kept walking, and finally she stopped, planting her feet.

"You know I'm gonna print something," she called after him. "Would you rather I use fact from you or rumor from 'an unnamed source'? Or maybe it'll be about the local sheriff bedding down with a nutcase, that nutcase almost getting burned to death—"

Nick rounded on her. "Don't go anywhere *near* that."

"I'm shaking in my stilettos. Now tell me about this."

He cursed, but needed for the media to keep putting Rebecca's name and face out there. And to stay away from Erin. "Rebecca Engel," he said.

"You found her? Found Ace Holmes?"

"We found Holmes, but not Rebecca. We just pulled her suitcase from the Dumpster."

"Is she dead?"

"We're looking for her."

"Did Holmes kill her?"

"We're looking for her."

"Is she really a suspect in the murders of Jack Calloway and Carl Whitmore?"

"We're look—"

"What does that bum over there have to do with it? He rape her and kill her or something?"

"Well, Leslie, that would've made a great story," Nick said sardonically, "but I'm afraid we're still hoping she's alive."

"Can I quote you on that, Sheriff, that it would've been great to—"

Nick advanced on her, felt a tingle of satisfaction when she backed up a step, then became dimly aware that Leslie's photographer was no longer the only one shooting. The press had arrived, cameras rolling all over the place. Television now, not just the local newspaper milking the Calloway story. Cleveland, Columbus, Toledo. Hopewell TV news and weather came from all three, and each of them had sent someone in to feed on whatever carcasses they could find in Hopewell. If Nick could keep it in hand, the coverage might help find Rebecca, and maybe Shelly Quinn and Robin Weelkes. The flip side, though, was rumor and mayhem that served no purpose but to destroy anyone caught in it.

Nick bent his head to Leslie, boom mikes coming at them like cobras. He kept his voice low. "You took a scared single mom and a possum and turned it into a circus about misuse of county funds. You crucified Calvin

Lee. You put Katie Engel on the front page looking like a murderer. If you think I'm gonna give you one single, fucking thing, *Miz* Roach, you are out of your fucking mind."

He straightened, skimmed the collection of reporters surrounding them and pointed a finger at one. "You," he said. "Come here."

The towheaded reporter slid from the pack, hesitant, and inched toward Nick. Nick felt a pang of concern; this guy might be twenty. Didn't matter. "You wanna break this story?"

The guy danced on his feet. "Sure, Sheriff."

"Follow me."

While Leslie Roach steamed, Nick took the bubbling young reporter to where Quentin stood next to Lud. "What's your name?" Nick asked the guy.

"Jimmy—uh, James Forrester, Channel Twelve, WBH-TV, Cleveland."

Nick looked at Quent. "Deputy Vaega, this is James Forrester, with Channel Twelve, WBH-TV, Cleveland. Fill him in on Ferguson twenty minutes before we break it. Let Channel Twelve have it first."

And he walked back past Leslie, ignoring the growl deep in her throat. To the pack of other reporters, he said, "A lesson for all of you: Don't fuck with me."

Talk to Katie. Tear apart Lud Ferguson. Question Margaret. Find Robin Weelkes and Shelly Quinn. Track down the printer of the suicide note. Keep Erin safe . . .

Nick stretched out on the vinyl sofa in his office, the list of things to do reeling through his mind. He draped his arm across his forehead and closed his eyes. He'd sent the day crew home—they'd been up almost twenty-four hours. The night deputies and some guys pulling overtime were doing their normal shifts, plus plodding through the steps necessary to get the FBI tips line set up, pull in some Feds to help go block-to-block for any sign of Rebecca, and stay with the college rosters as much as they could during the middle of the night. Nick called in the canines from Crawford County and put them on the streets. The dogs lost Rebecca at the corner where Ace had said he was going to pick her up, but found the place Lud said he'd stumbled across the suitcase.

Maybe Lud was telling the truth.

Within an hour, the team had resigned itself to searching the neighborhood for clues rather than for Rebecca herself. She wasn't in the neighborhood anymore. She was in the Dumpster, her back broken and her hips hoisted up over a window frame, saying "I'm scared" while a tiny voice somewhere on the streets cried, "Mommy, Mommy..."

"Sheriff."

A calm voice, not a motherless toddler. Not Allison.

Sher-eef.

He shot up, found Valeria holding a mug of coffee. Feeble gray light crept between the office blinds. "Jesus, what time is it?"

"Almost eight," Valeria said.

Nick was confused. "Eight? How the hell—"

"I keep everyone away. You needed to sleep."

He started moving, hoping his brain would catch up with his body. He checked the date on his watch. Still Wednesday. Justin wouldn't die today.

"There was nothing for you to do," Valeria said. "You have the FBI and the entire sheriff's department and half of Ohio working to find Rebecca. Deputy Fruth said you only came back in at four-thirty, so you only been sleeping three hours. You needed it."

"Damn you, Valeria," Nick said, running his hands through his hair. He took the mug of coffee.

She said, "There's an FBI agent named Louis Feldman in the conference room. He drove in from Pittsburgh and met some Cleveland agents. And Fruth and Bishop are on their way in from the Engel neighborhood. They stayed with the search all night."

"Anything?"

"I don't think so."

Okay. The search had gone on while he slept; the other cops who'd gone home in the middle of the night would be back soon, and the FBI had arrived. Things were moving. Erin was at Leni's, and Hannah with his mom and Luke.

Valeria pointed at the hall tree where his jacket hung. "I went to your house and got you clothes. It's not too bad. The great room and part of the deck, that's all. The Fire Marshall kept someone there all night and got someone from Ace Hardware to board up the window."

"Good." Nick was still catching up. Talk to Katie. Tear apart Ferguson. Question Margaret...The list he'd fallen asleep on started through his mind again.

"Do you think she's still alive?" Valeria.

A pulse of grief tapped Nick's heart. "I hope so."

"You know," Valeria said, her voice tentative, "my Rosa has worked there, at Hilltop, how many years? Do you think—"

Nick stopped her. "Rosa's okay, sweetheart. She's married, stable, a family friend. Not the type of woman Jack was sleeping with." But even as he said it, the name Robin

Weelkes came to mind. Who was she? What was her story?

Add it to the list.

Valeria said, "By the way, the mayor called. And the commissioner. And the lieutenant governor."

"The lieutenant governor?" He'd expected the others.

"They all want to know the same thing."

"Yeah: Where is Rebecca Engel?"

Valeria shook her head. "They want to know why you say 'fuck' on TV."

Feldman was in his early sixties, carried fifteen extra pounds at his belt and a wreath of white hair around his head. He held a phone to each ear and leaned over the shoulder of a woman Nick didn't recognize, who was looking at her computer screen. A half dozen strangers in dark suits and ties sat manning that many phones and laptops.

The Feds were here.

Feldman signed off the left ear and tapped something on the computer screen. The woman at the screen nodded, and he straightened. "Thank you. That's good to know, Mrs. Moody."

He signed off the second phone and said, "Eva Moody's good. After she left Mansfeld College she took a year off, then enrolled at Indiana University. Her mother talked to her last night."

"Got it," said the woman, and tapped some keys. "But I got one here that may be hot. Elisha Graham. She left Mansfeld a year and a half ago and never went home. Her parents are religious freaks, said she'd gone to the devil and wasn't welcome back. They don't know where she is."

"Any other leads?"

"A brother."

"Find him," he said, then turned to Nick and extended a hand. "Louis Feldman. I got here a couple hours ago. We could do this better from a field office, have a little more room to spread out."

"I want things close," Nick said. The nearest FBI field office was in Cleveland. "Thanks for coming."

"Sure. I'm three months from retirement. Wouldn't mind finding Shelly Quinn bef—"

"Sheriff." Brendan Madigan stood, waving something at Nick from across the room. It was a copy of the note from last night. "Robin Weelkes. Robin Weelkes."

"You found her? Is she alive?"

"Not even close."

CHAPTER
42

MADIGAN STUMBLED THROUGH tables toward Nick, who turned to catch Feldman up: "Someone left us a note with that name. It's the second note. The first had Shelly Quinn's name on it."

"You aren't gonna believe this," Madigan said. "Robin Weelkes was a firefighter in Minneapolis. Forty-four years old, joined the Eighteenth Firehouse in 1991. But here's the real kicker." He shook his head, as if he couldn't believe it himself. "She's a he. Robin. He was a man."

Nick went still. For the space of three seconds, his brain simply stopped. "Couldn't be."

"His wife begs to differ. I just got off the phone with her," Madigan said. "Her husband disappeared on October 3, 2003. He'd taken a week off to go hunting and fishing up in the lakes. He'd just gotten an award."

"What kind of award?" Feldman asked.

"For heroism. He pulled a little girl out of a burning trailer a couple months before, saved her life. The mayor gave him an award at a banquet on Saturday; then on Sunday he went off to the lakes. Had a cabin there and planned to meet his brother. He took his gear and his boat but when his brother got there, he couldn't find him. He was missing for six months; then his body turned up after the spring thaw."

Nick shook his head. They were looking at Jack for killing his lovers—lovers of a type: women who were pretty and adventuresome, younger than Jack and looking for love, dabbling with drugs. Women who were... *women.* "Can't be ours," Nick said, even as Feldman took the note from Madigan's hand.

"That's what I thought," Madigan said. "Then I looked at the ME's report. Weelkes was shot through the heart with a .38. Wolves had gotten to him, not much left—just pieces, preserved in the ice."

He handed Nick a photo, something marked with an evidence tag and coded for an autopsy. At first, Nick couldn't make out what it was. It was ragged and pale, and almost looked like there was hair on—

"Aw, Jesus," he said. His stomach turned. "Jesus."

"It's a piece of ear and temple," Madigan said, as Feldman took the photo from Nick's hand. "The ME found paint thinner on it."

"Paint thinner?" asked Feldman. Confused.

Nick felt like a brick had hit him in the chest. "Whoever killed Lauren McAllister shot her through the heart and cleaned up her face with paint thinner."

Feldman whistled. "I think you better catch me up."

It took ten minutes. When he was finished, Nick said, "You got guys in Minneapolis?"

"Of course," Feldman said. "I'll send someone to talk to the ME."

"And to Weelkes's wife."

"Right," Feldman said, and got on the phone.

Nick tried to piece it all together, but nothing worked. Keep going, keep going. But suddenly he didn't know what direction to go. A forty-four-year-old heterosexual male? He went back to Madigan. "Grab a Fed and get into every database you can find. Come up with someone else in the past twenty years whose face was cleaned off. Man, woman, old, young—doesn't matter."

"Christ," Madigan said, daunted. But he hurried out anyway. Every cop knew that sometimes the answer was a name on a list, an entry on a coroner's report, a date on a plane ticket. The problem here was that they'd started with a relatively small pool of possible victims: Jack's lovers. Suddenly, the victims could be anybody, anywhere.

And how many?

Fury got Nick by the throat. "Son of a bitch." Here they were, dancing like idiots to find dead women Jack might have seduced with sex and drugs, and all along, there was something else altogether that was getting people killed. And someone in his town knew: whoever left the note.

Nick pulled his brain back into gear, and remembered Fruth and Bishop. He'd asked them to find out where Margaret was when Rebecca disappeared, but then the fire happened and Lud Ferguson was found and the street search got under way. Nick looked at his watch: coming up on eight-thirty in the morning. Quentin and the guys who'd quit late last night ought to be back in the game by now. He dialed Quent.

"I'm on my way," Quent told him.

"Swing by Hilltop and get Margaret. Bring her in for questioning."

Then he called Dorian. The prick.

• • •

Margaret was not a happy camper. Rodney, who'd insisted on coming with her, appeared confused.

Nick didn't care. Someone in Hopewell was fucking with him.

He kept Rodney waiting in the lobby and walked Margaret past the holding cells—past Ace Holmes—and to the table in the interview room. He'd removed the coffee and snacks before she arrived, stripping the room as bare as possible. He'd always had a comfortable relationship with Margaret but didn't want her comfortable now. It needed to be like TV or a movie. Get a bare lightbulb, maybe, pump her full of coffee and refuse to let her pee... Something.

Quentin told Margaret to sit.

"What's this about?" she asked. "Have you found out something about John's death? Or about Carl Whitmore?"

"This is about Rebecca Engel." Nick watched her with an eye for reaction—any reaction. Nothing.

"You've seen the news?" Quent asked.

She moved her shoulders. *So what?*

"Then you know Rebecca Engel's disappearance wasn't by choice like we thought," Nick said. "She didn't run off with her boyfriend. In fact, as you just saw, her boyfriend is in custody here. We believe she was abducted from the street near her house, early yesterday morning."

Her eyebrows rose; then she seemed to lose her breath. "You don't think John... Oh, dear God, do you think he's alive?"

"No. I don't think he's alive. I think he was murdered, like Carl."

"Why?"

"Because you don't need to take your loaded gun with you to run your car over a cliff. And because there are people involved now who *weren't* Jack's lovers. Some look like cover-ups, like Carl. Others were connected to Jack—or you—somehow."

She shook her head. "This is too much—"

"You knew about Jack's affairs, except the one with Rebecca. Here's what I think, Margaret: I think you like to *say* you never loved Jack. But I think you do. And you found out about his affair with Rebecca from Katie Engel, after she dropped that note at Hilltop. And I think you went after Rebecca. And you want to know what else? I think you were afraid of what John might have confided to Carl Whitmore, and killed him, too. That's what I think, Margaret."

She looked flabbergasted. "You're out of your mind."

"Where were you between five and six yesterday morning?"

Her face went slack. "Are you serious?"

"Dead."

She started to get up, and Nick said, "Sit down, Margaret."

Startled, she sank back to the chair. "I want to call my lawyer now."

"No need."

"I know my rights, Nick."

Right on cue, Dorian came down the hall, Valeria calling after him in Spanish. Nick gestured him inside. "Margaret was just getting ready to tell me where she was yesterday morning when Rebecca Engel disappeared."

Dorian rolled his eyes. "You can't be serio—"

"I'm a little fucking tired of everyone thinking I'm not serious," he shot, and Quentin shifted. *Cool, man,* he said with his eyes. Nick looked at Margaret. "Five to six o'clock yesterday morn—"

"This is crazy, Nick," Dorian complained.

"I was in bed," she said, and the three men looked at her. "Where else would I be? Can I prove it? No. Was I alone? Yes."

"Then you wouldn't mind if we search Hilltop again."

"You think I have Rebecca Engel tied up in one of the guest rooms?"

Dorian: "Get a warrant."

"He doesn't need a warrant," Margaret said. "Go ahead, Nick. Search the inn. I didn't kidnap Rebecca."

Dorian puffed up. "Yes. He *does* need a warrant," he said, punctuating each word. He turned to Nick. "Anything else, Sheriff?"

Nick almost bared his teeth. "Yes." He homed in on Margaret. "Who is Robin Weelkes?"

She blinked, and Dorian's hand shot out to hush Margaret. "Wait." To Nick: "What's this about?"

"He was a firefighter killed in Minnesota in 2003, probably by the same person who killed Lauren McAllister."

Dorian cursed. "You don't have to answer, Mar—"

"He was a friend of John's," she said over him. Her body lost a little of its starch. "He died . . . a hunting accident. Or hiking or something."

"Did you ever visit him in Minnesota?"

"No," she said, but her hands were wringing.

"Did Jack?"

"I don't remember. Maybe."

"Try harder."

"Asked and answered, Sheriff," Dorian said.

Nick held her eyes until she broke the contact, then said, "Get out." After they were gone, he said to Quentin, "Go search the inn. With a forensics team this time. Take the Feds. And have one of the FBI geeks look up everything in

Margaret's history. I want to know about her life as Maggie Huggins. And," he said, with the bitter taste of betrayal in his throat, "put a tail on her."

Nick followed Dorian out and saw Rodney hunched over a newspaper at an empty desk, looking at it through a magnifying glass from an inch away. While Dorian pulled Margaret aside to talk, Nick looked at her nephew, considering. Jack, Margaret, Rodney. They were the three people who'd been in Florida when Lauren McAllister was murdered, in Virginia when Sara Daniels disappeared, and now, in Hopewell with Rebecca missing.

Nick narrowed his eyes, trying to be realistic. *Rodney?* They'd talked about it and decided *no*. He'd have been nineteen when Lauren was killed—old enough. But there were too many aspects of the murders that required sight, keen sight, as well as the ability to drive. Rodney wasn't a viable suspect. And they'd already pumped him for information about Jack, just as they'd pumped half the town.

Even so, Nick went over to him, pulling a couple of chairs out of his way as he walked. "Rodney, it's Nick," he said, and straddled a chair, laying his forearms across its back. "I was wondering...Do you recall Jack or Margaret ever going to Minnesota?"

His brows rose above the dark glasses. "Minnesota? Not for a long time."

Nick's pulse jumped. "When?"

"A few years ago, Jack went. I think it was Minneapolis. He had a friend there who was getting an award. Guy named Robin. He'd been in Miami the week before."

Nick glanced across the lobby at Margaret. She'd lied, pretended she could barely remember who Weelkes was.

Nick's throat went dry. It was the Hugginses, that was

for damn sure. Somehow and for some reason, it was the Hugginses. Now the only question was which one: Jack or Margaret?

Nick started to leave, then gave in to a ridiculous impulse. He looked at Rodney, trying to see his eyes behind the dark glasses. He could barely make them out.

"Is there something else, Sheriff?" Rodney asked.

"Where were you yesterday morning, early? Around five-ish?"

The hint of a smile curved Rodney's lips. "Good God, you're getting desperate."

"Humor me."

"Actually, I went to Kroger."

"At five in the morning?"

"Somewhere around there. I get headaches from my eyes, always have—ever since my surgery. I went to get a painkiller." He pulled a small container of Motrin from his pocket and shook it. It sounded full.

"You don't have a prescription?" Nick asked.

"I'd run out."

"How did you get there?"

"Same way I get most places: my three-wheeler. It has a headlight, but it's slow going in the dark. It took more than thirty minutes each way. So, I was out between, say, five and six-ish."

Nick's eyes narrowed; Rodney must have sensed it.

"Hold on," Rodney said, and dug out his wallet. "I might still have the receipt." He came up with a folded piece of paper, opened it up, and handed it to Nick. "Is this it?"

Nick looked. It was a receipt from Tuesday, November thirteenth, from the Kroger on Shallowford Road. That was a long way from Rebecca Engel's neighborhood, in fact, on the other side of town. The time was stamped five-thirty-two a.m.

"This is for orange juice."

"Oh. Whoops," Rodney said. "I went back inside for that after I bought the Motrin." He reached back into his pocket. "I must have tossed the first receipt."

"Is this where you usually shop for aspirin?"

He got a little cocky. "What else is open at five in the morning?"

"Okay," Nick said, standing. Rodney was right: He *was* getting desperate. Still, Nick pocketed the receipt and carefully slid his chair back under the desk. He carefully *didn't* move one of the others. "I think Dorian's done with Margaret."

Rodney got up. "Thanks."

He trailed his fingers along the desks to retrace his path, tripped on the chair Nick had left and almost went down. Nick caught him.

"Jeez. Sorry, man," Nick said. "You okay?"

Rodney turned in his general direction, and rubbed his leg. "Fine."

Nick watched him leave, then picked up the newspaper and read the top headline Rodney had seemed to be focused on. LOCAL DRUNK WITNESSES ENGEL DIS-APPEARANCE. That fucking Roach. But he'd deal with her later. Right now something else nagged at him. He walked to the command room and found Quentin talking to a female Fed wearing glasses the size of movie tickets, asking her to delve into Margaret's background. Nick wrote down Rodney's name and interrupted them.

"Include her nephew while you're looking. Find the doctor who operated on his eyes. I'd like to know just how much he sees."

The woman gave a dramatic sigh—he'd just added to her plate—and Nick went to Valeria. "Is Rosa at Hilltop this morning?"

"As far as I know."

"Would you call her for me?"

And when Valeria's eyes got big, he thought to add, "No, no, it's not about Calvin and nothing's wrong. I just have a question for her."

Rosa was on a minute later. "Can you check something?" Nick asked. "Rodney's here at headquarters, just leaving. I need for you to run out to his place and look in his fridge."

He explained only as much as he had to, and a few minutes later, she called him back as she went into Rodney's cabin.

"Whoo," she said, on a breath.

"What is it?"

"Nothing. It's just hot in here, that's all. Smells like pork." She paused. "*Dios.* That's where all those muddy towels came from. There's a whole pile of them here on the floor."

"Rosa, the fridge," Nick prompted.

"I'm going, I'm going. Okay, right here, Sheriff. Minute-Maid, calcium-enriched orange juice from concentrate. Pulp-free."

"Is it full?"

"Almost."

"What's the expiration date?"

Rosa hummed a note while she hunted for it. "December 15. Four weeks from now."

Okay. Nick hung up, bullied his brow with his fingers. Miami. Lawrenceville. Hopewell. Even Minnesota. No one else made sense.

Quent walked back in and Nick said: "Rodney says Jack went to Minneapolis for Weelkes's award ceremony."

"Really?" He blew out a breath. "Okay, I'll look. Virginia to Minneapolis, October 2003."

"Flights, trains, buses."

"Boats, balloons, carrier pigeons. I'll check."

Maggie drove with white knuckles; Rodney sat in the front seat, rewinding and replaying the scene with the sheriff in his mind. Did Mann actually suspect him? Was it possible?

He'd have to keep an ear to the ground. He didn't want to be caught off guard. Not when there was only one angel left to find.

The thrill of knowing it was almost finished gave him a heady sensation. The threat that Nick might catch up with him before the end too bitter to contemplate. He had to move quickly now.

Then again, there was a fly in the ointment: Lud Ferguson. Damn, he hadn't counted on that. The newspaper suggested he witnessed the disappearance of Rebecca Engel. Some stupid wino, for God's sake.

Maggie parked the Saturn and Rodney said, "I'll be back. I need to go home awhile."

She nodded in that way someone does when they're not paying attention; still, he swept his cane back and forth until he found his three-wheeler, then headed to the cabin at his normal cautious pace in case she was watching. A lot of legally blind people drove three-wheelers or bikes, even scooters. But they didn't drive them fast.

Once out of sight, he gunned it to the cabin and went inside. Whipped off the dark glasses and went downstairs to Rebecca.

His breath caught when he saw her, laid out like the dead on a slab in the morgue. One more, almost gone. The sensation was like flying. He looked at the shelf where just two figurines remained. One would die with Rebecca. The other? He still wasn't sure, but one thing was certain: it would all be over soon.

He touched the mask on Rebecca's face. Like leather, not like bisque. A couple more hours, then.

He cocked his head, looking at her, then touched her eyelid. It flickered, but barely. Still hanging on. Sometimes, depending how thick the clay was, they could breathe for a good long time. Clay was porous. Usually, they were still alive when he pulled off the mask and shot them through the heart. He liked that best. Easier to handle a body before rigor mortis set in.

Besides, the shooting always felt good. Made him feel nostalgic. Like he'd finally succeeded.

He climbed back up the wooden stairway, feeling good, then stopped. Got a *vibe*.

Someone here? He looked around, slowly, carefully. There, the kitchen door. He never left the kitchen door closed; the heat from downstairs collected there.

He stepped into the kitchen, scanning every inch. Rodney was scrupulous about keeping everything in its place—he'd learned it as a child when his world was little more than shadows, and even after his sight crept back following the surgery, he kept it up with convincing precision. He liked the order.

He *loved* the ruse. It was a ruse that fooled everyone but the angels.

His gaze touched the counters. Nothing different. He opened a cupboard, started to go through them, then remembered: The orange juice.

A smile blossomed, and he cocked his head. Really, Sheriff? *Really?*

He opened the refrigerator already knowing what he'd find. Sure enough, the OJ was on the second shelf. Not where he'd left it.

Rage began to swell but it morphed into excitement. Nick Mann was watching him.

Nick Mann *was* Number Ten.

A thrill shot through his veins. After all these years, taking the angels out one by one, it was finally coming to a close. The end of an era. From here, no one would follow him. No one would sit in the heavens keeping watch.

The Angelmaker smiled. The finale would be spectacular.

CHAPTER
43

ERIN WENT TO Leni's after the fire and stayed through the night, talking to Leni and waiting to talk to Katie. When the newspaper hit the front porch, she couldn't believe the headlines: LOCAL DRUNK WITNESSES ENGEL DISAPPEARANCE; CALLOWAY DOUBLE MURDER CONNECTED TO MISSING WOMAN; FIREBOMB ATTACK ON SHERIFF'S DAUGHTER; FBI TAKES OVER CALLOWAY CASE; COLLEGE CONDUCTS SEARCH FOR STRING OF MISSING STUDENTS. The stories, both on TV and in the paper, were melodramatic and, Erin thought, had the amazing ability to tiptoe around the truth while slogging through conjecture and speculation. She was starting to sympathize with Nick's hatred for the media when Katie wandered down from her room, looking shaken and exhausted.

"Hey," Erin said, straightening.

Katie jumped. Looked at her. Her gaze scanned the room until she saw her mother's toes peeking from the end of the sofa in the living room; then she looked back at Erin. "Dr. Baker said I wasn't allowed to talk to you. Sheriff Mann said you weren't allowed to talk to me."

"Things have changed," Erin said, and took a tentative step forward. "The sheriff was worried that my campaign against Huggins would taint anything you said to me, but we can't worry about that anymore." She paused. "Rebecca's not with Ace."

Katie's face went slack. "She isn't?"

"I'm sorry, no. They found him last night."

Her gaze veered to the living room, to her mother again. "Does Mom know?"

"Yes. She was up most of the night."

"Oh, God." Her eyes filled with tears. "What happened to Becca? Where is she?"

Erin herded her into the kitchen, hoping to let Leni sleep. "Ace says Rebecca was planning to meet him outside yesterday morning, after your mom went to work. When he came to get her, she was gone. The sheriff found her suitcase in a Dumpster behind some grocery store."

Katie pressed her fists against her eyelids. "Oh God, oh God, oh God."

"Katie," Erin said, her voice stern, "you're the one who knows the most about Becca and what she was doing the past few weeks. You have to think. Think about where she might have gone, or who might have taken her."

"I don't know, I don't know..." Katie was losing it. Erin wanted to pull her into her arms and tell her she didn't have to do this. No teenager should be responsible for keeping a sibling safe. It was too big a load. Too heavy.

But Katie wasn't going to confide to Andrew Baker. Erin was good at this. She knew psychology and she knew the court system; Katie was drowning in both right now.

"It might be something you heard her say, something you remember...It might be the key to finding—"

A sob rose from her gut and she whirled. "Stop it. Leave me alone."

She ran upstairs and slammed a bedroom door, and hopefulness drained from Erin's chest. She turned, surprised to see Leni standing in the doorway.

"I have to get to the restaurant," she said, "but you can go on upstairs."

"I don't think Katie will welcome me into her room right now."

"That's the point," Leni said, a little hope in her eyes. "She's not in her room. That was Rebecca's door that slammed just now."

Erin knocked on Rebecca's door and got no answer. "Katie?" she said. "I'm coming in."

She pressed the door open and stepped in as if expecting snakes to be hiding in all the crevices. Katie was curled up on an old daybed, a huge book in her lap. She wasn't reading it, just staring, rubbing her hands over it. When Erin sat down, the words tumbled out.

"I tried to stop her. She wouldn't listen to me," Katie said miserably. "If I'd just told Mom. If I'd told someone about her and Calloway, maybe this wouldn't have happened."

"Katie—" Erin reached for her hand but she snatched it away.

"You don't know," she wailed. "You don't have any idea what it's like to be the reason your sister might be dead."

Erin's skin constricted around her. "Let me tell you about Justin."

She did—about the beatings he took growing up, the emotional gorge he fell into after the man he both loved and hated disappeared, and the evidence against him she'd unwittingly given police. "So you see, Katie," she said, "I don't think you win the award for worst sister."

Katie had tears rolling down her cheeks. Erin moved to the daybed and took her hand. "We both have a sibling we're trying to save. Mine has until tomorrow night. I don't know about yours, but I do know this: We're going to have to do this together."

Lud Ferguson. The Angelmaker hadn't counted on some drunken bum witnessing Rebecca's disappearance. It wasn't insurmountable, but timing was key. Mann was too close. The orange juice, the chair. He was starting to see.

Had to be now.

He reached up to touch the knot at the back of his head; it felt strange. He yanked the whole wig a little to the left to try to center it, then tucked a few stray strands back up into the knot. His own hair was white-blond and to let it show would draw attention for sure. It had lost all its pigment in the weeks after his mother died. Rodney didn't remember that part, but then, he hadn't been able to see it happening the way others could. He didn't know what color his hair had been to start with. Brown, he guessed.

But he did remember his mother, and her fucking little angels. Rodney couldn't see a thing but always knew the angels were there. Every damn birthday, a new one. *To watch over you another year.*

Because she certainly didn't. She was too ashamed of him, too afraid someone would see him. *Mama's special,* she'd told him. *Men pay for that. But they won't pay for a blind little boy...*

And so he went to school, far away. Saw his mother only at Christmas and got another fucking angel every year.

Then Mother got in the car with John Huggins one night. After that, there was no more "special." No more men to keep her, or money for faraway school. Rodney came to live with her, in a smelly little apartment in New Orleans. For a year they lived together, and in that whole time he only had two memories of her: One was convincing her to go to Mardi Gras when he bummed a mask for her from their landlord.

The other was trying to kill her.

It should have been so easy. She'd been lying on the bed drunk, sobbing, sobbing with the Mardi Gras mask in one hand and a pistol in the other. He'd run his hands over hers and felt the gun, and all he'd had to do was press it into her chest and squeeze the trigger.

But she did it first. *Pop.* The wailing ended. She denied him even that.

He spent two days with her body, living on saltine crackers, thinking, planning. When he was ready, he wandered outside toward the sounds of the cathedral. A nun found him wandering outside: a ten-year-old boy, blind and scared, his hands smeared with blood and the thick makeup he'd smoothed over his mother's scars. Rodney had always thought it was the smeary hands that had been the crowning jewel in his plan—a nice touch. The nuns just about tripped all over themselves taking care of him, and when the police came, it was the same with them and then the same with Maggie.

Rodney became important. For the first time in his life, he was the center of a universe.

He wasn't going to give that up for sight. The corneal

transplants worked—not instantly, but over the next several months—but he wasn't willing to give up the power. Having sight only made him stronger: He still controlled everyone around him, and they didn't even know it.

Now he tugged at the wig and reminded himself *not* to pretend blindness. Today, he would pretend to be Leni Engel.

He looked nothing like her, of course, but with a big coat and hat and wire glasses, and the hair in a bun, anybody who saw him driving Leni's car would simply *assume* it was Leni.

Lud Ferguson had been to Hilltop House once, on one of those rare occasions when he had temporary employment. He'd worked with a yard service hired to landscape the area east of the barn. It had been a couple of years since Rodney had seen him, but he thought he could pick him out. Getting him to a safe location was the only issue.

Finding him wasn't hard. Rodney knew where to start, even this early in the afternoon. Everyone knew Lud Ferguson's passion, and on the fourth phone call, Rodney found him at a bar called The Pub.

Baiting him was even easier. "Mr. Ferguson," Rodney said, speaking in falsetto. The voice sounded ridiculous to his ears, like Mrs. Doubtfire, but Lud didn't have the brain cells to question it. "My name is Suzanne Fuller, and I'm an investigative reporter for the Ohio Morning news show."

"Fuller?" he asked. He was dazed, maybe a little bit drunk. But impressed, Rodney thought.

"I do research and interviews for Matt Laughlin and Lisa Gebhardt." Throw in the names of real anchors: Laughlin and Gebhardt had done extensive segments about Jack and Rebecca over the past couple of days. "We read about you in the paper today and we'd like to talk to you, and do an interview for TV. We'll pay you. We pay our sources very well, Mr. Ferguson."

"Uh, oh, well. Okay. That'd be good."

"Are you free this afternoon?"

"Uh..."

"We're shooting a story about crime in small-town America. We'll be there in about an hour. We're starting at the railroad tracks on Elmwood Road, you know, setting up the flavor of the town. There's an old station house there my producer wants to shoot."

"Yeah, I know it. Elmwood Road."

"Can you walk it, or can you get a ride?" A little solicitousness couldn't hurt.

"I can get there," he said, and Rodney thought he could almost hear Lud clearing his voice, straightening out his flannel shirt for the cameras.

Rodney smiled. Pure mastery. "An hour, then."

He disconnected. Now to Leni's car. This part carried some risk—broad daylight. She'd parked in the alley at the back of the restaurant, but he still wished she hadn't driven to work; it would have been easier taking her car from the house. No such luck, though, and he had to wait in a crook in the alley for nearly twenty minutes before there were no pedestrians in sight. Then he pulled out the set of keys he'd taken from Rebecca's purse, adjusted the bothersome bun at the back of his head, and walked to the car as if it belonged to him.

Head up, fast pace. Look straight at where you're going. Not very much like Leni, really, but more importantly, *nothing* like Rodney.

He got to the car and slipped into the driver's seat. Let out a little giggle.

Elmwood Road was an eighteen-minute drive. He slowed, scanning the railroad tracks, and tucked the car behind one of the abandoned buildings. The station had been condemned for years, except by rats and stray dogs; there probably weren't ten cars a day that came by here. Even if someone lived in one of the dilapidated houses in the distance, Rodney was far enough away not to be recognized. Woman's coat, Leni's car, wig—

And there he was. Ludwig Ferguson.

He walked along the tracks toward the old station, his body listing right as if he had a hitch in his side, his shirt tucked in to a beltless pair of jeans, an old denim jacket closed tight. Rodney couldn't be sure, but it almost looked as if his hair had been recently combed.

Gonna be on TV.

He waited until Lud was halfway across the second set of tracks, checked in both directions to be sure no cars were coming, and ran him down.

The police and FBI had already been through Rebecca's bedroom. Personal items—notes, receipts, a date book, PalmPilot—were gone. The things she had packed herself to take with Ace were gone. The clothes left behind had that feeling of pockets having been searched and the hangers returned to the closet ten at a time. Drawers had been riffled through and items returned to their places not quite right.

Still, Erin and Katie sifted through everything that was left, one piece at a time.

At two, Nick called. "Learning anything from Katie?"

"We're working on it."

"Okay." She could tell he knew Katie was standing right there. "How's Leni?"

"She went to the restaurant about ten-thirty. Needed to keep busy, I think." And maybe keep up a living.

"Look out the window, down the street half a block," Nick said. "Is there a gray sedan out there that only a Fed would drive?"

Erin looked. "I see it. That's a government car?"

"No. I told Agent Fisher not to use a government car because I didn't want him to look like a Fed, so he went and rented a fucking gray sedan."

"So it *is* a Fed?"

"Two of them. Fisher and Holt. They won't interfere, but they'll tail you if you need to go anywhere."

Erin closed her eyes. No fear when Nick Mann was on duty.

Nick started to say something, hesitated, then said, "Listen, Erin, I haven't really had time to think about things, but...you might have been right last night after the fire, at least about some of it."

"Some of it?"

"All of it. Especially the part about caring for you."

Warmth flooded her. "It was a bluff, you know. I wasn't sure."

"Christ."

Erin smiled. Felt a tingle: *Nikolaus Mann likes you.* She let it sink in, then got back to business. "Anything happening?"

He told her about Robin Weelkes and Margaret's alibi.

"I'm more confused than ever," Erin admitted.

"So am I. But for Justin, confusion is good. It means the Florida court has too much shit to sort out to go through with Justin's execution."

"Are you sure?"

"Not a hundred percent. Ninety-five."

She'd take it.

• • •

Except for the buzzards, they might not have found him.

Deputy Cutter—the man who'd thought it odd for Lud Ferguson to have an iPod—also thought it odd that buzzards had gathered above the old railway station. He tooled over, saw a lump, and the hairs on the back of his neck rippled. He pulled close enough to honk and scatter the birds in a cacophony of squawks and beating wings, then got out of his car and made his way toward the lump. It was human, he realized, his heartbeat quickening, and the jacket looked familiar. He hesitated, worried now: the arms and one leg were bent at an unlikely angle. Hand hovering over his pistol, he touched his radio and edged closer. Dark purple blood had puddled around the head, and when he stepped around to see the face…

Ah, God.

CHAPTER
44

WHEN NICK DROVE to the railroad tracks, Cutter was standing beside a lump, waving his arms at buzzards. A caravan of cars followed Nick: the press and others. The ME came in with Quentin, two minutes behind Nick, along with a couple of Feds, who then stood around in their long dark coats and small dark sunglasses, scratching their chins. Watching the small-town bumpkins handle a hit-and-run scene, Nick thought, and he might have smiled had there not been a dead man at his feet.

He peered down at Lud. He was half-sprawled, half-twisted on the train tracks. Until Cutter, no one but the buzzards had noticed.

"How long ago?" Nick asked the ME, who crouched over the body, touching the blood with a thin utensil. Looked like a meat thermometer.

"Not long. Blood's still tacky. Give me a chance to do a body temp and then I can tell you better." The ME stood, shivered. Nick didn't think it was from the weather.

Quent walked up. "No skid marks, no tracks. Be nice if we had a half-inch of snow or something. It's all just cracked up pavement and gravel out here. Nothing to see." He looked down at Lud's body. "You think we fingered him?"

Yeah, Nick thought, with guilt moving through his veins. They'd fingered him.

But not as much as the newspaper had.

He straightened, skimmed the growing crowd. Lasered in on Leslie Roach.

"Nick? You cool, man?" Quentin asked. He sounded worried.

"Fuck cool," Nick said, and stalked to the edge of the crime scene tape. He pointed a finger at Leslie, then crooked it at her. Her eyes got wide, a hyena spotting a meal, and she slipped through the photographers with a toss of her head and her chin in the air, as if proud to be The Chosen One.

He lifted the yellow tape and guided her under it by the elbow. When courtesy would have demanded that he let go, he tightened his fingers further and walked her past a couple of deputies, into the center of the scene. He felt her steps begin to drag but didn't stop until they were right over the body.

"Nick, what are you—"

"Take a look," he snarled, and she glanced down, then immediately looked away. Nick put a hand on the back of her neck and cranked her face back toward the body of Lud Ferguson. "I said, take a look." She tried to draw back against his hand, but he knew she was looking. At eyes that had bulged from the impact, then been pecked by buzzards, at blood crusted around Lud's lips.

"Let me go," she croaked.

"Lud Ferguson knew nothin' about nothin'."

"L-let go—"

"He didn't touch Rebecca Engel and he didn't see who did. He knew *nothing*."

Leslie whirled away and threw up. Nick watched with so much fury vibrating in his bones he thought his head might explode. He gave her another minute, her gut heaving in front of God and everybody, and when she looked at him, the back of her hand touching her mouth, Nick said, "You might as well have driven the car that bowled him down yourself. Why don't you print *that*?"

Leni Engel left the restaurant mid-afternoon, walked to the drugstore, and picked out a bottle of Sominex. Did a double take at a small TV behind the counter. A newsbreak in the middle of the afternoon: *"...authorities are now saying that Ferguson's death is considered part of the Calloway investigation, and may be connected to the disappearance of Rebecca Engel. Michael Wainscott is standing by at the scene...Michael? Originally, this looked like a tragic hit-and-run, maybe even an accident. Can you tell us what is leading authorities to believe that..."*

"Hey. Mrs. Engel?" The girl behind the counter touched Leni's hand. Leni blinked, took her change, and headed out. Lud Ferguson. She'd seen the newspaper, caught bits and pieces of the news on TV all day. Nick seemed certain that Lud was innocent. He didn't know where Rebecca was; he'd simply found her suitcase. And now...

She threaded her way through the city lot, to the alley behind the restaurant where she had parked. Stopped. Looked around for the car. There it was. A little farther down than she remembered.

Dear Heavens, she was losing her mind.

She walked past the rear of her car, coming to the driver's side door, slid the key into the lock, and—

Her jaw dropped. The hood was dented. For God's sake, someone had hit her car.

She glanced around, looking for the culprit, then pulled the key from the lock and went around to the front to get a better look. One time, years ago when her husband was still around, he'd hit a deer on the road. They'd eaten venison all winter long and paid a fortune to repair the car. Its front end was buckled, the headlight cracked, and the bumper hanging on for dear life.

It looked just like this.

Nick got the first call about Leni's mangled car as the ME piled Lud Ferguson into a county van and the newsmakers began dispersing. It wasn't from Leni, but from a passerby in the parking lot who'd heard the news about Lud and got to wondering. Nick got another call on his way to the Eatery. It wasn't from Leni, either.

Well, shit.

He and Quent went through the alley and eyeballed Leni's car, dispersed the onlookers, then posted a deputy to babysit the vehicle. They went through the back door of the restaurant—getting looks from the help still cleaning the kitchen—and straight to a little office Leni used for bookkeeping. She was sitting behind a small wooden desk. She looked catatonic.

"What happened to your car, Leni?" Nick asked.

She didn't react and he walked around the desk and folded to his haunches in front of her. "A man who might've seen Rebecca is dead now, and people are seeing your car. You need to tell us what happened."

"Did he know where Becca is?" she asked, her eyes seeming to look right through him.

He let a drop of venom leak into his voice. "We'll never know now, will we?"

"Oh, God..."

Nick glanced at Quentin, who said, "I'll go talk to the employees."

Quentin slipped out and Nick turned back to Leni. "Damn it, what happened to your car?"

"Did Lud Ferguson kill my Becca?"

Her words sank into Nick's chest like wet cement. "Jesus, Leni, I don't think he did. Honest to God, I don't think he did."

Another few seconds ticked by; then her eyes cleared. "All right, then. I didn't do it. I've been here since ten-thirty this morning."

He took her in anyway—there wasn't any choice—had the car towed in and let Feldman call in one of his forensics guys from the Cleveland field office. Before the Cleveland Fed even arrived, they knew: This was the car that had killed Lud Ferguson. Trace evidence on the car would take time to analyze, but the dead man's injuries matched the damage on the car, and a few grains of gravel and tar from the tire treads were distinctly the same as those found at the Elmwood Road railroad track crossing. Lud hadn't died instantly. He'd lived long enough for deep bruises to form at the points of impact, for blood to gather in a lung and pulse up his bronchial tubes and out his mouth. Long enough to have known he was dying, maybe even see the birds gathering, waiting.

Nick smothered that thought, shook off the media and the Feds and the commissioner, and buried himself in his office. He couldn't loosen up; his muscles and tendons and even his bones were clenched with tension. Most of the time, criminals were stupid; a few hours, a couple of days at the most, and the cops were hauling in some ass-hole with gun residue on his hands, or some other asshole who'd bragged about the crime, or some other one who never dreamed it was a bad idea to speed on the highway while fleeing the crime scene. Those chases—quick and down and dirty—always delivered a sense of victory, the kind of instant gratification that made cops high-five each other at happy hour and laugh at the stupidity of the criminal mind.

But once in a while, there was a guy—or gal, or even a group—who actually put on a *show*. Someone smart and careful and calculated. In this day and age of DNA and CSI, even that wasn't usually enough to get away with something. A criminal had to be *lucky,* too. And when brains and good planning converged with sheer luck, then it was something extraordinary. A battle of good versus evil, in which the stakes were literally life and death.

And Erin, damn her soul, was right: Nick got such a *charge* from those cases. Deep down and visceral. He'd never felt too guilty about that in the old days; he liked to hunt—it was how he was wired. But, God forgive him, now people in Hopewell were *dying,* and others—like Hannah and Erin—had been placed in harm's way. Carl Whitmore and Lud Ferguson and Rebecca Engel were dead. Nick shook his head at that last, hurrying to correct himself: Rebecca was *missing*. But in his gut, he thought she was dead. There was no movement surrounding her. No momentum.

But, dead or alive, *where*? He ran his hand through his hair. Of the enormous list of missing persons in the world, a huge number of them would never be accounted for. They just disappeared. But if Jack had really killed Lauren McAllister and three, maybe four other people over the years, where were all the bodies? Lauren's had been found in the Everglades and Robin Weelkes's in the wilderness of Minnesota. That left Sara Daniels and Shelly Quinn. Where were they? Dumped in a lake in Virginia, or on some remote mountain for the bears or coyotes to dispose of?

Could be, but if Rebecca was dead, discarding her body wasn't that easy here. For all its remoteness, Hopewell was transparent: People watched one another. A cornfield? A quarry? Weighted and dumped in Lake Erie? Multiple victims right here in Hopewell now, and besides Rebecca's suitcase, not a single piece of them found. Now *that* was a lucky killer...

And why not Whitmore or Ferguson? Why not bother disposing of them? Nick knew that answer and it sent a chill down his spine: Whitmore and Ferguson were left behind because they weren't part of it. They'd just gotten in the way. But the others—Lauren McAllister, Sara Daniels, Shelly Quinn, Robin Weelkes, Rebecca—they were about something else, and the idea that it came from being Jack's lovers didn't hold up anymore. Not with Weelkes thrown in. Not with Shelly, either.

He spent fifteen minutes rolling it around. In the end he didn't have any great revelations that solved the case, so he sat down and read through all the paper they'd collected—for the umpteenth time. Nothing there, either. He called Alayna and found her sitting in traffic on a Florida highway, on her way to the Attorney General's office. He caught her up on the murder of Lud Ferguson.

"I can't use that, Nick; it's not relevant," she said. "Ferguson's nothing like Lauren McAllister."

"But Robin Weelkes is. And Justin was in prison when Weelkes was murdered. You gotta tie Weelkes and McAllister to the same murderer."

"Gee, thanks. I'd've never thought of that."

"And get someone you trust to find the cop on the McAllister case voted Mostly Likely to Sell Out. There's a reason this never hit the light of day until now."

Rebecca had a small collection of books, thrown haphazardly in the bottom of a blanket chest: a handful of old teen novels, a couple magazines, and an oversized volume of fairy tales and nursery rhymes leftover from childhood. Erin sifted through a few of them, sighed, and sat back on her heels.

"I don't know what else there could be. I'm out of ideas," she said, looking at Katie. "Is there anyplace else she might have kept a diary or anything?"

"No. Becca wasn't much of a wri—" She stopped, catching herself, and hiccupped a huge sob. "Oh, God. Oh, God..."

Erin spoke firmly. "It was a slip of the tongue, Katie," she said. But she'd done it, too—caught herself referring to Rebecca in the past tense. She'd been close enough to court cases to know the statistics—those critical first twenty-four hours, the plunge of hope for finding a missing person after that. The probability of finding Rebecca alive was plummeting now.

Erin's cell phone rang. It was Nick.

"Have you been watching the news?" he asked.

"No. We've been searching Becca's room, looking for"—she felt like a fool—"clues, I guess."

"I have some bad news."

Erin's heart stopped. "Is it Becca?"

"No, no." His voice was strained. "Is Katie there? She okay?"

"Yes. Nick, what's wrong?"

"Lud Ferguson—he's the man we questioned last

night, who found Rebecca's suitcase and took her iPod—was murdered this afternoon. Someone ran him down with a car. He's dead."

"Oh, God." But Erin was confused. "Why?"

"Presumably because the news made it sound like he might know something about, or had something to do with, Rebecca's disappearance." Erin waited. He'd left too many blanks to be filled in. "Leni's car is the car that killed him," he finally said. "That's not just a theory; that's for real."

"Oh, no," Erin said. She looked at Katie, trying to keep her face from showing anything.

"Has Leni been home at all today?"

"No. She went to the restaurant around ten or ten-thirty, I think."

"Okay. What about Katie?"

Erin went still. "No."

"She's old enough to drive, Erin."

"She's been here with me all day."

"*All* day?"

"Yes."

"Okay." There was relief in his voice. "Look. I've got Leni here now. She's talking to a lawyer. I don't know what to do about Katie. Jesus. Maybe you should bring her here."

Erin looked at Katie, who was watching with unabashed interest in the conversation.

"No," she said, looking straight at Katie. "I'll tell her. And we'll keep working here. There's got to be something."

"You sure? She gonna be okay?"

"I'm sure. And"—she paused before answering his second question—"we'll see."

CHAPTER
45

CALVIN WANTED TO hide after school. Scared. Embarrassed about being in jail. Mad.

Mostly scared.

He got off the bus and headed to Rodney's cabin. Rodney liked him. He didn't see the weirdness, didn't care about it. His cabin was a good place to hide.

Calvin walked into the cabin like always, frowned. Something strange. The couch was different. The coffee table moved and the rug folded up.

Not good. Rodney would trip. Not good at all.

He went to straighten the rug and blinked. Stairs.

Stairs? A basement? Calvin didn't know there was a basement down there. Heat rolled up the stairs. It smelled like vanilla, the smell of the church his mom always took him to on Sundays.

Calvin started down the stairs. Hot. That was weird, too. Usually basements were cold. He slowed, moving quietly. Scared again. Didn't know why.

He came to a landing at the stairs and peered around the corner.

Oh, Jesus.

Calvin backed up, but couldn't stop staring. Rodney was there. He had eyes. They glowed red. Red, red, red, like the flames in the kiln. Calvin had never seen his eyes before, just glasses. Didn't know Rodney had eyes. Eyes like red fire.

He leaned back against the wall. So that's why Rodney needed medicine. *Tuesday, November thirteenth, two-thousand-twelve, five-thirty-two a.m., thirty-eight degrees Fahrenheit.* Kroger garbage bag. Bring the whole bag. For his eyes.

Rodney stepped back from the kiln and the red glow went away. Calvin ducked. Hide-hide-hide. Been here a lot but didn't know Rodney had a kiln. Giant, bigger than Margaret's. Didn't know he had a cellar, either. Creepy. Red, red, red. Flames in the kiln. Hot. *One-thousand-eight-hundred-and-fifty degrees Fahrenheit, Wednesday, November fourteenth, two-thousand-twelve, four-twenty-two p.m....*

Calvin slunk around the edge of the doorway. Didn't know why. Can't be scared. It's Rodney. Friend. Friend. Firing sculptures, like Margaret. *One-thousand-eight-hundred-and-fifty degrees Fahrenheit.* Hot-hot-hot.

Not right, not right. Too hot for sculptures.

Calvin began shaking, clutched his arms over his chest. He shook his head back and forth, bones trembling. He thought he knew something important but wasn't sure what. Didn't want to know.

Had to know.

He slipped back down the stairs, partway. A little farther to see around the corner. His nostrils twitched. Vanilla. But something else, too. Roasted meat. Burned.

Sweat popped out on his forehead. So hot down here. He took another couple steps. A motorcycle leaned against one wall. Motorcycle? He peeked past it, past the giant kiln to a table, and on the table—

Oh oh oh oh oh oh.

Calvin ran. He knew. He knew. Didn't want to know, but he knew. He ran, and thought about Mr. Reinhardt: *Don't talk, don't talk.* He was mean about it. Had scared Calvin. *Don't talk.*

That was okay—it didn't matter. Calvin hardly ever talked. When he did, it came out jumbled so no one understood. Sometimes the dates and times and temperatures didn't make sense to Calvin, either. Like the ones in his head now... *Tuesday, November thirteenth, two-thousand-twelve, five-thirty-two a.m., thirty-eight degrees Fahrenheit... Wednesday, November fourteenth, two-thousand-twelve, four-twenty-eight p.m., one-thousand-eight-hundred-and-fifty degrees Fahrenheit... One-thousand-eight-hundred-and-fifty degrees Fahrenheit...* Too, too hot.

Oh, God. Don't want to know this.

The candles had all burned out. The music was finished. Rebecca's breathing had gone from strained and raspy to almost imperceptible, but she was still alive—barely. The Angelmaker had poked a tiny hole through the clay in each nostril, like a kid putting holes in the top of a bell jar for lightning bugs. Just enough to keep her alive until the mask was ready. It was too hard to move the body once rigor mortis set in; he'd learned that the hard way. Had let Shelly Quinn suffocate beneath her mask, and had a helluva time handling her body afterward. Had to cut her into pieces.

Yuk.

But Rebecca was still hanging on and the clay was completely dry.

The Angelmaker picked up a rib, one of the smaller ones Maggie had in her collection of sculpting tools. Careful, now. Getting the mask off could be difficult. Go easy, or it won't be good enough to give to Maggie.

He tucked the narrow end of the rib barely under the edge of the mask beneath Rebecca's left jawbone, and pressed down on the flesh. *Fwsht.* The skin separated from the clay with the sound of a vacuum pack opening. The Angelmaker smiled.

Now work the rib around the edges, open the vacuum seal every half-inch or so, all around the perimeter of the face. The forehead was the hardest—the flesh there had little give—but a few moments later, the mask came off clean.

Rebecca wheezed with the increase in air, and the Angelmaker set aside the mask and looked at her. Her chest heaved, but her eyes were utterly blank. Seeing nothing now. He smiled. A little foreshadowing there.

He checked the temperature on the kiln—eighteen-hundred-and-fifty. Ready. Time to finish.

He picked up his .38 and placed the barrel against her breast, closed his eyes and remembered when he was ten, reaching out and finding the gun against his mother's chest, one of her hands shaking on the pistol and the other clinging to the mask he'd given her. Recalled his own hand sliding over hers—

Rodney stopped. A noise. He cocked his head and listened. Fucking Christ, what was that?

He slid around the table, peering up the stairs. Damn it, someone was there. Footsteps.

Mann? Maggie? Calvin? Fuck, this wasn't supposed to happen. He hadn't planned for this.

Rodney dashed upstairs, looked out the door and tried

to see, but there was no one. There was no one in his
house, outside, anywhere, yet his heart was going like a
trip-hammer.

Imagining things?

No, someone had been there. Someone had seen—with
the rug moved and the cellar door open.

Son of a bitch.

The story investigators got from Engel's was good but
not quite good enough. Yes, the employees had seen Leni
come in this morning. Yes, it was much later than usual.
Yes, she was there most of the day until mid-afternoon.

Was there ever a time when she might have been gone?

Well, she had holed up in her office for a while...

Long enough to slip out and get to Elmwood Road?

Four of Nick's better thinkers—Bishop, Jensen,
Hogue, and Schaberg—were working the Ferguson killing. Between restaurant patrons, restaurant employees,
and people who happened to be out and about downtown
today, they had compiled a list of about sixty names of
people who would need to be interviewed: people who
might have seen Leni getting in or out of her car, someone
else getting in or out of her car, or who might have noticed
her leave the restaurant. Keys? they asked at every junc-
ture. It was common knowledge that Leni hung her keys
on a hook just inside her office, with her coat and purse.
Anyone could have grabbed them.

Quentin stuck his head in Nick's office, waved a piece
of paper. "Forensics on your firebomb."

Nick blinked. God, his house had been firebombed last
night and things were so crazy today he'd almost forgotten.

Quent said, "They're looking for prints or tracks, but it's
mostly leaves and pine straw right now so they don't know

what they've got yet. No fingerprints on the cocktail itself. Rag, gasoline, and a wine bottle. Some Liquid Joy mixed in."

Liquid Joy. The back of Nick's neck prickled, as if something had crawled across it. Dish soap thickened the mixture, made it more likely to burn more.

"And the bottle was scored."

"Scored?"

"Like, with a glass cutter. So it would be sure to break."

Christ. Nick took a deep breath and thought about Hannah and his mom—safe with Luke. Erin, too—she was under the watch of two Feds at Rebecca's house. Of course, she'd been under watch at his house, too. His jaw ground.

"What about the .22s?" Nick asked.

"They found one in a tree. No one has shown up at any nearby clinics wearing the second under his skin."

Too much of a long shot to think Erin had hit anyone, given the circumstances.

Nick's phone rang and someone knocked at the door at the same time. At the door was Feldman, but Nick answered the phone before he could speak.

"I'm at the Pub." Schaberg. Nick put him on speaker so Quent could hear. Schaberg said, "A reporter from one of the morning news shows called here this morning and asked for Ferguson. Bartender doesn't know which show, but said Lud was bragging about going out and being on TV and getting paid for it."

"That's it?" asked Nick. "How'd he know where to find Lud?"

"Who?"

"The reporter."

"Anyone who knew Lud would know where to find him, Nick," Schaberg said. "Just start checking bars. But just for the record, he was a she."

She? Nick hung up and Quentin straightened.

"Aw, man: That looks like Leni. She thought Ferguson took Rebecca, so she posed as a reporter to set him up. Ran his ass down."

"Maybe not." Feldman, who'd listened from the door, walked in. "Want me to rock your world?"

Nick and Quent both looked at him. "So, we're poring over missing persons reports for the last two decades. Thousands, and no reason to think they might be in our orbit."

"But..." Nick's heartbeat picked up speed.

"Then we get to Eleanor Vann. A sixty-two-year-old woman in Lexington, Kentucky. She disappeared in 2005."

"When the Hugginses lived in Virginia."

"Three hours and fourteen minutes away, says MapQuest."

Feldman held up a picture. A gray-haired Bohemian woman, overweight, with gaudy jewelry and fingernails like red claws. Tammy Faye Baker makeup job.

Not the sort who would have been a lover of Jack. Of course, that was mattering less and less.

"She was a medium. *Madam* Vann."

Nick frowned. "What puts her in our orbit?"

"Keep listening. She and her daughter both disappeared in August, and her bones were found in Lake Cumberland more than a year later. Rib bone appeared to have been shot through near the heart; the bones were washed too smooth to tell the caliber. There was no skin left to look for paint thinner on her face. But—" He paused, milking it.

"For Christ's sake, *what*?" Nick shot.

"The week before she disappeared, Madam Vann had an appointment with Maggie Huggins."

CHAPTER
46

NICK'S BRAIN STUMBLED. A second later he picked up the phone, called the tail on Margaret.

"She's in the house," the guy assured him. "Came straight home with Rodney from talking to you, hasn't gone anywhere since."

"Don't let her out of your sight. I want to know if she moves so much as a finger."

Okay, she's covered. Think, now. Think.

Quentin was at the whiteboard, adding: *Eleanor Vann. Medium. And daughter.*

"We need that search warrant," Nick said, and turned to Feldman. "And I want that history on Margaret."

"Coming."

Feldman left and Nick stared at the last name on the list. "Why was Maggie seeing a medium?"

"Her parents? Her sister, maybe?" Quent said. "Rodney's mother was Margaret's twin. Twins are supposed to have a bond of some sort."

"Here," Feldman said, coming back with a woman in tow. She was the same woman Nick had seen handling phone calls to locate students who'd left Mansfeld.

Starched white blouse. "This is Agent Bidell. She's been pulling together the background on Maggie Huggins."

"We're beginning to think she's our murderer," Nick said. "Do you see anything that could support that?"

"There was some major sibling rivalry in that family. I've seen people kill over less."

"Tell me."

She pulled out some pages, laying them on Nick's desk. First, two pictures. They were the same ones Margaret had been wearing in her locket. "You've got a pair of drop-dead-beautiful twins. Identical. Except one's the apple of her father's eye and one's not."

"Why's that?" Quentin asked.

"I don't know. I only know that when sister Claire killed herself, their father pulled every string he could not to let Maggie get custody of Rodney. He got a lawyer and claimed that Maggie was unfit in the eyes of God."

"I take it he was a religious man?" Nick asked.

Bidell nodded. "Catholic, sort of. But not just everyday Catholic. Some fanatic strain. His criticism got even worse when John Huggins started hanging around her. Her father blamed him for Claire's death."

"Why?" Feldman said.

"John Huggins was driving the car the night Claire was scarred. They were together and he fell asleep at the wheel."

"Wait a minute," Nick said, "John knew Claire? Before he knew Maggie?"

"Well enough to take her out, but that might not be saying much. Claire Devilas was a call girl. She lived on the kindness of men with money."

"A call girl with a blind son?"

"She only saw her kid once in a while. He was at boarding school."

Nick rubbed his brow. Maggie's twin sister was a call girl who'd gone out with John. Weird, to say the least. "And a year after the accident," he said, trying to put it all together, "John married her twin, Maggie."

"Yes," Bidell said. "Believe it or not, it looks like John and Maggie met at the hospital, trying to visit Claire after the accident."

"Trying?" Quentin asked.

"She wouldn't see anyone. In fact, she lived like a recluse for the next year—which was the rest of her life."

Bidell laid out a photo of Magg—no, Nick corrected himself—this was Claire.

"Before the car accident," Bidell said; then she put another picture beside the first, and said, "After."

"Whoa," Nick said. The scarring was brutal. Even with a thick layer of caked-on makeup, Claire's face looked like a photograph that had been cut up and taped back together, the edges not quite fitting.

"This is why she became a recluse?" Nick asked.

"And why she killed herself. At least, that's what her father claimed," Agent Bidell said. "Turns out she never went out after the accident, refused to be seen. She and her little boy lived like hermits for that year. The only time she went out was the night before she died. She took her son to a Mardi Gras parade."

"Because she could wear a mask," Nick said, recalling the mask in Rodney's house. One of the few tokens he had from his life with his mother. "And then she came back home and killed herself."

"Right in front of her kid," Bidell said. "After she died, he was alone with her body for two days. Tried to put her makeup on for her. Finally, he found his way to a cathedral down the block where the nuns took him in."

Nick winced. Christ. No wonder Rodney's hair had turned. That would be enough to traumatize anyone, not to mention a ten-year-old kid who was blind. "So, then the fight started about who got Rodney. Where's her father now?"

"Dead. And her mother. They both died of cancer, six years apart. When her father died, Maggie was the last family member. Her father had written her out of the will, so everything reverted to the state. Maggie never saw a dime. She did break into his house and take a collection of figurines, though. There's a misdemeanor charge for it on file."

"What kind of figurines?"

"Angels. Ten little ceramic statues of angels. Court documents say she claimed that's all she wanted from the estate."

Nick tried to put it all together, but he couldn't get traction on anything. "Maggie is a beautiful woman, talented, and successful. Her sister was a hooker-turned-recluse. What would make an ultra-religious father claim *Maggie* was the one unfit in the eyes of God?"

Nick stared at the whiteboard, trying to imagine something that might make a fanatically religious father turn his back on a daughter. The answer came in one name: *Shelly Quinn.*

"Lesbian," Nick said, more to himself than to the room. But everyone heard.

"Nick?" Quent said.

He turned to Feldman. "The one thing you always said didn't fit about Shelly Quinn was that she was a looker and yet there weren't any studly frat boys around her. The one thing that seemed odd about Jack and Margaret was that they were a partnership except in bed."

The whole room grew still, but Nick's mind raced. Damn it, Shelly's roommates had just about handed it to him on a platter when he asked if she'd had an affair with Jack. *With his* wife *she might've... Not with* him...

Jesus. Maggie was a lesbian.

"Doesn't make her a killer," Quent said. "The fire-fighter in Minnesota still doesn't fit, and neither does the medium."

No, they didn't. But for sure this wasn't only about *Jack's* affairs. Maybe it was about Maggie's.

Nick picked up the phone. "Bishop, have you got the master list of people slated for interviews about Leni's whereabouts this afternoon?"

"Yeah. Sixty-three names who were at or around Engel's Eatery today, who might've seen Leni leave the restaurant. Will take another day to get to them all interviewed."

"Is Margaret Calloway on that list?"

"Hold on..." Shuffling papers. "Yeah. No. Oh, wait, I remember. No one saw Margaret around town today, but there were a couple people who said her Saturn was here."

"Where?"

"Behind the Sunoco station on Fir Street."

Nick's heart dropped. He hung up and told Quent and Feldman and Bidell.

"That's right behind Engel's," Quent said. "So, Margaret stole Leni's car and ran down Lud, then just came back and parked it?"

"Maybe. Except the car wasn't broken into, and everyone at the restaurant says no one went into Leni's office, where the keys were. Without doing that, how did Margaret get keys for Leni's car?"

It hit them all at once. "Rebecca."

CHAPTER
47

ERIN CLOSED HER EYES. There was nothing left in Rebecca's room. Not one item she and Katie hadn't picked up, looked at, talked about. Not one clue.

Her phone rang. It was Nick.

"Listen to me, and if Katie can hear you, don't say anything."

Erin stiffened. "Okay," she said. Katie was ten feet away.

"It's Margaret," he said. His voice was wired. He sounded like he was running, and there was commotion behind him.

"Nick?"

"It wasn't Jack, damn it; it was Margaret."

She almost lost her breath. "You're sure? Can you prove it?"

"I'm getting there. We're putting together a team now to take her at Hilltop. We're gonna go fall on her and finish this whole thing. I've called my sister; she's ready as soon as we nail down Margaret."

"Dear God." Erin could hardly breathe. It was happening. Justin was going to be exonerated.

"What can I do?"

"Nothing, I've got it cove—" He stopped. "You've done enough, sweetheart. I can finish it now. I just want to make sure you're here when it's over. Deal?"

Erin felt as if her heart would come out of her chest. She clutched her arms to her breast, holding him in her heart, and closed her eyes. "Deal."

Rodney seethed. Think, *think*. Everything had been just fine. Years, a lifetime, of everything perfectly controlled, and suddenly, things were unraveling. Someone had *seen* and he didn't know who.

Unacceptable. There was only one more angel, and that was Nick Mann. If there were more, then—that couldn't be. He'd spent the past twelve years hunting all ten down, his entire adult life eradicating them.

The rage came like a mushroom cloud, and with it a sense of panic he'd never experienced. For the first time since his surgery, he couldn't see straight. Suddenly, he didn't know who or how many were out there watching.

And it was Mann's fault. He should have been the grand finale. He should have been the end.

Rodney paced. He had to think, but there was no time. Whoever had just been here had certainly seen Rebecca. Police could be on their way right now.

The decision was quick—the only choice, really— and thanks to Jack, he could do it...false IDs and credit cards, a stash of money. For years, Jack had lived with his eye on the road and Rodney could make use of that now. Take it all and start over, without any angels watching. A new ruse, maybe—a paraplegic, maybe, or an autistic. He'd studied Calvin enough. He could pull it off.

But he couldn't leave anyone behind. Not Maggie, not Erin Sims, not Nick Mann.

Especially not Nick Mann.

He took two more minutes thinking it through, then kicked into gear. Brought the motorcycle up and pulled it into the woods where he'd be able to make a quick break if he needed to. Tipped the ninth figurine off the shelf and watched it shatter on the floor, then grabbed the tenth and dropped it into his pocket. Snatched up Rebecca's mask.

He paused on the way out, and went to the kitchen to have a little fun with Nick. When he was satisfied the sheriff would catch on, he grabbed a coat and hat and the white cane, and rolled down the path on his scooter.

First, Maggie. She was no angel; she'd never seen Rodney for what he really was. But she was in the way.

And after she was gone, the Angelmaker would get his grand finale. He'd turn it into a hunt and spread a little bait for Mann, just to make sure he showed up.

Erin Sims.

Erin hung up with Nick, her heart thrumming in her chest. It was coming to an end. She could hardly believe it.

When her phone rang, she grabbed it without looking at the number. "Nick?"

"No. Uh...sorry. Dr. Sims, this is Rodney."

He was whispering; he sounded strange. Maybe even afraid.

It's Margaret. She's the murderer. Did he know?

"Rodney, why are you calling me?"

"I need to talk to you. I think I have something important. I think—" He stopped, struggling with the words. "I know who killed Lauren and all those others."

Erin's pulse kicked up. *Don't say anything. Let Nick handle it.*

"It was Maggie. God help me, it was Maggie."

She let out a breath. He knew. "Rodney, I don't think she would hurt you—"

"I know that. But she knows the sheriff is coming, too. She's covered her tracks. You won't find the evidence, but I took something from her. It will free your brother."

Dear God. Erin's breathing went shallow. She didn't want to tell him he was right, and that Nick was already planning to take Maggie Huggins. But she didn't want to let Rodney crawl into a hole with evidence that would free Justin, or give Maggie a chance to destroy it.

"Can you meet me?" he said. "I'm afraid to go to Hilltop right now. She scares me."

Erin looked out Leni's front window. The gray sedan was still there, parked along the curb with two FBI agents. She could leave one with Katie and still have an escort herself.

"Where?" she asked.

"The corner of 219 and Grauter's Road…Can you find that? I can get there on my scooter in about fifteen minutes."

"Yes," Erin said. "I'll be there."

He hung up. Done.

Now get to Hilltop House. Hurry, but not too much. Mann considered Maggie a suspect; Sims hadn't denied that. And Rodney knew Mann well enough to know that if he'd caught a whiff of something at Hilltop, cops would be watching. Rodney didn't dare go wheeling in there like a sighted man. Keep up the guise, just for a little while longer.

So he put Rebecca's mask in a bag, checked the cartridge of his gun, and stuck his folded white cane in the basket on the scooter. Put on his dark glasses and tooled in slowly to the back entrance like he always did, then swept his cane back and forth along the path to go inside.

He took off his dark glasses and tugged on a pair of gloves. The gloves were unnecessary in the long run—sooner or later they would know it was him. But wearing them would buy him enough time to meet Erin and lay a trail for Nick Mann. After that, he'd be gone, on to a new life without any fucking angels watching him.

"Maggie?" he called, walking into the foyer. She came in, looking drawn and exhausted, yet still carrying that ethereal beauty shared by only one other person in the world.

"Rodney," she said. She seemed surprised that he'd come back to the inn. "There's no need to work today. No reservations or gues—" She stopped and tipped her head, looking at him oddly.

Rodney met her gaze head-on. No glasses, no looking off into the distance. He pulled out the pistol. "I'm sorry, Maggie. I hoped it wouldn't come to this."

Nick flew into the command room with one thing on his mind: Margaret Calloway.

The forces had gathered—the bulk of Hopewell's deputies, a half-dozen members of the Tactical Arms and Snipers Unit, and four Feds. A sniper was on his way in from Carroll County. Canine unit standing by.

Nick dove in. "I've had surveillance on Margaret Calloway since this morning: We think she kidnapped Rebecca. At this moment, she's inside the inn at Hilltop House." He pointed at three deputies, who each had the blank stare of someone trying to believe what he'd just heard, and at a woman who was a Fed. "You. Sling a net around her until we can get there. Keep it loose so she can't see it. If she goes *anywhere,* consider that she may be leading us to Rebecca Engel."

"Margaret?" Jensen asked, even as the four of them grabbed for coats and guns and started moving.

"We're operating on the assumption that Rebecca is alive and we need for Margaret to keep her that way. Don't spook her."

They left and Nick turned to everybody else. "Search warrant's on its way. Here's the Hilltop layout." He slapped an aerial map against the wall and Bishop jumped up to help hold it. "We'll take positions here, here..."

He got everyone up to speed. When he was finished, one of the Feds raised his hand and addressed Feldman. "Whose command are we?"

Feldman stared him down like a dog. "This one belongs to Mann. We all work for him."

Nick gave Feldman a nod. Okay. Everyone on the same page, then.

He said, "Go. Keep your positions until I get word the warrant is signed. Then we're gonna fucking tear that place apart."

"Wh—Wait..." Maggie backed up a step, her face clouded by shock. "Rodney, what are you doing? You can..." She looked more closely. "You can see?" And one realization led to another, and horror washed across her face. "You?" she asked, on a hush.

"I don't have any choice now. Nick Mann will be coming. Soon, he'll know everything." *But by the time he does, I'll be gone.*

"What will he know?" she asked, her eyes probing his. For a moment, he wondered what she was seeing there, in eyes she hadn't seen for years, the dark lenses always standing between him and the world. "John?" she asked, and dread filled her gaze. "You killed John?"

"Fuck John," he snapped. "He was never good enough for you. Or for me."

Something Rodney didn't recognize seemed to hit her in a wave. "Oh, dear God." It looked as if her knees threatened to give way. "Rodney," she said, on a hush. "He was your father."

Rodney's breath stopped. *Father?*

Her voice shook with emotion. "Dear God, he did everything for you. He built his life around being with you. Even marrying me, a woman who would never—"

She stopped, but Rodney barely noticed. The world was out of tilt.

"Oh, Rodney," Maggie said.

"Shut up," he barked, and she blanched. This wasn't right. "If he was my father, why didn't he tell me?"

"Because you hated him for the accident. You never hid that. He couldn't bear to tell you."

"Then where was he all those years?"

"Claire didn't tell him about you. Not until she made her decision to—" She broke off.

"Kill herself and leave her son."

Maggie swallowed. "She sent him a letter the day she died. He received it three days later. That was the first he knew about you." She stopped, glancing down at the gun and up again. "He couldn't change the lost time. All he could do was try to make a life for you. We tried. Together, we tried."

The rage jumped him. "Together? He was never a husband to you."

"Oh, Rodney," she said, in the saddest voice he'd ever heard. "I didn't want him. I've never wanted a man, not like that. It's the reason your grandfather detested me so."

Rodney stared, then shook his head. This was crazy. It was like a roller coaster set free at the top of a steep hill and there was nothing he could do to stop it. It kept on running, twisting and turning and picking up speed. Going by too fast for him to make sense of anything.

Maggie stared at him, her voice quavering on her lips. "How many?" she asked. "Besides John, how many?"

Rodney looked behind her at the grand display of masks. "Not enough," he said. "But I'm not finished yet."

He straightened the gun, and Maggie stiffened. *Kill her, kill her,* he told himself. But this was Maggie.

She looked at him. "He knew, you know," she said, as if she were figuring it out herself for the first time. "All this time, he must have known. That's why we left Virginia. It's why he set up everything with Dorian. The names, the identities, the money all set aside. I never understood. I thought he was afraid of Erin Sims. But all along, he was protecting you."

Rodney frowned. No. It couldn't be true. John was greed and lust and betrayal, and a murderer in his own right.

Maggie's eyes dropped to the gun. They glistened with tears. *Kill her. It's almost over.*

"Rodney, put the gun down. You can't fix it now. It's over."

But it wasn't over—not until the last angel. He glanced up at the blind masks on the wall behind Maggie, and could feel the porcelain of the last figurine in his pocket, cold against this leg. Still watching. No choice now.

He had to finish.

Maggie must have seen it in his eyes. She turned to run but he caught her, twisted her around and spun her back against his chest, pressed the gun to her temple. She cried out but he didn't dare stop. Roller coaster going fast.

Her left hand grabbed at his arm and a thought sprang up. Rodney shifted positions, correcting himself—Maggie was left-handed. He bullied her to his other side and transferred the gun to his left hand, brought it to her temple, and fired.

Fwp. Maggie dropped.

He straightened, looking down at her. A fleeting memory of his mother gripped him and for half a second, he was ten years old again, in the dark, alone, his mother's blood leaking between his fingers and the scent of death rising from her chest, and him smoothing on her makeup with bloody hands. He buried the image and stared down at Maggie, his chest an empty pit. Dead, and no time to even grieve for her.

Because Nick Mann was watching. *Mann* had made him do this. Fuck Mann. Fuck him, fuck him, fuck him.

Fury kicked in and with it, the clarity to set the stage. Rodney spent thirty seconds setting it up: gun in Maggie's left hand, mask of Rebecca in her right. He left her where she had dropped, tentacles of blood creeping through the rug beneath her head and Rebecca's mask faceup, her eyes now empty and seeing nothing.

He backed away, and a thought popped in the back of his mind. Rebecca wasn't dead. He hadn't finished her yet. He'd heard someone upstairs and panicked, and there were so many other things...

He looked at his watch, the clock beating down on him. He glanced around the foyer at the setup: It would take a little while to sort through, but not enough that he dared to go back to his cabin. God willing, the sheriff's department would be held up here long enough for Rebecca to take her last breaths. She'd been on that table almost two days already, so she wouldn't last much longer. Dehydration, exposure, pneumonia, what with the clay she'd sucked into her lungs.

It was more important to go meet Erin Sims. And let her deliver Mann.

He took a deep breath, straightened his jacket, and put his glasses back on. Walked out the back door of the inn the same way he'd entered, got on his three-wheeler, and drove slowly into the woods like he'd done hundreds of times before.

Nothing to see, bastards.

Erin went outside to the surveillance car. "I need to go to Rt. 219," she said, her cell phone calling up a map. "You're supposed to be my escort, right?"

The agent in the driver's seat—Fisher, Erin remembered—blinked. She was pretty sure he'd been dozing. "Uh, yeah."

"I don't want to leave Katie in there alone, but I need to meet someone."

"I'll stay here," said the agent in the passenger seat. "I can call another car."

Erin went around the car and took his seat. "Take care of her, okay?"

He nodded. "Will do."

And Fisher turned the ignition. "Tell me where."

CHAPTER
48

THE TEAM GOT INTO position around Hilltop House. They held for five minutes; then Nick got the call: "You got your warrant."

Nick gave the command. At once, small herds of law enforcement broke through every cavity of Hilltop's inn, barn, and carriage house. In twelve seconds, fifteen law enforcement officers were inside; two minutes after that, each of the buildings was cleared.

Except for Margaret, who lay dead in the foyer.

"Ah, Christ, Christ," Nick said. He pounded a fist on the wall, set the masks to rattling. *"Fuck,"* he said, even as the team around him started roping off the area. He felt as if his gut had been sliced open and tied into knots. "Damn you, Margaret. Goddamn you."

There was nothing at the intersection of Grauter's Road and 219. Nothing but Rodney, his light hair glowing like a moon in the settling dusk.

Fisher said, "Wait, I'll go with you," and Erin sat in the car until he came around to open her door. He walked at her side as she approached Rodney.

"Rodney," Erin said, "it's me. Erin Sims. This is Agent Fisher."

His chin cocked a little to the side. His eyes, behind the glasses, aimed somewhere in the vicinity of the two of them. "An FBI agent," he said. She didn't know if he sounded humored or put off. "You were afraid to meet me alone?"

Erin ignored that. "You said you have something for me to prove my brother didn't kill Lauren McAllister." She couldn't help the bitterness that came. "Why didn't you come forward with it sooner?"

"I didn't know. How long have *you* known that Margaret was the killer? I just found out myself."

Erin's unease slipped a notch. He was right; it was all just now beginning to come to an end. "What do you have that will help Justin? Give it to me."

He patted his jacket and reached inside. Fisher lifted his hand, ready, but didn't pull his gun. Rodney was blind.

And through the pocket of his jacket, Rodney shot him.

Erin screamed. Dear God. She ran but Rodney was on her in three strides. He tackled her on the gravel of the shoulder, taking her down. The air *whooshed* from her lungs and for a few terrifying seconds, she couldn't catch a breath. He shoved her down with one hand on the back of her neck, the other pressing the gun against her shoulder blade. She felt the weight of his knee in her back and struggled to breathe, spitting grit and gravel. For one shining second, the hand on the back of her head lifted and she came up, trying to dislodge him, but then something white flashed in his hand. A sound—*pzzt*.

And that was all.

The search for Rebecca at Hilltop House changed gears: Now it was also the scene of Margaret's suicide.

A crime scene unit took apart the foyer an inch at a time. Nick stood on the stairwell above Margaret's body, waiting for Martin Gamble to take a temperature reading. Quent stepped through the front door.

"Anyone here?" Nick asked.

"Rosa and Calvin. They're scared, but okay. Weren't expecting cops to bust through their apartment door, that's all."

Nick closed his eyes, wondering if anyone in his town would ever sleep soundly again.

"Sheriff," Gamble said. "You want to look at this?"

Nick stepped down to floor level but Gamble stopped him, saying, "Gloves," and a crime scene techie held out a box. Nick took two of the thin rubber gloves, handed a pair to Quentin, and they put them on. Gamble handed him the bare mask that had lain beside Maggie, beneath her right hand.

Nick's first thought was that it was more fragile than he expected. Unfired, a delicate bisque.

"Should've broken when she fell," Nick said.

"Yeah. And—" Gamble's face had gone pasty. "Doesn't Rebecca Engel have a jewel in the side of her nose? A stud?"

Nick frowned. He didn't understand.

"Look inside."

Nick turned the mask over and looked into the back. Shock washed over him.

Two columns of clay rose high inside the nose, sucked upward. And on one side, the imprint of a jewel, just above the left nostril.

Nick gasped. "Ah, God, God," he heard himself say, but beyond that, he couldn't speak.

Quentin whispered, "That's Rebecca?"

Nick swallowed back the taste of bile. He looked up at the wall of faces and horror seeped into his bones.

"No way," Quentin said, following his thoughts.

But Nick thought it just might be. Seven of them, all roughly the same size and shape, though crafted in different styles. Nick had seen the bare forms in Margaret's workshop—just like the one he now held in his hand. There were always a half dozen or more sitting around on the counters or on a mannequin mold. This was what she started with, made into her signature works of art, and then displayed in museums or sold.

Or hung them in her foyer?

He walked around Margaret's body, stepping over the little plastic tents that had popped up to mark evidence, and handed the mask in his hand to Gamble. Reached up to the wall and unhooked another, turned it over.

He had to force himself to breathe. No nostril columns on this one—no sign of someone sucking clay into their sinus cavity trying to breathe, but there was an indentation on this one, the size of a large pinhead, right above the corner of the left lip.

A Marilyn Monroe beauty mark. The mole of Lauren McAllister.

Nick reeled; Quentin ducked from the room.

"Take them all," Nick said, though a moment later, he wasn't sure he'd said it aloud. "Take them all. They're going to match the victims." And a moment later, he added, "Call Florida."

He forced air back into his lungs and looked to the other room where Quentin, all two-hundred-and-thirty-five pounds of defensive tackle tough-guy, had gone to throw up. When Quent came up for air, Nick said, "Margaret's workshop. Let's go."

• • •

They only made it halfway across the parking lot before one of Gamble's crew ducked out of the carriage house and jogged halfway up the hill. "You gotta see this, Sheriff," he called out, his voice strung with tension. Half horrified, half excited. "In the trunk of Maggie Calloway's Saturn."

They followed him down to the carriage house. The trunk of the car stood open, a high-powered lamp clamped to the edge and shining inside. Two tiny shards of something—bone?—had been photographed inside the trunk, beside their tiny tents that marked them as evidence. The techie was ready to pull them out.

"What are they?" Nick asked, and the woman went down with a pair of tweezers. A second later, she came up with one of them, turning it in the light. It was a slender wedge, black on one side, light on the other. Deep red smudges on one edge.

"Fingernail," she said. "Black nail polish. Someone was clawing at the carpet in here, trying to get out."

CHAPTER
49

ERIN TRIED TO MOVE but couldn't. She felt as if she were in a bowl, folded, cramped. She opened her eyes but nothing changed and when she tried to move her hands her wrists wouldn't come apart. She wiggled her fingers and a nail snagged, ripping. She winced, felt the white-hot chill of her nail bed exposed.

Her heart began to throb. She remembered walking up to Rodney, wondering, *What does he have for me?* Then his hand went into his jacket for it and instead of coming back out, the man named Fisher dropped. And she ran and she fell, and she slammed into the gravel.

Then, nothing.

Now she was bouncing—moving, she decided, but her brain still felt thick and soggy, like wool. It was pitch black and musty and cool, and smelled like...trunk.

Oh, God. She was in the trunk of a car.

Her hands were bound at the wrist, trapped against her belly. She tried to straighten her legs, was able to move them a couple of inches, no more. Started thinking about dying like this, running out of air in the trunk, never waking up. She thought of Nick finding her tomorrow or the next day, stuck in this fetal position, her face the pasty white of the dead.

Stop it. She tried to orient herself in the blackness... Where was the front of the trunk, the corner? There were taillights somewhere. As much as she could move, she started feeling around, wondering what taillights felt like from the inside. She couldn't reach, bend her arms, couldn't get any range of motion.

Never mind. Try the feet, keep feeling around. Tail-lights somewhere...

To Margaret's studio, the hounds of panic nipping Nick's brain. He and Quent had been here twice, maybe three times? And just yesterday, while they were talking to Maggie in her workshop, Rebecca Engel had maybe been there in the carriage house, trying to claw her way out of the trunk.

He tamped that down and pulled Gamble and two of the CSI team into the barn, saying: "We know Rebecca was here and Margaret made a mask of her face out of clay. We're looking for anything to prove that."

They stared at him as if he were crazy, but he didn't wait for them to ask questions. "Go," he ordered.

He and Quent took the largest studio, where Margaret held her classes, stored most supplies, and did the firing of her sculptures. They stayed out of the way of the forensics team but walked the workshop one step at a time, opening every cupboard, closet, drawer, hitting every light switch. It was bright, spacious, cool. An artist's domain, a place where masterworks were created. A ribbon of nausea twisted in Nick's belly at the thought of how those mas-terworks were created, and he had to force himself to keep moving, keep looking. There was no switch to a secret door or passage, no sign of struggle or hardship, no hint that this space had ever held a woman against her will.

Just a few stacks of bare facial molds ready for their destinies.

Quent handled them one by one, laying them facedown on a counter so they could see the inner contours. Across a window ledge sat a handful of wig blocks and a row of mounted mannequin heads, male and female. Three of them were covered with clay, drying.

"I don't know what to think," Quentin said, looking at both the molds and the masks. "These were made on plastic. They aren't human. You think the ones out there on the wall could have modeled for her willingly?" he asked.

"The one in Margaret's hands—Rebecca—had breathed clay into her nostrils."

Quentin's face fell. "Right." He came to the last mask in the stack and stopped. Nick frowned.

"What?"

Quentin's skin lost three shades. He held up the mask, turning it over to face Nick. A short gray hair was stuck to the edge of the temple.

"Ah, Jesus," Nick said.

It was Jack.

Rodney drove like a blue-hair—cruise control set for exactly the speed limit, complete stops at intersections, careful not to attract any attention. It was dark now, so his driving a car wouldn't attract any attention. At least not until Mann put an APB on this sedan in particular.

He turned on the radio—nothing. The news hadn't gotten wind of Maggie's death yet. But it didn't mean Mann didn't know. He might have been to Hilltop House already, found her, and gagged the press. Could have even started a search for this car already. Depended upon whether the dead agent had been discovered yet.

He drove for almost an hour, Sims beating at the inside of the trunk, falling silent for a few minutes, then starting up again. She'd have come around shortly after he put her in, and he imagined that in the quieter moments, she was probably frantically squirreling around inside, trying to knock out a taillight. She wouldn't be able to, not with her hands bound. Besides, he'd sealed off the taillights from the inside with some of the duct tape.

Taking no chances. He didn't need her for much longer but there was one more thing he wanted to do. She'd have to suffice as the last angel. When Nick came for her, there would be no chance to do a mask for him. There would only be time to kill him.

But Rodney would make sure there was still one more mask. And he'd leave it for Nick Mann.

A little gift, you son of a bitch.

Nick could hardly wrap his mind around it. Maggie's masks. He couldn't fathom it.

"It explains the paint thinner," Quentin said. "She didn't want the bodies found with clay on their faces."

That snapped Nick back like a rubber band to the face. "Just Lauren McAllister and Robin Weelkes," he said. "We don't know about Eleanor Vann 'cause she was in the lake too long. And none of the other bodies were ever found—including Jack and"—he stopped, then forced himself to say it—"Rebecca." He propped his hands on his belt and tried to think: Where the fuck were the bodies? Where the fuck was Rebecca? Jack and Margaret owned forty acres, woods in one direction and farm-lands in the others. Lake Erie, an hour's drive. He tried to remember if any unidentified bodies had been found in the past few years anywhere in the area, but couldn't. His brain was too full of Margaret's sickness.

Commotion erupted outside the workshop, and Nick snapped back. A woman cried out, and a deputy called after her. It sounded like—

"Rosa," Nick said, as she burst past the deputy. "What is it?"

"Calvin," she said. Her voice shook with emotion. "He needs to tell you something."

Nick followed Rosa out of the workroom. Calvin was in Jack's workshop in the main part of the barn, walking in small circles. Around and around. His head wagged back and forth in such tiny, fast movements it should have jostled his brain.

"Calvin?"

"...Thirty-eight degrees Fahrenheit, five-thirty-two a.m., November thirteenth, two-thousand-twelve...Thirty-eight degrees Fahrenheit, five-thirty-two a.m., November thirteenth, two-thousand-twelve..."

"Calvin." Rosa stood next to Quentin, a knuckle pressed against her lips. *"Madre de dios."*

"Thirty-eight degrees Fahrenheit, five-thirty-two a.m., November thirteenth, two-thousand-twelve..."

Nick took him by the shoulders, gave him a hard shake. "Calvin, look at me. What are you talking about?"

But Calvin's gaze never made contact and he sank back into his mantra, jumping dates and temperatures, making no sense. "Eighteen-hundred-and-fifty degrees Fahrenheit, November fourteenth, two-thousand-twelve...Too hot, hot, hot. Thirty-eight degrees Fahrenheit, five-thirty-two, November thirteenth, two-thousand-twelve..."

Nick closed his eyes. Goddamn it, what in the hell

was he supposed to read from that? Then he stopped. He ran over the last time and date in his mind, repeating it aloud. "Five-thirty-two a.m., November thirteenth, two-thousand-twelve...That was yesterday. When Rebecca disappeared."

Rosa looked at him in horror. "Calvin, what is this?"

Quentin stepped up. Calvin's eyes bounced around the barn like a scared animal. Nick took him by the arm, vibrating inside. "Five-thirty-two a.m., November thirteenth," he said. "Why were you outside, Calvin? How come you know the temperature?"

Calvin's eyes got big. His head swiveled back and forth.

"Did you see Rebecca yesterday morning?"

He shook his head. A violent shaking.

"You were outside. When Margaret was in bed and your mom would have been in the kitchen. Rodney went to Kroger." He grabbed Calvin by the shoulders, hard. "How come you know the temperature?"

"Kroger. Kroger. Eyes hurt. Red, red eyes, like a witch-witch-witch. Pills from trash bag at Kroger. Bring the whole bag whole bag whole bag. Thirty-eight-degrees Fahrenheit, five-thirty-nine a.m..."

Nick straightened, stunned. He looked at Quent and a knot of shock transformed to cold rage. "Rodney. He snowed us. That motherfucker snowed us."

CHAPTER
50

WEAVER'S CLAY RESERVES.

It was nine-thirty in the evening when Rodney got there. He'd been here dozens of times with Maggie. Knew just where to find the clay.

Except—he frowned—there were still lights on. Shit. He'd never come at night before. Didn't think about a second shift going.

He passed the mine—and the driveway that led to Nick Mann's vacation property—tooling around the perimeter of Weaver's as far as he could. The offices were all dark and there was no equipment moving the earth outside at this time of night. But steam still rose from the biggest building, where the clay passed through the hammer mill. And there was plenty of activity in the warehouse, where they packaged and stored the finished product. Lots of bright security lights outside.

Too many people. And most of them would know Rodney on sight.

He'd have to wait.

He turned around and swung into the Mann drive, pulling into the woods. Had always wondered what sort of place Mann had back here. Now he approached the house and got out of the car. Scoffed. Mann really had struck it rich when his wife was killed. The place was huge and desolate. A few trees looked as if they'd been hung with ghosts for Halloween and never taken down. The driveway was gravel, and with all the drizzle and sleet this week, the stones were slick with—

He stopped, reaching down. For God's sake, why hadn't he thought of that? There was a reason the Weaver brothers mined this area. Ohio was the fourth largest clay producer in the country and Weaver's one of the biggest games in the business. This whole area was rich with clay. He didn't need the fucking mine. Dig any hole. This mask didn't need to be pristine for Maggie to use. It only needed to be identifiable—for Nick.

He dug his fingers through the gravel, scraped out a handful of mud. Squeezed it a few times to test the consistency.

He straightened and looked around, and smiled. The irony was magnificent. There couldn't be a better place to leave Erin Sims in her mask.

Rodney's cabin door stood open. A couple of dirty towels lay on the floor by the door. The furniture was... shifted. Not quite in order.

"He's gone," Nick said, knowing it in the pit of his stomach. A couple of deputies went through anyway, making sure. When they came back, Nick nodded to Gamble and his techies. "Get busy."

"He can't get far," Quent said. "Three-wheeler. Bli—"

He started to say it, and Nick looked at him. Not blind. A blind man doesn't leave a stack of dirty towels on the floor to trip over. A blind man couldn't have maneuvered around the county the way the killer needed to.

"He's driving something," Nick said. "Gotta have a vehicle."

"Or could've scrambled out into the woods like some sort of survivalist."

Nick didn't think so. Rodney liked his creature comforts. But he didn't say so. He was too busy looking at the way the rug beneath the coffee table was cockeyed and wrinkled up at one corner. A loose woven rug, the kind that gets kicked up at the corners and becomes a trip hazard. Not something a blind man would have in his living room.

A tide of self-disgust welled up in Nick's body. *He* was the one who was blind. Unwilling to see what was right in front of his eyes.

And there was no place else...

He walked over and kicked up the rug, stomped on the floor, then shoved the coffee table aside and tore the rug away. A door. He ripped it open.

God help him. There was a room down there.

A techie handed him a flashlight. Nick stuck it under his arm and cocked his gun. Quentin and two others aimed their lights into the hole and Nick started down, Quentin right behind. It was a narrow cement staircase, dirty, cracked. It went down nine steps, then hairpinned around a landing.

The smell hit him first, then the heat, then the sounds. The smell: burned pork and vanilla wax. The temperature: too hot for a basement in November. The sounds: high singing like a women's choir or one of those English boys' choirs... *Regina coeli*... That's all Nick had time to notice before he heard the dull roar of a machine in the corner—and the wheezing of a woman.

"Cover me," he said, and Quentin fell in behind him. Nick rounded the hairpin landing far enough for his eyes to adjust to the darkness. He squinted and his gut wrenched. In the center of the room, a heavy workbench. On top, a woman.

"Ah, God," he breathed. "Rebecca." She was laid out on a table, faceup, dead still. Her breathing sounded like a freight train. Her teeth chattered behind lips that somehow didn't open, though it had to be over a hundred degrees down here. "Ambulance," Nick called up the stairs, while Quent walked around Nick with his gun and flashlight.

"It's clear," Quent said. He hit the stairs, calling out orders, pulling a string on a bare lightbulb on his way. Nick's heart stopped when the light came on.

Rebecca was duct-taped in place. Yards and yards of it, around and around her and the table, ankles to throat. Her face was immobilized by a strange looping of the tape under her chin and across the top of her forehead, and the powdery residue of clay left her looking chalky. Her lips were cracked and sealed shut, as she struggled to take in air through her nose. She shuddered with chills.

Nick bent over her face. "Rebecca," he said, touching his finger to her cheek. She was on fire. "It's Sheriff Mann. You're safe now, sweetie. We're gonna get you out of here."

EMTs were the enemies of a crime scene. Nonetheless, everyone cleared out to give them access to Rebecca, focusing on the upstairs while they waited. Nick called for Gamble, who found evidence of tire tracks in the living room—a small motorcycle—in and out the door several times, leaving mud that Rodney had tried to wipe up with the towels. Clean enough to have fooled Nick or a casual visitor, but not a crime scene crew. In the kitchen, everything was in its place, except for the orange juice Rodney had bought to match the receipt that served as his alibi for the time when Rebecca was taken. The juice sat out on the counter, unopened, with the receipt tucked underneath.

Nick's hands fisted. The fucker was taunting him.

He walked the small cabin, remembering being in here before. With Calvin and Rodney and Quent, nothing out of place. He stepped over to the ceramic bowl of Mardi Gras beads, remembered thinking it was an awfully sparse collection of souvenirs for a life almost thirty years long. He fingered the beads, then picked up the black mask beside them.

"Rodney's mother took him to Mardi Gras the night she killed herself," Nick said when Quent came over.

"Think that's hers?"

Nick turned it over. It wasn't worn, but had the feeling of being old, untouched. Dust had settled in a dull sheen over the satin and jewels and feathers. A dark spot stained one yellow feather.

Nick handed it to Quentin. "Probably."

"All clear." An EMT emerged from the basement, carrying a plastic bag of fluids with a tube running behind him. They pulled Rebecca up the cellar stairs on a stretcher, the fluids going into her veins and oxygen into her nose. Nick offered a silent word to a God he wasn't sure of, praying their efforts weren't too little, too late; then he and Quent went back downstairs. The place was lit up with floodlights now, but it was still hot and the air was cloying. A church choir floated from the CD player, the CD case sitting on top bearing a picture of a cathedral and a bunch of Latin titles.

Nick hit a button on the machine and the angel voices died. The dull roar that had hummed beneath the singing continued on from a machine in the corner. Nick narrowed his gaze on the machine. He remembered it: an industrial-sized kiln he'd once helped move into Margaret's work-shop, back when she still did large sculptures like the boy and girl statues in the garden. He'd helped Jack vent it out the back of the barn, but when Margaret started focusing on smaller works like her masks, she'd gotten rid of it.

Apparently not. Rodney had it now. It was vented through the fireplace in his living room upstairs.

A dozen thoughts crossed Nick's mind as he made his way around the table and over to the kiln. Rosa: *"It's hot in here. Smells like pork."* Calvin: *"Eighteen-hundred-and-fifty degrees. Too, too hot."* Erin, reading: *"Witches have red eyes, and cannot see far. When a child fell into her power, she killed it, threw it in the oven and cooked it."* And Nick's own question, over and over again... *Where are the other bodies?*

With a pit in his gut, he laid a hand on the kiln. Hot. He turned it off, heard the gas flames inside suck their last breaths, and moved around to open one of the port holes. He looked inside.

His turn to be sick.

Nick forced himself to keep thinking, keep moving. *No, don't think about the ash and bones in the kiln—almost certainly Jack—there's nothing to do about that now. Think about Rodney. Where he's going. What he'll do next. Sick bastard.*

He stepped away, giving Quent a look in the kiln, and stopped when he noticed a shelf on the wall. He frowned. It was covered in dust but too nice to be mounted in a musty, unfinished cellar: stained cherry with carved corbels and gilt trim. It should have been in a dining room or formal living room, or on display in the grand foyer at Hilltop. He aimed one of the floodlights at it. Dust rings marked the surface—five of them—where small items used to sit. The first had been absent so long its ring was barely visible, and the next had built up a good bit of dust, too. But the next two were covered with the finest sheen of powder, as if something had sat in those rings until only a few days ago. A fourth spot was oval and nearly clean, and a fifth marked the place where something with a square base had been removed just recently, and so hastily that a streak of dust had been wiped away.

Nick took a step closer and felt a crunch. He looked down. Shards of broken porcelain or china lay at his feet. And against the wall sat a bucket containing more. He squinted—made out a woman's head from one piece, an arm from another. And a wing.

"Angels."

"Figurines," Quent said, joining him. "You think these are the ones Margaret took from her father?"

Maybe. Nick picked up one piece, an oval base. It had handwriting on the bottom—*February 4, 1990—Mom.* It fit perfectly over one of the dust rings.

"February fourth is Rodney's birthday," Nick remembered. "Gifts?"

Quentin dragged the bucket out. "Could be. There are more angels here than there are spots on the shelf. And there's writing on all of them. Not just the dates." They dug through for another minute, putting together the bigger pieces into piles that appeared to make the other angels, piecing together what was written on each.

" *'To watch over you another year,'* " Nick read, then used the inscriptions to arrange the angels by year.

"Nineteen-eighty-three to 1993. Rodney's first ten

years. And Claire Devilas died during Mardi Gras right after he turned ten."

"So you're right. They were birthday angels. So what?"

"I don't know. But it would explain why both Margaret and her father wanted the collection. They would have wanted for Rodney to keep them."

"Except it looks like Rodney didn't want them," Quent said. "This is pretty meticulous destruction, not to mention keeping the pieces after they were broken."

Yeah. And something else was bothering Nick. "They weren't broken all at the same time. I mean, we don't know about the first five, but these from the last five years—you can see from the dust rings when they came off the shelf. This one's been gone for years. This one not quite so long, but a while. This was probably there just a few days ago and this one—" He stopped, a terrible notion rising to the surface. "Jesus. What if—"

"What if, what?" Quentin asked.

Nick pointed at the piles of porcelain on the floor that had once been the earliest angels, the ones that hadn't been on the shelf but that Rodney had kept in a bucket. "Lauren McAllister," he said, then went to the next. "Robin Weelkes. Sara Daniels. Eleanor Vann and her daughter. They were all killed before the Calloways moved here, before this shelf went up."

Quentin picked up the idea, moving the base of each angel now sitting in a pile onto the shelf. "Shelly Quinn." He looked at Nick, then back at the broken figurine. "She was the first murder after they moved here."

Nick picked up the next. "Elisha Graham—the girl whose parents wouldn't let her come home."

They did the same with a figurine for Jack and one for Rebecca. Then, they ran out of angels.

"So, where's the last one?" Quentin asked, as Nick's phone rang.

It was Feldman, his voice wired with tension. "Special Agent Fisher—the one assigned to Dr. Sims—is dead."

Nick stared at Quent. *Fisher? The last angel?* "What happened? Where's Erin?"

"His body was just found at the intersection of 219 and Grauters. He was shot. It looks like his car was stolen from the scene and there's a motorcycle there."

Nick's throat clogged. "Where's Erin?" he said again.

"She left the Engels' house an hour ago. Her purse is sitting on the road with Fisher's body."

Footsteps. Erin held her breath. He was coming.

A tidal wave of terror washed through her. Suddenly she was sixteen again, lying in bed with her eyes squeezed closed and her fingers curled around the gun under her pillow, straining to hear if Jeffrey was coming.

Only this wasn't Jeffrey. And she didn't have a gun. She didn't even know for sure if, when the lid to this dank, musty trunk finally opened, she would have the strength to use her limbs. She'd lost all sense of time and direction. Spent every ounce of energy she could muster trying to make noise or move. She had no idea where they had stopped. She only knew Rodney had gotten out of the car and disappeared for a little while.

And now he was coming back. Footsteps on the gravel. Closer.

The footsteps stopped, and Erin couldn't help the horrible surge of panic that raced through her veins. It wasn't just fear for her life. It wasn't even just the fear that she'd come all this way to prove Justin innocent and he would die, anyway. It was the fear that she'd never see Nick again, or Hannah.

No, stop it. She couldn't think like that. She had to keep her head. Rodney was a mental case and she was a shrink. Get into his head, figure him out. Stop him from taking this horrific string of murders any further.

Stop him. Sure. That notion was so ludicrous she might have laughed if the stakes hadn't been so high. For God's sake, he was an animal—a brutal, keen-eyed manipulator who had taken pleasure in a twelve-year ruse. The extent of that deception was flabbergasting. The depth of his evil, mind-boggling.

Keys jangled. Erin held her breath and heard the key slide into the lock, heard the catch of the clasp and felt a sudden *whoosh* of air. She opened her eyes, blinking even though there was little but moonlight. Took a deep breath and smelled the scents of pine trees and clay. Felt the cold muzzle of a pistol touch her cheek.

Erin turned to stone.

"Ah, she's still alive," Rodney said, sounding gleeful. "That's a relief. I would have been sorely put out to come all this way and then find you were dead before your time." He bent down close, his breath whispering against her cheek. "This is a reminder to you that I'm the one with a gun. Get out of the car and walk in front of me, peaceably, mind you, or I won't hesitate to use it. On an elbow or kneecap, or something fun like that."

The threat hit its mark. Erin tried to move, but her muscles were tied into cramps and her equilibrium off. Rodney cursed and hauled her out of the trunk. She crumpled to her knees.

She gritted her teeth against the pain, gravel biting into her knees, and struggled to right herself. Dared to look around. Trees, darkness, gravel. And something else. Scraps of white hanging on a tree trunk.

Astonishment whipped through her breast. Nick's cabin.

She tried to think, but Rodney didn't give her a chance. He snagged her arm—her wrists still bound with duct tape in front of her—and yanked her upright, poking the gun into her back.

"Move. Into your lover's house. We don't have all night." He chuckled. "Well, at least *you* don't."

Nick, Quent, and all the Feds hit the intersection of 219 and Grauters. Panic gnawed at Nick's gut. An unbearable swelling of fear he hadn't felt since Hannah lay in the hospital with a bullet wound in her head, and Allison lay on a slab.

He shoved that thought down and forced himself to focus. The Fed, Fisher, was shot at close range, from maybe ten feet away. It made sense. He wouldn't have been worried about walking right up to a blind man. Rodney's motorcycle, the one whose tread marked the cellar stairs, had been tucked in the ditch along the road, almost out of sight. The gray sedan—the cheap rental that wasn't supposed to look like a Fed car—was gone.

And Erin's purse, with her gun and cell phone sitting on top, sat in the middle of the road. A driver had thought it was an animal and stopped, and that's how Fisher's body had been found.

Rage gripped Nick's bones. The orange juice out on the counter. The purse, neatly placed in the road. The motherfucker was playing with him.

Nick looked at his watch: ten o'clock. To the best they could determine, Erin and Fisher had come here around eight-thirty. Her phone showed a call from Rodney at 7:48, and Katie confirmed that Erin had left right after. Did she say where? No. Did she say why? No.

For one-and-a-half fucking hours, she'd been in Rodney's hands.

When his phone rang, he actually jumped. He saw Luke's number and a brand-new finger of terror touched his chest. "Hannah?" he said.

"She's fine. Mom's fine. I'm fine, too, thanks for asking." A beat passed while Nick closed his eyes, trying to hear Hannah's laughter, remember the way she felt hugging his neck. He walked to the perimeter of the crime scene tape and braced an arm against the top of a van just outside the floodlights.

"Christ, Nick, what's going on up there?" Luke asked.

Nick told him.

"Okay, keep your head, man. Rodney knows the jig is up," Luke said. "He's in a car you can identify, so he's not gonna stay on the road. He's holed up somewhere, and enjoying fucking with you."

"I know that, damn it. Where?"

"Get into his head. Think like a shrink. The bastard's too far gone to do something sane."

Nick cursed. He wasn't the one who could think like shrink; Erin was. He'd sworn off psychology for manhunts years ag—

An idea darted through his head. "Luke, I gotta go. There's someone I need to talk to."

Erin moved with the gun pressed into her back. She took slow, mincing steps, pretending more weakness than she actually felt. She had to think. This was Nick's front porch—the one where she'd seen a cooler and black marker, shell casings on the floor. What else? What was inside? The house was empty; she remembered that. No phones, no electricity. Would Nick have left any guns here? No, he wasn't that careless; he wouldn't arm a place he only visited once a year.

And what about outside? Dark, eerie woods with the leftovers of Nick's ghosts hanging on trees, acres and acres of—

No. It wasn't just acres and acres of woods. There was a clay mine nearby. She'd passed it driving up here before, and knew there were people there late at night. How late? She didn't know. But it wasn't that far—a hundred, maybe two hundred yards. If she could get away just for a little while, she could find some help.

She kept walking, making a show of the difficulty, and wondered if Nick even knew yet that she was gone. What if she simply disappeared, like Sara Daniels and Jack and Rebecca? What if there was never any sign of her again?

She wriggled her hands together, loosening the pearl ring she wore. It dropped to the driveway without Rodney's notice. A silly thing—like Hansel and the breadcrumbs—but it soothed her to do it. At least Nick would know she'd been here. Someday.

Maybe next November ninth.

They came to the front steps of the porch and Rodney nudged her. Erin swallowed back a lump of terror: She couldn't let him take her in there.

She started up the steps and kicked one with her toe, pretending to trip. She dropped, spinning as she fell, and shoved at Rodney, but he stuck out a leg and she plowed into the ground. She landed on her own bound arms, working her legs to get them beneath her. A bullet whizzed past her head into the ground.

She went still. Rodney dragged her to unsteady feet, lodged the gun beneath her chin and spoke through gritted teeth.

"You're even more foolish than I imagined," he said, and hauled her up the stairs. He pulled her across the porch and over the threshold into the house, then shoved her against a wall and held up his free hand. Something white was in it and he reached out.

Pzzt.

Nick moved out of the melee of the crime scene to the backside of a county van, where he could talk. Checked his watch. Not just past seven o'clock in L.A.

He dialed his former partner. Randy picked up on the second ring.

"HOPEWELL CO SHER DEPT," Randy said, apparently reading the caller ID. "It's about damn time."

"I've been busy," Nick said.

"I heard. I thought you didn't have shit like this out there."

Me, either. "Randy, I need to talk to Rita Yardin. Tonight."

"Rita Yar—Are you crazy?"

"She always said so."

"Jesus, Nick. That broad spent a year messing around in your head. And all she ever did was try to get you committed."

"Can you get me a number?"

"Geesh . . ."

Dr. Yardin sounded both surprised and cocky. "Nick," she said. "When Randy told me you wanted to talk to me, I almost fell over."

"I've got a problem."

"I remember. I'm the one who diagnosed it."

His jaw tightened. "It's not about me. I need to shrink someone and I don't know how."

"You don't have psychologists in Ohio? Or none who'll talk to you?"

"There's one who will talk to me," Nick said, a knot of pain tightening in his throat, "but she's out of commission. Doctor, this is important."

A few seconds of silence gathered across the miles and finally she said, "What is it?"

He laid it out. Gave her everything he knew about Rodney—his mother, his blindness, his life with Margaret and Jack. Then he gave her what they'd found at Hilltop and his cabin. Felt her cockiness transform to horror.

"Mother of God," she said, when he was finished. "And you're sure this woman is with him now?"

If she's not, he's already killed her. "Yes," he said. There was no other choice.

"Then he has a plan for her. If he'd wanted to kill her, you would have found her with the body of the agent. He's using her for something."

"I know that much. A mask?"

"I don't know. Certainly, that's the theme. From what you said, it sounds like he's replaced his mother's angels with the masks. Why? A person doesn't do that sort of thing unless they get something out of it. What do the masks do?"

"Christ, they're decoration. What the fuck do masks do, mounted on a wall? They can't do anything." He paced, then stopped. "They're trophies."

"On display, while the angels are crushed and in the garbage. They're reminders of how cunning he is."

"The angel figurines came from his mother." *Always the mother.* " 'To watch over you another year.' " Most people would think that was nice.

"Nick, you said his music was Latin church music. What was it?"

Nick closed his eyes, tried to remember. "*Regina coeli.* I remember hearing that. And on the CD case, I saw a word like 'angel.' *Angelis* something or other."

"*Angeli me custodiunt?*"

"Maybe. I can check. Why?"

"I'm Catholic and I know some of these texts. *Semper angelis conservabor* means 'I will be watched over by angels.' *Angeli me custodiunt* means about the same."

"Watched by angels," Nick said.

"And not liking it. Wanting them crushed."

"He didn't have to kill people to break statues."

"No, but that's where the power comes in. He was a kid who couldn't see anything, while he was always being watched. As a man, he could see, but felt powerful not letting anyone know. I imagine it tickled his fancy to have Maggie hang real faces on the wall without knowing it, and to have people admire them. It makes everyone *else* blind."

"So, he replaced his mother's angels with dead people who have no eyes at all."

"Or ears or mouth, for that matter."

"And he'll do the same with one more. He'll do it with Erin."

"Yes, I believe so. But he won't do it where no one can see. He'll want it on display."

"He doesn't have a place to display them anymore. We just took apart his fucking art museum."

"Then he'll find someplace else. Someplace where you'll be sure to see his—"

Nick didn't hear anymore. He disconnected and ran like hell.

CHAPTER
51

RODNEY WATCHED ERIN drop to the floor and smiled. The woman had balls. She'd regret that, but he wouldn't. It would make for a more satisfying climax, that's all.

He reached into his pocket and touched the statue, could almost feel the weight beginning to lift from his shoulders. The last one.

And because this was the last play of the game, he was going to make sure it was special for Nick Mann.

But he'd have to hurry. Mann may get waylaid for a while blaming Maggie and tearing apart Hilltop House, but sooner or later, someone would find the dead FBI agent or notice that Sims was nowhere to be found. It wouldn't do to still be the Angelmaker then.

Thankfully, Jack had made that easy. Everything ready for a new identity. Thanks, *Dad*.

He bit back a surge of hatred and left Erin in a heap in the hall, walked through Nick Mann's vacation home, using his cell phone as a flashlight. Frowned. For God's sake, the man came here every year. One would think there would be a creature comfort or two.

But there wasn't. The place was abandoned. What must have once been a beautiful great room was desolate and lonely, with naked wires clawing from the outlets and a heap of ash huddled in the fireplace. The ceiling joists crisscrossed in a matrix ten feet up, the floors and walls stripped to bare concrete and plaster, making the tiniest sound ricochet in the rafters. Even a faint moan from Erin's throat echoed like a whisper in a cathedral.

Rodney got busy; not much time. He moved a rickety table to the middle of the room, lit the lantern, kicked some beer and tequila bottles out of the way. He pulled the duct tape from his coat pocket and set the last angel figurine on the empty mantel.

Watch this.

Erin was just starting to stir. He stood back and watched for a minute, enjoying her efforts, and when she got halfway up, that glint of mutiny flashed in her eyes.

I don't think so, Rodney thought, and walked over and kicked her in the stomach. She hit the wall and he pulled her back up and slapped her hard across the face. Her head snapped to the side, striking the doorjamb. Blood began to seep from the row of stitches in her temple.

Rodney straightened, breathing hard. He'd never done that before—beaten one of his victims. It felt kind of amazing, actually. A different kind of power.

He hoped Nick would like it.

Nick dodged the crime scene team's markers, grabbing Quentin on the way to his truck. "Let's go."

"Huh?" Quentin said, jogging after him. They piled in the Tahoe. "Who's chasing us?" Quentin asked.

"We're doing the chasing."

Quent buckled up. "About damn time."

They ran without headlights or sirens until they were well outside the perimeter of the media, Nick taking mental inventory of the firepower locked in the back of his truck. The pair of 45-caliber Hechler & Koch machine pistols, a 12-gauge shotgun, the scoped Remington rifle, as well as the County pieces—an AR-15 and the standard 9 mm pistol. Plus Quent's.

Oughta do it.

"Call Carroll County," Nick said. Quentin did, and Nick dictated what he wanted them to do: Send guys to Weaver's. Set up a perimeter around the property, anywhere Rodney might find good clay and a place to lay out Erin. Conduct a search. And get some armored cops ready to hit Nick's cabin.

Quentin relayed the message, saying, "I don't care how many acres it is. You got a crazy man up there who might be trying to get in with a hostage."

He hung up. "Wanna tell me what's going on?"

Nick explained the call to Dr. Yardin.

"So you think he's at Weaver's, looking for clay? Gonna put her on display for everyone to see?"

"No," Nick said. "That would require that fucking *no one* up there has seen the news. Besides, the collection of masks doesn't matter anymore. All that matters now is crushing the last angel."

"He could have done that anywhere," Quentin reminded him. "He could have done it already".

"But he hasn't," Nick said, growing more certain of it with every passing second. "Remember the orange juice, the purse. This display is just for me. The fucker is using my cabin."

Quentin whistled. "Gun it, man."

• • •

Don't close your eyes. Stay awake, stay awake. Erin repeated it to herself over and over again, like when she was young and Jeffrey was out there. *Stay awake.* Pain seared her skull and she could feel the cut on her head gaping open. Her ribs ached and there was no blood in her hands. She was still bound, humped in a corner on the floor.

Stay awake. She wiggled her fingers as if her mother's Derringer were there. It wasn't.

She forced herself to look around. Rodney was... cleaning up. Moving a table, picking up bottles. Humming, a flowing tune with a few words here and there... Latin? He stopped at the mantel and set something down. Stood back and studied it, his body going rigid.

Erin swallowed. *It's Maggie.* Dear God. She hoped Nick knew he was wrong.

Rodney turned and noticed her watching. "You're here again?" he asked, with such a cocky tone of voice it rippled down Erin's spine. "Just in time. I was hoping you wouldn't miss the main attraction. Especially since it's you."

She made a show of working at the words. Don't show strength; he'll just try to crush it. "What are you doing?" she asked, and let her head loll against the wall. "You'll never get away with this."

He chuckled. "I *have* gotten away with this. For twelve years. Ask Justin."

Erin closed her eyes. God. Justin. *Ninety-five percent.* Nick thought Justin would live. How cruel to think that after all this, she wouldn't be there to greet him coming from prison.

Rodney sauntered over to her, gloating. "And now you and your lover will be the denouement."

Fear squeezed her heart. "Where is Nick?"

Again, the chuckle. "At my cabin, I would wager. Cleaning up what's left of Rebecca. But I imagine he'll be here soon. To clean up what's left of you."

A knot formed in her throat but she pushed past it. He was enjoying himself. He'd manipulated his entire universe for all these years. Being blind had been a game. The people in his life were pawns.

"How many?" she asked, but she was almost afraid to know.

He walked to the mantel. Stopped a few feet from it and looked at whatever he'd set there. A statue of some sort, just a few inches tall. "Ten," he said. "Ten fucking angels from my mother. They watched, they saw. And when they did, I crushed them. Every one of them." He turned back to her. "Do you want to know what I turned them into? You'll be impressed, I think." She might have answered—to keep him talking—but didn't need to. He went on without any encouragement. "I turned them into blind mutes. I put the clay on their faces and then handed them to Maggie, and she made them beautiful and hung them on the wall. It was all my mother wanted, anyway, to be beautiful." He was laughing now, a gleeful sound. "No one else could see what they were. Only the blind man. Isn't that wonderful?"

God, he was crazy. Stay with it. Pay attention. His mother had committed suicide. Erin remembered that. "So your mother left you. But her angel kept watching."

Rodney sneered. "Angel? Singular? Not one, you stupid bitch. Ten. Ten. It's taken me years to find them all. Every time I killed one, another was there." He fingered the angel on the mantel and his posture got a shot of steel. "But this is the last. I don't care who it is. Maggie. You.

Mann. It doesn't fucking matter anymore, as long as it's gone."

He knocked the angel statue off the mantel, a sweeping motion that was filled with rage. It flew across the room and hit the mattress on the floor, bounced twice, and lay there.

Looking up at him.

He stared. His frame was vibrating. Erin thought he couldn't breathe.

Then he turned and marched straight to her. Rage in his eyes. She tried to scoot from reach, but his boot caught her in the chest. She rolled, and another kick hit her chin. He went at her, again and again, and Erin rolled into a ball and prayed she could fool him.

CHAPTER
52

RODNEY STOOD BACK to catch his breath. She was gone. He bound her ankles anyway and hauled her to the table. Deadweight. Damn her.

So your mother left you.

Fuck you. It doesn't matter now.

He straightened, feeling the gaze of the figurine on the mattress. Unbroken, but not for long. He just had to kill Erin first.

He studied her, bound on a wooden table with duct tape around her wrists and ankles, her eyes staring into the rafters in a daze. *What do you see now, bitch?* Nothing, he thought, and got the stun gun and glue ready. He stretched her out straight. Several minutes had passed since he'd used the stun gun; she ought to be coming around again. But she wasn't.

Shit. He shouldn't have cut loose on her quite so hard. She'd just made him so fucking mad. And now she was nearly gone.

Didn't matter. He would have enjoyed taunting her more, enjoyed explaining everything to her psychologist's mind, but time was ticking. Nick would be here soon. Gotta move.

He pried a hunk of earth from the pile he'd brought in, kneaded it like artist's clay, then reached down and smeared it onto her face. Got another dollop and pushed it over the edge of the first, over the slender nose, over the high cheekbones, over the seam of ugly stitches at her temple. He smiled at that. On the inside of this mask would be something special: the imprint of stitches and the swell of a nasty welt on the side of her face. When the authorities found this one, there would be no doubt whose face had provided the mold.

The mighty Erin Sims. Just in time to join her brother in hell. A twofer.

The dregs of his anger drained at that, and he worked faster, pushing more mud onto her face. He hadn't been a hundred percent certain it would work, the earth unrefined and a little too dry, but it did. This one wasn't going to be art, after all. This one would just be a death mask.

He smeared it on until he ran out, one side of her face half-caked, the other still pale and clear. He held a hand over her nose. Her breaths were barely there.

He picked up the lantern from the hearth, turned up the flame and headed for the basement. It was almost as empty as the rest of the house, but he found a shovel.

Good enough.

He peeked in on Erin Sims's unmoving body and carried the shovel outside. He got in the car and angled it to face into the woods, then left the headlights on and followed the twin beams, looking for a spot clear of trees. Didn't want to run into big roots six inches down.

He found a spot that looked hopeful, and began digging. *Tick-tock,* Dr. Sims.

Erin held her breath, listening. Her cheek and nose were nearly covered, the sharp tang of earth in her nose.

Pain rolled over her in waves, but she didn't care. She was alive. He'd stopped kicking and hitting when she went limp and sank into a ball—no sport in beating a dead woman. She'd struggled not to move, to let her body be deadweight.

Not as far gone as he thought.

But maybe not as strong as she'd need to be? She wasn't sure. Her feet felt swollen; the bastard had bound her tight. She gave her hands a try. They were taped, even tighter than before.

And she was on a table, afraid to move. She listened, straining to hear footsteps. He was gone.

Easy, now. Keep your head.

She took a deep breath, braced for the pain, and swung her legs around. Bound, the movement nearly threw her off kilter, but she hung on and swiveled to her side on the table. One more try and she got her legs over the edge to sit up.

And nearly passed out. The room whirled. Erin swallowed back a chunk of fear in her throat and the sensation of the mud tightening on her face brought a wave of panic. For a few seconds, she could do nothing but lift both hands and scrape at her face like a madwoman. "Get it off, get it off," she whispered, frantic, as the mud hit the floor in pieces.

Stop it; don't be crazy. There's no time for that.

She slid to the floor, her heart beating like that of a cornered hare. She found her balance and straightened, carefully, unable to separate her feet. She turned around and braced her hands on the table, scuffling a few inches at a time toward the door. A kitchen back there; she could see it. It was dark and unused, but if there was a sharp object anywhere in the house, it would be there.

The length of table ran out—she had to go without. She hopped once, swayed and almost fell, then bunny-hopped to the wall.

Her heart raced, but the wall held her up. She caught her breath and started moving, getting the hang of the locomotion: a two-footed scoot and then a hop to catch her balance, staying close against the wall. Scootch, hop. Scootch, hop.

She made it to the kitchen door and nearly wilted with relief, then rounded the doorway and lost the wall at her back. Erin fell, face-first. *Thwack,* she hit the bare cement. Pain rolled through her head on a cloud of dizziness, and a slippery heat pooled between the cold surface of the concrete and her skin. Forehead, she realized, as the pain began to throb, and then decided her eyebrow must be split. Blood in her eye.

She rolled, trying to get it to drip the other way, and waggled upright again, using the lower kitchen cupboards as her wall. Vertical, she pulled drawers open, one after another, bending close in the dark to see. A knife, a corkscrew, ice pick. *Anything* sharp. Duct tape would tear, if she could just get an edge started. Of course, Rodney had been thorough: The lengths of tape were looped around four, maybe five times. Still...

Nothing. *Damn you, Nick.*

She fingered the edge of the countertop...Sharp enough? No. Granite, of course. Expensive, smooth, granite with rounded edges. Nick's kitchen. Nothing but the best.

Damn you, Nick.

She inched farther along the counters, trying to listen for Rodney past the thunder beating in her chest and the pain pounding in her head. Scootch, hop. Scootch, hop...

Then she saw the sink, another six feet away. Something in it? Something sharp? Too dark to see, and it was a deep sink—the kind a chef would want. *Damn you, Nick...*

She scooched and hopped her way there and almost cried for joy. There, in the depths of stainless steel, was how Nick Mann spent his annual hell weekend. There, in the darkness, lay two empty tequila bottles.

Bless you, Nick.

Nick rolled past Weaver's. Lights flared all over the plant, cops conducting a search and questioning employees. He swerved to a stop beside a Carroll County cruiser.

"Any sign of him?" he asked a deputy posted at the main entrance.

"No, sir. We've got a search going."

He looked at Quent. "This site's covered. Let's go."

Erin broke the first bottle against the granite counter top without much trouble—and without bringing Rodney running—but it snapped high on the neck, cutting her fingers and leaving her with too little to use as a saw. Her second try was better—she held the bottle by the bottom rather than the top and broke it lower—then bent down in the dark to saw the edge into the tape around her ankles. Her feet were free in no time, but her hands were slick with blood. She couldn't get an angle to reach the tape on her wrists.

She kept trying, her heart in her throat. Dear God, Rodney would hear and come back, and she couldn't get the sharp edge to—

It cut. Just like that, the glass slid through and the tape gave way. She was free.

Her heart raced. She used her forearm to wipe blood

from her eye, then stood there panting, trying to decide what to do. Where was Rodney? The garage? The basement? She'd have heard him if he'd gone upstairs; he'd have heard her if he were in the house.

Outside, then, still digging up clay. Unless he *had* heard her, and was waiting, just around the corner, gun in hand…

She closed her eyes. She couldn't think like that; it would paralyze her.

She glanced around, wishing she knew more about this house. She had to decide: Stay inside and be cornered by the gun or run outside and try to elude him in the dark. Inside there was warmth, limited space, and no weapons besides these bottles. Outside was darkness and cold, the same weapons but room to run, places to hide. A clay mine with people not far away. A bullet could reach out and grab her from dozens of yards away, but not reliably. Even a sharpshooter missed nine out of ten times when the target was moving. And in the dark…

In the end, Erin decided there really wasn't a choice. She went out a side door from the kitchen, the broken bottle in her right hand. Scooped down to pick up a beer bottle for her left.

She looked around. A gray-white column of light— headlights—pointed off to her left, and darkness stretched to her right and in front of her.

She went for the darkness. Kept rubbing blood from her eye with her sleeve and noticed, with a twist of her stomach, that her sleeve was drenched and sticky. She kept walking, light-headed through the dark. The ground had a strange way of shifting underfoot. The biggest trees made dark shadows but vines and shrubs were like invisible wires that tangled her feet—

BOOM.

CHAPTER
53

E RIN DROPPED, SCRAMBLED TO A TREE.
    BOOM-thwack.

A second bullet followed, a different sound. This one had hit a tree ten feet in front of her.

God, he saw her.

She whirled to go the other way. Tripped and dragged herself over the ground in an army crawl for a few feet, then lumbered upright and dodged in a different direction. She lost one bottle but hung on to the broken one.

"Bitch," Rodney called. "Stupid, stupid bitch."

BOOM.

Erin stumbled, then found her feet and zigzagged between the trees, blood blinding her left eye. The beam of the headlights stretched out in front of her.

BOOM.

She hit the ground. Dear God, her silhouette must be visible in front of that beam. Rodney had seen exactly where she was.

She crawled, blinking at blood and cold sweat, wishing she could take off her jacket and tie the sleeves around her forehead. She couldn't. The shirt underneath was light yellow—it would look white out here. She kept moving, knees and elbows dragging across the ground, needing to get out from in front of those damn headlights.

Thirty yards out, forty. Need the dark, need the dark.

Need to rest.

A shred of paper marked a tree and Erin put her hand out, bracing herself to catch her breath. She leaned back against the tree and winced. Something caught her in the back. She pulled away and reached behind her, feeling for it.

A knife. It was stabbed through the target and holding it in place.

Thank you, Nick.

Rodney seethed, stopping to reload the pistol. *Bitch.* He'd just about screamed with rage when he saw her come out of the house, then thought better of it. Instead, he doused the lantern and stalked her in the dark. Evil, damnable bitch. She'd tricked him. When he left her, he'd thought she was almost dead.

But he had the advantage. Aside from having a gun, the headlights had stretched out behind Erin like a backdrop. He fired, and Erin dropped below the light. For a moment of sheer thrill, Rodney thought he'd hit her; then her silhouette reappeared, and he squeezed the trigger again. Missed. Kept the bitch on the run, though.

Rodney wasn't running. Once Erin managed to get out from in front of the headlights, it was harder to keep track of her, but she was hurt, and she'd already been weak and running before he took that first shot. And Rodney didn't need to be careful where he went. His hair would catch the moonlight, but it didn't matter if Erin knew where he was. She didn't have a gun. He did.

He followed the direction he'd seen her go, taking measured steps, peering into the darkness. Erin Sims was no match for him. She hadn't been for twelve years and she wouldn't be now. *Relax. Keep looking. You'll find her as soon as—*

A sound stopped him. Rodney whirled toward the driveway and dropped to a crouch. A truck pulled up the drive.

Son of a bitch.

Nick saw headlights through the trees from fifty yards out. He came in fast, running without lights, and put the Tahoe in a fishtail. Grabbed the AR-15 from the back through the window and pushed the Remington to Quentin.

They cracked their car doors to get out and a gun went off. The bullet hit the truck bed.

"Shit. Get down."

Quentin crouched back inside the truck. "From over there," he said, pointing into the spread of darkness beyond the two columns of headlights. Nick led with the assault rifle, moving toward the gunshot. The .38 fired again, hitting just behind him. He dropped to the ground.

"Nick," Quentin whispered. "Damn it, use the truck for cover. You can't fire."

Nick clenched his teeth. Jesus, Erin was out there. He couldn't fire, not until they knew where she was. Rodney could be holding her up against him just now, using her body as a shield.

He darted back to the truck, and crouched behind it. Nick called out. "Erin," he yelled. "Erin!"

"You're fucking crazy," Quent whispered.

"He knows where we are, anyway," Nick said. "I have

to let her know I'm here. The motherfucker was firing on her."

"Then for God's sake, quit calling to her. If she answers you, he'll have a bead on her."

"We gotta know where Erin is. My hands are tied without knowing where Erin is."

Quentin was a good friend: he didn't point out that Erin hadn't answered and might already be dead. He didn't point out that Rodney might be the only one out there. Instead, he said, "Cover me and I'll get to the house. Got your radio?"

"Don't use it. I'm gonna move into the woods. If I'm close to Rodney and you use the radio, he'll finger me."

Quentin didn't like it, but Nick was right. "I'll flip a light inside—twice if I find her, once if I don't."

"There's no electricity," Nick said. "Take a lighter from the glove compartment."

"Okay. Ready?"

"Go."

Quentin stumbled to the front of the truck for the lighter, then ran for the house. Nick sprayed an arc of bullets into the sky, too high to hit Erin if she was out there but intimidating enough to keep Rodney from shooting back. When Quent was in, Nick started working his way into the woods.

Erin heard her name and felt the earth shift. *Nick.* But she couldn't answer. Rodney was close, twenty feet away. She'd caught his silhouette crossing through the pale reach of the headlights, his light head shining like a moon.

Coming after her.

Don't breathe, don't move. He didn't know where she was just now. He'd gotten distracted taking shots at Nick.

She pressed back against the tree, praying Nick wasn't hit. She closed her eyes and stuck the knife under her arm long enough to wipe blood from her fingers, then got a new grip on it.

Rodney came nearer.

A tiny light shone in the second-story window, flicking back off a second later. Nick watched. *Twice if I find her* ...

No more light. Ah, Jesus. He reeled. So, Erin was out here. Somewhere—dead or alive or maybe hurt—Erin was out here with a madman who had nothing left to lose. Or, she wasn't here at all ... Rodney had already killed her and dumped her—

Stop it. *Stop it*.

"Erin!" he called out, a stupid thing to do, pinpointing himself like that, but he had to let her know he was here. He crouched with his back against a tree, waiting, then shouted again. *"Erin."*

And the answer that came back was *BOOM*. Right past his ear.

CHAPTER
54

INSTINCT TOOK NICK to the ground. He trained his rifle in the direction of the shot, then cursed and forced his fingers to loosen on the trigger. For seven years he'd been shooting at demons in these woods. Their light-colored remnants still dangled from the trees, the trees themselves worse for wear.

Now a new ghost haunted him: the image of Erin, caught by his own bullet.

His woods. His hell. And he didn't dare shoot.

But behind him, he heard footsteps rustling and recognized them. The armored cops, running in lines, flanking his sides and taking up positions in the dark.

Thank you, Quentin.

Erin swallowed, forcing herself to think. The last shot had come from fifteen feet ahead. And there were other sounds now, too, like scurrying animals. Police? She couldn't think about that. She had to think about Rodney. He'd moved, and she didn't know where. She clasped the knife in her right hand, the bottle in her left. She got an idea, thought about it for three seconds—worried it would distract Nick as much as Rodney—and then decided to try. Nick wasn't likely to react blindly to something. Rodney, on the other hand, might tumble to it.

And the animals?

It didn't matter. If there *were* other cops out there, Rodney was hearing them, too. The time to distract him was now.

She threw the bottle fifteen feet behind her, into the column of headlights. It smashed against a tree and she held her breath, pressing tight against the big tree with massive holes shot through the trunk. Twenty feet away, Rodney moved—his pale head catching the light. He crept toward the place the bottle had hit, looking for her, moving in a path that would bring him right past her. Closer, closer, five feet away, three...Erin tried to still her pulse as he passed the tree with the holes. Surely, he could hear her breathing, her heartbeat, could *smell* the fear. But he kept going. Erin could actually look through the holes in the tree and see him pass.

And when he took one more step, she lunged.

Nick heard a scream—like a war cry—and shouted, "Hold your fire!"

He bolted toward the voice and a stream of cops descended, flashlights and guns all hunting for the source of the screams. Nick led with the AR-15 and then, in the overcast light of the headlights, saw Erin wobble back on her knees. A body lay at her feet, facedown.

She shuddered, struggling to back away, blood everywhere. Rodney rolled and groaned in agony, and the lights of a dozen cops all converged on his white head, catching him in an eerie spotlight like the star of a gruesome show.

A knife jutted out from his neck.

"Erin," Nick said, starting toward her. Rodney let out a moan that sounded like death, but Nick saw his fingers move, and a split second later, saw the gun on the ground. Rodney touched it, blood leaking from his throat. He gasped for air but managed to wind his fingers around the butt.

Nick blew him away.

CHAPTER
55

IT WAS A LONG NIGHT. Yet another crime scene, and when they could finally leave, Nick took Erin to the sheriff's office for the remaining few hours of morning. He had some things to wrap up and wasn't about to let her out of his sight. She was patched up again and insisted on flying home tomorrow. Nick didn't want her to, but there was Justin to think about. Always Justin.

A little before nine, Nick stood at his whiteboard making a list. Erin stirred and he turned.

"You look like hell," he said, handing her a cup of luke-warm coffee.

"You sweet-talker, you."

Nick put her chin in his palm and tilted her face to one side, then the other. Every mark and bruise caught him in the chest.

"I'll be all right. Stop acting like a father." Then she asked, "How's Rebecca?"

"Docs say she'll make it. Aspiration pneumonia from the clay, but she'll be okay."

Erin closed her eyes. "And have you heard from Hannah and Luke?"

"Hannah called. She and my mom are gonna stay a couple more days. Luke left as soon as he heard that Rodney was dead." Nick smoothed a flyaway lock of hair behind her ear. "Hannah's afraid you won't still be here when they get back."

Erin shook her head. "We've been through this already. I have to go."

"Layna can handle it," Nick said. "She's pretty sure Senator McAllister is gonna be pulling strings right and left, trying to make up for all the terrible things he's said about you over the years."

She snorted. "More than a third of Justin's life has been spent in that prison. How's the Senator going to make up for that?"

"Justin will figure it out. You'll figure it out." He bent in to kiss her, but a knock at the door pulled him back.

"Sheriff." *Shereef.* Valeria poked her nose in. "Dorian Reinhardt just arrived. He said you asked him to come in."

"I did." Nick took a deep breath. First time in five years he was looking forward to seeing the prick. "Bring him back."

"*Sí.*" She didn't leave.

"Is there something else?" Nick asked.

"I'm deciding."

"Deciding what?"

"What bet to place. There's a new pool going, with all sorts of wagers . . . When Erin moves in, when you get married, how long until she's pregnant. A lot to think about."

"Get out," Nick said.

Valeria smirked, but it was short-lived and she gave Erin a sad look. "Jensen is waiting for you. You need to go if you're going to catch your flight."

A weight dropped on Nick's shoulders as Jensen ducked in and took her bags, Dorian lagging a few steps behind him. Erin gave him a parting smile, then left with Jensen.

Nick looked at Dorian. He looked like a man who'd lost a fortune in a game of craps.

That's not all you've lost, Nick thought.

"You wanted to see me, Sheriff?" he asked, a bitter edge to his voice.

"Yeah," Nick said. "But, listen, I gotta step out for a minute. I'll be back."

Dorian paced Nick's office, petted his tie, and paced some more. Nick hadn't told him what he wanted. Had just *summoned* him to his office and then left him there.

Cocky bastard.

He paced another five minutes, complained to Valeria—who told him to *seet back down*—and finally sat down on the vinyl couch. He stared at the wall for a couple of minutes before he realized he was staring at the whiteboard covered with ideas Nick had explored during the course of the Calloway case. He let his eyes roam from box to box, thinking of the case. How big it could have been, and how he'd have been a household name by the end of it if things had gone the way he'd hoped.

Seeing his name in a box.

He came to the edge of the sofa.

DORIAN REINHARDT. Nick had scrawled his name in capital letters and drawn a rectangle around it. An arrow dropped down from that box to another, in which was printed: VANDALISM. And from that, scribbled along vertical lines:

Jack Calloway's lawyer—knew about Jack's past
Having financial problems—wanted big case
Needed for Sims to get attention—spreads paint
Keeps Calvin quiet.

Dorian swallowed, the walls closing in. He moved to the next box, which said, ASSAULT. He wanted to get up and leave the office, but like a man passing a gory accident, he couldn't keep himself from reading:

Wants hype for Sims—takes run in parking lot
Relatives in south Georgia—car rental in Starke, FL

It couldn't be. Nick didn't know any of that. He couldn't. This was just some power play to jerk Dorian around. And yet, there was a third box, and the tightness in Dorian's throat turned into a noose. *MURDER.*

Accessory to Calloways' deaths
Knows Jack is covering, provided false IDs
Tips sheriff about Weelkes and Quinn

Dorian thought for ten seconds, breathing like a marathoner, then grabbed his jacket and yanked open the door.

Nick Mann was waiting.

EPILOGUE

Seven days later . . .
Thanksgiving Day, November 22
Outside the Florida State Prison, Starke, FL
5:15 p.m.

Erin stood in the drive of the prison, Alayna Mann at her side. Senator McAllister spoke to the press—a string of *mea culpas* that would have made Erin sick to her stomach if it hadn't been for the fact that they had helped speed up Justin's release. McAllister's role in Justin's trial wouldn't go undisclosed forever—Alayna Mann was collecting evidence—but right now it didn't matter.

"There," Layna said, and Erin's blood raced faster. Collie gave her a wink.

Justin. He walked out of the prison carrying a small bag in his hand, and skimmed the crowd that had gathered. Stopped when he laid eyes on Erin.

Her breath caught. He was a man, timeworn and hard, not a scraggly seventeen-year-old who couldn't seem to understand what was happening. His frame had bulked up from having nothing to do besides use the gym every day for nearly twelve years and his eyes—those piercing blue eyes— seemed to look right through her even from forty yards away.

The prison door opened behind him and another man stepped out. Erin gasped. "Nick," she breathed, and glanced at Alayna, who shrugged. Nick walked up to where Justin stood with a pair of guards, and all four of them approached the inner gate, the median, then the outer gate. There, the guards fell away and Nick and Justin came out to Erin.

Tears gathered in her eyes. She was shocked to see Nick—and thrilled—but she couldn't stop looking at Justin. Dear God, she didn't know him at all. She didn't know if he'd even want to know her.

They stopped in front of her. Nick crossed his arms while Justin's gaze locked on hers.

"This man tells me I better treat you like a queen," Justin said, and Erin's heart did a little flutter. "If I don't, he's gonna beat the shit out of me."

A smile shuddered on Erin's lips. "He talks pretty, doesn't he?" she asked, and the faintest glint lit Justin's eyes. She sobered and looked into that blue gaze. "Can you forgive me?"

His features twisted, a fleeting, tortured expression. "You've got that backwards," he said, his voice like gravel. "It was never you." Then he nodded to something behind her. "And what about her?"

Erin turned. At the edge of the parking lot stood a woman, wearing a full, calf-length skirt and a hat. An image from two weeks ago flitted through Erin's mind, seeing that same silhouette in the darkness at the edge of the prison parking lot, an onlooker to Justin's stay of execution. Now, in the daylight, Erin could see who it was.

"Mother," she said, emotion knotting in her chest. She turned to Nick. "You?"

He shook his head. "I got in to have a chat with Justin, but I don't know anything about her." He paused, as Erin tried to unravel it all. She hated her mother, loved her. The woman who let it all happen, the woman who never tried to stop it.

Or who couldn't.

I wasn't strong enough to protect Justin, Erin had said to Nick. And he'd replied, *You did your best.*

Was it the same for her mother?

Nick stepped forward. "Give us a minute," he said to Justin and Alayna. Layna stepped out of earshot and Justin walked out to see their mother. It was an awkward greeting, Erin could tell, but it was a greeting. A start.

She turned to Nick. "Layna didn't tell me you were going to be here."

"I had to come. Turns out you left something in Ohio."

"I did?"

He pulled a small box from his pocket. "Your ring. The crime scene crew found it in the driveway of my cabin. It was a good idea on your part, even though it turned out not to matter."

Erin took the box. "You didn't have to fly down here to give me that. It was just a little pearl."

Nick cocked his head. "Really? Huh. It didn't look like a pearl to me."

Erin frowned. She opened the box and her knees went weak. A diamond glittered up at her. "Oh," she said, in a stroke of brilliance. She couldn't think. "It's...it's beautiful."

"But will it replace your pearl?" Nick asked. His voice sounded tight.

Erin looked up at him. "Ohio?"

He shrugged. "I dunno. I'm not sure there's much to keep me busy up there, and Hannah would like the beach. And I was thinking Miami might be a lot like L.A. Palm trees. Heat. Ocean."

"Drugs. Violence. Murder."

A half smile curled his lips. "Who can resist?"

"Not I," Erin said, and stepped into his arms. "Not I."

When prosecutor Kara Chandler's
ex-husband and son were killed by
a drunk driver, she had no reason
to think it was anything more than
a tragic accident. Now cryptic
messages on her cell phone make
her realize it was murder, and just
the beginning of a killer's
twisted plan.

Please turn the page

for a preview of the next

pulse-pounding novel of

ROMANTIC SUSPENSE

from Kate Brady

CHAPTER
1

It was an odd place to find a woman like Kara Chandler, at an odd time: a squalid alley in the armpit of Atlanta, nearly midnight. The air sweltered—orange-zone breathing quality, said the news, with dramatic warnings for asthma sufferers and the elderly to stay inside. And here, behind a Dumpster in an alley off Vine Street, the odors of sweat and urine and rotten trash hung in the air like fog.

Luke Varón heard a noise and inched left to peer past the Dumpster to the sidewalk. An odd place indeed for Kara Chandler, yet there she was, and looking nothing like he'd expected. The jewels and spiked heels were gone; the evening's upswept hairdo now falling in waves over her shoulders. In place of the classic black dress that had hugged her curves an hour earlier, she wore jeans and a short-sleeved blouse, and instead of the fashionable clutch purse, a shapeless woven sack hung over one shoulder with her right hand buried deep inside.

Gun.

Luke held to shadows. Two aluminum-caged security bulbs hung under the eaves behind him but he'd broken the nearest one, forcing what was left of the sickly light toward the street. Kara Chandler paused there, tension rising in the alley like a third presence. She took a few steps and peeked into a culvert that wasn't visible from the alley's entrance. Luke's hackles lifted: Ms. Chandler had been here before.

"Mr. Varón?"

Her voice stroked the night and every fiber of Luke's body tightened. Damn, he shouldn't be here, shouldn't need to give a second thought to Kara Chandler. In less than two weeks, eight-and-a-half tons of cocaine cut with levamisole would arrive off the Georgia coast. Luke had spent the last six days securing the route from Ecuador, making sure every last mile was covered and that nothing could go wrong. He'd returned to the States only hours ago, longing only for a clean bed and about sixteen hours to languish in it.

What he'd found was a message from Kara Chandler, Assistant District Attorney for the City of Atlanta and Andrew Chandler's wife. Either identity would have made her a concern. Together, they made her downright dangerous.

"Mr. Varón?" she said again.

Luke strung the silence out a bit longer, then said, "Here."

She whirled, a bulge forming in the canvas of her shoulder bag. "Where? Come out, damn it."

"So you can shoot me through a wall of macramé?"

"I didn't ask you here so I could shoot you." But the bulge in her purse moved. "You're not worth the effort."

"Flattery," Luke drawled. "There's a saying about where that will get you."

"I need to talk to you. Come out."

He did, leading with a G18. Her gaze dropped to the weapon and he watched the details register in her eyes: a lightweight, 9 mm shooter with a threaded barrel to accommodate a silencer, and just now sporting an extra magazine that held thirty-three rounds. Tonight, he'd added the extra clip just for show, but in fully automatic mode, the G18 could fire all thirty-three bullets in less than two seconds. It was legal only among law enforcement and the military.

Luke Varón was neither.

He didn't know what she was carrying, but it didn't take her long to determine she was outclassed. The bulge in the bag loosened and Luke tilted the Glock skyward. "Your turn," he said, but Kara Chandler didn't move. He put an edge of steel into his voice. "Lady, pull your fucking hand out of the bag. I'd hate to fill you with bullets, then find out you were going for lipstick."

An inch at a time, she withdrew her hand—empty. Luke lifted the edge of his Armani suit coat and tucked his gun in the holster. He took a couple of steps to his left so when she angled to keep her eyes on him, the frail light caught her face. Not that he needed any reminders of what she looked like: hair like a waterfall of honey, bottle-green eyes dulled by tragedy, pale skin with two, teasing little tucks in her cheeks that flashed like lightning when she was angry and perhaps—Luke could only speculate here—when she smiled. Without her heels, she claimed only a few inches above five feet, but she carried herself as if meeting him eye to eye. On her turf, in a courtroom trying to convict him of murder, for example, Kara Chandler was the definition of cold control. Out here, she was wired so tight Luke thought she might snap if she so much as took a deep breath.

Better that way. Composed, this woman was a force to be reckoned with. Off balance, he might have a chance figuring out what the hell she was up to.

"Did you enjoy Berlioz's Third Symphony?" he asked, and she winced—surprised. "Personally," he continued, "I prefer a slower tempo in the fourth movement. It loses the ominous character of the guillotine when played too fast."

"You were watching me?"

He tilted his head. "I was watching Spano conduct the *Symphonie Fantastique*. And for what it's worth, I don't think you were paying much attention."

"There was no need to keep tabs on me. I asked you here because I have a proposition for you, that's all."

Luke touched his chest, feigning delight. "Now, what could a faithful public servant like you want with a common criminal like me?"

"This has nothing to do with the DA's office. It's personal."

"Even better," Luke said, and used the opportunity to let his gaze run down her figure and back again. Christ, Andrew Chandler had been one lucky son of a bitch. "If that's true, I have to tell you I'm a little disenchanted. Until tonight, I was under the impression you were one of the few members of the justice system possessed of integrity."

"I want to hire you," she said, and Luke almost blinked. He caught himself and arched a dark brow instead.

"I'm not a stockbroker or private chef, Ms. Chandler."

"I know what you are," she spat. "You're an arsonist and a murderer. So this job should be right up your alley. I want you to blow up a boat and make sure its owners die in the fire."

Luke was flabbergasted. Christ. It was an effort to keep his jaw hinged in place.

"I'll pay you twenty thousand dollars," she said. "Half of it now and the other half when the job is done. We can set up a drop for the money so we don't have to meet a second time."

"Twenty thousand," he said, hoping he sounded disapproving.

"It's all I can give you."

Luke narrowed his gaze on her. He didn't know what she was doing here but the part about the money was probably true. Her husband, architect Andrew Chandler, had been killed by a drunk driver a year ago. Luke was half convinced the bastard deserved it, but his family hadn't deserved what he'd left behind. Shortly after Chandler's death, his estate collapsed in a web of fraud, his architectural firm was implicated in the activities of a drug ring, and his wife was left to handle the scandal and a mountain of debts while raising their teenage son alone. In addition, Luke knew, the year since Chandler's death had been peppered with other personal tragedies— the death of her father and a college girlfriend. It was as if a cloud of doom had been hovering over Kara Chandler for the past year.

"I want it done tomorrow night, late. There's only one neighbor who can see the dock, and she flew to Florida today for a cruise…"

She spoke right past him, as if she'd rehearsed a script, and Luke's skepticism climbed to the surface. He'd already checked the area. There were no electronics and no surveillance, and there had only been one person hanging around—a homeless man Luke had run off with a hundred-dollar bill. The thought passed that Chandler could be wearing a wire, but she was an unlikely choice for a sting. The Atlanta Police Department had people especially trained for undercover work.

Besides, this didn't have the feel of a scam. The DA's office asking him to commit murder? No one would believe he'd be stupid enough to buy into that.

"Wait at least two hours after dark—"

"Why me?" he asked.

She stopped, glaring at him. "Because you can get away with it. You can get away with anything. You proved that when you walked out of court a month ago."

"More flattery," he said. "But you're a prosecutor. You must know dozens of good criminals."

Her gaze might have melted steel. "Besides you, the criminals I know are behind bars."

"Ah, yes," Luke said, with the ghost of a smile. "You aren't accustomed to a checkmark in the LOSS column. I'm sorry I tarnished your record."

She took a step toward him. "It wasn't a loss; it was a mistrial. And you were guilty. You know it and I know it. You killed a man in that warehouse fire—some poor, unidentified soul who went to an unmarked grave and whose family will never know what happened to him. You should be in prison for the rest of your life."

"Lucky for you I'm not. Who would you call to commit *your* felonies?"

She quailed, but spoke through gritted teeth. "I don't know how the evidence against you disappeared but I know there was enough that you would have gotten life— if you were lucky. The fact that you're a goon for Gene Montiel and have access to his resources is just proof that he's as dirty as the DA's office has been saying."

"And as powerful?" Luke suggested. Kara Chandler

wasn't a gracious loser. Apparently, that was especially true when the freed defendant—Luke—worked security for a multi-millionaire land developer who owned a good portion of Atlanta's businesses, police, and justice department. A man whom the DA's office was convinced had become involved with a major drug cartel. "I appreciate the *film noir* character of this little charade, Ms. Chandler. But is the DA really so desperate to nail Montiel that he's sending you into dark alleys to entrap one of his... goons?"

"This isn't a charade and I'm not here as part of some undercover operation. I told you, this is personal."

"Prove it."

"Excuse me?"

He skimmed the buttons down the front of her blouse. "Show me you aren't wearing a wire."

"You're crazy," she said, but Luke could see that she was thinking about it. Considering stripping her clothes in a lonely, dark alley with the likes of Luke Varón, just to prove she wasn't wired. Proof enough, Luke thought, and couldn't quite believe his eyes when her fingers rose to her blouse and the first disk slipped through the hole. Jesus, she was going to do it. He felt like a twelve-year-old who'd just stumbled on a *Playboy* magazine under a mattress, watching her cleavage and her pale, flat belly come into view an inch at a time. His blood drained from his brain as she slipped her arms from the blouse and let it drop to the pavement with her bag.

You don't have to do this. The words rose to his lips but went no further. She unzipped her jeans and Luke's pulse kicked up. She shimmied the denim over her hips— an unconsciously seductive move from any woman in any circumstance, and almost unbearably so in the heat of night with a woman of Kara Chandler's lithe curves and unexpected mystique. Luke's mouth went dry as she stepped from the jeans; then she straightened and squared her shoulders.

The notion of sixteen hours in bed took an unexpected turn. Luke swallowed, taking his time looking. Long, slender limbs and gently flaring hips, lace-edged underwear cut high enough and low enough to accentuate a shapely figure usually encased in power suits. Her breasts strained against pale satin cups, and Luke's fingers curled into fists with the desire to trade the bra for his hands.

"Satisfied?" she asked.

"Hardly," Luke said, with more honesty than he'd intended. He stepped toward her, noting a trickle of perspiration trail between her breasts even as a shiver drew her nipples tight. "You and I both know transmission devices are sophisticated enough to be almost imperceptible, except upon close inspection." He circled around her, stopping at her back and brushing a hand beneath her hair to lift it from her shoulders. The scent of something sweet rose to his nostrils from the pulse point on her throat, an incongruous touch of elegance in the fetid alley.

But there were no electronics. If she was wearing a wire, it was installed someplace that would require exploration to find. That thought sent a surge of blood against his zipper, but a wave of anger flowed right behind it. Kara Chandler was no blushing virgin. She was the Assistant District Attorney in a major metropolis, a woman who'd taken him to court once for murder and whose boss was committed to ruining Gene Montiel. And she was playing a game. Luke didn't like games when he didn't know the rules.

He coiled the mass of gold around his hand and tightened

the slack, tipping her head back to expose a pale stretch of throat. "You think you're safe, presenting yourself to me like this? Perhaps you don't know what I'm capable of."

"I know exactly what you're capable of," she said, through clenched teeth. Tension rolled off her in waves. "It's the reason I mailed a letter today that identifies who I'm meeting, when, and where. It's somewhere in the U.S. Postal Service's channels right now so there's no use trying to find it. And, it contains a piece of evidence against Montiel that would be the final straw. If you let that letter be opened, your boss will be finished. So will you."

Luke was careful not to react, but inside, his gut tightened. She didn't know that Montiel was untouchable; Luke didn't give a damn about him. But if there was a letter, even if it only contained enough to get police sniffing around, the drug shipment would be dispersed instead of being unloaded at the mill. Eight-and-a-half tons of levamisole-laced cocaine would hit the streets and thousands of people looking for a short-term high—junkies, yuppies, kids—would come down with fever and find their skin turning black. Some would die.

Like Seth.

Luke's jaw ground, even as the backs of his knuckles brushed the warm flesh on her neck. Damn her. She could fuck up everything.

"You're lying," he said against her ear.

"Maybe," she acknowledged, and despite that her voice sounded firm, a breath shuddered between her lips. "I'm fully aware that you have Gene Montiel's resources at your disposal, and that you can disappear on a moment's notice to a nation without extradition. But understand that if I am murdered here tonight, nothing short of disappearing will keep you from being arrested."

Luke tightened his grip on the gold hair, and Chandler's nearly naked frame came against him. "Murder wasn't what I had in mind," he whispered. A bit of bald truth in a tangle of lies. He waited for a shiver of fear, but instead, Kara Chandler jerked from his grasp and whirled, teeth bared.

"For God's sake, do it then."

Luke stared.

"You think I don't know what kind of man you are? You think I didn't know before I came here what you might demand? Your mistake is in thinking I care. If sex is the currency you want, then get it over with. It's hot out here and it stinks."

Luke was stunned. Kara Chandler stood in front of him in an alley with nothing but scant inches of silk and lace between them. She didn't care about her own safety or what little money she had left. If she was telling the truth and this was a personal matter, then she didn't care about her job anymore, either.

It made him wonder what she did care about.

Warning bells went off. *Walk away.* He'd spent too much of his life waging war against the Rojàs cartel in Ecuador to let this woman and her groundless accusations against Montiel get in his way now. He couldn't let any more bodies pile onto his conscience. Seth's weighed too much already.

So, don't ask. Don't wonder. Walk away. Let Kara Chandler find someone else to play games with.

Luke stepped back, his body now wound as tight as hers. He scooped up her clothes and fired them at her chest. "Count yourself lucky that I'm partial to brunettes," he said, but didn't bother turning away while she hurried back into her clothes. He tried not to notice the sense of loss in his gut when she covered herself, tried not to wonder what—besides a setup—would drive a woman of the law to try to hire a hit.

That thought snapped Luke back. She grabbed her bag and started to step away, but Luke stopped her with his voice. "Ms. Chandler," he said, "you never told me: Whose boat and whose death?"

She looked him straight in the eyes. "Mine."

THE DISH

Where authors give you the inside scoop!

♥ ♥ ♥ ♥ ♥ ♥ ♥ ♥ ♥ ♥ ♥ ♥ ♥ ♥ ♥ ♥ ♥

From the desk of Kate Brady

Dear Reader,

People always ask: "Where do you get your ideas for books?" Usually I don't have a clue. But in the case of WHERE ANGELS REST, I actually recall the two seedlings of ideas that ultimately grew into this story. The first was a trailer on TV for an upcoming talk show. The interview was to be with a mother who had chased her child's rapist from state to state for years, basically raising hell wherever he tried to surface.

I never saw the show, but I remember thinking, *That would make a great heroine:* a woman who has dedicated her life to exposing someone she knows is dangerous.

Dr. Erin Sims was born.

The second idea evolved more gradually, but I can still name it: It's the town where I grew up. You see, I'm from Hopewell, Ohio. Well, not really, because there is no "Hopewell" in Ohio—at least not one I could find on a map. But I grew up in *a* Hopewell. Towns like my fictitious Hopewell are scattered all over the Midwest and, for that matter, the whole country. They're chock-full of sleepy charm, and they provide the perfect haven for someone battered and beaten by the evils of the larger world.

Sheriff Nick Mann was born.

When the two ideas merged—a man protecting the

sanctity of a town that appears peaceful, and a woman who knows that appearances can be deceiving—I knew I had the makings for a story.

In WHERE ANGELS REST, Erin Sims takes her hunt for a demented serial killer to a quaint town that couldn't possibly harbor such evil. There she unearths secrets Nick Mann refuses to believe—after he's spent years working to make Hopewell his refuge from a tortured past and a safe haven for his daughter's future. Eventually he can't deny the truth, no more than he can deny that the fire in Erin Sims has reignited not only his long-buried passion for police work but also his long-denied desire for love.

I hope you'll enjoy the ride as Erin and Nick set out to unravel a demented villain's compulsion to silence the angels who are privy to horrific, long-hidden truths. And while you're at it, catch a glimpse of my next hero, Nick's brother, who will hopefully whet your appetite for the second book in the series, coming soon!

Happy Reading!

Kate Brady

www.katebrady.net

♥ ♥ ♥ ♥ ♥ ♥ ♥ ♥ ♥ ♥ ♥ ♥ ♥ ♥ ♥

From the desk of Laurel McKee

Dear Reader,

For as long as I can remember I've been a "theater geek"! My parents took me to see a production of *A Midsummer Night's Dream* when I was about six, and I loved everything about it—the costumes, the music, the way it felt like an escape from the real world into Shakespeare's fairy-tale woods. I decided right then that I wanted to be an actress. I put on productions at home (recruiting my little brother and our family dog to be the other performers) and made my parents buy tickets. (Until I got in trouble for using my mom's antique lace tablecloth for a costume.)

Then I got older, did some community theater, and found out I was lacking one essential element for being an actress—talent! But I've never lost my love of going to the theater. There is just something about settling into one of those velvet seats, reading the glossy program, waiting for the curtain to go up and a whole new world to be revealed. I was so happy to "meet" the St. Claire family and have the chance to live in their world for a while, to vicariously be part of the theater all over again.

The Victorian age was a great era for the theater. The enthusiastic patronage of Queen Victoria meant that the theater was becoming more respectable, and actors and actresses were more accepted in society. People like Ellen Terry and Henry Irving at the Lyceum Theater were celebrities and artists, and a new style of theatergoing was taking hold. The audience actually sat and watched the play in silence instead of having supper and gossiping with their friends! Our modern idea of theater was born in this time period.

I loved seeing my own St. Claire family in the very thick of this exciting period, on the cusp between scandal and respectability! But with them, I think they will tend more toward the scandal side of things…

I'm thrilled with how TWO SINFUL SECRETS turned out, and hope that you all enjoy it!

Happy Reading!

Laurel McKee

www.LaurelMckee.net
Facebook.com
Twitter, @AmandaLaurel1

♥ ♥ ♥ ♥ ♥ ♥ ♥ ♥ ♥ ♥ ♥ ♥ ♥ ♥ ♥

From the desk of Cara Elliott

Dear Reader,

For those of you who have been asking me about the maddeningly mysterious Cameron Daggett, well, the wait is over! Connor and Gryff—those two other devilishly dashing Lords of Midnight—have been tamed by love, and now, in TOO DANGEROUS TO DESIRE, it's Cameron's turn to meet his match. But trust me, it wasn't easy to find a way to unlock his heart.

The most cynical of the three friends, he had good reason to keep his feelings well guarded, for he had been hurt in the past. Luckily I knew just the right lady to turn the key. (Be advised that opening locks is not as easy as it might seem. Sometimes it takes some very deft and clever manipulations to release all the little levers—as several scenes in the book will show!) But of course, as this is a romance, Cameron finds his happily-ever-after with Sophie Lawrance.

I, however, must confess to shedding a few tears on having my Lords of Midnight trilogy come to an end. All of the characters have become such dear friends, so it's hard not to feel very sad as they move away from the cozy little neighborhood of my desk to live in far-flung places all around the world. I'll miss their wonderful company—we had coffee together most every day for so long! However, it's time to let them go off and have their own future adventures, so I'm looking forward to making new friends who will share my morning jolts of caffeine (along with those afternoon nibbles of chocolate).

And speaking of new friends, I've already met a delightfully unconventional trio of sisters with a passion for writing. Olivia, the eldest, pens fiery political essays; Anna, middle sister, writes racy romance novels; and Caro, who is not quite out of the schoolroom, is a budding poet. Of course, proper young Regency ladies of the *ton*—especially ones who have very small dowries—are not encouraged to have an interest in intellectual pursuits. Indeed, the only thing they are encouraged to pursue is an eligible bachelor. Preferably one with both a title and a fortune. So the headstrong, opinionated Sloane sisters must keep their passions a secret.

Ah, but we all know that secret passions are wont to lead a lady into trouble…

Alas, I can already report that Olivia has set off sparks with the Earl of Wrexham, a paragon of propriety, who—

Oh, but that would be spoiling all the fun! I'll let you read all about it for yourself. All I'll say is that I'm so excited about starting my new series! Please be sure to check out my website www.caraelliott.com for more updates on the Hellions of Half Moon Street!

Cara Elliott

Find out more about Forever Romance!

Visit us at
www.hachettebookgroup.com/publishing_forever.aspx

Find us on Facebook
http://www.facebook.com/ForeverRomance

Follow us on Twitter
http://twitter.com/ForeverRomance

NEW AND UPCOMING TITLES

Each month we feature our new titles
and reader favorites.

CONTESTS AND GIVEAWAYS

We give away galleys, autographed copies,
and all kinds of exclusive items.

AUTHOR INFO

You'll find bios, articles, and links to personal websites
for all your favorite authors—and so much more.

GET SOCIAL

Connect with your favorite authors, editors, and
other Forever fans, and share what's important to you.

THE BUZZ

Sign up for our monthly romance newsletter,
and be the first to read all about it.